THE THUG AND HIS DOLL

PRINCETOWN HEIRS
BOOK 1

BEA PAIGE

THE THUG AND IS

NOTE TO READERS

This book is a work of fiction, but with everything I write, I do
delve into difficult topics.
This book contains discussions of past child abuse, domestic abuse,
talk of past suicide attempts, and has some scenes of violence.
(None of the above mentioned is between the love interests)
Please be mindful when reading.

BOOK PLAYLIST

Book Playlist

As you all know I love a book playlist! I write to music always, and scenes are often inspired by the songs I choose, and a lot of thought goes into each song choice. All of the songs that inspired this story can be found on my Spotify playlist - ***The Thug And His Doll.***

"Behind every beautiful thing, there is some kind of pain."
Bob Dylan.

HAMMER
Lia and Drix

PROLOGUE

"WHAT A FUCKING NIGHT," Sterling remarks, letting out an exhausted sigh from across the table, his hand raking through his unruly brown locks. Next to him his suit jacket is tossed carelessly over the vacant chair, and as he lifts his tired gaze to mine, I'm struck by the bright blue of his irises, a stark contrast to the dark circles beneath them. Every line and crease on his face tells a story of the long and eventful night we've all just experienced.

"I'm guessing you've had about as much sleep as the rest of us," I remark, glancing at my best friend Dalton, who's rubbing his hand across his neck and watching me warily, then at Ben, who's staring at the empty glass in his hand, no doubt savouring the harsh burn of the whisky he's just downed. The table is littered with empty glasses, evidence of our need to numb ourselves from the events of the past twenty-four hours. The bitter aroma of whisky lingers in the air, mingling with the scent of desperation.

"Yeah, that would be none then," Sterling states, exhaling sharply.

It's the morning after his father's lavish wedding, and we're all gathered in the opulent bar of the only five-star hotel in town, owned by Dalton's wealthy father, Carl.

A palpable tension fills the air as we sit in brooding silence, the only sound that dares to break the stillness is the soft clink of ice cubes swirling around our glasses. My mind can't help but wander to the events that brought us together this morning: four women who have left us all feeling emotionally tangled and raw inside. Each sip of my drink brings a bittersweet taste to my tongue, mirroring the complex emotions swirling through my mind.

Waiting outside, the rabid tabloids would have a field day if they knew how the heirs of Princetown's four founding families were so easily brought to their knees.

Four sons. Four friends. Four men carrying the weight of their fathers' legacies.

There's Dalton, a self-confessed rogue and heir to the Gunn family's billion-pound fortune.

Sterling, a gifted artist and recluse set to inherit the Blade family's wealth.

Benedict, owner of Bandits Bar, with a genius IQ who is expected to carry on the Pike family legacy.

And then there's me, Hendrix, the adopted son of the late Hubert Hammer, who is bound by a debt that has forced me into a role I hate, and a life I never wanted.

Together our families own Princetown, a picturesque town nestled in the English countryside, where rich men reside in their lavish estates and hold power over the working class. It's a concept that makes me uneasy given my own humble beginnings.

My late father, Hubert Hammer, used to tell me that there are three sides to every man. The side he presents to the world, the side he wishes he could be, and the side he hides from himself.

As I look at each of my friends in turn, I can't help but wonder which side they are showing me right now.

I made my choice to be the man everyone else wanted me to be in order to secure my sister's future. I accepted my role.

That is until Lia walked into my life and made me question everything...

ONE

"BLACK COFFEE, FOUR SUGARS… *PLEASE*, DAPHNE," I add, when the owner of The Rock Cafe–a sixty-something, takes no bullshit kinda woman–glares at me for momentarily forgetting my manners.

"That's better," she grouses, giving me a wink to let me know she gets me before placing my order on the table. I should've known she'd already have it ready. It's not like I order anything else. I'm not into any of that oak milk, latte bullshit.

"Sorry, Daph," I reply, rubbing my hand over the back of my neck and giving her a wry smile as I stretch my legs out beneath the booth I always sit at. I'm a creature of habit, and I like what I like. A black coffee with four sugars being one of them. This particular spot in the cafe, another.

"It's a bad day already?" she asks, looking at her wrist which, by the way, has no watch adorning it. She's cute like that.

"Bad night. I've yet to go to bed."

"And you're drinking a black coffee with four sugars at seven in the morning? You need a nice relaxing cup of chamomile tea and the arms of a good woman... or man?" She winks.

"Woman," I grunt, swallowing a mouthful of the best coffee you'll find this side of Princetown. "And sleeping is for the dead."

Shaking her head, she tuts. "This is exactly why you need a good woman. Someone's gotta take care of you."

"Are you offering?" I ask, giving her my most devastating smile.

Her skin flushes right up into the hairline of her silvery brown hair as she wags a finger at me. "If only I were thirty years younger," she laughs. "As it is, this woman needs her beauty sleep, and I haven't got the energy to chase a strapping, blonde, tattooed bear of a man around town."

"Oh, I don't know, I reckon you've still got it in you," I flirt.

"You, Hendrix Hammer, are a charmer."

I shrug. "If the shoe fits."

She drops her gaze to my size thirteen feet, then slowly raises her gaze up my body, letting out a peel of laughter. "Frankly, I don't even know *how* it would fit."

Now it's my turn for my cheeks to flush. "And there's me thinking you're one of the innocent ones."

Her laughter erupts as she turns her attention to the only other occupants in the cafe at this ungodly time in the morning. "I've had my fair share of bad boys in my time," she throws over her shoulder.

"I've no doubt," I mumble, rubbing at my temples as a headache starts to bloom. "Fuck, I really need to get some sleep."

"Mama, he swore!" a childish voice accuses, reminding me that I'm not the only person in the cafe this morning.

"Sorry," I mumble, eying the kid sitting at the table opposite. He eyes me right back.

"It's fine," the woman with him replies, her hand wrapping around her kid's shoulder protectively.

Well, I'm assuming he's hers given they look so damn alike in every way but the shade of their eyes and the colour of their hair. Where his are both dark brown in colour, her eyes are a pale shade of green, her hair the colour of warm honey. She's pretty in an understated way.

My eyes flick to meet hers, and I give her a polite dip of my head as she brushes a strand of hair behind her ear. I can't help but notice the lack of a wedding ring, and the way her fingers tremble.

"Don't mind him," Daphne pipes up, chucking a grin over her shoulder. "He might look like someone you wouldn't want to meet in a dark alley at night, but he's one of the good ones."

"Thanks, I think?" I mumble, catching the look of... *fear* scattering across the woman's features. I guess she sees what most people do. It kind of comes with the territory.

Besides, I'm used to that kind of reaction. If I look like I could crack a person's head open with one punch it's because I can. I might look like a thug on the outside, and act like one when the need arises, but that's the reputation I'm required to maintain, not want.

"May I have the bill, please?" she asks Daphne, and something about the way she draws her son closer and the skittish way she flicks her gaze away reminds me of a time I'd sooner rather forget.

"Sure thing, sweetie. Just give me a moment," Daphne replies, heading off to the counter to ring up her bill.

"I apologise," I say after a beat, as she quietly reminds her son not to stare. "For swearing in front of your boy."

"It's fine," she mumbles, not lifting her head as she swipes a napkin across her little boy's face, collecting the chocolate smudged around his lips from the hot chocolate he's just guzzled down with gusto.

"You know, Mama says it's rude to swear," the little boy adds, pushing his mum's hand away so he can give me a curious smile. "Why do you have so many drawings on your body?"

I chuckle, resting my tattooed hand against the counter, the word *love* written across my left knuckles to match *hate* written across the right. Original, I know. "Well, firstly, your Mama's right. It *is* rude to swear."

"Toby, that's enough. Leave the man to drink his coffee in peace," the woman warns, shushing him.

"It's okay. You're right to teach him his manners." I give her a warm smile, hoping it makes her relax a little. I don't like the idea of making this woman uncomfortable. I might spend some of my nights scaring the shit out of the men who fuck off the families I work for in this town, but that doesn't mean I want to do the same here. I'm not a *complete* arsehole.

"I also told him not to speak to strangers," she mutters, casting me another concerned look as she drops her gaze to my thick tattooed arms, and the numerous tattoos inked into my skin.

Pulling the sleeve of my hoody down, I grin. "Well, if you know my name, I won't be a stranger anymore, right?" I say to her son. "Toby, is it?"

"Yes," he nods, brushing a flop of hair out of his eyes that just falls back into them seconds later.

"Well, Toby, my name is Hendrix Hammer, but everyone around here calls me Drix. Nice to meet you."

"Except that lady, *she* called you Hendrix," he points out, grinning at me.

"Very observant, kid. And whilst that's true, most people call me Drix." I lean across the aisle, holding my hand out to him. He takes it instantly, his tiny hand slipping into mine as I gently shake it. Behind him, his mother stiffens.

"Toby," she warns.

I let the kid's hand go. "And your name?" I ask, resting back in my seat, curious who this woman is, and why I've never seen her before. I know everyone in this town.

"That's none of your—" she begins, but her son cuts her off.

"It's Amelia Pearson, but everyone calls her Lia," Toby replies proudly, oblivious to the stuttered way his mother draws in a breath. For a small kid, he sure has impressive vocabulary. I'm guessing he's around four or five, but I could be wrong.

"Well, Lia, pleasure to meet you," I say, curiosity getting the better of me as I ask another probing question. "Are you just passing through or visiting family?"

"Like I said that's none of your—"

"We're on an adventure!" Toby pipes up. "We left my Papa sleeping, and this place is as good as any place to stop, right Mama?"

Lia's skin pales as she flicks her gaze from her son to me, and back again. "That's enough, Toby. We should get going. We've got a long drive ahead of us."

"So you're just passing through then?" I question, feeling the tension rolling off her.

This woman is spooked, and I don't think it's just me who's doing the spooking. Given what the kid just said, she's running scared. That knowledge triggers me in a way that I wished it wouldn't.

"Yes. Exactly," she replies tightly, casting her gaze over her shoulder to Daphne who seems to be taking her merry time fetching the bill.

"I thought you said we could stay this time? I wanted to go on the swing, Mama. You *promised* me."

"Maybe it's best if we just kept going, sweetie," she says. "They'll be other playgrounds."

"Not with a huge caterpillar slide!"

"We'll find another playground just as good."

"But you promised," he whines. "You said this would be the

last time. I want to stay *here*. I don't want to sleep in the car again. It's cold, Mama."

"I–"

"Wait, you're sleeping in a car?" I interrupt, knowing it's none of my damn business, but asking anyway. Why is she sleeping in her car with her kid? It's fucking winter, and soon the snow will drop and the temperature will plummet even further. It's only then that I notice that she's not as well turned out as the majority of the women in Princetown are, and whilst her kid is as clean as a whistle, as much as any kid at such a young age can be, on closer inspection Lia looks a little... *dishevelled*, for lack of a better word.

"Toby, please," she whispers, refusing to meet my gaze and searching in her handbag for her purse, presumably.

"Hey, is everything–" I begin, but Daphne appears, laying the bill on the table, cutting me off before I can finish my sentence.

"There we go, darling," she says, casting a look over at me, frowning at the look on my face no doubt. "Everything okay?"

"It's fine. *We're fine*," Lia insists, grabbing the bill and quickly casting her gaze over it. She opens up her purse, her cheeks colouring a deeper shade of pink as panic scatters across her face.

"Sorry. I erm... Just give me a moment," she mumbles, unzipping her purse, upending the contents as she counts through the coins that have tumbled onto the formica table.

"Take your time," Daphne replies kindly, giving me one of her looks as she passes by.

Pretty sure she's thinking the same as me. Pushing up from my seat, I follow Daphne to the back of the cafe, out of earshot of Lia and her son.

"Can't get enough of me, huh?" Daphne asks as she steps behind the counter and busies herself sorting through the freshly washed cups and plates, stacking them onto the shelf behind her.

"How much does she owe?" I ask, ignoring her question and flicking my gaze to Lia as she counts out the cost of the bill, piling up the coins onto the small silver dish Daphne left to collect the money.

"Six pounds, eighty pence," Daphne replies. "Why?"

"I got this," I say, throwing down a twenty to cover her bill and mine, then adding another fifty on top. I'd leave more, but it's all the cash I have in my wallet. "When I'm gone, give that to the lady. Looks like she could use it."

Daphne raises a brow, her look one of curiosity. "When I said you needed a woman, I didn't mean the first one you came across, and especially not one who's as jumpy as a jack rabbit."

"You noticed that too, huh?" I ask, ignoring her other remark.

"A lot of people pass through these doors. After a while, you get good at figuring out their situation."

"And what's *their* situation?" I ask, curious to know if her thoughts match my own as I stare at Lia and her kid.

"One to avoid, I'd say."

"Daph, that's not what I asked."

She sighs, following my gaze. "I'd say she's a woman on the run."

"From what?"

"Well, I'm guessing someone bad enough to run from."

"Yeah, I think you might be right," I agree, feeling a surge of protectiveness barrel out of nowhere as I swipe a hand through my hair. "Ah, fuck."

"Now, Hendrix," Daphne warns.

"Don't give me that look. I'm just paying her bill. That's all."

"And a bit more on top," Daphne replies, as I wave off her concern and stride towards their table.

"Don't worry about that, it's been paid for," I say, making Lia jump as she reaches for the tray of coins and pushes it to the edge of the table.

"What?" she questions, her gaze barely meeting mine.

"I paid for your bill."

Toby grins widely, his smile dropping when he looks over at his mother. "But that's *nice*," he whispers, picking up on her wariness.

"We don't need your charity," she bites back.

"It ain't charity," I retort, bristling a little at her reaction, not because she's pissed me off for being rude, but because some arsehole, somewhere along the line, has made her so fucking distrusting.

"Then take this," she says, pushing the pile of coins towards me.

I keep my arms folded across my chest. "Just call it a random act of kindness."

"I don't want to owe you anything," she counters, round spots of colour tingeing her cheeks pink.

"Then pass it on."

"What?" she questions.

Toby looks between us, his brown eyes absorbing this awkward as fuck interaction. "Next time you see someone in need. Pass it on. It's no big deal," I shrug.

She swallows hard, and I expect her to protest, but instead she meets my gaze with a steely one of her own. "I'm *not* in need."

We both know she's lying. "Regardless, it's done now. Have a good day, yeah?" I reply, forcing my feet to move so I don't sit down at their table and demand to know what the fuck has happened to them. It's none of my damn business, anyway.

But as I step out into the biting November wind, I can't help wondering who Amelia Pearson is running from and more to the point, why the hell I care.

TWO

"IT'S OKAY, sweetie, just cuddle up to me okay. I'll keep you warm," I murmur, holding Toby close to my chest and wrapping him up tighter in the threadbare blanket I grabbed in my rush to leave.

I should've planned better. I should've squirrelled away more money. I should *never* have trusted Martin. My mother knew. She had told me he wasn't a good man, and I ignored her, believing his lies, ignoring the red flags. Marrying him anyway.

She'll be rolling in her grave, so disappointed in me. But if I had listened to her I wouldn't have Toby, and despite the hell I've lived through, I won't ever regret that.

At least we have each other.

"I'm so cold," Toby cries, his sobs breaking my heart as I stare out of the window into the darkness of night. My back and arse ache from the bruises littering my skin and my body shivers from the cold as puffs of warm air escape my lips. I stifle a sob, thankful for the fact that Martin had avoided hitting my face, not because I wanted to protect the arsehole from people finding out he's an abuser, but because I have to protect Toby from the truth. Just like I'm protecting him now.

"This is *our* adventure. Yours and mine," I remind him, plastering on a smile despite the well of fear churning in my stomach.

"But who will bring Papa his breakfast?"

"I guess he'll have to get it himself," I reply, handing him Blue Bear, his favourite teddy. He wraps his arms around it, holding it tight. As old as Toby, Blue Bear is looking a little worse for wear after five years of accompanying my sweet boy everywhere.

"Doesn't he miss us?" Toby asks.

"In the morning we'll go back to that cafe and I'll buy you another cup of hot chocolate, okay?" I say, distracting him, avoiding the difficult questions. "Maybe this time we can ask for a squirt of whipped cream on top too."

"Really?" Toby asks, his cheek pressed against Blue Bear, his big brown eyes wide with happiness. They're the only good thing he got from his father.

I choke back a sob, hating that's all I can offer him. What kind of mother am I? I can't even provide him a safe roof over his head, let alone a decent breakfast. The only reason I can promise him a measly hot chocolate is because of a stranger's pity, but at least it bought him a decent meal tonight. I still feel prickly about the whole situation. I saw the way Hendrix, *Drix*, was looking at me, like I was a charity case. Not to mention the fact that I didn't like how he'd pried into my situation despite me clearly not wanting to tell a complete stranger my problems. No doubt he thought I was an easy target. But I'm wiser now. I know men like him, I fell in love with one of them after all, and look how that ended up for us. Didn't stop me from accepting the fifty pounds he left for me though.

God, how could I have let this happen?

"Mama?"

"I promise," I reply, pressing a kiss against his head as I struggle to hold in the tears.

"Okay, Mama."

Okay, Mama.

Somehow those two words are bloated with meaning. Okay, Mama, I trust you take care of me even though I haven't slept in a real bed in over a week. Okay, Mama, you're plastering on a smile even though I see the sadness in your eyes. Okay, Mama, this is our fun adventure, even though I'm cold and hungry, and it doesn't feel very fun anymore.

"It will get better, I promise," I whisper against the soft hair of his head, knowing that what he really needs right now is a warm bath, a safe place to sleep and a future filled with happiness and joy, not fear and uncertainty.

After a few more minutes of rocking Toby, he finally falls asleep, relaxing in my arms, unaware that with every mile that I've put between us and the bastard who stripped me of my self-esteem, joy and zest for life, my heart has barricaded itself in an impenetrable stone casing, vowing to never fall in love again.

For the next hour I stay awake, acutely aware that I'm a woman alone with a small child in an empty car park of a shopping mall we'd spent the day keeping warm in. Toby had so much fun wandering around the stores, playing in the free soft play area whilst I watched him like a hawk and worried myself sick about what to do next given I'm completely broke.

This morning when I checked my joint bank account that I share with that piece of shit we left behind, all the money in it had been withdrawn.

Every. Last. Penny.

A thousand pounds, gone. Just like that.

Why hadn't I opened up a separate savings account? How could I be so stupid? The first thing I should've done after leaving was withdraw the cash before Martin had a chance to. But I had been running scared, intent on getting as many miles between us as possible, that I just hadn't thought of it.

"Stupid. Stupid. Stupid," I berate myself.

Swiping at the tears that fall, I continue to curse myself for my lack of foresight, forever believing Martin when he said he would change, that he would do better. I believed him, every time. When the verbal abuse began, my foolish heart had made excuses for him. He'd had a bad day. He didn't mean it. I thought that my love would change him, would make him a better man. Of course, it never did. In fact, somehow I think it just made him hate me even more.

It wasn't always this way. In the early days of our relationship he'd been attentive, showering me with gifts, attention, and love. Only now when I look back, I can see that it wasn't real. He had controlled me, not loved me. He isolated me from my friends, claiming that all I needed was him, that I didn't need anyone else, that it was us against the world.

I'd fallen for it. Hook, line and sinker.

Then as soon as Toby was born a year into our relationship, things began to change. He became angry at every little thing I did. He started staying late at work, then going on *business trips* for days on end, whilst I struggled to bring up a newborn baby who was often colicky and kept me up all hours of the day and night.

We needed him, and he let us down.

But that wasn't the worst of it. When I found out about his *indiscretions*, he blamed me. I wasn't putting out, my figure wasn't attractive to him anymore. I had a fuller figure from carrying a child, *ugly stretch marks* and *saggy tits*. His words, not mine. He made me hate the body that carried our child. He made me feel ugly, worthless.

But still I stayed. Stupidly, foolishly believing that if I started working out again, if I coloured my hair a lighter blonde, just the way he liked it, and poured my body into too tight-fitting clothes I hated wearing just to please him, that he would see me again, would love me again.

But the name calling just got worse, until one day when Toby was three, he didn't just hurt me with his words, he hurt me with his fists too.

Before Martin, I was always one of those women who would wonder why someone wouldn't leave an abusive relationship. I didn't understand the psychological damage that living with a violent narcissist can have on a person. He made me feel like I couldn't leave, that no one else would love me, and on the rare occasions he would show me affection–normally when he would sense I'd grown courageous and was about to leave–he would turn on the compliments, the affection, making me believe that the man I fell in love with had finally returned for good.

Of course, he never did.

A man like him isn't capable of love. A violent man. A man who'd rather use his fists to beat on a woman than look into himself and try to figure out why he needs to make someone else feel like shit to make him feel better about himself.

"No more. I refuse to let you control my thoughts and emotions a second longer," I say, my words huffing out of my mouth in wispy clouds as I press my eyes shut and fall into a fitful sleep, knowing my words are empty. That I'll never be free of the damage he caused me.

"MAMA, Mama, wake up. I need to go to the toilet!" Toby exclaims, pressing on my bladder as he wiggles in my lap.

I blink open my eyes, feeling worse for having fallen asleep, not better. "What time is it?" I ask, knowing full well Toby can't read the time to tell me.

"It's dark," he says, cupping his hands against the windowpane as he peers outside.

"Shit," I whisper, clearly not quietly enough.

"Mama, you swore!"

"I'm sorry, sweetie. As soon as I can buy a jar, I'll add a coin to it," I say, shifting him off my lap and strapping him back into his car seat. I don't mention the fact I have no money to do that.

"Do you need to wee or poop?" I ask, briefly considering whether we can risk dashing into the bushes on the far side of the car park if it's just a wee he needs.

"Poop," he groans, clutching his stomach.

"Okay, let's see if the garage down the road is still open," I reply, turning on the engine and starting the car up. She splutters to life, and I back out of the parking spot, heading towards our destination. It's clear as we get closer the garage is closed. Another swear word leaves my mouth, causing Toby to burst out laughing.

"Mama, you're being very naughty."

"I know," I reply, slowing the car as we drive past the garage. "I'm sorry. I just really need the toilet too."

At least that's the truth, about the only truth I've been able to share with him this past week since we ran away. He groans, shifting in his seat.

"Mama, I really need to go!"

"Okay, hang on sweetheart. There must be somewhere open."

A couple of minutes later I notice a neon sign in the near distance flashing the words *Bandits Bar* in bold green lights. In the parking lot there are a few cars and some motorbikes lined up outside the front door. Not to mention a couple of beefy looking men sporting beards and leather chaps hanging around outside.

"What about there?" Toby asks, pointing to the place I have no intention of taking him to.

"I don't think that's an appropriate place for a child," I say, biting on my lip as Toby releases another rather smelly fart.

"Mama, I'm desperate!" he pleads, pulling a face.

"Okay. Okay," I reply, and against my better judgement, I pull into the parking lot.

A minute later I'm locking the car up, grabbing hold of Toby's hand and striding over to the entrance. Forcing my shoulders back, I keep my head held high even though I'm terrified. Fake it until you make it, right? The two men smoking cigarettes cast me a look that has my hackles rising, and I almost, *almost* turn around but Toby tugs on my arm, hopping on his feet as he clutches his stomach.

"Mama! I'm going to shit!"

"Toby!" I exclaim.

He clamps a hand over his mouth, tears welling in his eyes as the men lingering outside chuckle under their breaths. One turns towards me, opening his mouth to speak, but I don't give him the opportunity, instead I pull Toby into my side and push open the door into the bar.

Inside the air is cloying and thick from a combination of sweat and the sheer number of people enjoying the music being performed by a live band called Princetown Bandits, according to the name scrawled across the bass drum. I've never really been into rock music, preferring folk and indie, but despite that, I appreciate they're good musicians and pretty popular given the reaction of the crowd.

"MAMA! WHY IS IT SO LOUD?" Toby shouts up at me, his need for the toilet momentarily forgotten given the mixture of awe and horror on his face as he lets go of my hand and wraps his arms around my thigh.

"Let's make this quick," I reply, although at this point I'm pretty sure he can't hear me as I pick him up and nudge my way through the crowd towards the bar, apologies spilling from my lips with each step. A few people eye me and Toby a little strangely, not that I can blame them given it's past midnight and I've entered a bar with a child on my hip.

Like the rest of the place, the bar area is crowded with people, all vying for the bartender's attention as they wave their money in the air. Right now he's talking to someone at the other end of the bar, clearly finding something they've said amusing given he throws his head back and lets out a peel of laughter. Eventually, he makes his way towards the next punter, and all the while Toby is squirming on my hip. I'm not sure if it's because he's about to poop his pants or is enjoying the too loud music. Either way, I'm not going to get the bartender's attention anytime soon. It's not that I need a drink or anything anyway, I just need to know where the toilet is.

Turning to the man standing next to me, a tall guy with a black bristly beard and dark eyes under even darker eyebrows, I tap him on the arm. He looks down at where my fingers touch his arm, then slowly raises his eyes to meet mine.

I blanch at the look he gives me. "I'm so sorry to disturb you, but can you tell me where the toilets are?" Toby, sensing the same thing as me, seems to shrink a little under the man's stare.

"This is no place for a child," the man replies.

No shit, I think.

"We just need to use the toilet," I reply, glad my voice is steady even if I feel far from it.

He points to the back of the bar. "Over there."

"Thanks," I mumble, stepping around him and through the crowd as Toby clings onto me like a spider monkey. I pull him close to my chest, hoping for once that I am as invisible as Martin always made me feel.

THREE

"WHAT THE FUCK?!" I exclaim, my attention drawn to the blonde from the cafe pushing her way through the crowd as she carries her son in her arms. They both look fucking terrified.

"What's up Drix?" Dalton asks me, placing his glass of bourbon on the table and loosening the top button of his shirt, his Armani suit and Rolex better suited for the five star hotel he manages and not our friend's bar. Not that anyone would try to rob him, he's Dalton Gunn, only child to Carl Gunn, the head of one of Princetown's four founding families, manager of Princetown Manor Hotel and Spa, and my best friend.

"Just give me a minute, okay? I've got something I need to deal with," I reply, getting up just as one of Dalton's regular *booty calls* steps up to the table.

"Drix," the redhead says, flashing me a cocaine induced grin that does absolutely nothing for me.

"Heather," I nod, casting Dalton a warning look that he completely ignores.

Instead his lips spread into a leisurely smile, his dark blue eyes sliding over her tight-fitting, low-cut dress that barely leaves anything to the imagination.

"Bring us both a drink on your way back," Dalton orders, dismissing my glare and switching on his arsehole persona just like he always does whenever there's a woman he wants to fuck around.

"She ain't the one," I caution, ignoring his cuntish remark.

Number one, I'm not his fucking servant, and number two he's supposed to be finding himself a wife, not fucking around with women who use him as much as he's using them.

"Tonight she is," he throws back, pulling her onto his lap as she giggles.

"Then be sure to wrap it up," I offer, knowing full well I won't be seeing him for the rest of the night.

Dalton might be my best friend, but he's also a sex addict who likes to piss his father off on the regular by fucking women and living up to his playboy reputation. Blowing out a breath, I leave one mess and walk right into another.

Pushing open the door to the corridor that leads to the toilets, which is where I'm assuming Lia was taking her son, I lean against the wall and wait outside the ladies room. After five minutes, and no sign of the pair, I push open the door and step inside. The first thing I hear is Lia cursing, and the second, the kid crying.

"Oh Toby, don't cry, it's not your fault," Lia soothes, the soles of her shoes sticking out of the bottom of the stall.

"But I pooped my pants, and now I stink," Toby replies, crying harder.

"Ah shit," I mumble, stepping fully into the room, the door clicking shut behind me.

Frankly, I'm not sure this is something I should be getting involved in, and I consider leaving them to it, but when Toby cries in earnest I can't bring myself to leave. Clearing my throat, I approach the stall.

"Can I help?" I offer.

She swears again and Toby just sobs harder.

"Who's that?" Lia asks, a note of trepidation in her voice.

"It's Drix Hammer... We met at the cafe," I add just to be sure she knows it's me.

"This is the *female* toilets," she replies, as if I didn't already know.

"I'm well aware."

"Then go next door," she continues, her voice tight.

"I don't need to use the toilet. I saw you in the bar, and figured–"

"You'd follow a lone woman with a child into the toilet," she finishes, her voice tense.

"It's not like that," I reply, then continue on when she doesn't respond. "It's past midnight. You're in a bar. With a child..." I add, wincing at how fucking judgemental that sounds.

It doesn't take a genius to figure out that her coming here was an act of desperation. Guilt climbs up my spine for not pressing her further when we first met. What kind of man knowingly walks away from a woman in need? They're obviously in some serious kind of trouble.

"I know it's past midnight and I'm in a bar with *my* child," she adds.

It's clearly her way of telling me to back the fuck off, but I'm here now and I can't in good conscience walk away.

"I just want to help. Is there anything I can do?"

She doesn't answer right away, instead I hear her whispering words of comfort to her son, before she unlocks the door and steps out of the cubicle. I catch a whiff of shit, and the tear streaked face of Toby perched on the toilet behind her before she positions herself between me and the door. Her face is flushed, and I can tell by the way her eyes are red-rimmed that she has been doing some crying of her own too. I have the sudden urge to pull her into my arms and comfort her.

Jesus fucking Christ. I'm in over my head here.

"Toby has an upset tummy. I need to get a change of clothes for him from my car, but I don't want to leave him here on his own," she blurts out.

"Okay, so give me your car keys and I'll go fetch him some clothes. Just tell me where to find them."

She considers my offer, chewing on her lip as she does so. "I don't know."

"You're in quite the predicament, and need help. I can do that."

"Are you sure?"

"I wouldn't offer if I wasn't," I reply, holding my hand out.

"Here," she murmurs, her shoulders sagging a little as she fishes her keys out of the back pocket of her jeans and drops them into my hand. "My car is a red Toyota with the fuzzy pink dice hanging from the rearview mirror."

"Got it. Where will I find his clothes?" I ask, pocketing the car keys.

"In the blue suitcase on the back seat. There should be some Smurf pyjamas right on top of the other clothes."

"Smurf?"

"It's his favourite cartoon," she explains, licking her lips nervously.

I nod, meeting her gaze. "Give me a minute. I'll be right back."

"I want Blue Bear!" Toby cries from the stool.

"Blue Bear?" I question, frowning.

"His teddy. It's in his car seat."

"Right. I'll grab that too," I reply, and with that I turn on my heel and head back out into the bar.

As I step into the heaving crowd, the music from the Princetown Bandits is loud enough to burst an eardrum, and I ask myself why I chose this place to have a serious heart-to-heart with my best mate, but thankful I did given the circumstances.

As I pass by the bar, Ben, my friend, owner of this bar, and Princetown Bandits Manager, motions me over. "You got a minute?" he shouts out over the din, whilst simultaneously pulling a pint.

"Not right now, Ben. Got something I need to do," I shout back, nudging my way through the crowd and heading out into the carpark. Whatever he needs it'll have to wait. Lia and Toby come first.

Lia and Toby come first...

Huffing out a breath, I question why this woman and her son are having this affect on me, but here I am, so I'll just fucking go with it and figure the rest out later.

I spot Lia's car immediately, the tin rust-bucket looks about as safe as the clapped out old bangers me and Dalton used to drive around his father's estate when we were teenagers. I stopped racing cars for fun when I realised I wasn't actually all that good at it. But Dalton? He went from cars to motorbikes, and continues to compete when he's not fucking women, managing the hotel, or pissing his father off. He's actually pretty good.

Opening up the door I find the suitcase exactly where Lia had said it would be. Unzipping it, I pull out the Smurf pyjamas and grab a pair of the tiniest underpants I've ever seen, figuring if he's shit himself he's gonna need them. There are also some baby wipes tucked into the pocket on the back of the driver's seat, so I grab them too.

Slamming the door shut, I open up the front passenger door, and grab the teddy Toby was desperate for, taking a moment to check out the rest of the items in the car. Even if the kid hadn't given the game away, there's no doubt that she's run. Two suitcases are piled in the boot of the car, as well as a box of what look like cookery books, a couple of woollen throws, and some toys.

"Now what, genius?" I ask myself as I tuck the teddy and Toby's clothes under my arm, and lock the car.

"You stay the fuck out of my bar!" a familiar voice shouts from behind me.

I turn around to find Ben facing off with a guy who is clearly looking for some trouble tonight. He's gesticulating aggressively towards my friend who remains unflinching, glaring back at him.

Without hesitation, I place the items I'm holding onto the roof of Lia's car and jog over to them.

"What's happening here?" I growl, catching Ben giving me a look I know only too well.

This one's a wildcard, and whilst I know that my friend is more than capable of dealing with the dickhead, I'm not afraid to step in when the need arises.

"What the fuck has it got to do with you?" the man retorts, whirling on me.

He's a big bastard, as tall as me, and also under the influence of alcohol, and probably cocaine, given the wild look in his eyes. It's a dangerous combination.

"You clearly aren't from around here, because if you were, *mate*," I add, my nostrils flaring, "You'd know not to fuck with me or my friends."

"Fuck you," he laughs, his glassy eyes narrowing at me.

"Seriously, get out of here," I warn, losing my patience fast.

"I ain't going nowhere until that bitch gives me what I want," he snarls back. "What's a man gotta do to get a bit of pussy around here?"

I glance at Ben who sneers at the prick. "This arsehole won't take no for an answer. Tried roughing the woman up when she refused his offer of a dance."

"I see," I reply, turning my attention back to the prick, anger boiling in my chest. "So you think you can go around assaulting women?"

"This ain't got shit all to do with you."

"That's where you're wrong. Now fuck off!"

"Whatcha gonna do, make me?" he asks, pulling a knife from his back pocket and jabbing it towards me.

Before the fucker is even able to get close enough, I've grabbed his wrist with both of my hands, pushing his arm out from his body, and land a brutal kick to his groin, kneeing him in the stomach for good measure. He lets out a roar, falling to his knees with a loud crack. I'm no stranger to jerks like this, or men carrying weapons, and I act with confidence, twisting his arm behind his back, bending it painfully. With a cry of pain he releases the knife, and I kick it away from his body in one smooth motion.

"That was fucking stupid," I snap, more pissed off that he's tried to assault a woman, and has kept me from Lia and Toby, than the fact he's just tried to gut me.

"Get the fuck out of here, and don't come back!" Ben warns.

The arsehole on his knees responds by clearing his throat and spitting at my friend, earning him a punch to the side of the head from me that has him careening sideways as I shove him to the ground with a boot to his back for good measure. Ordinarily, a man in this situation would realise that the wise thing to do is to back the fuck off, but he pushes upright, his expression telling me he's not backing down anytime soon.

Time to teach him a lesson.

"Drix!" Benedict calls, and in the few seconds it takes for the arsehole to launch himself at me, Benedict has kicked the discarded knife towards me. I crouch down, scooping it up, slashing it across the guy's cheek as I rise before he's even realised what's happened.

Blood seeps from the wound that runs from his lip to his ear, and he stumbles backwards, his hand covering his face as he reels off a stream of curse words.

"You have a choice. Fuck off now, or die. It's up to you," I warn, stepping towards him.

Violence is as familiar to me as breathing, and even though I dislike that part of me, it comes in useful when the need arises. Fortunately for him, common sense kicks in and he backs up, putting as much space between us as possible.

"You fucking crazy arsehole! I'm outta here."

"Wise move," I shout after him, watching as he climbs into his car and drives away like a bat out of Hell.

"You know, I had that handled," Ben says, taking the knife from me as he grins.

"I know you did, but you got a bar to run. So I figured I could see him off and save you the trouble," I reply with a shrug.

"Drink on me?" he offers, swiping the knife clean on a washcloth he's got tucked into his back pocket.

"Nah, I got something to do," I reply, checking myself over to make sure I haven't got any of the arsehole's blood on me. "Got to grab something real quick. Catch you later?"

"Sure thing," Benedict replies, shaking his head with a laugh. "It's not a good night at the bar unless some kind of brawl breaks out, I guess?"

"Yeah," I mutter as he pushes open the door and disappears out of sight.

I take a minute to shake off the thrumming violence in my veins before grabbing Toby's things and heading back inside the bar. The last thing I want to do is scare either of them.

By the time I return, Toby has stopped crying and Lia is kneeling at his feet, his dirty clothes piled in the corner of the cubicle.

"Here we go," I say, handing her the clothes and wipes, and Toby his teddy.

He takes it from me, hiccupping as he sucks his thumb. Naked from the waist down, he's shivering a little.

"Thank you," Lia murmurs as I avert my gaze so she can clean and dress him.

"It's no problem," I mutter, taking a step back to give them some space.

Once he's dressed, she picks up the dirty clothes, and takes his hand in hers. I drop my gaze to the filthy floor and his bare feet. "This floor ain't too clean. I should probably have a word with Ben about that."

Lia drops her gaze to the floor, and automatically reaches down to pick Toby up, but she's juggling the dirty clothes, wipes and her handbag, so I act on instinct and scoop the kid up in my arms.

"You all better now?" I ask gruffly, resting the little guy on my hip.

He nods, sniffling as he looks up at me with his thumb in his mouth and his teddy clutched in his arms. The kid looks worn out.

"I've got him," Lia says, reaching for him.

"It's okay, I ain't gonna run off with him," I reply, giving her a smile that she just frowns at.

The tension between us makes me feel as uncomfortable as she's clearly feeling right now.

"Look–" I begin, but she shakes her head, cutting me off.

"I don't know what you want from me, but I can assure you I'm not the type of woman who..."

"Who what?" I ask, as Toby heaves out a sigh and rests his head against my chest, his eyelids drooping. Without thinking, I haul the kid closer, rubbing my hand over his back. He lets out another sigh, as Lia's brows draw together.

"Who puts out just because someone has given her a *random act of kindness*," she hisses, her mouth thinning with displeasure.

"You think that this is what that is? Some kind of convoluted booty call?" I shoot back just as quietly, given the kid seems to have dozed off.

"Then what is it then?" she asks, her cheeks flushing angrily, her suspicion thick and cloying between us.

"Look, I ain't like that. I meant it when I said that I just wanted to help."

"Why?" she counters, her worried gaze flicking to her son.

"Because you look like you need it."

"I can look after my son just fine," she replies techily, moving to grab her kid from my arms. He lets out a stuttered sob, cuddling closer against my chest. Her hand drops away.

"Yeah, but who's looking after you?"

Her eyes snap up to meet mine, heat flooding her cheeks. "I can take care of the *both* of us."

"Is that why you're sleeping in your car?" I reply, instantly regretting my harsh tone of voice. Whatever she's been through, she's projecting it onto me, and *that* makes me mad, not her need to protect her son.

"You've no right to judge me," she counters shakily.

"I ain't judging you," I sigh, wishing I was better equipped to deal with this situation. She's so fucking skittish, and I do my best to even my features to stop her from ripping the kid out of my arms and running out of the bar.

"Then what is this exactly?"

"Just hear me out," I say, wondering why I'm about to say what I am, given she clearly wants to get the fuck out of here and as far away from me as possible. "I have a spare room at my place. You can stay there for the night. Clean the kid up properly. Take a shower. Have a good night's sleep. Then tomorrow you can decide your next move."

"You want me to go back to your place?" her voice rises with every word, and I wince at how my offer sounds.

"To sleep. To rest. There's nothing more to it than that. I swear." I add.

She bites on her lip, uncertainty a dark cloud marring her pretty face. "I don't know you."

"You're right. You don't," I reply, trying to put myself in her shoes. It doesn't take a genius to figure out she ran from her partner given Toby mentioned his dad earlier, and from the way she's acting there's no doubt he's abused her in some way. My offer of help seems a lot more loaded, and frankly, down right scary for a woman who's cleary fucking terrified. I need to approach this differently. "Okay, look. I have a friend whose family owns a hotel here in town. I'll get you a room no problem. You can stay there."

"I don't have money for a hotel room," she quickly replies, more heat flooding her cheeks.

"That's okay. He's my best mate, he owes me a favour."

More like a thousand. The amount of times I've helped Dalton out when he's gotten into trouble with his womanising ways is a joke. So asking for a room for one night in the hotel he manages for his father isn't going to be an issue. Besides, I know for a fact he keeps at least one room free so he can take women back there to fuck. Looks like tonight he'll have to find somewhere else to go if there isn't any other rooms free at the hotel.

"I have no means of paying you back," she whispers after a moment.

"Just call this—"

"A random act of kindness?" she finishes for me.

"Do you have an alternative to sleeping in your car tonight?" I counter, ignoring her sarcasm.

She flicks her gaze away. "No," she eventually whispers.

"Then you stay at the hotel. Sleep in a decent bed. Wash up. Rest. You can have a big breakfast in the morning."

"A big breakfast?"

"Like I said, my best mate owes me. A room for the night, and a full English breakfast is the least he can do."

"I don't know..." her voice trails off with indecision, but I can tell she's close to agreeing. She looks dead on her feet, physically exhausted and no doubt emotionally and mentally too.

"Just one night, okay? It's below zero out there with snow in the forecast, and unless you run your engine all night to keep the heat on in your car, you'll be at risk of getting really sick. The kid has already had enough fun for one night, don't you think?"

She grimaces, her gaze dropping to Toby, tears welling in her pretty green eyes, making them glassy. Blinking them back, she nods once. "Okay."

"Okay," I repeat, feeling a deep sense of relief. "You should grab whatever you need from your car. I'll drive you both."

"You'll drive us?"

"You'll need to preserve your gas to get you to wherever it is that you're going to, right?"

She chews on her lip, deliberating. "Look, I'm not going to hurt you. I promise," I add, hoping to fuck by now she'll know I'm not going to hurt her despite her preconceived idea of me.

She lets out a strained laugh as she jerks her chin up and levels her gaze with mine. "I might seem feeble to you, but if you do anything to hurt my son, I promise you I will fight to the death to protect him."

Shifting Toby on my hip, I meet her heated gaze. "I don't think you're feeble, Lia. In fact I think you're the type of woman who's dangerous for a man like me."

She considers me for a moment, and I don't know if it's what I just said that changes her mind, or if she's finally reached rock bottom, but either way she nods and says, "Let's go then."

FOUR

THE QUIRKY LOOKING woman with pink-streaked, strawberry blonde hair, thick batwing eyeliner, and unicorn earrings gives me a sweet smile from behind the reception desk. I can tell she's curious as to why Drix is bringing some random woman and her son to this beautiful hotel, and checking them in a room for the night.

"And *Dalton* agreed to this?" she asks, her eyebrows rising a little in surprise as she hands over the keycard to the room she's just checked us into. Drix takes it from her while I stand a little way back, feeling wholly uncomfortable not just because this situation screams *woman in need*, but because this hotel is clearly five stars and I simply don't belong here.

"Yeah, I just reminded him about that night I saved his arse from a beating when he got caught with his dick—"

"Drix!" the receptionist exclaims, her eyes flicking to Toby who's stirring in his arms. Aside from the twenty minute drive over here, Drix hasn't put him down. I'm not entirely sure how I feel about that.

"Sorry, Daise..." Drix mumbles, shifting on his feet, his cheeks colouring a little. "Ain't used to having to hold my tongue."

I look between the two curiously. They seem incredibly relaxed in each other's company. Drix must notice my confusion because he jerks his chin at the receptionist and says, "This is my sister, Daisy. Daisy, meet Lia and Toby."

I give her a tight smile. *Sister?* Okay, now I get it. Although I would never have guessed they were related, they look nothing alike. Where Drix is a huge, somewhere over six foot, wall of a man, with dark brown eyes and hay blonde hair, Daisy is a petite woman in both height and stature with freckles dusting her nose and cheeks, and the palest blue eyes I've ever seen.

"Well, it's nice to meet you Lia," Daisy says, her genuine smile making me feel a tiny bit more comfortable. "I'm on the night shift and don't clock off until nine am, so if you need anything at all, just ring zero and I'll be here to help, okay?"

"Okay," I reply, my smile tensing a little when I hear someone close by commenting about the *state of the clientele these days.*

Drix must hear the comment too, because he throws a look at the obviously well-to-do couple and says, "I'll pass your concerns onto Carl Gunn, shall I? I'm sure he'll be interested to hear all about how you just insulted his son's guests."

The woman, who's dripping in jewels and expensive clothing, gasps, and the man I'm assuming is her husband clears his throat and says, "Apologies Mr Hammer, my wife has had one tipple too many. Pleasure to meet you," he adds, his gaze flicking to me as he steers his wife towards the lounge bar at the far end of the corridor.

"Yeah, that's what I thought," Drix mumbles, and Daisy grins.

"Go on, get this woman and her son to their room," she orders. "Sleep well, Lia."

"Thank you," I reply, readjusting my bag on my shoulder and following Drix across the marbled floor to the elevators on the other side of the reception hall.

The journey to the tenth floor only takes half a minute, but the tension in the small space is enough to make me catch my breath a couple of times. I don't even know how I got here, standing in an elevator with a man who, apparently, has no issue helping a complete stranger. I'm both confused by his apparent kindness, and suspicious of his motives. Despite that, I couldn't argue against his offer, not when Toby is clearly exhausted, unwell, and we have literally nowhere else to go.

"You good?" Drix asks me, his gaze falling to my hands that I'm currently wringing in front of me.

"I'm fine," I lie, dropping my hands to my side and refusing to look at him. I'm on the verge of tears, and I really don't want to lose it in front of him.

"I'm sure you'll feel better after a good night's sleep in a comfortable bed," he offers, clearing his throat when I don't respond. Because, honestly, I'm dreading waking up in the morning knowing I have to face the fact that I'm literally homeless with no money to my name, and no way to take care of myself, let alone Toby.

Moments later we hit the top floor, and the doors to the elevator slide open onto a richly decorated hallway that I almost don't want to step onto with my dirt-encrusted trainers. The carpet is a plush maroon, off-setting the golden flecked wallpaper and decorative sconces.

"Your room is to the right at the far end of the corridor," he says, handing me the keycard.

"Thanks," I mumble, taking it from him. Picking up my suitcase, I walk down the hallway.

"If you place the keycard in the holder to the right of the door, it will automatically turn on the lights," Drix instructs from behind me.

I feel his presence like a wall of heat, and even though I'm not a short woman, standing at five foot nine, I feel tiny in his presence. There's something about that which makes me feel simultaneously fearful and protected. It's a feeling I don't particularly like.

Forcing myself to move, I push open the door and place the keycard in the holder. The room is immediately flooded with soft lighting, and by room, I mean suite.

"This is..." My voice trails off as I step into the huge space that's larger than the entire footprint of the house I'd left behind.

"Where you'll be very comfortable," Drix finishes for me, striding towards the bed with Toby who is fast asleep in his arms.

He lays him down on the huge bed on the far side of the room, and Toby immediately rolls over, snuggling into the soft pillows and plush eiderdown. I watch as Drix pulls the throw that's folded at the end of the bed, over his body.

"There we go, kid," he mutters, gently brushing his knuckles over Toby's cheek before turning to face me.

My heart pangs inside my chest, and I swallow down the lump in my throat at the kind gesture. I don't ever remember an occasion when Martin had been as sweet to Toby.

"This must cost a fortune to stay at," I exclaim, avoiding his penetrating gaze as I cast my eyes around the opulent suite.

The polished wooden floors are buffed to perfection, the walls a dusky pink and the furniture and soft furnishings an expensive cream. Carefully selected paintings are hung on the walls, the art abstract but tasteful. Even the fixtures and fittings are gold instead of plastic. Every inch of this space is stunningly thought out and highly inappropriate for a five year old rambunctious boy. Fortunately for everyone we're only here for the night, and Toby is sleeping peacefully.

"Dalton likes to impress the women he brings up here," Drix says, almost apologetically.

"I see," I reply, not sure what else to say to that. From the little

I've heard, Dalton sounds like a womaniser, and someone I'd avoid at all costs.

"I could show you around, make sure you know where everything is?" Drix offers, tucking his hands in his jean pockets, his dark eyes seeking mine.

"I can figure it out by myself," I reply, chewing on my lip and feeling more than a little overwhelmed by his kindness. I don't understand it. Not at all.

"Of course you can..." His voice trails off as he stares at me.

I don't really know what to do next. This whole night has been an ordeal, and I just need a moment to gather myself. To think.

"Well, I think I'll take a shower then get some rest."

"Right, yes. Of course," he replies, stepping towards me, his huge frame suddenly even more intimidating now that I'm alone in a room with him.

I back up as he approaches, feeling more and more uncertain the closer he gets. He seems to be a decent man, and has been nothing but kind, and yet I can't bring myself to relax in his presence. I didn't use to be like this, so... *frightened*. I hate that about myself. I hate that I allowed myself to get to this point.

"The fridge is full of soft drinks. There's a tea and coffee machine," he says, pointing to the plush kitchenette behind me. "And there's a menu by the phone if you want to order some room service. Don't worry about the cost, that's all covered."

"I don't want to owe you anymore than I do already," I say, raising my chin with as much dignity as I can muster.

"You don't owe me a damn thing, Lia," he replies softly, and I feel tears clogging my throat at his kindness. A kindness that I simply can't bring myself to trust.

He steps closer, slowly, hesitantly, and I force myself to stand still even though every part of me is telling me to back up, to put space between us.

"Do you have a phone?" he asks.

"I do."

"Let me add my number to it. Just in case you need me."

"*Need you?*" I question, my gaze snapping up to meet his.

Something about the gruffness of his voice and the intensity of his stare makes me question his intentions once again. I hate feeling like this, oscillating between wary gratitude and fear. If it's confusing to me, then God knows what it must be like to be on the receiving end.

"You don't know anyone in town, and in case there's an emergency you'll have at least one person you can call," he explains, frowning a little at my harshness.

"I'm sorry," I mumble, instantly feeling ashamed.

Here he is being kind, showing concern and all I can do is bite his head off. I swipe a hand over my face, and this time the tears that have been threatening to fall ever since he appeared tonight, begin to tumble from my eyes. Turning away from him, I wrap my arms around myself and cry.

"Lia, fuck. I didn't mean to upset you. I just..." he begins, and I can feel him step closer, his pity thick between us. It's humiliating.

"Please, just give me a moment. It's been a long night," I manage to choke out.

"Of course it has."

Thankfully he doesn't press me further, giving me breathing space to cry without interruption, and I do. I hug myself tighter and sob quietly, unable to stop now that I've started. Like a cork being unplugged, tears stream down my face unbidden.

Martin hated it when I cried. Despised it even. He'd call me a *weak-ass crybaby bitch,* and a *fucking ugly cunt* for crying when he ridiculed me or hit me. My tears always fuelled his wrath, so having a man allow me to let go like this without hateful words or physical abuse just makes me cry even harder.

"Lia, do you need a hug?" Drix asks tentatively.

The concern in his voice sounds so genuine that I almost,

almost answer with a nod of my head, but I quickly remind myself that Martin had been just as genuine when we first started dating and look where that got me. I'm not exactly a good judge of character.

"I'm sorry. I'm okay now," I sniffle eventually, drawing in a ragged breath as I wipe my eyes and turn to face him. God, what must I look like? What must he think of me?

"You've nothing to apologise for," Drix replies, trying his best to reassure me as I pull out my phone, tapping the screen to open it up.

"What's your number?" I ask, unable to meet his gaze as my thumb hovers over the screen. I'm shaking so badly that when he begins to reel off his number I make a mistake and have to start over again.

"Here, let me," he says, gently cupping my hand, his thick tattooed fingers curling around mine as he takes my phone. Too shocked by his touch, and exhausted by all the crying, I just watch as he taps his number into my phone before handing it back to me.

"There you go."

For a beat I'm unable to speak, caught in this tense moment between us as his warm fingers linger on my skin. A shiver scatters down my spine, and this time I can't tell if it's from fear or attraction, a feeling that I've not felt in a very, very long time. A feeling I push deep down inside of me. No. I will never let myself feel anything for anyone other than Toby, ever again.

Blowing out a tremulous breath, I shiver with fatigue and emotional exhaustion.

"Thanks... for everything."

"You're welcome, Lia." He reaches for me, but I shake my head, wrapping my arms around my chest. His fingertips, so close to brushing against my arm, fall away, taking their heat with them. "I'm going to go now, okay?"

"Okay."

"Rest up. I'll swing by tomorrow morning at ten to drive you back to your car."

"I'd appreciate that," I reply, forcing myself to give him a tight smile.

"See you then," he says, then swivels on his feet, and strides towards the door.

Only he doesn't get very far.

If I thought tonight couldn't get any worse, I was sorely mistaken, because right at that moment, when Drix pulls open the door, Toby sits up in bed and projectile vomits all over himself and the very expensive Egyptian cotton bed linen.

FIVE

"HERE, TAKE THIS," I say, handing Lia a glass of water for Toby to sip from.

He sits in the bath, his knees drawn up to his chest as Lia cleans his face with a washcloth. The poor kid looks wrecked, Lia not much better, and yet she still pushes on, handling the situation like a champ. I admire her so fucking much.

"Thank you," she murmurs, taking the glass from me and handing it to Toby, helping him to take a sip before placing the glass on the ledge beside the bath. It's been an hour since he last threw up, so it looks like the worst of it is over.

"I'm sorry, Mama," Toby whispers, his skinny shoulders rolling over as he drops his head.

"You've nothing to be sorry for," she replies, cupping his chin and lifting his head. "It's not *your* fault you're ill."

I hear the unspoken words she doesn't say, she blames herself. I see it in the tense way she holds herself, the concern in her eyes, and the sadness that silently gathers in the bathroom around us.

"How about we get you back into bed?" she asks him, plastering on a smile as she pushes upwards, taking the soft towel that I silently hand to her.

"But I threw up all over it. Where will I sleep?"

"That's okay, buddy. The cleaners came up to change the bedding whilst you're Ma got you all cleaned up. It's like nothing ever happened," I explain, grateful that my sister didn't question why I needed the bed sheets changed fifteen minutes after we entered the room. Pretty sure she'll have a hell of a lot of questions for me tomorrow, but right now she's leaving me to deal with this on my own.

"I'm so sleepy," he says, flicking his gaze back to Lia as she helps him out of the bath.

Stepping back out into the suite to give them some privacy, I stride over to the kitchenette, flipping on the switch to the kettle. The expensive machine silently heats the water as I busy myself grabbing a couple of chamomile tea bags from the vast selection of expensive teas and coffee displayed on the counter. If Daphne says it can help to relax a person, then I'm gonna pour a cup for Lia and me. Can't hurt to try.

Leaning against the counter, I scrape a hand through my hair questioning what the fuck I think I'm doing. Lia and Toby aren't my responsibility, and yet the longer I'm in their company the more protective I feel, which is fucking ridiculous since I've only known them for such a short amount of time.

No doubt Daisy will find great pleasure in psychoanalysing me. She'll tell me it's because of my past and the experiences I had as a kid. To a certain extent she'd be right, but there's more to it than the urge to help out someone in need. I can't deny that I'm attracted to Lia's soft curves, pretty eyes and full lips. She's a beautiful woman, and you'd have to be fucking blind not to notice. Not to mention a fucking incredible mother. Whatever her story is, she's protecting her son out of a fierce kind of love. A love both me and Daisy were sorely lacking from our own parents growing up. Fortunately for the both of us, we were adopted by a man I was proud to call my father; the late, great, Hubert Hammer. He was always such a good judge of character, and he appreciated, and respected women as much as I do. And I sure do appreciate Lia.

"Fuck, get a grip man," I scold myself. This ain't the time to start thinking sinful thoughts about a woman who has the weight of the world on her shoulders.

When Lia finally enters the suite with Toby cuddled against her chest it's past three in the morning, and none of us have had a wink of sleep. I'm usually a night owl, but fuck, this whole experience has been exhausting. Christ knows how Lia has kept going, she's a fucking saint cleaning up after her kid without uttering a single complaint. I've watched her take care of Toby, reassuring him and keeping him calm these past few hours, and my admiration for her has only grown. I may not know anything about her, but I do know that she's a good woman.

I watch as she lays him down on the bed, pressing a soft kiss against his cheek. He immediately closes his eyes, and within seconds he's asleep. For a moment she just watches him, her fingers gently stroking his damp hair. Then with a deep sigh, she pushes upwards and walks towards me.

"That was pretty rough going," I say, handing her the cup of chamomile tea that she takes from me, placing it on the marble island separating us. "Do you think he might throw up again?"

She rubs at her forehead, glancing over at him. "I hope not."

"You should drink the tea, sleep," I encourage her, taking a sip from my own cup and wrinkling my nose at the taste. It ain't as tasty as the black coffee I usually drink, that's for sure.

"Actually, I could really do with taking a shower," she sighs wearily.

"Then you go do that. I'll keep an eye on him."

"I'd appreciate that." Her gaze meets mine, and the tense lines of her face relax a little, but still she remains standing where she is, uncertain once more.

"I've got this. Promise," I reassure her.

"Okay," she agrees. "Thank you."

I watch her walk across the room and reach for her suitcase, pulling out some clothes and a washbag, cursing myself again for staring at her arse. With one last glance at me she heads into the bathroom and quietly closes the door behind her.

Moments later my phone vibrates in my pocket and I pull it out, answering the call from my best mate. "What's up, Dalton?"

"Have you fucked her yet?" comes his immediate reply. I can hear the smirk in his voice and, frankly, it pisses me off.

"No, I haven't," I snap, annoyance littering my voice. "Not everyone is like you."

"So you steal my shag-suite and don't even fuck the woman you take up there?" he asks amused, not in the least bit put off by my anger. "You need to up your game."

"Firstly, she's got a kid with her, arsehole, and secondly this ain't no game," I growl into the mouthpiece.

"Then what is it? Have you grown a conscience in your old age?"

"I resent that remark, dickhead. Besides, it ain't me who needs to grow a conscience. I'm not the one fucking every woman who looks his way."

"Fuck, tetchy much," he counters, and I hear the distinct sound of a woman moaning.

"Please don't tell me you're calling me whilst fucking your hook-up."

"I can mutli-task," he laughs back.

"Really?" I ask incredulously.

"You should try it sometime."

"You know what Dalton, you need to take a long hard look at

yourself. This conversation is over." With that I hang up, slamming my phone down onto the counter.

"Mama?" Toby whimpers, and I curse under my breath as he sits up in bed, blinking sleepily. My stomach drops at the terror on his face as I rush to his side.

"Hey, kid. Your Ma's just in the shower," I say, perching on the edge of the bed, not entirely sure what I'm going to do if he projectile vomits again.

"I want Blue Bear," he says, his bottom lip trembling.

"Here he is," I reply, grabbing the teddy from the far side of the bed and handing it to him. He takes it from me, wrapping his arms around it tightly. "Better now?"

Shaking his head, Toby's eyes fill with tears, and on instinct I draw the kid into my arms, hugging him. When he doesn't protest, I kick off my shoes, and shift myself on the bed, propping myself against the headboard and resting my jean clad legs on the mattress. "There we are, kid. You just sleep, as soon as your Ma's done with her shower, I'll leave you both in peace."

Toby snuggles against me, turning his face to look up at me. "I like you," he murmurs.

My fucking heart squeezes in my chest. "The feeling's mutual," I whisper as his eyes droop shut and he falls back to sleep once more.

Ten minutes later, as Lia enters the suite, my own eyes are heavy with sleep. Stifling a yawn, I give her an apologetic smile. "He was a little unsettled, so I thought I'd..."

My voice trails off as she frowns, her cleanly washed hair dripping onto her white t-shirt, the water seeping into her top and sticking it to her ample breasts. She's not wearing a bra.

Fuck.

My gaze lifts, and I clear my throat as my eyes rest upon her face, and despite the dark circles ringing her eyes, and the long cotton pyjama bottoms she's wearing, I don't think I've ever seen anyone more beautiful. Forcing myself to look away, I shift on the bed. "I should really go now."

"Do you live far from here?" she asks, placing her wash bag and dirty clothes on top of the overnight bag she'd left beside the bed.

"About a fifteen minute drive away. Not far."

She looks over to the window, her frown deepening. "It's snowing pretty heavily."

"It is? I hadn't even noticed," I reply, turning my attention to the drift of snow already piling up on the windowsill outside.

She chews on her lip, looking between me and her son. "Perhaps you should stay? I can sleep on the sofa," she offers.

"Absolutely not," I shake my head, gingerly trying to lay Toby back down on the bed, but he whimpers in his sleep and Lia holds her hand up.

"No, don't. He seems... *peaceful* in your arms," she whispers, a look I can't interpret fluttering across her face.

"I can't let you sleep on the sofa," I protest.

"Believe me that sofa looks a thousand times more comfortable than my car."

"Which is precisely why you need to sleep on the bed. Lia, *please...*" I say, grabbing one of the plump pillows and laying it down beside me, building a wall between us. "Now you've got some protection." I smile, but she doesn't.

"Do I need protection from you?"

"Fuck, no. That's not what I meant. I just... Fuck, I'm not good at this."

"Good at what?" she asks, approaching me. Her wariness slipping into weariness as she stifles a yawn.

"I don't need to know what kind of trouble you're in, or why you're running, but I do want you to know that I won't hurt you or Toby. I swear on my sister's life, *my own.*"

"I fell for that before," she mutters before she's able to stop herself, her arms instantly wrapping around her chest and, not for the first time, I wish it was me holding her. That thought is shoved aside as the truth of her words trickle into my consciousness.

"You've been hurt, physically, emotionally?" I ask her tentatively, knowing that there is no other explanation, that I've no right to ask something so personal, but do so anyway.

"Beyond measure," she replies softly.

"The boy's father?"

She nods, her expression crumbling as she brings her hands up to cover her face, her shoulders curving inward as she tries to gather herself.

"I'm so fucking sorry," I say, meaning it, feeling this ball of anger coming alive in my chest, but I push those feelings aside too, she doesn't need to bear the weight of my feelings on top of her own. Her shoulders are already weighted heavily by the shit she's been through, and I'm not going to add to it.

"Tomorrow we'll be out of your hair, and you can get back to normal," she eventually says, swiping at her eyes and rounding the bed. Gingerly she sits down and twists her body to face me. Her beautiful eyes are swimming with more unshed tears, and my gut fucking knots itself up in empathy for her.

"I chose to be here, Lia," I remind her. "You're *not* a burden."

Licking her lips, she nods, her features softening just a fraction. I know I don't have her complete trust, I don't even expect it, but at least she's willing to rest. Small steps are better than none at all.

"Is this okay?" she asks, laying on the edge of the bed, as far away as she can get without falling onto the floor.

"You're asking me that?" I counter, resting back against the headboard as I cant my head towards her. She lets out a broken laugh, and the sound fucking guts me. That piece of shit who hurt her deserves to be crucified for causing her so much fucking pain. I've put men in hospital for far less than that.

"Old habits die hard," she replies cryptically, lying on her side as she stares at her son.

"Just sleep, okay? I'll be here when you wake up."

She shifts on the bed, drawing her knees up slightly, and I can't help but notice the way she winces as she moves.

"Thank you," she mutters, fatigue finally pulling her under moments later.

I don't fall asleep immediately, instead I listen to the soft puffs of Lia's breath as she slumbers, and the sweet murmurs from Toby's mouth, his body warm and relaxed against mine.

Outside the soft patter of thick winter snow falls against the windowpane and I find myself wondering how I can stop this incredibly strong woman and her sweet boy from leaving in just a few short hours. But most of all, I wonder how I can hide the truth of who I am from a woman who's already been deeply scarred by way too much violence in her life.

SIX

BLINKING back the last dregs of sleep, I automatically reach for Toby, remembering too late that he fell asleep in Drix's arms as my hand slides upwards across the firm planes of a warm, muscular chest.

"Where's Toby?" I ask, panicking as I'm suddenly all too aware that my body has been pressed against a man I barely know as I untangle my legs from his.

"I'm taking a poop, Mama!" his voice calls from the bathroom. "Don't worry, it's a good one this time."

"A good one?" I groan, a relieved breath whooshing out of my chest as Drix chuckles, the rumble of his laughter reminding me that I still have my hand pressed against him. "Sorry."

"No need to apologise, Lia," he replies, swiping a hand through his hair as I pull my hand back, my cheeks heating.

"What time is it?" I ask, floundering a little at the mussed up way his hay-blonde hair sticks up on his head, and how my body is still warm from evidentially cuddling up to him all night. Objectively, the man is good looking, and whilst I don't dislike tattoos,

I've never been drawn to a man who has them covering every inch of his skin right up to his jawline. There are even a couple of smaller ones tattooed onto his face.

Yeah, the type you go for are usually well dressed men, with dazzling smiles that hide the evil inside, a little voice inside my head goads. I ignore it.

"Around nine. Sleep okay?" Drix asks, rubbing the back of his neck, wincing a little.

"I'm guessing by the look on your face you didn't?" I throw back, chewing on my lip. "I'm sorry if I..."

My voice trails off as his gaze drops, and I'm suddenly acutely aware of how tight my t-shirt is, and how I stupidly didn't put a bra on last night. I guess I was too exhausted to think straight.

Drix quickly forces his gaze back upwards and my cheeks heat as I fold my arms across my chest, wishing I'd worn a jumper over the top. I don't need to look down to know my nipples are pebbling against the material. Not because I'm turned on, but because since having Toby they're permanently erect. A combination of breast feeding him for the first eighteen months of his life, and how my body has changed since having him.

"Nothing that a long hot shower won't cure. I slept just fine," he replies, clearing his throat.

His eyes rest on mine, and for a moment the air between us thickens with unspoken things.

"Can I get you a coffee? Maybe that will help?" I climb off the bed and rush towards the kitchenette on the other side of the suite, grabbing my jumper from on top of my suitcase and pulling it on as I go.

"Sure, that'd be good," he replies, climbing to his feet just as Toby comes running out of the bathroom and throws himself into Drix's arms.

"Good morning, Drix!" Toby shouts, laughing as Drix picks him up and messes his hair.

"Morning, buddy," Drix greets him, grinning.

"Toby, leave the man alone. I think he's had quite enough of you clambering all over him," I say, a little tersely. Mostly because I'm still embarrassed by the fact I've practically flashed my breasts at Drix, but also because I'm scared that Toby is becoming way too attached.

"Sorry," he mumbles, his smile fading, and I instantly regret my words.

"What's with all the apologies today?" Drix asks goodnaturedly, bopping Toby's nose with his finger. "We're all good."

"We *are* all good, aren't we Mama?" Toby asks.

I nod, caught by the moment of Toby so happy in a stranger's arms.

"We sure are," Drix chuckles, setting him down on the bed.

Toby immediately starts jumping up and down on the bed like it's a trampoline, laughing and flapping his arms around as he enjoys the bounce from the springy mattress.

"Toby stop that! This isn't a playground," I say, worry coursing through me. I love Toby with everything that I am, but he's full of energy at the best of times, and this room is so posh, I'm worried he'll break something.

Drix just chuckles, waving away my concerns. "It's fine. You bounce away, little man, you have my approval."

"You really shouldn't encourage him," I counter, busying myself with making us both a cup of coffee as Drix approaches. His tall frame, broad shoulders, and body covered in tattoos are somehow even more intimidating in the light of day.

"I can assure you, that bed has survived way more action than a kid's energetic bouncing."

"I'm not sure I want that visual in my head," I reply, pouring a dash of milk into my mug, offering him some.

Drix shakes his head. "I prefer mine without."

"Sugar?"

"I'm sweet enough," he jokes.

"I doubt that very much," I mutter under my breath, remembering the flare of heat in his eyes when he forced himself to look away from my breasts just moments ago.

The sheer fact he didn't look at me with disgust like Martin would do all the time makes me feel uncomfortable in a different way. It's been a long time since anyone has looked at me like I'm an attractive woman, and I have to remind myself that I don't know this man, that I have to be cautious, that I can't let myself trust him. Which seems ridiculous since that's exactly what I've done these past twenty-four hours. I guess desperation makes you do stupid things.

Sliding the mug across the counter, I take a sip of my own coffee.

"This is good," I mumble, feeling wholly uncomfortable about the situation I've found myself in.

"The breakfast is even better," Drix replies, looking at me from over the rim of his mug as he swallows a mouthful.

My gaze flicks to my suitcase. "I don't think I've got the right clothes to wear for breakfast."

Drix frowns. "The right clothes?"

"You know, it's posh here..." My voice trails off as I remember the well dressed couple from last night. This hotel seems to cater to the well to-do, and I really don't fit into that bracket.

"You don't need to dress up for breakfast," he reassures me, amusement in his eyes.

"Even so. I don't feel comfortable."

"But you are hungry, right?"

My stomach takes the opportunity to rumble loudly right at that precise moment. "I'm fine—"

He raises a brow, unconvinced. "If you don't want to go down for breakfast. I'll order room service for the three of us. How about that?"

"Room service? What's that?" Toby asks, flopping down onto the bed, a wide grin spreading across his flushed face as he flips on his stomach and looks between us.

"That, my friend, is when we get food delivered right to our door."

"Like a takeaway?" he asks, pushing up onto his hands and knees and doing a forward roll off the end of the bed. We both stiffen as he drops, hitting the floor hard. "Did you see that, Mama?" he exclaims after a beat, jumping up and bouncing on the spot like he hasn't just given us both a heart attack.

"I saw that," I exhale.

Drix looks at me wide-eyed. "I heard kids bounce back, but that takes the cake," he says, shaking his head in disbelief.

"I imagine you were just as lively as a child," I say, my lips twitching with a smile, that I shut down just as quickly as it appeared.

"Believe me, I was worse," he snorts.

"I bet."

"So what do you fancy eating?" he asks Toby, casting a look at me. "If you think his tummy can take it, of course."

"Given how lively he is this morning, I'd say he's good to eat. But maybe something simple like scrambled eggs and toast?" I suggest.

"Sounds good to me." Drix nods. "And what about you, what would you like to eat?"

"I'll have the same," I say automatically. It's not that I wouldn't like to eat more, because I would, it's just I don't want to take advantage.

Sensing that I'm holding back, Drix grins. "I'll order you the same as me. A full English breakfast with all the trimmings. May as well make the most of my friend's generosity."

"You'll have to thank him for me," I reply, glad that I've got my hands full with the mug of coffee, because if I didn't, I know I'd be wringing them with guilt. I shouldn't be leaning on this man the way that I am.

"I spoke to him last night whilst you were in the shower, believe me he's happy to help," Drix replies, but there's something in his eyes that tells me he's stretching the truth there a little.

"If you're sure?"

"Leave it with me."

Half an hour later we're seated at the table by the huge floor to ceiling windows, a feast laid out in front of us as Toby stuffs his mouth with toast whilst simultaneously bouncing up and down in his seat, utterly entranced by the view, and the thick snow covering every inch of the grounds surrounding the hotel.

"Can we build a snowman after breakfast, Mama?" he asks, bits of food flying out of his mouth as he speaks.

"Toby, don't speak with your mouth full," I chide, giving Drix an apologetic look, knowing only too well that we'll be on the road again after breakfast.

"Don't mind me. The kid's excited. Nothing like building a snowman, is there, fella?"

"I don't know. I've never made a snowman before," Toby replies, eyes wide with wonder.

"Well then, we'll have to change that, won't we?" Drix answers indulgently, wiping his mouth with a napkin. "If that's okay with you, of course," he adds.

"Mama, can we?" Toby asks, his face lighting up with happiness.

Happiness that I'm going to have to put out. I hate that I'm the one to smother it, but we can't stay here. We've already outstayed our welcome. Building snowmen with Drix is out of the question.

"Drix, can I speak to you for a minute?" I ask, pushing back my chair and motioning him to follow me to the otherside of the suite, and out of earshot of Toby.

"Sure thing," he replies, getting up and following me.

Nearing the door to the suite, I turn to face him. "I appreciate everything that you've done for us, but you can't be building snowmen with my son."

"Why not? It's just a snowman," he replies, stepping into my personal space. It's not meant to be an intimidating move, more to ensure our conversation is only heard by the two of us, but I react like it is, stepping back.

"We both know that it isn't just a snowman," I reply, my back hitting the wall as I look up at him.

He considers my reply for a moment, then reaches for my arm, cupping it gently. "If I'm honest, maybe it isn't just about building a snowman. Maybe I'm insane for saying this, but I'm going to anyway."

"Say what?" I reply softly.

Like a deer caught in headlamps, I freeze, uncertain about every decision I've made in the past twenty-four hours. The intimate way he looks at me, and the gentle way his thumb rubs up and down my arm has my fight or flight instincts kicking in.

"Lia, I want—"

"Please, don't touch me," I warn, cutting him off as tears of anger, of fear, of *hope*, brim in my eyes. It's the hope that's blooming inside of me that spurns me into action as I push at his chest, forcing him backwards and away from me. I can't afford to let my guard down. I chose wrong once before, I won't do that again.

"Fuck," he murmurs, pulling back, giving me the breathing space I so desperately need.

"You have been unbelievably kind," I say, struggling to find the words to thank him for what he's done for us. "But I *can't* do this."

"I won't lie and tell you that I don't want you to stay," he counters, taking me by surprise with his honesty. "There's something about you Lia. I want to get to know you more. I want to help you and Toby. Stay?"

"Stay where? I have nowhere to go. I have no friends here, no family. All I have is Toby. He's all I've got."

"It doesn't have to be that way. Let me be a friend to you both. Let me help you, at least until you get on your feet."

"I can't do that."

"Why? Have I not shown you that I'm someone you don't have to fear?"

"I'm not a very good judge of character, Drix. I've made that mistake before."

He runs a hand over his face in frustration, his brown eyes filled with concern, with empathy, and if I'm not mistaken a dash of anger.

"You're mad at me."

"Christ, no," he replies, shaking his head. "I'm mad at the man who hurt you. I'm mad at *him*, not you."

"Believe me, the feeling's mutual."

I don't tell him that I'm also terrified of Martin. What if he comes after us? What if he finds us, hurts me and takes Toby? I *have* to keep moving. I've travelled hundreds of miles and it still doesn't feel far enough away.

"You know running isn't going to solve your problems, Lia," he comments, gently. "You'll be in the same position in the next town you stop at. "Perhaps even worse off."

"I'll figure something out. I'll find a way somehow."

"How? You have no money, and presumably no plan beyond getting in your car and driving aimlessly until your gas runs out. You must see how irresponsible that is."

He's right of course, but that doesn't stop me from snapping back at him. "You've no idea how it feels to be scared for your life. So fucking out of your depth."

Drix's eyes flash with compassion, with *knowing*. "That's where you're wrong. I do know. I know only too well."

"Drix, I–" I begin, but he cuts me off, refusing to elaborate further.

"Regardless of how I feel about this whole situation, the snow is staying. Your car has no snow tires, you'll end up getting in an accident before you get a mile down the road. I can't in good conscience let you put yourself or Toby in danger like that," he argues.

My shoulders sag. He's right, again, and honestly, I'm not even sure how my car got us this far as it is. The last fifty or so miles before I reached Princetown, its engine had been rattling like a dying man's chest in the last hours of his life. It's a miracle we even made it this far.

"So what do I do? Let you build a snowman with Toby, and pretend everything's okay, that he has a home here?"

"You let me help. No strings attached. I want nothing in return. When the snow clears, you'll be free to leave, I'll even give you some money to help you on your way."

"You don't have to do that," I protest.

"I know that, but I want to."

"I don't understand why," I admit, confused by this man's kindness. Wary as hell.

"Just call it a random act of kindness," he says softly, tipping his head to the side as he regards me.

"I used to believe that it exists... Kindness, I mean," I blurt out.

"And now?" he asks.

"Everything comes at a price. The question is, what's yours?" I probe, folding my arms across my chest, ignoring the pain from the bruises on my back which only serve to remind me how little kindness I've experienced the past few years of my life.

Drix heaves out a sigh, then levelling his gaze at me says,

"When I was a kid, a man called Hubert took me in. I was fourteen, and by that time had been in foster care for almost five years of my life. He took me under his wing, gave me a home, his name. He had no reason to be kind other than the fact he was. He taught me that for every shit person in the world, there is a good one, a *kind* one. He never wanted anything in return, but he always said to me that if I ever met someone who needed my help, to give it without question. That's what I'm striving to do now. *I'm* paying it forward, Lia."

I blanch, surprised by his honesty. "He sounds like a great guy."

"He was," Drix replies. "Been dead for over a year now and I miss him."

Silence descends between us, interrupted only by Toby's excitement over the snow as he gazes out of the window and claps his hand in glee.

Drix looks over at Toby, his gaze softening. "He's a good kid," he says.

"He is," I agree.

"And you're a good woman. A good mother," he adds, turning back to face me. "You deserve a chance to rest, a moment's reprieve. I can give you that at least."

"Just until the snow clears?" I question him.

"I give you my word. If, by the time it's safe to drive, you still want to leave. I won't stop you."

"Okay," I reply before I can change my mind. What does a few days matter in the grand scheme of things? Whether I can learn to trust this man or not, Toby needs this.

"Okay?" His tone is filled with warmth and relief, and it's such a change to what I'm used to that I don't know how to act in the face of such empathy, concern and... *kindness*.

"I'll stay until the snow clears," I reply, my voice fading to a hushed stillness as Toby comes running over, hopping on his feet as he tugs on Drix's hand.

"Can we make a snowman now?" Can we? Can we, please?" he cries, his happiness making Drix grin widely and my heart break a little knowing that we'll be leaving this place behind just as soon as the snow clears.

SEVEN

WE PULL into my drive an hour later, Toby chatting incessantly about the huge snowman we built together on the front lawn of the hotel. I don't think I've smiled as much in a while. His exuberance, his joy, was like a breath of fresh air, and I gulped it down like a man who hadn't breathed deeply in a long, long time.

"You did good, buddy. That was the best snowman I've ever seen," I say, grinning, my gaze flicking to Lia who has been quiet for the entire drive here.

She stares out of the window now, her slender hands folded in her lap, lost to her thoughts, and even though she'd helped us build the snowman, smiled the whole time, laughed when Toby lay flat out in the snow and rolled around in it like a puppy might, I could tell her thoughts were elsewhere, that her heart wasn't really in it.

It makes me wonder when she last smiled, laughed even, not because she wanted to make the experience better for her son, but because she truly *wanted* to. It's clear to me that it's been a long time since she was relaxed enough to experience that kind of happiness for herself.

"Here we are," I say, parking the car right outside the front door of the home I share with my sister, Daisy.

"*This* is your home?" Lia asks, surprise littering her voice as Toby gasps at Brownstone Estate, a sprawling homestead built around two-hundred years ago when Hubert's great-great grandfather settled in Princetown.

Sitting on ten acres of land, it's less flashy than the three other founding families' homes, but it is impressive nevertheless. With its brown tiled roof—mostly hidden now by the snow—tan stucco walls, wooden windows with shutters, it's a nod to the Spanish architecture the Hammer family left behind in their homeland.

"It's bigger than a palace!" Toby exclaims excitedly.

"Not quite," I chuckle. "Besides, there are no Kings or Queens living here. Just me and Daise. Just us."

"You're rich," Lia states, and it comes out as an accusation rather than a statement, as though I hid that fact from her. Truth is, it never occurred to me to mention it. What was I going to say, hey my name's Drix and I'm a millionaire, in property at least?

"My father, *Hubert,* was a wealthy man. Daise and I inherited his home when he died," I reply, tiptoeing around the complicated details of our inheritance. Even Daisy is unaware of the true extent of our predicament. "Truthfully, I'm more comfortable sleeping at the flat above the gym I run in town than here. I earn my own living."

Lia frowns, colour seeping into her cheeks. "I'm sorry, that sounded really judgemental," she apologises.

"It's no big deal."

"Why?" she asks after a beat, looking out of the window at my home, taking it all in.

"Why what?" I reply, switching off the engine.

"Why are you more comfortable sleeping elsewhere? You have a beautiful home."

I shrug. "I guess it doesn't feel like much of home without Hubert living in it."

"Not even with your sister here too?"

"That came out wrong. I love Daisy, she's the best, but this place hasn't felt the same since he's been gone. His absence has left a huge hole, one both me and Daisy have struggled to live with."

Lia nods in understanding. "I'm sorry for your loss, Drix."

"Thank you," I reply, grief hitting me so suddenly that it feels like a punch to my gut. Clearing my throat, I open my door. "Shall we head inside?"

"Sure."

Grabbing their suitcase from the boot, I wait for Lia to get Toby out of the car. She gathers him in her arms, trudging across the snow-covered drive behind me, white puffs of air escaping their lips as we walk towards the arched wooden door that opens up into the main living area. Decorated simply, with white walls, wooden beams, and neutral cushions and throws, it's a welcoming home. Warm despite its apparent grandeur.

As soon as I close the door behind us, Lia removes Toby's shoes and coat, then her own. Brushing a dusting of snow off his hair as she straightens up. The minute she lets him go, he runs straight to the leather sectional situated in front of the huge widescreen TV hanging on the wall opposite.

"Can I watch some cartoons, Mama?" he asks, swivelling his head around at us as she hangs up their coats on the hook by the front door.

Lia grimaces. "I'm sorry. If you just show us where we're sleeping, I'll settle him down. He's very excited right now. We'll stay out of your way."

"No need to apologise, and you're not in anyone's way. How about Toby watches some cartoons whilst I show you around?" I offer, trying to put her at ease.

"I don't know," Lia replies, casting her gaze around the space, wringing her hands.

I wish I could take them in mine and reassure her with my touch that she doesn't need to feel awkward. Instead I use my words, hoping for the time being, that's enough.

"He's perfectly safe where he is. If he decides to go for a wander, all he'll find is a kitchen through there," I say pointing towards the back of the room. "Apart from the gym that's off the kitchen, the doors to the other sections of the house are locked up as Daise and I don't tend to use them all that much given there's only two of us living here."

"Please, Mama. I promise to stay *right here*," Toby adds, patting the seat as he grins at the both of us. Pretty sure those puppy eyes he also gives her win her over every time.

"So long as you don't move a muscle," she concedes, nodding. "And just in case you break your promise, remember what I said about handling anything dangerous in the kitchen."

"No touching anything sharp or hot," he reels back.

"That's right, good boy. You enjoy the cartoons then."

"Thank you, Mama!"

"Perfect! Let me find you the right channel," I say before she can change her mind.

Placing her suitcase on the floor, I stride over to Toby and pick up the remote that's resting on the coffee table in front of the sectional. It takes me a moment to find the right channel, but as soon as a cartoon appears, Toby squeals with delight, his attention utterly focussed on the screen.

"I may have trouble dragging him away," Lia remarks, a soft smile on her lips that falters as I near.

"Come on, let me show you to your room," I say, stooping down to grab her suitcase right at the same time she does. Our fingers brush against each other, and I swear I feel a bolt of electricity zing up my arm from that brief touch.

Fuck.

Her hand falls away, and she straightens up. "I can carry the suitcase," she says softly.

"I know, but I want to," I reply, picking it up and turning on my heel so she can't see how affected I am by her brief touch.

Fuck knows how I kept my hands off her last night as she lay next to me in bed, metaphorically speaking of course. I would never have come on to her, or touched her without her express permission. I'm not like Dalton who just assumes everyone wants to fuck him. Granted, he has a one hundred percent success rate with women, but that doesn't mean he'll eventually find one who doesn't want to sleep with him. I'd like to see that moment, that's for sure. He could use a little humbling.

Besides, I respect the women I choose to sleep with, and consent is really fucking important to me. Not that's what this is. I meant it when I said I wanted to help them both, no strings attached.

Even so, I couldn't stop myself from watching her sleep for a little while last night. My gaze had traced the curve of her hip and the dip of her waist, appreciating the softness of a woman who's carried and birthed a child. Even in sleep she had been tense, as though she had no respite from the monster she's running from. Perhaps she hadn't. Perhaps that fucker who hurt her continued to do so in her nightmares.

"Will your sister be home soon?" Lia asks me, interrupting my thoughts as we hit the top of the wooden staircase and start down the hallway towards the guest suite. I can't help but notice how she follows me quietly a few steps behind, as though she's used to being unseen, small somehow.

"She usually pops in to see Daphne at the cafe for breakfast after her shift at the hotel. I imagine she'll be home soon," I explain, pushing open the door to the room she'll be staying in with Toby.

"And she won't mind us staying here?" Lia asks, following me into the room.

"Not at all. Daisy is cool like that."

"She seemed friendly," she recounts, nibbling on her lip as her eyes dart around the room. I don't like the way she holds herself as though she's about to bolt. Or worse, that now I've got her alone she expects me to switch on her, to do something she doesn't want. Her body is stiff, a coil pulled tight with tension.

"Daisy is the sweetest, kindest person you'll ever meet," I say, hoping that gives her the kind of comfort that I clearly can't. "My sister doesn't have a bad bone in her body. As a kid she was always bringing back waifs and strays, both people and animals. Hubert always humoured her, encouraged it even. He was good like that," I chuckle.

Lia stiffens, and I curse myself. "Is that what I am to you?" she asks, her expression growing serious. "A waif or stray?"

"No," I immediately answer, because it's true. She might be someone I want to help in the same way Daisy always helps people but, shockingly, she is fast becoming more than that.

Truth be known that thought kind of terrifies me. I meant what I said about her being a woman dangerous for a man like me. She arches a brow, unconvinced, and that fire in her eyes I've seen a couple of times since meeting her flickers to life. Looks like Lia Pearson is a proud woman too, and maybe, underneath all that distrust and fear, someone to be reckoned with.

Dropping the suitcase onto the leather ottoman at the end of the double bed, I say, "What you are is a woman who has done the one thing my mother couldn't do for me. You put yourself and your kid first, and escaped a violent relationship. Can't say I was as lucky."

"Drix..." Her voice trails off as a look of sympathy passes across her face.

"I know what it feels like to live in fear, Lia," I explain. "My biological father was a violent drunk, a misogynist. He was the worst kind of person. If it hadn't been for Hubert giving me a home, a family, I may have lived my life believing the same thing that you do now."

"And what's that?" she cautions.

"That accepting kindness comes with a price. That everyone I meet has an ulterior motive. That I'm not worthy of acceptance, empathy, happiness, *love*."

That statement hangs in the air between us. Maybe I've said too much, shown my hand too early. Maybe, like Lia, I should protect myself from disappointment. But if Hubert taught me one thing, it's to be honest even when you've got everything to lose. Lia could walk away with Toby just as soon as the opportunity arises. I expect her to, and yet I'm willing to take that risk even if it means I'll be the one left damaged at the end of it.

The sheer fact that I already know I will be hurt if she walks is one of the scariest things I've ever had to face. But I ain't lived the life I have without learning a few things myself, and trusting my gut is one of them. Lia might not know that we could be good together, but I do.

Rubbing her forehead as though she has a headache, she blows out a breath. "Can we start over?"

"I'd happily do whatever you want," I reply gruffly because, at this point, that too is true. I think I might just burn the world down for this woman and her son if she asked me to. Across her beautiful face a dim flush races like a fever, and I have the sudden urge to chase it with my fingers.

"You've done more than enough already," she replies, stepping aside as I head towards the door.

"I'll go check on Toby, grab him a drink whilst you settle in," I say, casting one last brief gaze her way before stepping out of the room, hoping to fuck I find a way to earn her trust, and maybe later, something more.

EIGHT

FIFTEEN MINUTES LATER, after taking a moment to just sit with my thoughts on the huge teak double bed in this beautiful room that houses a matching wardrobe, plush taupe carpet and pine green bedding, I head back downstairs.

As I wander back down the hallway, my emotions are all over the place. I have mixed feelings of relief and guilt. Relief because at least Toby and I don't have to sleep another night in my car, and guilt because of all the mistakes I've made, not just this past week, but the last few years staying with a man who I knew, deep down, was incapable of ever changing.

They say hindsight is twenty-twenty. Of course now that I've been able to distance us from Martin, I can see clearly, but whilst you're in the thick of an abusive, toxic relationship it's hard to do that. So very hard.

Bit by bit I allowed Martin to chip away at my self-esteem and confidence. I've lived for so long in fear. Fear of saying the wrong thing to set him off in a rage. Fear of doing the wrong thing. Walking around him on eggshells constantly. If I didn't dress in the clothes he wanted me to wear, he would abuse me. If I looked at him in a way he didn't like, he'd raise his fists.

God forbid standing up to him.

As I reach the top of the stairs, a sudden memory of that morning he'd beaten me so badly I knew I had to leave comes rushing back in, and I have to grip the handrail to steady myself as a wave of nausea washes over me. I'm littered with bruises, all because the coffee I brought him wasn't big enough.

"Are you fucking stupid?" he'd shouted at me. *"I asked for a large!"*

My mumbled apology had been met with a sudden explosive rage as he'd thrown the coffee cup against the wall and launched himself at me. The rest is a blur of fists flying, of pain and humiliation. He only stopped because the postman had knocked at the door with a delivery.

I've thanked my lucky stars ever since, knowing that if Martin hadn't been interrupted he may well have killed me. That morning, as I struggled to my feet, I knew we had to escape, wholly believing that it would be just a matter of time before he'd take his rage out on Toby too.

Dragging in a few deep breaths, I force my feet to move and head back downstairs. With each step I lock away the memories and plaster on a smile. Protecting Toby from my pain, from any kind of heartache, is my top priority.

"Toby?" I call, my stomach rolling when I don't see him sitting on the sofa. The television still plays cartoons, but he's nowhere to be seen. "Toby?!" I shout a little louder this time, panic making my heart race.

For one awful, terrible moment, I think the worst.

Then I hear Toby's childish giggle and Drix's deep chuckle, followed by a more feminine one. My stomach coils, the sound both comforting and terrifying all at once. Toby is such a sweet and loving kid, and I know he's already becoming attached to the man who's shown us both such kindness, the likes of which I've not experienced in a long, long time.

"Hey, what's happening here?" I ask, stepping into the beautiful shaker style kitchen that's almost as large as the open plan living space I've just passed through. Cabinets run the entirety of the room, and the thick wooden countertops and flooring give it a lovely warmth, or perhaps that warmth is coming from the huge Aga cooker that looks like it hasn't been used in quite some time, given the pristine condition it's in. If I were ever in a position to own such a beautiful home, this would be the exact kitchen I'd like.

"Mama, we're making cherry pie!" Toby exclaims, his eyes lighting up as I approach them. Perched on a stool next to the large kitchen island, Toby's hands are covered in flour. Next to him Daisy watches Drix roll out some dough, amusement in her eyes.

"Well, trying too anyway," Daisy explains, smothering a giggle as she casts a dubious look at the dough Drix seems to be having trouble with. She gives me a warm smile. "Settled in okay?"

Our eyes meet, and I see the empathy in hers. "Yes, thank you."

She nods. "Of course."

"So you're making a cherry pie?" I ask, avoiding Drix's gaze as I look at the ingredients scattered across the island.

Toby bounces on his seat. "Drix says that it's even better than chocolate cake!"

"I do love a slice of cherry pie," he grins, his hands covered in sticky dough. There's a dusting of flour across his cheek as he looks over at me. "And it *is* better than chocolate cake."

"You might be good at *demolishing* a cherry pie, but I'm not so sure you're as good at making one," Daisy giggles as Drix pulls a face, the dough way too sticky to roll out.

"I'm not sure that dough is going to cut it," I observe, approaching them.

"Yeah?" Drix frowns. "I swear I've followed every step in the recipe."

"May I?" I ask, rounding the island.

"You bake?" he asks, stepping aside so I can assess the damage.

"It's one of my favourite things to do," I say.

"Mama is the best baker ever! She makes the yummiest chocolate cake. Before she had me, she made birthday cakes for a living!" he says proudly.

"Thank God for that, because I think I could use some help here," Drix admits, swiping at his face and depositing more flour.

"Your face," I say, pointing to his cheek. The flour has scattered across his cheeks and chin, collecting in his short blonde beard.

"My face?"

"You've got flour on your face," Daisy points out, surreptitiously swiping at the flour sprinkled on the counter. "Right there," she adds, reaching up and pressing her palm over his mouth, laughing at her handiwork as Drix coughs, flour puffing from his lips in a white cloud.

"You little brat!" he laughs, his eyes darting to the bag of flour as a smirk slides across his face.

"Don't even think about it, Drix!" she squeals, backing up as he stuffs his hand into the bag and grabs a handful.

"Don't dish it out if you can't take it," he warns, stalking towards her as she laughs, holding her hands up.

It's a reflexive action, and I know she's enjoying the playful moment, but despite that, I feel anxiety creeping up my spine. The way he stalks towards her reminds me too much of how Martin has done the same to me on so many occasions I've lost count.

"No, don't!" she cries, laughing as she backs up, hitting the counter.

Toby is laughing with them too, his childish glee lifting up into the air, joining the chorus of their mutual joy. But joy is the last thing I feel. Fear shudders through me as another memory crashes through my mind. I grip hold of the countertop, my knuckles turning white as I hold on.

"Please stop," I whisper, partly to the ghost of the memory, and partly to them.

"Drix, don't!" Daisy squeals.

"Too late," Drix chuckles, not hearing me as he drops flour all over Daisy's head. It falls in a puff of white cloud, covering her strawberry blonde hair, colouring it white.

She tackles him, laughing and shaking her head so more flour scatters over his chest and arms. Toby, finding the whole episode thoroughly amusing, climbs down from his seat, his small hands covered in flour too as he pats his hands against them both. Joining in on their fun.

Only it isn't fun for me.

It's triggering me in a way I wished it wouldn't. I can feel myself spiralling, and I don't want to lose it in front of them. "Please stop," I repeat, pressing my eyes shut, trying and failing to block out the sounds of Martin's voice as he goads me.

"Look at you, proper little servant covered in flour. You think that baking me a cake is going to make up for looking like some ugly, washed-out, old hag?"

My hands come up to cover my ears, as I press my eyes shut and begin to tremble. "Please, stop it!" Their laughter somehow twists into sobs, and I realise too late that it's *me* who's crying.

"Lia?" I feel the gentle touch of someone's hand on my arm, and I flinch away from it, forcing my eyes open as I blink back tears. Drix is standing in front of me, his expression crestfallen. "Lia, what is it?"

"I–" my voice cracks as I back away from him, dragging in deep, even breaths.

"Mama?" Toby whispers, his voice trembling.

"I'll be okay. I'm okay," I mumble, but despite my words, I'm not okay. I'm not sure that I'll ever be okay again.

"Daisy, take Toby to wash up. We'll be with you in a moment," Drix instructs, realising that what I need most of all is Toby elsewhere so that I can try and regain my composure.

"Mama?" Toby questions, and I look over at him, forcing a tight smile on my face.

"It's okay, go with Daisy. I'll be there in a moment."

"But you're crying," he protests, running towards me. I drop down to my haunches, folding him into a hug.

"I'm just super tired. Think I might have a little headache coming on, that's all," I lie. Forcing brightness into my voice, I gently ease back and say, "Mama will be fine. Promise."

"Promise?" he asks, his own eyes welling with tears.

"Cross my heart," I say, pressing a kiss to his forehead.

"Come on, sweetie, let's get cleaned up, shall we?" Daisy suggests, her expression filled with concern as she gently rests her hand on Toby's shoulder.

I stand, nodding, feeling ashamed all of a sudden. I can't even keep myself together for my son. When Toby doesn't go with her immediately, she adds. "I can show you my collection of toy unicorns. I keep them in the den with all my books."

"You have *toy unicorns?*" he asks, looking up at her wide-eyed.

"Pretty sure they've been waiting for me to introduce you to them," she replies, looking over at me, searching for my approval.

"Can I go see the unicorns?" Toby questions.

"Go on. It's okay," I urge him, touching his upturned cheek.

After a beat Toby nods. "Okay, Mama."

Okay, Mama. Those two words linger in the air as Daisy steers him out of the room.

Okay, Mama, I know you're sad, but I'll pretend you're not, just like you keep pretending.

"Lia, I'm so sorry. I didn't think," Drix says as soon as they're out of earshot.

I shake my head, forcing myself to meet his gaze. "It's not your fault. You were having fun. It's just…"

"It's just what, Lia? You can talk to me. There'll be no judgments from me, just an ear to listen."

I chew on my lip, wanting so much to relieve myself of some of the burden of my memories, but I don't. I'm feeling way too vulnerable right now. Sensing my indecision Drix blows out a breath, eying the mess that is the kitchen island and the sticky dough and flour covering it.

"So you bake?"

"Yeah," I nod.

"Do you want to help me do this properly?"

I swipe at my eyes, glad for the distraction. "Sure."

Twenty minutes later, the pie crust is chilling in the fridge ready to be rolled out in a couple of hours, the pitted cherries, sugar, cornstarch, vanilla and almond extract mix is almost ready to remove from the heat, and the kitchen is clean and tidy.

"That smells delicious," Drix remarks as he leans against the counter, drying his hands with a kitchen towel. "You're good at this."

"It's easy when you know how."

"Toby said you make birthday cakes?"

"Other things too. Baking was a passion of mine."

"Was? You don't bake any more?"

"I stopped baking professionally a long time ago," I reply, turning down the heat and carrying the pan of cherries to the island. I set it down, placing the sieve above the bowl, then pour the mixture from the pan into it.

The sweet juices flow into the bowl, whilst the softened cherries collect on top. "We just need to let them cool," I explain as Drix quietly watches me. "Once the dough is ready in a couple of hours, we can line the tin with the dough, add the cherries then top it with a lattice crust."

"Why did you stop baking?" he asks me, though I'm guessing he can already figure out the answer to that all on his own, but I answer anyway.

"Because Martin didn't like it."

"He didn't like you baking?" Drix asks, perching on one of the stools.

"Martin didn't like me doing much of anything. He didn't like to see me happy," I sigh. "He took great pleasure out of making me miserable. Those china dolls Toby mentioned, he smashed most of them to smithereens the day I finally found the courage to leave."

"Arsehole," Drix mutters, and when I glance over at him I can see a muscle feathering in his jaw as he holds back from saying more.

"You're right, he *is* an arsehole." I give him a half-smile that doesn't reach my eyes.

"I'm sorry you had to live through that," he replies, swiping a hand over his face, dislodging some of the flour that still sticks to his beard.

"Over the years he stripped me of my independence. The sad thing is, I let him. I let him chip away at every piece of me until I no longer recognise myself when I look in the mirror," I admit. "I'm just as much to blame for letting him."

"No," Drix argues firmly. "You are not to blame for that bastard's behaviour."

"But I didn't leave him," I counter, more shame piling on top of the ton that already sits on my shoulders. "Not after the first time he called me names, not after the first time he beat me or the countless times he treated me with hatefulness."

"Lia, you have to know that none of this is your fault," he urges.

"I know that I was once someone who loved to dance in the

kitchen whilst I baked," I say, my voice catching. "I was once someone who laughed at stupid jokes until her belly ached and tears poured from her eyes. I was once a girl who liked to walk in the rain, who loved to watch the sun set, who collected china dolls, who found pleasure in the simple things life offered. I was someone who loved tulips and strawberry cheesecake, who would like to go on picnics and eat red wine with smelly cheese, who would sing badly in the shower, who'd wear the clothes she loved, not the ones I was forced to wear. I was once a woman who had passion in her heart and fire in her soul. Now look at me."

"You can find joy in those things again," he presses. "You can be that woman again, Lia."

I laugh bitterly. "How can you be so sure?"

"Because if a man like me can still feel the things I do despite everything, then you can find your way back to the person you once were."

"*A man like me?* What do you mean by that?" I ask.

Drix drops his gaze, staring at his large hands that are pressed against the countertop. The words love and hate tattooed across his fingers "Lia, there's something you should know..."

"There you are, arsehole! I've been calling you all morning. How about you answer your phone for once!"

Drix's head snaps up as he looks over at the smartly dressed man entering the kitchen, followed by a flustered looking Daisy.

"Sorry, Drix, he just barged right in. Like he always does, the stupid oaf," she scowls accusingly.

The man, with well-styled mahogany-brown hair and deep set blue eyes, swings his head around to look at her. I notice that he too has tattoos, the black ink edging just above the collar of his shirt. "You do realise that I'm your boss, right? I'd be careful at how you address me," he warns. "Nice hair by the way," he smirks, laughing at the flour that still clings to the strands.

"Would you prefer it if I called you a pig-headed womaniser?"

she counters, folding her arms across her chest, challenging him with her gaze.

Drix covers his laugh with a cough. "It's okay, Daisy, you can back down now. I've got this. What's up, Dalton?"

"Dalton?" I question, looking between the three of them, then back at the man who slides his gaze around, meeting mine. "Aren't you–?"

"You must be the woman Drix took back to my hotel," he says, cutting me off as he strides towards me, his hand outstretched. I can't help but notice the assessing way his gaze slides over me.

"I wouldn't touch him, Lia. You might catch something," Daisy snaps, still bristling from his intrusion.

Drix pushes up from his seat, rounding the island, and stepping between me and Dalton. "This is Lia Pearson. *My friend*," he adds, the tone of his voice protective, threaded with warning.

Dalton grins, holding his hands up. "Of course she is. Nice to meet you, Lia," he says, smirking in a way that makes me feel uncomfortable.

"You too," I reply, not meaning it in the slightest.

Daisy lets out an annoyed sound. "Want to join me and Toby in the den?" she asks me, and I'm filled with relief at her offer.

"Sure," I reply, stepping out from behind Drix, glancing warily at Dalton as I pass them by.

"I won't keep him too long. Business to discuss," Dalton says to our retreating backs.

Neither me nor Daisy reply.

"Sorry about him. He's a douchebag," Daisy says as I follow her to the den.

"You don't think much of him then?" I ask.

"Not particularly. He's an arrogant, cock-sure arsehole. Thinks he's God's gift to women too."

"And clearly you don't think that."

Daisy laughs. "He's been Drix's best friend since we were

kids. Didn't much like him back then, and I sure as hell don't now. He has become more of a jerk over the years. Frankly, I don't understand what all the women he sleeps with see in him."

"But Drix seems to like him, given their best friends," I observe.

"Drix likes an awful lot of people he shouldn't, present company excluded, of course." She gives me a smile and shakes her head. "Sorry, Dalton just rubs me up the wrong way. Always has."

"So he was never one of the waifs or strays you brought home as a kid then?"

Daisy blows a breath through her pursed lips. "Hell would freeze over first. Besides, Dalton comes from old money, the Gunn's aren't short of a pound or a billion."

"A billion? You're joking, right?"

"Nope," she replies, popping the 'p' with an exaggerated breath.

"Wow. That's a lot of money."

"Yeah, it is."

"What made you take a job working for Dalton then?" I ask, curious as to how she ended up working as a receptionist of the hotel he owns, or why, given she too is wealthy.

"Carl offered me the job, and I happen to like working at the hotel. Been doing it since I was a teenager. Hubert, our father, wanted us to understand the value of hardwork and earning our own money. Besides, most of the time Dalton's not around anyway. He's one of those managers who doesn't actually manage all that much. He spends most of his time being a player and getting his dick wet at every opportunity."

"Sounds like Dalton doesn't understand how privileged he is."

"Oh, he knows. He just doesn't care. No doubt he'll eventually swan back off to the Maldives living his playboy life for months on end, sleeping with everyone he meets whilst everyone else works their arses off to keep him in the lifestyle he's accustomed to. At least Sterling and Benedict are more down to earth and willing to work for a living."

"Who are Sterling and Benedict?"

"They're Dalton and Drix's friends. Been friends ever since Hubert adopted us both. Sterling is Robert Blade's son, another wealthy man in Princetown. Sterling is this really talented artist, much to his dad's annoyance. I honestly don't understand why he doesn't support him, but I guess he wants Sterling to take over his business too, just like the other heirs."

"Heirs?"

Daisy gives me a sheepish smile. "To their families' fortunes. There are basically four families that run this town. The Blades, the Gunns, the Pikes and the Hammers. Well, up until Hubert passed away of course."

"Run this town? You make it sound like the wild west, not some picturesque town in England."

She shrugs. "I guess it does sound like that, doesn't it? But basically they own most of the businesses in town between them, supporting the families living here."

"And does Drix do that now?" I ask curiously.

"Since Hubert passed away, in terms of the business side of things, not so much. Though honestly, I think Drix prefers it that way."

"And Drix's other friend you mentioned, Benedict?"

"He's Walter Pike's son," she explains. "Walter owns Bandits Bar, and a few other pubs in the area. Benedict runs the bar and manages Princetown Bandits, a local band."

"Oh, yes. I saw them play briefly when Toby had to use the toilet in the bar the other night. They're good."

"They're fantastic! Maybe you could come watch them live with me sometime?" she offers, enthusiastically.

"Maybe," I reply, stepping into the den and stopping short when I see Toby sprawled out on a thick sheepskin rug playing with the prettiest looking toy unicorns I've ever seen. "Well you look like you're having fun."

"Mama, look at them, aren't they great?" he asks, sitting up and grabbing a blue sparkly unicorn with rainbow coloured hair.

"They're pretty," I agree, crouching down beside him.

"That one is called Trixy Bluebell the third," Daisy says, winking at me when Toby gasps.

"That's a *cool* name."

"It sure is," Daisy agrees.

"So these are yours?" I ask after Toby has picked up each one and Daisy has named them all.

"Yep. I was obsessed with the movie Stardust as a kid. It was the first movie Hubert took me and Drix to see when we came to live with him. I wanted to be Yvaine so badly. She rode a unicorn in the movie," she says, wistfully.

"Drix told me Hubert adopted you both, that your dad was—"

"Oh no, Drix isn't my biological brother. We just happened to live with the same foster family and became close. Despite not sharing the same blood, he is my brother in all the ways that count. I love him very much."

"I'm sorry, I just assumed," I apologise.

"That's okay. I'm not offended in the slightest. Anyone would be lucky to have Drix as their brother. I know I am."

"So Hubert adopted you both at the same time?"

"Initially Hubert just wanted to adopt a son, not having one of his own to carry on his family name, and with no viable options, he chose Drix."

"No viable options?"

"He was firing blanks," Daisy replies, smiling ruefully. "Anyway, when he realised how close Drix and I were he couldn't bear to break us up, so he adopted me too."

"That's incredibly kind..." I say, my voice trailing off as I stare at Toby, unable to comprehend ever being parted from him.

"And Drix's mum," I ask, frowning "Didn't she try to get him back?"

Daisy shakes her head. "Didn't he tell you?"

"Tell me what?"

"Oh sugar, I've said too much." Her skin pales, and I get this sinking feeling in the pit of my stomach.

"Please don't tell me..."

Daisy nods, lowering her voice. "Drix's mum died the night his father killed her. That's why he ended up in care."

NINE

"DIDN'T THINK you'd go for a single mother, Drix. Though, to be fair, I can see the attraction. She's good looking in a *mother-I'd-like-to-fuck* kind of way," Dalton observes, eying me.

My back stiffens at his crass description of Lia. "You might be my best friend, but I'm warning you, dickhead, you speak about Lia in that way again and I'll knock you the fuck out," I growl, my fingers curling into fists.

I've never hit my best mate before, in fact I've defended him on countless occasions. I guess there's a first time for everything. Dalton raises his brows as he loosens his tie and undoes the top button of his shirt.

"Whoa, it was just a joke."

"Not to me it ain't. So cut it out!" I reply, forcing my fingers to uncurl.

After a beat, he smirks. "I've not seen you this riled up over a woman... Well, *ever*."

"I'm just helping her and her kid out," I lie.

Dalton smirks. "Yeah, and I'm a monk."

"Whatever, man. Wanna tell me why you're here because I got

shit to do."

"Does the shit you've got to do involve baking...?" He frowns, staring at the cherries in the bowl. "Very domesticated of you."

"I need to head over to the gym in a bit. Gotta sort out the staff rota," I reply, avoiding his question and picking up the bowl of cherries, placing them in the fridge.

"Well, you're going to need to swing by our place first," Dalton says, lowering his voice and casting his gaze to the door. "Dad's got a job for you."

"Yeah?" I roll my head, feeling the weight of that remark sit on my shoulders. "What does your dad need me for this time?"

"What do any of our dad's need you for?" Dalton throws back. "We all know I bring brains, beauty and talent to the table. You're the muscle."

"Correction, we all know that *Sterling* has the talent and beauty, and *Benedict,* the brains," I remark, knowing it will piss him off, because whilst Dalton is a charmer with the kind of classic good looks that are better suited to black and white movies of old, Sterling is by far the best looking and most talented of the four of us, and Benedict the smartest with his genius level IQ.

"Fuck you, there's no accounting for taste."

I scoff. "I think your brain has been well and truly addled by all the fucking you've been doing lately."

"It's just my way of relieving the tension," he retorts with a grin that doesn't reach his eyes.

"I can think of better ways."

"Better ways than fucking? You really have been sleeping with the wrong kind of woman. If I'd known you were having below par sex, I'd have hooked you up."

"What you do ain't healthy. You've got an addiction, Dalton."

"Addiction?" he scoffs. "I have a *healthy* appetite for beautiful women and multiple orgasms."

"If you say so."

"Look, you know how it is. My dad is constantly on my arse about finding a wife and carrying on the Gunn family name. He's fucking obsessed. May as well try out all the goods on offer before I finally have to choose the lucky lady to impregnate, right?"

"Lucky lady?" I laugh. "I feel sorry for whoever you set your sights on."

"Me too," Daisy scoffs

We both turn our attention to Daisy, flour still clinging to her hair as she heads towards the kettle, switching it on.

"Are you offering yourself up for the role?" Dalton says, deflecting like he always does when a touchy subject comes up.

"I'd rather eat horse shit," she replies deadpan.

"I thought unicorn shit was more your style?" he asks, his voice as cool and clear as ice water, a little of his father shining through. His dad, Carl, is about as warm as a frozen lake, and just as fucking dangerous.

"There's no way in hell I'd let you anywhere near my sister," I add, just in case he was considering chasing her, because that is *never* going to happen. I can tolerate a lot of things, but Dalton messing about with my sister's feelings isn't one of them.

"Don't worry, Drix, she's not my type," Dalton drawls, and I can't help but notice the way Daisy's eyes flash with something that looks an awful lot like hurt. She covers it quickly though.

"I wouldn't sleep with you if you were the last man on Earth. I'm not *that* desperate."

Dalton laughs. "I prefer my women with at least some experience under their belt. Virgins really aren't my thing."

I open my mouth, about to tell him to shut the fuck up, but Daisy cuts me off.

"And I prefer my men with *depth*, not some vacuous, forty-something, self-centred, egotistical arsehole who lets his dick rule his actions. You might want to get yourself tested, pretty sure I can smell the rot setting in from all the way over here."

Dalton looks at her wide-eyed, bristling. He turns to me, and I just shrug my shoulders. It's not like he didn't ask for it.

"I'm thirty-two," he protests, choosing to hone in on her jibe about his age over the others. Vanity should be his middle name.

"Tell that to your greying hair and the lines around your eyes," she retorts cattily. "Either way, isn't it about time you grew the hell up and stopped acting like a selfish prick with no concern for anyone but himself?!"

"And here I was thinking I'd have to punch you for being such a dickhead towards my sister. Looks like her verbal lashing is just as harsh as any punch to the gut I could throw at you," I observe, pride filling my chest. Daisy might be the nicest person I know, but she's no wallflower.

"Sticks and stones, and all that," Dalton mumbles, clearly put out.

Daisy smirks. "You just keep on pretending that you're happy messing around with women who are more interested in your inheritance than what little you have to offer, and I'll enjoy spending my time with real men who aren't afraid of their feelings."

"What men?" both me and Dalton question at the same time.

"Wouldn't you like to know," she replies cryptically before busying herself making tea. I make a mental note to ask her about these men when I next get the chance.

Beside me Dalton's mouth opens and closes like a fish out of water, until eventually he says, "Well as much as I'd like to stick around and exchange insults with a prickly, unicorn-loving, flower, Drix and I have business to attend to."

"You're going out?" Daisy asks, ignoring Dalton and focussing on me.

"Just for a bit. Got to check in at the gym and swing by Carl's place," I explain.

"Well don't be long, okay?"

"I won't. I'll have this wrapped up soon, and be back in time for dinner."

"You'd better."

TWENTY MINUTES later we're pulling up the drive to Carl Gunn's stately mansion. Overlooking Princetown, it's prime real estate worth over twenty million pounds. With enough bedrooms to sleep thirty couples, a ballroom that can comfortably seat over a hundred, a huge indoor swimming pool, gym, library, cinema room, elaborate gardens and stables, it's as obnoxious as it is beautiful, just like the heir to the family fortune.

"I can see the whole gang's here," Dalton comments, eying the other expensive cars parked in his drive. Whilst I appreciate the beauty of Dalton's very own matte black, Aston Martin Valour, Benedict's sage green Bentley, and Robert Blade's silver Rolls Royce Sweptail, I'm not into overly flashy vehicles worth a shit ton more money than most people could ever dream of earning in a lifetime. Hubert may have been a relatively wealthy man himself, but he was also a humble one. Flashy, outlandish cars weren't his thing, and they're not mine either. I'd take his ten year old Landrover that he left me in his will any day of the week.

"Sterling's here?" I question, surprised to see his car—a top of the line Tesla—amongst the others.

"He was ordered home for his dad's wedding next month."

"Wedding? Since fucking when?"

"Since Robert found a younger version of Sterling's mum to keep him company until he tires of her too."

"Bet Sterling was happy about that," I comment. "The ink has only just dried on his parent's divorce papers and Robert's already replacing her with some self-absorbed gold digger, no doubt."

"About as happy as I am about my dad's obsession for a grandchild."

"Yeah," I acknowledge. "Let's get this shit over and done with, shall we?"

Heading inside, we exchange pleasantries with each member of the families present. They're all sitting around the huge table in the billiard room, repurposed for business meetings just like this one.

"Ben, Sterling," I nod, greeting my friends. It's been a few months since we've all been in the same room together, and whilst Sterling and Benedict are five years younger than Dalton and me, we've all been friends since Hubert adopted me.

"Drix," they reply in unison.

Neither of them look happy about being here. Can't say I blame them.

"You were supposed to be here half an hour ago," Sterling's father, Robert Blade, says sharply, his countenance as cold and unyielding as his steel grey eyes.

With as much money in the bank as Carl Gunn, his patience for time wasters is zero. He believes that being a billionaire alone should garner immediate respect, and for the most part he gets it from all the fake-arse, simpering people that he surrounds himself with. I, on the other hand, am polite to him out of respect for Hubert. I don't like him. Never have. Pretty sure his son feels the same way given the tight look he throws his way. The guy's an arsehole, no wonder Sterling bailed as soon as his mum left their family home.

"You can blame me for that," Dalton retorts. "I got sidetracked."

"Yeah, with pussy," Ben coughs, his emerald eyes dancing with amusement. Beside him, his dad chuckles. Of the three older men sitting around the table, he's the only one I like.

"You good, Walter?" I ask.

"As good as an old man past his prime can be. You?"

"Couldn't be better."

"Take a seat," Carl instructs, cutting the niceties off as he eyes his son with the same look of disappointment he always seems to wear when it comes to Dalton. Similar in looks, Carl is a sixty-five year old version of Dalton, except where his son has a smattering of silver streaks in his auburn hair, Carl is a self-proclaimed silver fox with a gaggle of women he likes to rotate on a regular basis. I guess the apple doesn't fall far from the tree.

"So what's up?" I ask, not keen on partaking in small talk myself. The sooner I'm back home with Lia, Toby, and Daisy, the better.

"As you all know, Robert's wedding is coming up soon, and he's asked whether he can use the hotel for the wedding and reception party, and a place for all his guests to stay. Of course, I've agreed," Carl explains.

"Okay," I say, not actually knowing this was happening until just now. I guess my involvement with the families only extends to when they need *hired muscle*. "So what do you need me for?"

"Security. We have a number of high profile guests, including Counsellor John Hoxton and his wife Elodie."

"Fuck!" Benedict mutters, his jaw gritting.

"Isn't that your ex, Ben?" Dalton asks, a smirk playing around his lips.

"Shut the fuck up, Dalton," Benedict growls, his normally bright countenance dimming with anger. Pretty sure she's the only woman he ever loved. Fucked him up good and proper when he found out she left him to marry that old bastard. Benedict fell hard for her, and she walked away from him like he didn't matter.

"I need a security detail arranged around the clock to cover the few days leading up to the wedding as our guests arrive, during the ceremony and celebrations, and until the last guests have left," Robert adds. "At least a week's worth."

Next to him Sterling rolls his eyes. "You're not marrying royalty, Robert. Isn't this overkill?"

Robert bristles. "There'll be a lot of wealthy people in attendance, and you know as well as I, *son*," he adds with contempt, "That there is always a target on the wealthy. Plus, we are having the whole event covered by select media outlets."

"So your fiance's wealthy then? Not that I know, given I haven't even met her yet," Sterling bites back.

"She's high profile, that is why I've not introduced you. Besides, you've not been around. I haven't had an opportunity to do so."

"I've been with Mum, someone had to look out for her after you replaced her because she no longer met your unattainable *standards*," Sterling sneers.

"Now listen—" Robert grinds out.

"I'll get started on the arrangements as soon as possible," I say, cutting in, because as much as I'd enjoy watching Sterling give his dad a hard time, I've got better shit to do. "What date is the wedding?"

"New Year's Eve," Robert replies.

"So you're making Drix work over New Year's?" Sterling shakes his head, giving me an apologetic look. "I'm sure, like the rest of us, he's got better things to do."

"It is a huge social event. What better way to celebrate my marriage than on New Year's Eve. Everyone wants to attend," the egotistical bastard replies. "Besides, Drix won't be required to work the whole day of the wedding. He will be present at the marriage vows and reception representing Hubert now that he's the head of the Hammer family."

A role I neither want nor need. Of course I don't express that thought out loud. Instead I say, "I'll need a list of the guests' names, details of the wedding arrangements, which media establishments are attending, and any plans you have for entertainment. I'll handle the rest."

Carl nods. "Good. Robert will get those details sent to you asap."

"If that's all?" I ask, pushing up from the table.

"That's not all. Sit!" Carl demands.

I remain standing.

Walter chuckles. "Good lad," he says, winking at me. Beside him Ben smirks.

"What is it?"

"I want you to pay Fraser a visit."

"Fraser? Why would I need to visit that cocksucker? He's just some two-bit thief."

"Exactly. He's a ticking time bomb. I need him in line," Carl says.

"He also *needs* to understand that this isn't an opportunity to steal from any of our guests," Robert adds. "The only reason either of us haven't sent you to *deal* with him already is because his parents are respected members of our community. But our patience is wearing thin. One more wrong move and it won't be just a chat you'll be having with him. Do I make myself clear?"

"Crystal," I reply, my fucking gut twisting.

It's not that I give a fuck about Fraser. He's a thorn in our side and a sleazeball with a rap sheet of violence, theft, burglary and aggravated assault as long as my arm, but I do give a fuck about bringing trouble to my door, especially now I have Lia and Toby to think about too.

"Then I suggest you get going. Report back to me once you've paid him a visit," Carl says, dismissing me with a flick of his hand.

I have no choice but to do as he demanded If I don't then my agreement with Carl will be null and void, and there's no way I'm going to allow him to fuck up Daisy's life like he's intent on fucking up mine. I'd rather die first.

TEN

"YOU DIDN'T HAVE to cook for us," Daisy says as she sits down at the kitchen island a few hours later. She's dressed in pyjamas covered in cartoon unicorns, her freshly washed hair piled up on her head in a loose bun. Despite being a rich woman, there are no airs and graces. I like that about her. She's down to earth.

"It's the least I can do," I reply, busying myself with dishing up the lasagna onto four separate plates and placing the freshly made garlic bread onto the centre of the kitchen island. "Besides, cooking makes me happy."

"It's a wonder you found enough ingredients to put this together."

"You have a freezer full of meat, and I was able to make the pasta, garlic bread and sauce from scratch using the ingredients in your pantry. Believe me, there's enough food to feed the five-thousand in your cupboards."

Daisy meets my gaze, grinning. "Well that's just perfect because me and Drix love to eat. It's been a while since we've enjoyed a home cooked meal."

"Neither of you cook then?"

She shakes her head. "Hubert was the cook in this house, and since he's been gone Drix and I have basically eaten takeaways most nights, or at the cafe. Pretty sure that we've single-handedly kept Daphne in business."

"Who's Hubert and where did he go?" Toby asks innocently.

Daisy gives him a soft smile. "Hubert was mine and Drix's dad. He had to go on a new adventure, someplace that Drix and I can't follow."

"An adventure like mine and Mama's?"

"Not quite, no," Daisy replies quietly, looking to me for help.

"You remember when I explained how Nana went over the rainbow bridge into the sky, Toby? Hubert has gone to that special place too," I explain, hoping that's enough to keep his questions at bay.

He frowns. "The place where angels go?"

"That's right. Where all the good people go," I reply as Daisy turns her head away, blinking back tears.

At a loss for words, we fall silent as I pass the plates to them both.

"It smells so good, Mama," Toby says, watching me closely as I cut up his portion so it's easier for him to eat.

"Thank you, darling," I reply, pressing a kiss against the top of his head before glancing at the clock on the wall. "Do you think I should put Drix's to one side so he can heat it up when he gets back?"

"I texted him half an hour ago. He said he'd be home for dinner. I'm sure he won't be long now. We should get started," she replies, digging into her food, her eyes lighting up as she chews. "Oh my God, this is amazing!"

I smile, a warm feeling thrumming in my veins at her appreciation. It's been a long time since someone has complimented my food. It feels good.

"Mama is the best cook *ever*," Toby adds, stuffing his mouth with a forkful of food.

"She sure is!" Daisy agrees.

Taking a seat, I begin to eat, glancing at the plate left for Drix. Daisy notices.

"Drix is like a bloodhound when it comes to food. He won't miss this, especially not since I told him you were cooking us all lasagna. You wait, he'll be here any minute." And, as if she called him into being, the front door slams shut and Daisy chuckles. "Told you!"

"Is that lasagna I smell?" comes the deep timber of Drix's voice, nerves fluttering through me at the sound.

"Drix!" Toby exclaims, his eyes lighting up as he steps into the kitchen.

My stomach does a flip-flop at Toby's obvious happiness at his return. There's something about Drix's presence that makes me feel uncertain. Not in a bad way per se, but in a way that's far more scary. I push it down, I have no business feeling anything towards Drix other than gratitude. This is just temporary. I refuse to allow myself to get emotionally attached in any way, I can't fall into that trap again.

"Hey, Toby, Lia," he says, meeting my gaze before flicking his eyes to Daisy who has practically wolfed down half of her portion already. "I can see you started without me."

"Sorry, I'm starving and this is *so good*," she mumbles around her food.

"I can see that," he chuckles, grabbing the plate that I set down for him and pulling up the seat beside mine. "Thanks for this, Lia. I appreciate it."

"Like I said to Daisy, it's the least I can do," I mumble, concentrating on eating and not at the warmth emanating from him, heating me up in a way that I refuse to look too closely at.

"The cherry pie is cooking in the Aga as we speak, and Lia

whipped up some homemade custard to go with it. So don't go pigging out on multiple helpings of lasagna, you need to leave room for all that yummy goodness," Daisy adds.

"Oh don't worry, I've always got plenty of room for cherry pie," Drix replies, his voice appreciative.

"Did you get everything sorted at the gym?" Daisy asks after a beat.

"Yep. I just needed to make sure the rota was covered for the next couple weeks. The guys have got shit covered for me."

"Drix!" Toby exclaims, wide-eyed as he looks between us both.

Drix pulls a face, his forkful of food inches from his mouth. "Sorry, Lia, Toby. I really need to watch my mouth."

"Don't worry about it," Toby interjects good-naturedly. "Mama swore a lot the other night too. She owes *four pounds* to the jar. Don't you, Mama?"

"Is that so?" Drix asks, side-eying me, a smile playing on his lips as he chews his food.

"It was a bad night," I respond quietly.

"Looks like you *both* need to cough up then," Daisy comments, biting back a laugh.

"Well, I did wrong, so I guess I should pay for it." Drix says, reaching into his jeans pocket and pulling out a ten pound note, placing it on the table between us.

"That's too much. It's one pound per swear word," I point out.

"That's for any future mistakes I might make, and for the ones you owe," he replies, pushing the note towards me.

"You don't need to cover mine. I can pay my own way," I reply, pushing it back towards him, knowing that, actually, I can't.

Drix's hand covers my own, and I stiffen at his touch, my heart racing in my chest. "It's cool. I got this," he offers, squeezing my fingers before letting go.

With my hand still warm from his touch, I pull back, leaving the note where it is. It sits between us like a promise of something more. I don't know what that is, but I do know I can't lean on this man more than I already have.

Daisy watches the exchange with interest until eventually she says, "Well I guess it's up to me to be in charge of the swear jar then."

Leaning across the table she snatches up the note, then slides off the stool and walks to the far side of the kitchen, pulling open a cabinet next to the Aga. Reaching down she brings out a screw top jar and unscrews the lid, placing the note inside.

"There, all sorted," she says, placing it on the side. "Now when you fill this to the brim with all the money you'll owe for swearing, Drix, me and Toby can use it to pay for a trip to the amusement arcade in town. What do you think, Toby, does that sound like a good plan to you?"

"An amusement arcade? What's that?"

Daisy claps her hands together in glee. "It's only *the* best place on Earth to win unicorns!"

"Win unicorns? Mama, can I go? Can I?" he asks, whipping around his head to look at me.

"Oh dear, you've gone and done it now," Drix says, scooping up another mouthful of lasagna, his hum of appreciation like a soft caress against my skin.

I clear my throat, prepared to let Toby down gently, but his wide-eyed wonder stops me. Instead, I say, "Well, if we're still here when that jar fills up, I guess it would be okay."

"Pretty sure that jar will be full before the snow clears," Drix mutters with a shrug of his shoulders.

Daisy's eyes sparkle as she plops back down onto her seat. "That's a date then."

Twenty minutes later, after we've all finished eating, Toby is begging to watch more cartoons, and Drix is collecting the dishes from the counter to wash up. Outside darkness has fallen, more snow trickling from the sky in soft puffs.

"I'll sit with Toby," Daisy yawns, rubbing at her eyes. "I could do with letting all that yummy food settle a bit before filling it right back up with cherry pie. Are you okay cleaning up?"

"Take a load off," Drix says, rolling up his sleeves as he fills the sink with water and washing-up liquid. I can't help but notice the intricate tattoos on his forearm and appreciate the thought gone into the designs. Whoever the tattoo artist is, they're talented, that's for sure.

"You sure?" Daisy asks, taking Toby's hand in hers, winking at him as he hops on his feet.

He giggles, and the way she makes him feel comfortable in her presence is really appreciated. Martin was always too busy, or too caught up in his own selfishness to ever really give Toby the attention and love he deserved. So, no matter how I feel about him forming attachments to Daisy and Drix, I can't deny him this affection when it's given so freely.

"Of course. You too, Lia. I've got this," Drix adds, jerking his chin towards Daisy and Toby.

"Cartoons really aren't my thing," I reply. "Besides, I'm happy to help. Got to earn my keep somehow."

Drix frowns, but doesn't comment.

"Well, see you in a bit then. Just give us a shout when the cherry pie is ready, okay?" Daisy asks, as she guides Toby from the room.

We work side by side in silence as Drix washes up and I dry the dishes, the sound of Daisy and Toby laughing at whatever cartoon they're watching, filtering into the room. I wonder why he doesn't use the dishwasher, but I don't ask, suspecting that it's got more to do with spending time with me than it does because he cares about ruining the delicate china.

When the final dish is put away, Drix reaches for me, his fingers gently resting on my arm.

"You know you don't have to feel like you have to earn your

keep around here. You and Toby are my guests. I want you to feel at home."

My stomach churns at the pity in his gaze. Letting out a sigh, I rest my hand over his, removing it. "Cooking for you all is my way of saying thank you," I explain.

"That's not what I meant, Lia."

"Then what did you mean?"

"You love to cook, I love that you want to cook in my home, and I appreciate it. If that makes you feel more comfortable staying here, then you're welcome to cook all you want. But don't feel you *have* to do that."

"But I have nothing else to offer. I don't have any money of my own. I can't even pay for groceries, let alone the four pounds I owe to the swear jar."

"You don't need to pay me for anything. If it makes you any happier, I will probably swear a hundred times more, and that jar will be filled, rightly so, in no time. Toby won't miss the money you owe."

"You have to understand, I want to pay you back somehow. I will cook, clean for you even, anything you want. I don't want to freeload whilst I'm here. I *need* to do this, please."

I don't say to him that living here, under his roof, eating his food, and accepting his hospitality feels like something more than just a kind man helping me out. Despite his words, I know he wants more from me, and that's something I just can't give. At least this way we're on an even playing field. Kind of.

"You're not my maid, Lia, and as much as I love your food, you're not my cook either."

"Then I'll get a job whilst I'm here? Maybe at the hotel? I could work in the kitchen, clean the rooms? Do you think Dalton might hire me? I could do some shifts, see if there's a nursery that will take Toby..." My voice trails off as he frowns.

"No, you can't work for Dalton. It's bad enough that my sister's working under him."

"But he's your best friend."

"And a terrible boss. The only reason I can just about cope with Daisy working there is because she knows how to handle herself around him."

"And you think because of my past, I don't?"

"It's not that. Despite appearances, Dalton is a complicated man. I don't want you getting caught up in any of his shit."

"His *shit?*"

Drix smiles ruefully, trying to ease the tension growing between us. "Told you I'd fill up that jar in no time."

"That's not what I meant. Is he really that bad?" I ask, knowing that he probably is both a rogue and a terrible manager given my short interaction with him earlier today, and everything Daisy has told me.

Drix blows out a breath. "He's not for everyone, that's for sure."

"But I'd really like to try and get a job. Aside from being able to pay towards my keep here–"

"Lia, I've already said, I don't want your money."

"I want to keep busy," I push on. "I want to show Toby that whilst your generosity is something to be thankful for, *grateful* for, that's it's important to earn my own way. Can you understand that?"

"Okay, look," Drix concedes. "I do understand your need to take care of yourself and Toby, and I don't want to prevent you from doing that. Let me think about it, there might be a solution that doesn't involve you having to look after my sorry arse or work for my obnoxious friend."

"You know someone else who might be able to give me a job whilst I'm here?" I ask, hopeful.

"Possibly. Leave it with me, yeah?" he replies, just as the timer dings on the oven letting us both know the cherry pie is ready.

"I appreciate it," I reply softly. "I've made so many bad decisions, Drix. I just want to do right by Toby."

"You, Lia Pearson, have done nothing but do the right thing. Every decision you've made since I've met you has been for your son's well being. You've got nothing to be ashamed of. I, for one, think you're an incredible woman," he replies, his voice raw with honesty as he cups my face, stroking my cheek gently. It's an instinctive move, one born on the back of his kindness and need to comfort me. Yet, still I question it.

"Drix..." My voice is quiet, edged with caution, but this time I don't remove his hand, and neither does he.

For a brief moment as I look up at him, and he down at me, I allow myself to relax into the intimacy of his touch. Call it a moment of weakness, a deep sense of gratitude, even. Either way, I can't seem to break the spell even though my head is telling me to spare myself the heartache I know will come, because it always does.

"Did I hear the timer go off?" Daisy asks as she steps into the kitchen with Toby hot on her heels.

Drix draws back his hand, and I turn away from him, grabbing the mitt and pulling open the oven, my cheeks flaming with heat. I daren't look around at Daisy, feeling acute embarrassment. What must she think of me? Here I am in her home, eating her food, sleeping in her guest room all the while looking like I'm making a pass at her wealthy brother. She doesn't know me, and even though she doesn't seem like someone who would judge, my anxiety doesn't seem to care in the slightest.

"It's ready," I say, averting my gaze as I pop the pie on the island. The crust is a perfect golden brown, the juice bubbles between the gaps of the lattice scenting the kitchen with memories of a time before Martin. A time when I was a brave woman, someone open to making new friendships. Not this terrified shell of a person I am now.

"Oh wow, look at that," Daisy exclaims, helping Toby climb back onto one of the chairs before grabbing some clean plates. "Looks even better than the pies Daphne makes at the cafe."

"It sure looks delicious," Drix agrees, grabbing a knife and cutting us all a slice.

"Cold or hot custard?" I ask, opening the fridge and grabbing the jug I prepared earlier.

"Cold!" they all agree in unison.

As I pour the custard over everyone's slice, Drix's mobile rings. He reaches into his pocket and glances at the screen.

"Sorry I need to take this call," he apologies. "Don't eat my portion whilst I'm gone."

"Then you'd better be quick or I will," Daisy jokes.

By the time Drix returns, we've all finished our slice and Daisy is eying his greedily. "Everything alright?" she asks.

"All good," Drix replies, striding over to the table and digging into the cherry pie with enthusiasm, and even though his expression is relaxed, there's no hiding the fact that his body language seems to tell a whole other story. He's hiding something, and I have this terrible sinking feeling that I'm not going to like whatever it is.

ELEVEN

"YOU, MOTHERFUCKER, NEED TO EXPLAIN YOURSELF," I growl, the breath whooshing out of Fraser's chest as I pin him against the wall of his workshop an hour after eating the best meal of my damn life.

"Drix, I–" he stutters, panic seizing him.

"You can imagine my surprise," I continue, cutting him off, "When I arrive here to have a word about Robert Blade's upcoming wedding, and find my friend's car trashed instead!"

Behind me Lia's car is stripped of its wheels, even the fucking seats and carpet have been removed. Clearly he's moved on from burgling houses to nicking and stripping cars for parts. I should've picked up her car sooner. It's my fault this chancer stole it. She'll be devastated when she finds out.

"I didn't know this car belonged to your friend!" he protests, his eyes wide with panic as I lean in closer, the stench of his tobacco breath making me almost gag.

"Don't lie to me!" I roar, my fingers tightening around his throat.

"I swear it," he bites out, turning a deep crimson as spittle flies from his lips.

"You've got about five seconds to explain yourself before I pick up that crowbar you've been using to demolish a good woman's car and use it to rearrange your face instead!"

He garbles some nonsensical response as I start to count.

"Five!" I snarl, anger raging through my blood at the fucking audacity of this prick.

"Drix, man—" he chokes out.

"Four!"

His feet scramble against the dusty floor as he tries to regain his footing, but I don't let up. A red haze settles over me as I think about what this means for Lia and Toby. Her car might have been easy pickings for this prick, but it was all they had left.

"Three!"

Fraser's fingernails dig into my hand, and I don't even register the pain. I don't even give a fuck about what Carl and Robert want out of this *conversation*, right now all I care about is settling the score for Lia and Toby. He's done them wrong, and I intend on making him pay.

"Two!" I grind out, his eyes starting to bulge as veins pop in his forehead. "One!"

Fraser lets go of my hand, slamming his palm against my arm. I could easily murder the bastard here and now, but when I press my eyes shut ready to do just that, all I see is Lia and Toby in my mind's eye and this wave of fucking shame punches me in the gut, forcing me to uncurl my fingers. They'd be terrified of me if they knew what I was doing right now, and I can't live with that. I want them to trust me, not fear me.

"Start talking," I demand, letting him go. He drops to the floor, sucking in ragged breaths as tears stream from his eyes.

After half a minute or so of him struggling to regain his breath, his skin begins to return to a more reasonable colour, and he's swiping at the tears on his face. Snatching up the crowbar, I rest it beneath his chin, forcing him to look up at me.

"Listen, the car was abandoned at Bandits. I figured I would–"

"That you would steal it and fucking take it to pieces? You shit."

"A man's gotta earn a living. My parents cut me off. What else was I supposed to do?"

"Hey, I don't know, get a fucking job?" I reply, my voice thick with sarcasm as I push the tip of the crowbar against his Adam's apple.

"No one will hire me," he chokes out.

"Because you're a fucking no good, thieving shithead, that's why!" Fury like nothing else rages through me as I look at the strewn and scattered parts of Lia's car. Most of the engine is in pieces on the floor, as well as her other belongings we'd left in the car to pick up later. The way he's just thrown her belongings about like their worthless riles me up further. "I should fucking kill you!"

"I'm sorry, man. I was desperate," he whimpers.

"So tell me what I should do now? Because we both know that Carl and Robert are loosing patience with you, and I've got every fucking reason to rip your damn head off and dump your body where no fucker will find it."

"L-let me make it u-up to you," he stammers.

"How? How the fuck are you going to make this better, because you know as well as I do that car ain't gonna magically put itself back together again. It's a fucking write off."

"I'll do anything, just don't kill me."

Not so long ago, I would've ignored his plea and ended him right here and now. But I don't want to be that man anymore. I never wanted to be that man, but circumstance and the fucking hold Carl has over me meant that I've had to be. My hands are covered in too much blood already, I don't want to add anymore to it.

"Gather up all my friends' belongings and put them in the boot of my car. Then take what's left of this car to the landfill. Ask for Kentucky. I'll call him, let him know you're coming," I order, releasing the pressure from the crowbar, and stepping back.

He nods, lifting his shaking hands up as I motion for him to get a fucking move on. "You got it."

"And don't even think about running. Your cards are marked. One more step out of line and I won't hesitate to pay you another visit. Understand?"

"I u–understand," he mumbles, moving away to collect the strewn recipe books and placing them back into the box he'd dumped them out of. I watch him as he works, using all of my willpower not to go back on my word and cave his head in with the crowbar.

As soon as he's finished, he steps back into his workshop, eyes wide with fear. "I'm truly sorry."

I shake my head, my lip curling up in disgust. "No, you're just sorry you got caught, and the *only* reason you're still breathing is because I ain't willing to fuck up a good thing for your sorry arse."

"I appreciate that."

"Don't get fucking comfortable, Fraser. No more shit. Get a real job, tidy yourelf up, and stay the fuck away from Robert's guests when they arrive in town for his wedding next month."

"You have my word."

"Your word means shit to me. I'll have my people watching you very closely. Stay out of fucking trouble," I growl, stepping towards him menacingly.

"I will. I swear it," he replies, backing up.

"Your parents are good people, and I don't want to be the one to tell them you died after getting into an *accident*. Catch my drift?"

"I swear to you, this is the last time. I'm done with all that shit."

I nod tightly. "Get rid of this mess." With that I yank open the door, and stride towards my car. Ten minutes later I'm pulling up to Bandits.

"WHAT'S THE DEAL, DRIX?" Ben asks me as I sit at the table my friends are gathered around in the back of the bar. We've got about thirty minutes before he opens the doors for the punters, and I need time to fucking vent.

"I just paid a visit to Fraser," I explain, taking a gulp of the black coffee Ben had waiting for me after I called him on the drive over and told him to gather the others. Honestly, I could do with a stiff drink like the rest of them, but I've got to drive home, and I don't want to be stinking of alcohol. That's not the kind of impression I want to give Lia. I like a drink when the occasion calls for it, but now is not the time. I need to calm the fuck down, not get drunk.

"Yeah, how did that go?" Sterling asks, sitting forward in his seat as he pulls back the hood of his sweater, his thick brown hair falling into his light blue eyes. It's the first thing everyone notices about him, followed quickly by the fact that his hands are always covered in paint. As a gifted artist, it's unsurprising. At least for him it's not blood.

"He had a car pulled apart in his workshop, ready to sell on for parts," I say, looking between my friends in turn.

Dalton raises his brow. "Why am I not surprised?"

"That dude needs his head checked. Carl and Robert are this close to forfeiting his right to breathe," Ben says, pinching his thumb and forefinger together, leaving just a slither of space between them.

"Believe me, I was that close to caving his head in," I grind out, part of me wishing I had.

It's one thing me giving the fucker a second chance for the sake of Lia and Toby, but I have a reputation to uphold, and if word gets out I've gone soft, there could be repercussions for all of the families.

"Then why didn't you?" Sterling asks. "No one would've missed the vermin."

"Because it was Lia's car he stole," I reply, my voice constricting with concern. "She'll be fucking devastated when I tell her."

"The woman you picked up here, the one who's staying with you?" Ben asks, letting out a low whistle.

"The woman I *helped*," I correct him. "She's not a fucking booty call."

Ben and Sterling exchange looks, but wisely don't say anything.

"And you said you *didn't* kill him?" Dalton adds, looking at me with surprise. "What gives?"

"I didn't for precisely the reason you think I should've. I need Lia and Toby to trust me, they ain't got no one else to look out for them."

Dalton cocks his head. "You need to?"

"I *want* them to trust me. They mean something to me."

"Drix, you're playing with fire here," Dalton warns. "You know she comes with baggage, and I'm not just talking about her kid."

"You think I can't protect them? You know me better than that," I shoot back, challenging him. "If her ex comes for them, I'll be waiting."

"Hey, I know you can. But that's not what I meant. If my dad finds out that you're keeping shit from him, he won't take it well. There'll be consequences. You *know* this," he reminds me.

"I'm not keeping anything from him. I did my fucking job and paid Fraser a visit."

"Yet instead of telling him what you found, you're here with us," Dalton reminds me.

"Who I choose to invite into my home has nothing to do with your dad. She's my guest. That's all he needs to know."

"With an abusive ex who could bring trouble to our town. Drix, I'm just looking out for you," Dalton insists. "I know my dad better than anyone, he won't take kindly to being kept in the dark."

"I don't give two fucks. I will introduce her to him and the others when the time is right, and not before," I say forcefully, leaning forward in my seat and hoping to fuck they've got my back like I've always had theirs. Over the years, one way or the other, I've helped them all out. It's what I do for the people I care about, and these three men are brothers to me. Always will be. I hope I have their loyalty in return. "I need you all to promise me, this conversation goes no further."

Ben and Sterling nod. "You've got it," they say in unison.

"So long as you know what you're doing," Dalton adds, puffing out a breath.

"Of course I do," I snap.

"So what are you going to tell Lia?" Dalton asks after a beat.

"The truth, that her car was stolen."

Ben takes a sip of his rum. "Then what?"

"She stays with me. I was taking the next few weeks off from the gym anyway." I reply, meeting his gaze before looking over at Dalton. "I do have a favour to ask you though."

"Yeah, what's that?"

"Lia needs a job. She wants to earn her own money, pay her way, and whilst I've already said I don't want anything from her, she's insistent. I was going to ask Daphne to take her on at the cafe, but given the circumstances, I think she'll be safer at the hotel working for you. The place is filled with cameras, has round the clock security, and if by chance her ex finds out where she is and comes looking he won't have a chance at getting close to her before I can intervene."

"I can do that," he agrees. "What about the kid? Who's looking after him whilst she works?"

I level my gaze with his. "Me, of course."

Pretty sure that their looks of surprise would make a perfect meme.

After I leave the guys at the bar, I make sure Fraser has dropped what's left of Lia's car with Kentucky at the landfill, then store her cookery books at my flat above the gym. Still feeling out of sorts, I spend the half-an-hour driving around town, using the time to cool off and to get my head on straight. My gut keeps telling me that I need to get rid of her cookery books too because how else would I explain being in possession of them when her car was stolen? But I can't bring myself to do it. Besides, she'll have no reason to visit my flat, so I can keep them there until I figure out what to do.

Part of me, a really shitty, selfish part, is relieved that Fraser stole her car because leaving town is a lot harder when you haven't got a vehicle to escape in. It doesn't make me feel good knowing that, but at least she'll be here for longer and perhaps it will give me time to give her a reason to stay.

By the time I step into the house, everyone's gone to bed and there's this peaceful kind of quiet that makes my shoulders relax. It's as though the house itself knows that it's starting to become a home again after Hubert was taken from us all. It's a good feeling, one I have every intention of cultivating.

As I climb the stairs and head to my bedroom, I can't help but go over the events of the last couple days. To the guys, Lia and Toby are a complication I could do without. There might be plenty of single, childless women in this town who'd be more than happy to warm my bed, but that's all they'd be warming. With Lia it's different. I don't know why, and I can't explain it, but it is.

Passing Daisy's room first, I peer inside. She's wrapped up in her blanket like a caterpillar cocooned in its chrysalis. She's always slept that way. It's because she fears the dark, which is why she also sleeps with a nightlight on. During our time in foster care together she would have regular nightmares, and I would climb into bed with her, wrapping her up in my arms until she felt safe enough to fall asleep. That stopped when we came here to live with Hubert, not because I didn't want to comfort her, but because we each found our own way to deal with the memories of our past. Filling her life with brightness in the form of colourful clothes, magical creatures, kindness and laughter, is her way of coping.

My way of coping... Well, I just don't think too much about my life before Hubert adopted me. It's better that way.

Gently drawing her door closed, I make my way towards the guest room Lia and Toby are sleeping in. Pushing it open a little, I heave out a relieved sigh at the sight of them both sleeping peacefully, the light from the hallway falling across Toby. He's curled up on his side, wrapped in his mother's arms, his mouth popped open as he sleeps. Behind him Lia is pitched in darkness, only her arm visible as she holds him close.

My fucking heart squeezes inside my chest, and another sudden rush of a protectiveness almost knocks me sideways. I grip the doorframe, forcing myself to stay where I am and not head into the room and curl my body around Lia's, holding them both. Instead I allow myself a moment to watch them sleep, finding comfort in their peacefulness.

"Sweet dreams," I whisper, hoping to fuck that Lia will eventually take down her guard and let me in, and more importantly, that I can be the man they both deserve.

TWELVE

"THIS IS THE HOTEL," I observe a few days later as Drix parks the car, snow crunching beneath the tires.

As the daylight dwindles, the hotel looks even more beautiful, the windowsills and roof covered in a thick layer of glistening snow. Two Christmas trees, adorned with twinkling fairy lights, flank the grand entrance, and outside the grounds are blanketed in at least three more inches of snow that fell last night, adding to its already picturesque setting. This morning when I asked Daisy how long she thought the snow would stay, she'd given me a bemused look and shrugged her shoulders. I'd checked the weather app on my phone and was surprised to find that the long-term forecast suggested at least two more weeks.

"It is," Drix replies, dragging my attention back to the warm gravel of his voice. He sits beside me, effortlessly handsome in his scuffed brown boots, dark denim jeans, plaid shirt and shearling lined, brown leather jacket.

"And we're here because?" I ask, forcing myself to concentrate.

"Because Dalton is offering you a job as a part-time pastry chef. If you want it, that is?"

"But I thought...?"

"Dalton has promised to be on his best behaviour, and Daisy here will make sure he stays in line, won't you, Daise?" he questions, throwing a look over his shoulder at Daisy who's currently whispering something in Toby's ear. He looks at Daisy, smothering a giggle with his hand.

"Of course I will," Daisy replies. "I'll give you tips on how to handle him should he ignore Drix's demands. Seriously, it's not all that hard to keep him in line. You just need to know his weak spots, mainly the fact he's as vain as they come. If he upsets you, just point out that he needs to get a new supply of *Just For Men,* and he'll leave you alone."

"That'll do it," Drix snorts.

"I'm sure that would just get me fired."

"You're Drix's... *friend,*" Daisy says, using her words carefully. "You've basically got a licence to say whatever you want to him, and he can't do a thing about it."

"Damn straight," Drix confirms. "If he's being difficult, just mention the night I had to use bolt cutters to get him out of a tricky predicament."

"You never told me about that! Oh my God, I'm going to live off this for the next six months!" Daisy barks out a laugh, and Toby joins in, not understanding what's so funny.

"Bolt cutters?" I ask, eyes wide as I imagine the situation Dalton had got himself caught up in to warrant Drix freeing him in such a way.

"Yeah," Drix says, lowering his voice as he leans towards me. "His date upped and left with the key to the handcuffs when she found out that she wasn't his only... *friend.* The maid who cleaned the room in the morning found him butt naked and called me after he had offered her a bonus to keep her mouth shut."

"That'll teach him," Daisy giggles, unlocking Toby's car seat. "Shall we head inside then?"

Drix looks over his shoulder at her. "Would you mind taking Toby? Show him the kids playroom. I want to have a chat with Lia about something. If that's okay with you, of course?" he asks me.

"Sure," I agree.

"No problem. See you inside," Daisy says, climbing out of the car and hauling Toby into her arms. We watch her trudge through the snow, her bright yellow wellington boots sinking into the softness as warm puffs of air lift up into the sky from their laughter.

"She's so good with him," I observe, smiling softly.

"Daisy is good with everyone," Drix replies, grinning. "Except, maybe, Dalton."

"Yes, she told me about her dislike for him," I reply, my voice fading out when his expression grows serious. "What is it?"

"Lia, there's something I need to tell you, and you're not going to like it."

"That sounds ominous," I reply, trying and failing to prevent my heart rate from kicking up a notch.

"There's no easy way to say this, but..." He hesitates, swiping a hand through his hair.

"Just rip the plaster off, Drix. I'm an adult. I can deal with whatever it is." *I hope.*

"Your car's been stolen."

"What?!" Air rushes out of my chest as I stare at him, hoping he's joking. When he doesn't crack a smile, my heart plummets.

"Your car. It's been stolen," he repeats, reaching for my hands and taking them in his. "I'm so sorry, Lia."

I stare at his hands gripping mine, his thumbs rubbing gentle circles onto my skin. My mind is reeling. Stolen? My car's been *stolen?* What did I do to deserve this? Tears prick my eyes as I realise what this means for Toby and me.

"This is..." I choke out, willing myself not to cry. "What am I going to do now?"

Drix tips my chin up with his finger. "You're going to carry on, that's what you're going to do. You're gonna walk in there and meet the other kitchen staff and chefs before you officially start tomorrow, then I'm taking you all to dinner, and we're going to figure out a plan of action."

"But, I have *nothing* left," I murmur, a rogue tear slipping from my lashes. "Not even my cookery books."

Drix swipes the tear away with his thumb. "I'll buy you more cookery books."

"They were special to me. Some of them were my mum's. They're irreplaceable," I say, shaking my head. His hand falls away from my face as he cuts me a look I can't interpret.

"Fuck, I'm sorry. I feel responsible."

"How is my car getting stolen your fault?"

"I should've picked it up sooner," he replies, averting his gaze.

"All we have left are a few clothes," I mumble, disbelief rolling through me as I try to absorb the news.

The lights decorating the Christmas trees behind Drix draw my attention, and I suddenly realise that I won't be able to buy Toby all the things he deserves to make this Christmas special. An overwhelming feeling of grief presses down onto my shoulders at the thought.

"You have each other, Lia. That's the most important thing, and you have *me* and Daisy. You have a safe place to live and people who want to care for you."

"It's Christmas soon," I mutter. "I haven't got any presents for Toby."

"I can guarantee you the best Christmas present for that kid will be seeing a smile on your face and knowing you're happy. Besides, now you have a job. You can buy him some gifts if that's what you need to feel okay about all of this. "

"Aside from Toby, that's all just temporary," I whisper.

"It doesn't have to be," he replies just as softly.

"But I can't just–"

"You have a home with me and Daisy if you want it."

"We've only known each other for a few days, Drix."

"That doesn't matter to me. I really like–"

"Don't, Drix. Don't say it."

Drix drops his gaze, staring at his hand that still holds mine. The heat from his touch makes me feel things I shouldn't, that I can't allow myself to feel.

"If life has taught me anything it's to grab something good and hold on to it tightly," he says, squeezing my hand gently. "I want to be the man who'll make you feel safe enough to laugh freely, to experience the joy you deserve. Even if it's just a friendship you're comfortable with, I'm willing to be that friend for you. Either way, I'll wait until you're ready. "

"You can't mean that. I'm a single mum with nothing to offer you. We don't even know each other, not really."

He looks up, the deep brown of his eyes filled with empathy. "I know that you're a wonderful mother, that your eyes light with this endless love every time you look at Toby, that you make the best lasagna and a cherry pie that I would request as my last meal on Earth." He smiles ruefully then and my chest aches. "I know that you have a son who worships you. I know that you've been through the shittest time, but you're still here fighting to regain your life back."

"I have to be, for Toby," I whisper, knowing on more than a few occasions than I'd care to admit I'd thought about leaving this world to escape Martin's abuse. Leaving Toby with his father stopped me.

"I know that you're scared, *terrified* that I'm going to hurt you like that bastard did," he continues as though picking up on my thoughts.

"Drix, please," my voice breaks, and this time I can't prevent the tears from falling. All I've done is cry in front of this man. I feel like a failure. I feel *weak*, just like Martin always said I was.

"I also know that you're *going* to get through this, because that's the woman you are. You're *strong*, Lia."

"I don't feel all that strong right now. I'm a complete mess. How can you be interested in me?" I ask, swiping at my face.

"You really don't see what I see, do you?"

"I just—"

"Maybe I shouldn't say this..."

I shake my head. "Then don't."

"But I'm going to anyway. Lia..."

"Drix, please. I don't have anything to give you."

"Then at the very least, let me give you a compliment," he presses on. "You've lived with a man who has made you feel like shit, who's treated you in the worst way possible. He's knocked your confidence, and I fucking hate that, because to me, you're fucking beautiful, Lia. I'm attracted to everything you are and all that I see."

I'm too overwhelmed to reply. Instead I turn my head away, staring out at the quiet peacefulness that snow always seems to bring, trying to ignore the burning heat between us and the promise of something more.

"Lia, shit. I've made you feel uncomfortable," Drix says after a while.

"You know, I haven't felt beautiful in a very, very long time," I admit, slowly meeting his gaze once more. "In the early days, Martin used to compliment me all the time. He'd shower me with gifts, take me out to fancy restaurants. They call it love-bombing."

"That's not what this is," Drix says quickly, and I can hear the panic in his voice. "Shit. I've fucked up. This is too much too soon. I'm sorry."

"This is no reflection on you, but you have to understand why I'm so wary," I say.

"I do understand, Lia, and I hope that one day you'll feel beautiful again. I hope that I can be the man who can give you the space and the time to get back to that confident, fun-loving woman you spoke about."

"This is just all so overwhelming. I'm not in the right head-space to even consider falling into another relationship. There's too much at stake. I can't risk breaking Toby's heart... and *mine*," I add quietly.

He nods. "I get it. There's no pressure from me for anything. I'll take whatever you're comfortable with giving, and that will be enough."

For a moment we just sit quietly, neither one of us speaking as snow gently falls around us. Eventually, I break the heavy silence.

"Martin broke me, Drix. I don't know if I can ever get back to that woman I was. He took away my confidence, my self-love, my power, my trust in people. Truthfully, I'm afraid I'll never be able to love another man again. The little I have left in me is for Toby."

Drix gives me a soft smile. "He's the most important person in your life, and he should always be your priority. Just know that I'm here in whatever capacity you need..." His voice trails off and he blows out a steadying breath before continuing to speak. "Okay, so hear me out. I know you said that you find it hard to trust people, and I understand why, but if you're going to take this job you'll need someone to look after Toby, and I want to be that person."

"Don't you have better things to do?" I ask, hating myself for how that sounds.

Drix shakes his head. "I've already taken time off from managing the gym for a few weeks to plan the security for Robert Blade's upcoming wedding, but that's flexible."

"You're planning security for a wedding?" I ask, avoiding responding to his offer because I honestly don't know how I feel about it. Despite the fact he's never given me any reason to be concerned when it comes to Toby, I can't help but feel the way I do.

"My friend's dad, Robert Blade, is getting married again on

New Year's Eve. He's a wealthy man, with a lot of friends in high places, and he needs security. It's a big event, the press will be here covering the wedding. It's a whole thing," he explains.

"And you're the man for the job?"

"It's what I do for the families. I'm their unofficial head of security."

"I didn't know that," I say.

"I took over the role from Hubert. It's what he used to do."

"Daisy mentioned something about four families running this town, including your family. I didn't know that kind of thing still existed. It seems a little archaic to me."

"It is," Drix agrees. "But money buys you power, and Robert Blade, Carl Dunn and Walter Pike have a lot of that around here. They're influential. Own many of the businesses in town between them."

"And you don't have money or power?"

"I have my own money, but a lot less comparably."

"And the power?"

Drix winces, shifting his gaze out the window. "Let's just say when Hubert died things changed. Not that I mind, I don't want that kind of... *responsibility*," he replies, choosing his words carefully.

"I see," I reply, not sure that I do.

"So, that means I have time to look after Toby whilst you work the morning shift, and if anything crops up Daisy is willing to help too. As you can see, she already adores Toby."

"Isn't there a nursery in town?" I ask, biting on my lip as I try to think this through.

A nursery will cost money, money that I don't have. Drix has already shown me over and over again what a good man he is, and Toby adores both him and Daisy. This could be a perfect arrangement for all of us.

"There is. I could take you to view it later today, if you'd prefer?" he replies, and I can't help but notice how his eyes flicker with disappointment.

In that moment, I'm reminded of all the times he's shown Toby such kindness and affection in such a short space of time. Making a decision, I shake my head.

"That won't be necessary. I'd love it if you could look after Toby for me, if you're absolutely certain you're okay with that?"

Drix grins, his smile is so genuine it takes my breath away. "I wouldn't have offered if I wasn't. Thank you, Lia, for trusting me with Toby. That means a lot."

"It's me who should be thanking you," I say, earnestly, giving him a wavering smile. "I will never forget this kindness, and one day I hope that I'll have the opportunity to pass it on."

"You're welcome, Lia," he replies, reaching for the door handle.

I grab his arm, and without allowing myself to think too much about it, I lean in and press a kiss against his cheek. It's both brief and eternal; this soothing kind of warmth floods through me at the contact. He smells of pine and warm leather, like everything my broken heart needs, yet my head tells it to be wary of. Pulling away, I feel heat flush my cheeks, and tiny sparks of electricity scatter down my spine as our gazes meet. God, what is this man doing to me? *This feeling*, that's what frightens me the most.

He clears his throat. "Come on, let's head inside."

AN HOUR later we sit down for dinner in a quiet corner of the hotel's restaurant. Toby is tucking into a bowl of spaghetti, Drix and I enjoy roast beef with all the trimmings, and Daisy is demolishing duck confit. The conversation flows easily between Drix and Daisy, but I'm lost in thought, more than a little overwhelmed after meeting everyone I'm going to be working with and the conversation I had with Drix earlier. Overwhelm seems to be a feeling I'm constantly living with right now, but I'm hoping once I get into some kind of routine, things will get better. Drix certainly seems positive they will, and maybe I should allow myself just a tiny bit of hope that he's right.

The kitchen staff and the chefs were welcoming, the kitchen itself well equipped with everything I could need to do my job. To be truthful, just thinking about starting work tomorrow fills me with an excitement that I haven't felt in a long time. It's a feeling I'm not used to.

"Penny for your thoughts," Drix says, catching my eye as he lines up his knife and fork on his empty plate.

"Everyone seems really nice," I reply with honesty.

"The staff here are amazing, no thanks to Dalton," Daisy adds, her attention drawn to someone over on the other side of the room. That someone being Dalton himself. He's dressed smartly in a black fitted suit, talking with a couple at another table. On the surface he appears to be professional and charming, yet going by the look on Daisy's face she doesn't buy it for a minute.

"You know you really need to try and lay off him," Drix says. "The guy has sh- *stuff* going on," Drix corrects himself when Toby snaps his head up, a smile pulling up his sauce-covered lips.

"That stuff being husbands wanting to murder him for sleeping with their wives?" Daisy counters, visibly bristling.

"Look, I get it. He's a womaniser—"

"What's a womaniser?" Toby asks, swiping his mouth with the back of his hand.

It's kind of cute the way Drix screws up his face trying to figure out a child-friendly way to explain to Toby that his best friend likes to sleep around with people he shouldn't.

"Erm, it's kind of when a man makes friends with a woman who's already married to another man," Drix says.

"Like you and Mama you mean?" he replies, and Daisy coughs

on her mouthful of drink, her eyes widening as she drops her gaze to my ring finger. Which is ring-less, given I threw the damn thing away the first moment I could after escaping.

"No, not like that," I say, suddenly feeling nauseous.

"You're married?" Daisy whispers, as Drix draws Toby's attention to the waitstaff heading towards us with pudding.

"I'll explain later," I reply, shaking my head.

Daisy frowns, looking over at Drix who's doing his best to not listen in, even though he's the one who deserves an explanation the most. It's not that I lied to him, it's just I couldn't bring myself to admit that I actually married my abuser even though at that time there were no signs of who he really was beneath all the charm. The truth is, when I left, I didn't just leave Martin, but every commitment I ever made to the man. He's not my husband. Not anymore.

"Okay," she nods, shifting in her seat as one of our waitresses clears our plates and the other serves our pudding.

"Wow, this looks incredible," I say, forcing a lightness into my tone that I don't feel.

"This is a blackcurrant and strawberry mousse with passion fruit drizzle and white chocolate flakes," the waitress explains, grinning at Toby when he picks up the spoon and dives right in.

"YUM!" he exclaims, smacking his lips. "THIS IS THE BEST!"

The waitress smiles. "I'll be sure to pass on your compliments to the chef."

"Make sure he knows that now my Mama's gonna work here, he'll have to make sure his puddings are *way* bigger."

"Toby!" I exclaim. What's that saying? Out of the mouth of babes?

But when Drix, Daisy and the waitresses burst out laughing, I can't help but join in.

"What's so funny?" Dalton asks, stepping up to the table as the waitresses leave. His gaze falls to their retreating backs, or should I say arses.

"Really?" Daisy mutters, noticing too.

"Did you enjoy your meal?" Dalton asks, ignoring her.

"It was delicious, thank you," I reply, keeping things polite given he's my new boss.

Dalton nods. "And you met the staff you'll be working with, Lia?"

"I did. They were very welcoming."

"Good. Well, I better head off, I've got work to do."

Daisy snorts. "Like getting handcuffed to a bed by one of your... *lady friends*, you mean?"

Dalton blanches, cutting a glare to Drix.

"It just slipped out," Drix says, smothering a smile.

Dalton lifts a brow. "See you tomorrow then?" he says, looking at me then Daisy.

She lifts her eyes to meet his. "Not if I can help it."

"Daisy," Drix mutters, and she just shrugs. "Thanks Dalton, I'll give you a call later?" he adds.

"Sure thing. Goodnight," he replies, before twisting on his heel and striding off.

Toby screws up his face. "You were rude to that man," he points out.

Daisy gives him a rueful smile. "It's no more than he deserves."

BY THE TIME we get home an hour later, Toby is fast asleep. Rather than wake him up to get washed and ready for bed, I simply carry him into our bedroom, remove his coat and shoes, and tuck him into bed.

As I head downstairs, I hear Daisy and Drix moving about in the kitchen, and I mentally prepare myself for the conversation to come. I owe them my complete honesty, and that's what I'm going to give them.

"Has he gone down alright?" Drix asks me as I approach. He's sitting at the kitchen island drinking black coffee whilst Daisy leans against one of the cabinets taking a sip from a glass of water.

"He's out cold," I reply softly, looking between the two. "About what Toby said—"

"You don't need to explain yourself to us," Drix interrupts.

I shake my head. "I want to. You've been so kind, and I don't want you to think I'm keeping secrets, because I'm not."

"So you are married then?" Daisy asks, giving Drix a concerned look.

"Daisy," Drix warns.

"No it's okay," I say to Drix, then turn my attention to Daisy. "Legally, I'm still married, but in here," I say, pressing a hand against my chest, right over my heart. "I'm not anymore. He lost that right to be my husband the first time he laid hands on me. Before, honestly."

Daisy nods, her features softening. "I'm sorry for everything you've been through. Did he ever hurt...?" Her voice trails off, and I understand what she can't bring herself to say.

"He never hurt Toby, no. At least not physically, but he also didn't really love him either. In the short time you've known him you two have shown him so much more kindness and affection than Martin managed in the whole of Toby's short life so far."

"God, what a dick!" Daisy exclaims, her sweet, friendly nature shadowed with anger as she roughly places her glass of water on the counter. "How could he hurt you like that? How could anyone not love Toby? He's amazing."

"He really, really is," I agree, my throat thickening with tears. "I just wish I'd made different choices. What if he's damaged in some way? I kept the violence and abuse hidden from him as much as possible, but I just..." I drop my head, trying to control my emotions, feeling so much guilt.

Daisy rounds the kitchen island and pulls me into her embrace. "Hey, don't you dare blame yourself. Toby is going to be just fine. He has a fantastic mother, and now he has us, okay?"

"Thank you," I mumble as she pulls back and gives me her own watery smile.

"I can't imagine how hard this has been for you, and I know Drix has already said this to you, but you can stay here for as long as you need. In the past few days, this house has become more of a home with you both in it. I want you to know that."

"That means a lot, and I truly, *truly* appreciate it. You're good people, I *do* see that," I say, flicking my gaze to Drix who's watching our interaction quietly.

After drawing me in for another quick hug, Daisy steps back. "I'm going to head to bed, I've got the day shift tomorrow on reception, and need my beauty sleep. I can drive us both to work?" she offers.

"I'd like that, thank you," I agree.

"Good. Perhaps you should get some rest too?" she suggests.

"I will. I just want a moment to talk with Drix, if that's okay?"

"Of course. Goodnight. See you both bright and early!"

"Night, Daise," Drix says.

I wait until she leaves before taking a seat beside Drix. "I never meant to keep the fact I'm married a secret from you."

"I know you didn't," he replies.

"And I don't take marriage vows lightly either, but I meant it when I said that he's no longer my husband, not in any of the ways that count. If I could divorce him, I would, but that would mean letting him know where I am and I can't do that..." My voice trembles and my body shudders at the thought.

"God, Lia," Drix exclaims, his voice tight. "I could murder him for what he's done to you."

Forcing my head up, I look at him. Baring myself, I say, "I'm so afraid, Drix. I'm so scared he'll find me, that he'll hurt us both."

Drix shakes his head. "Come here," he says, reaching for me, his strong arms wrapping around me as I stumble from my seat and into his arms. Shifting, he hauls me against his chest, his legs widening so that I can nestle between them. I lean into his hold, realising how much I need this hug.

"I'm sorry," I mumble against his neck, my lips grazing the warmth of his skin.

On instinct, I wrap my arms around him tighter, my eyes pressing shut as I allow myself this one moment to feel cared for. My body begins to tremble in earnest now as years of fear and sadness are unleashed. It's as though somewhere deep inside, despite the reservations I still hold, a core part of me understands the safe space Drix has provided me with in this simple gesture of human kindness.

"Never apologise for finding comfort in my arms, Lia," he whispers against the top of my head, his hands rubbing up and down my back as he holds me.

"Thank you," I whisper.

"He will never hurt you again, you hear me?" Drix reassures me, the sound of his voice rumbling through his chest.

"You can't possibly know that."

"I know that," he insists, his arms tightening around me. "I swear, I'll keep you both safe. And you can trust me when I say, I will never hurt you or Toby. *I promise.*"

Held in the comfort of his arms, I begin to believe that what he says is true.

THIRTEEN

WITH MY PHONE pressed against my ear, I listen to Robert drone on about the wedding arrangements, my attention focussed on Toby playing on the caterpillar slide in the children's playground. It's the fifth day of me looking after him and he's wrapped up warm in his coat, green tracksuit and snow boots, his cheeks red with cold, eyes bright as he scrambles up the slide, pushing off the top with a shriek of happiness.

"Drix, did you hear what I just said?" Robert asks.

"I got it. Everything's sorted," I reply, placating him.

"Good. it's imperative this all goes smoothly. I'm relying on you, Drix."

"Listen, I had a good mentor in Hubert. You don't need to worry about anything. I have an excellent security team lined up. The arrangements I've put in place are watertight."

"DRIX, watch this!" Toby calls from the top of the slide as he grips the bar that crosses above his head right at the top of the slide and starts swinging his legs. My heart fucking does a summersault in my chest at the potential danger.

"Who's that?" Robert asks.

"I gotta go," I reply, hanging up just as Toby flings himself from the top of the slide. He goes down with a hard bump, bashing the back of his head against the slide from the force. By the time I reach him he's slid down at top speed, landing in a heap at the bottom, covered in snow.

"Owwwwwww!" he cries, tears spurting from his eyes as he rubs the back of his head.

"Shit!" I shout, scooping down to haul him into my arms. "Are you okay?"

Toby hiccups as I check the back of his head for any lumps. "You swore!" he says, still crying, but this time with a smile creeping up his face.

"And you, buddy, are gonna get me into so much trouble with your Ma!" I reply with a shake of my head as I internally curse myself for bringing him to the playground. Probably not the smartest move given he's only been in my care a few days.

"I won't tell," Toby replies, sniffling as he looks up at me with his big brown eyes.

"Hey, there'll be no lying to your Ma. Truth always, kiddo," I reply, realising how that sounds coming out of my mouth.

"Okay," he mumbles as I dry his tears with my thumb.

"How about we make everything better with a mug of hot chocolate and a doughnut? I'm sure Daph would be glad to see you," I suggest.

"Yes please!" he replies, grinning now.

Two minutes later we're sitting in The Rock Cafe, and true to form, Toby is thoroughly enjoying his treat. Sprinkles of sugar surround his lips as he eats with the enthusiasm of a small kid who clearly has a sweet tooth.

"Hendrix, I could use a hand," Daphne calls, motioning me over from behind the counter.

"Sure thing," I reply, tapping Toby's arm. "I'm just going to help Daph with something. You stay put, okay? I won't be a second."

He nods, taking another bite of his doughnut.

"What do you need me for?" I ask Daphne as I approach.

"An intervention, maybe?" she replies, casting a look over at Toby.

"Daph, I know what I'm doing," I say, leaning against the counter.

She lifts a brow. "You, Hendrix Hammer, are a kind soul."

"But?" I ask, knowing there's more.

"But you and I both know that things are complicated for you. Does that little boy's mum know what you do around here?"

My eyebrows lift in surprise. "And you do?"

"Hendrix, I've known you a long time. Hubert, God rest his soul, longer before that. I may be old, but I'm not a fool. Does she know what you do?" she repeats.

I swipe a hand over my face. "I'm going to tell her when the time is right."

"And when is that going to be? Before or after they've both fallen in love with you?"

"Daph, it's not that simple."

"The truth never is," she agrees, resting her hand on mine. "But that woman deserves to know what getting involved with you means."

"Fuck," I mutter, knowing she's right. Knowing my past, *my present*, is littered with the kind of violence Lia would run screaming from. It's not something I'm proud of, but it is part of my life here, given I'm not just the families' Head of Security but also their enforcer.

"What do I do?" I ask, feeling fucking helpless. "If I tell her, she'll run."

She gives me a sympathetic smile, squeezing my hand. "I know your heart, Drix. I know you'll do the right thing."

"Yeah," I mumble, not sure that she does because right now I'll do anything to keep Lia and Toby, even if that means hiding who I really am.

"YOU HAVE SO MANY!" Toby exclaims loudly as he looks around my office filled to the brim with Funko Pops. "There are hundreds and hundreds and hundreds!"

"Two hundred and fifty-two to be exact," I say, laughing as we both glance around the room.

"Is that Spiderman?" he asks after a beat, bouncing up and down on his feet as he points to one of the boxes that sits on the middle shelf running the entirety of the room.

"Yes, my friend, that is indeed Spiderman. Wanna look at it?"

"Yes, yes, yes!" he yells happily.

Reaching up for the box, I grab it from the shelf and pass it to him. He takes it in his hands, dropping to his bottom as he stares at it wide-eyed.

"It's a limited edition," I explain, pointing to the gold sticker embossed on the box saying as much.

He looks up at me, confusion in his eyes. "What does that mean?"

"It means it's special, just like you are."

"Like me?" he asks.

"Yeah, just like you."

"Wow."

"Do you want it?" I ask, crouching beside him.

"To play with?"

"To keep," I say, taking the box from him and undoing the lid, reaching inside.

"Really, I can have it?"

I smile, handing it to him, his happiness such a fucking joy to be around. "It's yours."

His small hands fold around the toy as he drops his gaze.

"Thank you," he whispers, as if I've just handed him the world.

My throat tightens remembering what it felt like for me when Hubert bought me my first Funko Pop. I was fourteen and a half, a bolshy teen with the weight of the world on his shoulders. We'd been living with Hubert for six months but I still didn't trust him, despite the fact he'd been nothing but kind. Daisy had fallen in love with Hubert almost immediately, when he'd offered to take us to the movie she'd chosen after a winning coin flip. She'd dragged us to see Stardust over my request to watch some action movie out at the time.

Afterwards, when we were walking down the highstreet, she'd stopped at the toy store, staring into the window at the unicorns on display. Ten minutes later she'd walked out with her first unicorn, and Hubert had bought me my very first toy. It was a Fred Flinstone Funko Pop, and even though I pretended like it meant nothing to receive the gift, it had meant *everything* to me.

Growing up with an alcoholic father meant most of our money was spent on his addiction. Anything left over was spent on the essentials, so toys were a luxury we simply couldn't afford.

"You're welcome, kid," I say, ruffling his hair, blinking away the memory as my heart pangs for the only man I'd ever called Dad. Fuck, I miss him.

"Hey, is anyone home?" Lia calls from the hallway. I swipe at my face, surprised to find it wet. Toby immediately jumps up, running out of the room towards his mum whilst I pull my shit together.

"Look what Drix gave me," he says, holding up the Funko Pop, beaming.

She smiles, dropping her gaze as she takes it from him. "Well, that's awesome. It's Spiderman."

"A limited edition!" Toby exclaims, grabbing it back from her as she looks over at me.

"Are you sure?" she asks, removing her coat and draping it over her arm. Her cheeks and lips are flushed from the cold, her hair pulled up into a ponytail, tendrils framing her face. God, she's fucking beautiful.

I nod. "Of course."

"I'm gonna go play with it in my bedroom," he shouts, running up the stairs and out of sight.

"You don't need to do that, give him things, I mean," she says softly, hanging up her coat and kicking off her shoes, placing them by the front door.

"It's fine. It was only sitting on my shelf gathering dust," I respond with a shrug.

"Well, thanks." She yawns, apologising with her eyes.

"Busy day?" I ask, motioning her to follow me into the kitchen.

"I'm surprised I'm this tired, but it was so much fun," she replies with a small smile that makes my heart ache even more. "I made panna cotta today. It was delicious, if I do say so myself."

"I'm glad you're enjoying it. How did you get back?" I ask, grabbing a couple of mugs from the counter and flicking the switch to the kettle on.

"Daisy let me borrow her car. She's getting a lift back from a coworker. She asked me to tell you not to wait up."

"What coworker?" I ask, frowning.

"A guy named Lewis. He's one of the hotel porters I think," Lia replies, taking a seat at the kitchen island.

"Yeah, I know the guy," I grind out, feeling that dangerous protective streak rearing its ugly head.

"You don't like him?"

"I don't particularly like any man who makes a pass at my sister," I admit.

"She's a grown woman, Drix. I'm sure she can make her own decisions about who she chooses to spend her time with."

"Doesn't mean I have to like it..." My voice trails off as I remember the prick she'd dated in college, the bastard treated her like shit. "I'm a little protective when it comes to Daisy, really anyone I care about," I add.

"There seems to be a story here, do you want to share it?" Lia asks, picking up on my vibe.

"There was this guy she went out with in college. He was an arsehole to her. Not in the same way you've been treated," I add hastily when Lia stiffens.

"How so?"

"During the last few weeks of college he dated her on a dare, only to humiliate her in front of her peers during the Summer Ball they all went to for celebrating passing their exams."

"Humiliated her, how?" Lia asks quietly, taking the mug of tea that I pass to her. She wraps her hands around the mug, waiting.

"She told him that she loved him and he publicly revealed the dare, dumping her in front of everyone. It was fucking horrible."

"What a dick," Lia exclaims.

"Yeah, he was," I let slip, stiffening when Lia's gaze snaps up to meet mine.

"Was?"

"He moved away. Left to go to university abroad," I lie, because the truth is, I beat the shit out of him and he ended up spending a month in hospital. Hubert and Carl covered the whole thing up, paying off his family to save my arse from jail. The family moved away from the area as soon as he'd recovered from his injuries. Daisy has no idea what I did for her, and that's the way it's going to stay.

"Well, I'm glad he's no longer around."

"Yeah, me too."

I take a sip of my coffee, feeling like a bastard for not telling her the truth. Keeping this kind of shit from her has been playing on my mind ever since Daphne brought it up earlier today. It doesn't feel good lying to her, but I can't reveal that side to me. I just can't.

"So how was today? Did Toby behave?" Lia asks me after a while.

"He was great. We had a nice time," I say honestly. "He did, however, bump his head."

"What happened?" Lia asks, worry clouding her features.

"Hey, he's good. He just did what little boys do and threw himself down the slide at the park, bumped his head on the way down. Nearly had a fucking heart attack," I explain, pulling a face. "Recovered pretty quickly after a doughnut and a hot chocolate at Daphne's though."

"That'll do it," she says, her shoulders relaxing. "Sorry, he can be a little overexcitable."

I laugh. "He's just being a kid. I like his exuberance. I like him a lot."

"He likes you too, Drix," Lia says quietly, her smile soft as she looks over at me.

There's something in her eyes that makes me pause, a quiet calmness, a glimmer of something more that I haven't seen before. It makes me believe that maybe there's a chance for us.

"Lia, how would you feel about going–"

My fucking phone rings, interrupting my attempt to ask her out on a date. Probably just as well, I need to remind myself about what she told me. She's not ready for anything more.

"I should take this," I say, pulling my phone out of my pocket and glancing at the screen.

It's Carl Gunn. *Fuck.*

"Sure, I'll just go check on Toby," she says, stepping off the stool, taking her warmth with her as she leaves the kitchen.

I answer the phone, the ring insistent. "Yes?"

"You and I need to talk," comes his prompt response.

"About?"

"Seems like you've got a woman and her kid staying with you... Lia, I understand." He lets that comment hang in the air as I abandon my coffee and push up from the table. "I want you to bring them to me."

"She's just got back from work."

"At *my* hotel," he counters. "I think it's prudent I met one of my employees, don't you?"

"It's not a convenient time."

"Regardless, you bring them to me. Now."

"But–"

"This is not a request."

"We'll be with you within the hour," I bite back.

With that, I hang up, the ground beneath my feet fucking lurching.

FOURTEEN

"SO YOU MUST BE LIA?" a suave, silver-haired man with piercing blue eyes asks me, his tailored suit and polished appearance exuding sophistication.

"I am, and this is my son, Toby," I reply as Toby hides behind me, his arm wrapped tightly around my thigh.

"Carl," Drix acknowledges, his hand resting gently on the small of my back as I take Toby's hand and he guides me into the opulent lounge where Dalton's father sits on a plush plum couch, a glistening chandelier hanging overhead.

The grandeur of Carl's mansion is as unsettling as the man who owns it. He reeks of money and entitlement, right down to his handmade leather loafers and arrogant disposition, solidifying his image as a man who has everything he desires at his fingertips.

"Take a seat, I'll have Tessa bring some refreshments," he replies, waving a hand as a woman, not much older than me, enters the room as if by magic. "Some tea, Tessa, and a..." His voice trails off as Toby settles beside me on the pristine white couch. Carl's gaze rises up from Toby's scuffed and dirty trainers. "What would you like to drink?"

"A glass of whatever juice you have will be fine," I reply for Toby, who for the first time in his life is lost for words.

Toby is usually so chatty, so the sheer fact he's not around this man is a warning in and of itself. Kids are incredibly instinctual when it comes to understanding whether someone is a good person or not, and going by his reactions, Toby is just as keen on this man as I am. Which is not at all.

"Fine," Carl says with a dismissive shake of his hand towards the poor woman.

"Thank you," I add, shooting her a smile, making sure she knows I appreciate her given this man clearly doesn't. She dips her head, leaving the room as quietly as she entered it.

"I understand that you're both staying with Drix," Carl says, taking me off guard with his abruptness and steely tone of voice.

Dislike crawls up my spine like an unfriendly spider, and I suddenly feel some empathy towards Dalton. No wonder he seeks comfort in the arms of women because I've no doubt he got very little from a man like this. Carl's cold, matter of fact, and entirely too much like Martin than I'd care to admit. My hackles rise.

"They're my guests," Drix adds tightly, a warning tone to his voice as he takes a seat beside me.

"I see. And how did you meet exactly?" Carl asks, flicking his gaze from Drix to me. When neither of us answer immediately, because what business is it of his anyway, Carl plasters a smile on his face that reminds me more of a snake about to strike. "Drix is the son of my very good friend, so you see I have a vested interest in knowing who he chooses to bring into his home."

"And Drix is a grown man who doesn't need to explain himself to you," I bite out, anger rising in my chest at his words.

Carl smiles, leaning back in his chair as he regards me. "You'll have to excuse me for sounding so..."

"Rude?" I suggest, and Drix stiffens beside me.

"*Interested,*" he corrects. "Drix is like family to me. Hubert was my best friend and I need to ensure that his son and heir is protecting himself. You understand?"

"Carl, you're out of line," Drix growls, his body stiff with tension.

I bristle. "I can assure you that I'm not interested in Drix's money, if that's what you're getting at."

"That would seem to add up given you're working at my hotel. Pastry chef, no?"

"If you're unhappy with my work, then you can ask Dalton to fire me," I snap back, refusing to let the tears stinging my eyes fall. In all of two minutes this man has made me feel worthless.

"That is not the issue here," he says curtly.

"Then what is?" Drix asks tightly.

"No need to be so defensive, this is just a friendly chat," Carl replies, crossing his leg as he gives us all an empty smile.

Friendly? This is about as friendly as Martin used to be before he flew into one of his rages.

"Like I said," he continues, "I have a vested interest in who Drix chooses to invite into his home," Carl says, cutting his gaze to Drix who flinches.

"What do you want to know?" I ask just as coldly.

"Where you're from, your background, that kind of thing."

"You don't have to say anything," Drix says. "This was a mistake bringing you here. I'm sorry, Lia." Drix reaches for my hand, squeezing it tightly. Carl notices and raises a brow.

"My name is Amelia Pearson, this is my son Toby."

"And what brought you to Princetown?"

Drix gives my hand another squeeze, and despite not saying a word I know it's a warning of sorts. I get a feeling he doesn't want me to tell the truth, so I give Carl as little information as possible.

"My car broke down, and when the snow fell, Drix was kind enough to offer us a place to stay until I could get on my feet." It's not the complete truth, but it's not a lie either.

"I see," Carl replies, steepling his fingers beneath his chin before resting his eyes on Toby. "Where's his father?"

I silently thank God that Toby is too scared to speak. "Not around."

"And you have no family you could call to assist with your... predicament."

"No. My mother died not long ago. I don't have anyone else."

"So your car breaks down. Drix is kind enough to put you up, and you take a job at my hotel. That about it?"

"My car has since been stolen," I say.

"Stolen?" he questions, flicking his eyes to Drix. "That's indeed very unfortunate. You've not had much luck have you, Ms Pearson? Or perhaps you've fallen very nicely on your feet. I guess it all depends on how you look at this situation."

"This isn't a situation. I'm helping Lia and Toby out. Dalton offered her a job which, by the way, Lia is incredible at," Drix replies forcefully.

"How long do you plan on staying?" Carl asks.

Up until recently, I was determined to leave as soon as the snow cleared with or without a car, but now... I shift uncomfortably. Things between Drix and I are... I don't even know, but I was willing to see where things would lead. Now, with this man staring at me like I'm some kind of golddigger after Drix's money, that thought makes me feel uncomfortable.

"As soon as I have enough money saved to take care of Toby and me, we'll be on our way," I say instead.

"Is that right?" he asks, turning his attention to Drix.

"I've already told Lia she is welcome to stay for however long she likes. If she chooses to leave I won't stop her, but if she wants to stay you best believe I'll have her back in whatever capacity she needs."

Carl smirks. "Indeed."

"Mama, I want to go home," Toby murmurs, curling into my side. I place a protective arm around his shoulder.

"You can leave when I'm finished talking with your mother," Carl says, his tone sharp.

Toby lets out a sob.

"We're done here," Drix growls, climbing to his feet. He holds out his hand and I slide mine into his, needing his support as I'm suddenly feeling very unsteady as I rise to my feet.

"We're done when I say we're done," Carl snaps back.

"That's where you're wrong. You've insulted my friend, my intelligence, and upset Toby all in the space of a few minutes. Who I choose to invite into my home is no business of yours," Drix replies coolly. "We're leaving."

Tessa re-enters the room holding a tray, stepping towards us until Carl holds his hand up. "Take it back to the kitchen. Drix and his *friend* are leaving."

Tessa nods, her eyes flicking to mine. She gives me a sympathetic look and my stomach coils as she backs out of the room once more. Carl remains seated, watching me with narrowed eyes.

"I don't know what you think I'm about," I say angrily, Drix's presence making me bold. "But I can assure you that Drix's wealth is of no interest to me. He's my *friend*, and I happen to treat people I like with the respect they deserve. Perhaps you should consider doing the same?" I add with a strength I didn't know I possessed.

Carl cocks a brow, rising to his feet, his demeanour changing from out and out dislike, to a begrudging respect. "I can see why he likes you. It's been a while since a woman has stood up to me. Nice to meet you, Lia. I look forward to tasting some of your work. Dalton tells me you're quite gifted."

I'm thrown by his sudden change of heart, but not fooled by it. I know men like him.

"Come on, Lia, Toby, let's go," Drix urges.

I follow him, Toby's hand clenched tightly in mine. As we

reach the door Carl clears his throat, and Drix stalls as we turn to face him.

"Drix is an important cog in a very smoothly running wheel. His position within our families' businesses is exceedingly important," he says to me before looking at Drix. "I expect you to adhere to our arrangement. Understood?"

A muscle in Drix's jaw flickers as he gives him a sharp nod in response. Carl smiles and it sends shivers down my spine.

"Good. So long as we're clear."

Ten minutes later, Drix is pulling into the car park of the shopping centre that I parked in on the night we first arrived in Princetown. It seems like ages ago now when we were forced to sleep in my car, when in reality it's only been about a week and a half.

"Are we going to the ballpark, Mama?" Toby asks, cheering up a little now that we're far away from that awful man.

"I thought we could do some shopping," Drix says, plastering on a smile for Toby. "But you can visit the ballpark first, then we can shop and have dinner after. How about that?"

"Yes please," Toby exclaims, clapping his hands together with excitement.

"Drix, I haven't been paid yet," I say quietly as he climbs out of the car, fetching Toby from his seat.

He doesn't reply, he simply waits for me to join them both. Reluctantly, I step into stride beside them as we enter the shopping centre and head towards the children's play centre. Around us people are shopping for Christmas gifts. Couples walk hand in hand, chattering, happy, bags filled with their purchases swinging from their hands, but all I feel is a dark cloud over my head despite the Christmas lights decorating the place.

The discussion with Carl has made me feel out of sorts, and I don't know what to think or how to behave. I certainly don't want Drix thinking that I'm after him for his money like Carl insinuated.

When we reach the children's play centre, Toby runs off to the ballpit, throwing his body into the huge pile of coloured plastic balls the second we enter. Within minutes he's made a friend and they're running around the netted climbing frame hooting and laughing.

"Lia, I'm sorry about how Carl treated you," Drix says as we sit at one of the plastic tables watching Toby play.

I shake my head. "I guess he was just looking out for you," I reply, not sure why I'm making excuses for the man's appalling behaviour.

"He was being an intrusive bastard. There's no excuse. I apologise," he says firmly.

I nod, my gaze following Toby as he enjoys himself. "I want you to know, I'm not after you for your money. That isn't who I am," I add.

Drix swivels in his seat to face me. He reaches for my hands holding them gently. "I know that. Carl is suspicious of anyone new to town. He has more money than sense and it clouds his judgement."

"Even so, I never want you to feel like I'm some gold digger. I'm only staying because I have no other choice." Drix removes his hands from mine, and I feel bereft from the loss of his touch, my gut twisting at the hurt look on his face. "That's not what I meant," I mumble.

"So you're still planning on leaving?" he asks me.

"I– I don't know," I admit. "My head is all over the place."

"Don't let what Carl said make you feel like you have to leave as soon as you're able. I like having you both around. I mean it, Lia. I *want* you to stay. I don't give a fuck about what Carl Gunn has to say. All I care about is you and Toby, and how you make me feel."

I sigh. "I know you like having us around."

"But?"

"But where can this really lead? I'm still married, Drix. My life is complicated."

"I happen to like complicated things," he replies, shooting me a small smile.

"And it seems like your life is complicated too," I note, remembering Carl's parting shot as we were leaving. "I don't know what hold that man has over you, but I'm not stupid, Drix, I sense that there's something going on."

Drix swipes a hand over his face. "You don't need to worry about that. It's just... *business*," he falters.

"Don't do that. Don't treat me like I'm stupid, Drix," I say, looking away from him, feeling my slowly building trust for him beginning to crumble.

"Lia, please look at me."

"I can't," I whisper out, barely holding myself together.

"Lia, look at me," he quietly urges.

I lift my gaze, my lips trembling.

"What do you see?"

"I don't understand," I reply.

"What do you see when you look at me?" he repeats.

"That's kind of an odd question," I reply, biding my time.

"Okay then, tell me what you feel when you look at me. You can be honest. I can take it."

I heave out a sigh, honesty all that I have left. "I feel scared, Drix."

"I frighten you?" he asks, flinching.

"Not like the way Martin did, not like that," I reassure him.

"Why do I scare you, Lia?" he gently asks.

"Because you make me feel..." My voice trails off as I press my eyes shut, trying to gather myself. When I open my eyes, the intense way he looks at me catches my breath.

"I make you feel what?" He flexes his fingers and I know he wants to reach for me again but doesn't.

"You make me feel safer than I've felt in a long, long time," I admit in a rush of breath, and then as though a dam has been breached my words come flooding out. "You make me feel like I'm worth something, that I'm interesting, worthy of your attention. You make me feel good about myself."

"You are amazing, Lia. God, it's me that's not worthy of you," he says with a shake of his head.

"You make me believe that there's a chance..." I drag in another faltering breath as he waits, staring at me intently. "You make me believe that there's a chance I could be happy again."

"I want you to be happy, Lia, and I want to be that man who makes you happy."

This time he reaches for me, his palms covering my hands, enveloping them in their warmth. "Ignore Carl, he means nothing. Trust what you feel, Lia. If you can't fully trust me, trust that."

"I'll try, Drix."

"That's good enough for me," he replies, smiling broadly now.

Toby yells from the climbing frame, and we both turn to face him. "This is so much fun!"

We both laugh, his childish exuberance the tonic we both need.

"We should probably get him out of there or we'll never get any shopping done," Drix says with a chuckle.

"About that," I begin.

"I know you don't want me to buy you anything, but will you at least allow me to treat Toby?"

I consider his offer as Toby runs over to us both, his happiness a remedy to my barely stitched together heart. How can I possibly deny him?

"Okay," I say, nodding as Toby throws himself into Drix's arms.

"It might just be your lucky day," Drix says, hauling him into his arms as they both laugh.

"Why?" Toby asks.

"Well, kid, I happen to know a really good toy store that is filled with stuff I think you'd like."

"You're going to buy me a toy?" he asks.

"I sure am!"

Toby's smile spreads impossibly wider as he reaches up, his small hands gently cupping Drix's cheeks. For a moment they just stare at each other, my throat clogging at the sweetness of the moment, my heart aching at their growing bond.

Drix's features soften, and in that moment I realise that it isn't my feelings I should trust, but Toby's. There's no doubt that he lights up with happiness whenever he's around Drix, and his happiness means more to me than my own. It's with that thought that I decide to entrust our hearts to Hendrix Hammer, hoping to God he never gives me a reason to regret that decision.

FIFTEEN

"I'M sorry Dad gave Lia a hard time, Drix," Dalton apologises as we step out of the hotel and into the fading daylight a couple of days later. We've spent the afternoon going over the arrangements for Robert's wedding, double-checking that the hotel's security system is up to par for the reception.

"He told you then?"

"It came up in conversation."

"I bet. How the fuck do you put up with him?" I reply, grabbing my keys from my pocket and unlocking my car. "He's an arsehole."

"You've only just noticed?" Dalton jokes, giving me a wry smile as he tries to lighten the mood, but it falls flat as the memory of the conversation Lia and I had with Carl resurfaces.

"Didn't drive to work this morning?" I fire back when I notice his car isn't parked in his space, not wanting to get into a conversation about his dick of a father.

He shrugs. "Stayed at the hotel last night."

I raise a brow. "Let me guess, another late-night hook-up?"

"Don't look at me like that, I have needs."

"What you *need* is an intervention, Dalton. This shit has got to stop."

"I appreciate your concern, but I'm good, thanks."

"Whatever, man," I retort. It's not as if I haven't tried over the years to get him to see sense. We both know he's struggling with deep-rooted issues, but like a stubborn idiot he refuses to acknowledge them.

"If you're passing by my place, I could use a lift home."

"Sure, hop in."

As I reach for the handle of my car door, my phone buzzes in my pocket, signalling an incoming call. No doubt it's Daisy calling to remind me to get my arse home for dinner. Despite what I'd said to Lia when she first arrived, I enjoy returning to a home-cooked meal, and so long as she enjoys cooking for us there'll be no complaints from me.

Only it's not Daisy, it's Benedict.

"Ben?" I ask, pressing the phone to my ear as I slide behind the wheel and slam my door shut.

"Need you at Bandits," he bites out.

I'm immediately on high alert. "I'm with Dalton. We're just leaving the hotel."

"You might want to let Dalton drive," he retorts.

"That urgent?" I press, jumping out of the driver's seat and motioning for Dalton to take my place as I jog around the car. He takes the hint, swapping places with me as I connect to bluetooth, so Dalton can listen in as he gets behind the wheel.

"You remember that prick you saw off that night outside the bar?"

"Yeah."

"I've had a tip-off that he's heading this way and bringing some friends."

"We'll be there in ten," I snap out, buckling up as Dalton fires up the engine.

"Make that five," Dalton says with a grin as he presses his foot on the clutch and puts the car in first, the back wheels of the car spinning as he floors the gas.

Adrenaline courses through my veins as the car lurches forward with a powerful surge, and I grip on to the edge of my seat as we race through the winding roads, narrowly avoiding collisions and leaving a trail of startled honks in our wake. Dalton handles the car with cool precision, his hands gripping the steering wheel with unwavering determination.

"Am I going to need a lawyer?" Dalton jokes as we screech to a halt outside Bandits, our car coming to rest amidst a cacophony of shouting and crashing sounds. He knows as well as I do that whatever is about to happen will never get close to the courts, let alone any police.

How many times have we been in this position? Too many to count. Mostly I'm the one left to deal with the arseholes threatening the families, but there have been occasions when my friends have been involved too. Over the years they've had my back, as much as I've had theirs, and I'm grateful for their friendship, their loyalty. Without uttering a word, I spring out of the car, storming through the entrance, Dalton close behind me.

Inside, Ben stands near the counter, his muscles taut with determination as he wields a bat with deadly precision. Five men surround him, their faces twisted into malicious grins as they circle him. I catch the eye of the bastard who started all this shit the night Lia and Toby entered Bandits, the wound I gave him is sewed together haphazardly, making him seem even more menacing.

"Watch out!" Dalton shouts, the sound of shattering glass echoing throughout the room as one of the men smashes a bottle against the surface of a table, lunging for Ben who, thanks to Dalton's warning, bats it out of his hand with a loud crack.

"Motherfucker!" the man shouts, holding on to his injured hand as he staggers backwards.

Without hesitation, Dalton and I join the fray, our bodies moving in sync as we charge towards the intruders. The atmosphere crackles with a primal energy, each swing of our fists punctuated by the deafening thud of knuckles meeting flesh. The air becomes a maelstrom of chaos and fury, bodies colliding and curses reverberating throughout the bar.

I catch a glimpse of Dalton, his eyes ablaze with righteous anger as he unleashes a flurry of powerful blows, sending his opponents sprawling to the ground like discarded puppets. Together, we fight as one, the rhythm of our violence echoing throughout the room. Blood stains the floor, mingling with spilled drinks and shattered debris. My vision becomes blurred as I unleash a volley of strikes, my body moving on pure instinct.

Amidst the chaos, Ben's gritty determination propels him forward as he wields his bat with unwavering purpose. One by one the men fall, their bodies crumpling to the floor from our relentless onslaught, leaving only one man standing. The prick who I cut.

"You were warned never to come back," I shout, swiping my bloody knuckles against my jeans as I step over one of the men who's out cold. There's only one way to end this, and that's this bastard's broken body thrown into an unmarked grave, alongside the rest of his men.

"You think I'd let that go?" he asks, his snarl turning into a deranged grin as he lunges forward, swinging wildly at me. We exchange more blows, blood spraying from the barely healed knife wound that I inflicted the last time he decided to fuck with us. Each punch is more brutal than the last.

His fist connects with my jaw, sending a shockwave of pain through my body, but despite his ferocity, he's no match for my pent-up rage. I am merciless, raining down a storm of punches until he crumples to the ground on his hands and knees, panting like a dog.

With a savage grip on his hair, I violently jerk his head back and continue to unleash my fury upon him. Each strike of my clenched fist delivers a sickening thud as I scream.

"YOU."

His jaw shatters under the force of my blows.

"ARE."

A brutal punch to the bridge of his nose sends blood flying outwards.

"DEAD," I roar, my fist raised high as I prepare to deliver the final strike.

Crimson blood flows from his broken nose, lip and brow. His eyes are swelling shut, the skin around them a grotesque shade of purple, and his hastily stitched scar is ripped open once again.

"You should never have come back," I spit, my whole body vibrating with violence.

"Fuck. You," he retorts, gathering all the saliva and blood in his mouth and spitting at my face. The putrid mixture splatters across my skin and slides down my temple. Rage overtakes me and I clench my fists so tightly that my nails draw blood from my palms. My vision blurs as I imagine all the ways I could kill him right now.

But instead of ending this with one last fatal punch, a sudden eerie stillness creeps into the room, suffocating any thoughts of revenge. My heart races as I struggle to resist the urge to end his life. Once again, images of Lia and Toby flash through my mind reminding me of the man I want to be, not this thug everyone needs me to be. With great effort, I release his hair and take a step back, refusing to give in to the violence inside of me.

My clenched fist lowers.

I won't fucking do it.

"Drix?" Ben questions as I meet Dalton's gaze.

Understanding passes between us and he nods.

"Walk away," Dalton says, his voice calm. "We'll take care of this mess."

I nod, swallowing the knot in my throat. There's no denying the anger that rages inside of me, or the fact that I'm more than capable of finishing this, but there's a larger part of me that doesn't want to fuck up the possibility of a future with the amazing woman waiting at home for me with her son. Dalton understands that.

"What's your plan?" I ask.

"You're not the only one with contacts," Dalton replies, giving my shoulder a squeeze. "We've got this. Go home."

"Ben?" I question, looking at my friend, needing his approval too.

"You were never here. Go."

"Text me when it's sorted," I say, for once in my life relinquishing control as I walk out of the bar and into the cold night air.

A couple of minutes later I unlock the door to my flat above the gym, thankful that the entrance is around the back of the building. It's early enough for people to still be out and about, but dark enough for me to slip inside without being noticed. There's no way I can go home covered in blood, I need to clean up first.

Tossing my keys onto the table beside the front door, I head for the shower, needing to wash off the grime and blood that clings to my skin. Removing my clothes, I step into the shower. The water cascades down my body, washing away the remnants of tonight's chaos. For a moment, I close my eyes, trying to forget the violence - the sounds of bones cracking, the blood splattering on the floor, the screams of the men we fought.

"Fuck!" I grind out, my thoughts conflicted.

There's no way I wasn't going to help Ben deal with those bastards, and yet I resent my position as the enforcer for the families. This isn't who I want to be.

Turning off the shower, I wrap myself in a towel and stare at my reflection in the mirror. A face I barely recognise stares back at me, the hard jawline, the shadowed eyes, the rage that still flickers within them. This is the man I've become and there's no hiding from it. But tonight, just like with Fraser, I hesitated before causing irreparable damage.

I hesitated for them. For Lia and Toby.

Swiping at my split lip that still weeps blood, I force myself to regain some semblance of control. A bruise is beginning to form on my cheek, another on my jaw. How am I going to explain this away? As far as Lia, Daisy and Toby are concerned I've spent the afternoon at the hotel. The thought of lying to them makes me feel even more shit, but what choice do I have? I can't tell them the truth.

As I contemplate what to do, my phone vibrates on the countertop, snapping me out of my thoughts. I pick it up, swiping it open to see a text from Dalton.

It's done.

Relief floods through me, and I fire him a quick text back.

I've got a split lip. Some bruises forming. Need a story. I'm going to say I was checking one of the cameras in the hotel lobby. Fell off the ladder. I got some blood on my clothes so I went to change at my flat above the gym.

I watch as the three bubbles dance as he writes his response.

You got it.

Taking a deep breath, I ignore the guilt I feel and head into my bedroom, slipping into a pair of clean boxers and a t-shirt, the soft fabric brushing against my skin providing little comfort. Grabbing some jeans and a sweater, I get dressed, pull on my shoes, pick up my car keys and head home, my eyes catching on the box of Lia's recipe books stored in the corner of my closet. The sight of them makes more guilt pile on the mountain already sitting on my shoulders.

As I drive through the streets of Princetown, my mind is still reeling from tonight's events. But as much as my mind seems to want to dwell on it—to wallow in self-pity or berate myself for getting caught up in this lifestyle—I refuse to let it.

Instead, I focus on Lia and Toby. They've brought out a part of me that has been buried beneath all the violence and chaos that my life has become. Their presence reminds me of the person I truly am, who I want to continue to be, and the only thing I care about is helping them have a better life. I just need to figure out if that's with or without me.

Because after tonight, I've no fucking clue.

SIXTEEN

AS I CLEAR the dinner plates away, I surreptitiously glance over at Drix, who has been uncharacteristically quiet this evening. His usually bright eyes are clouded with something that I can't quite decipher and it makes me feel a little off-kilter. Gathering the courage to break the silence, I clear my throat and turn towards him.

"So," I start tentatively, "You fell off a ladder while checking a security camera?"

A slight crease appears between his eyebrows as he nods, but his lips remain tightly pressed together. The soft glow of the dimmed lights in the kitchen cast shadows across his face, making it hard for me to read his expression.

"Yeah, toppled right off the darn thing, caught my face on the edge of a chair," he replies eventually, rubbing his jaw where a bruise is beginning to form. There's another on his cheek, and his lip is split too. "My shoulder took the brunt of the fall, luckily I remembered not to put my hand out, might've broken something otherwise."

"Does it hurt?" Toby asks him, sliding off his seat to gently prod at the darkened bruise on Drix's cheek.

"Nah, I'm good," he replies, ruffling Toby's hair with a small smile.

"You know, you should sue Dalton," Daisy remarks, before swallowing a mouthful of homemade lemon sorbet, her face lighting with pleasure. "Oh my God, Lia, you could sell this to the masses. It's delicious," she adds with a groan.

"Sue him?" Drix shakes his head. "He's my best mate, Daisy, why would I do that? Besides, it ain't his fault I'm a clumsy idiot."

"Because he's loaded, and it would be *fun* to piss him off," she replies with a mischievous smile.

"Daisy!" Toby laughs. "You said a rude word!"

"Who me? No, I didn't," she argues playfully.

"Yes, you did. That means you owe a pound to the swear jar," Toby says, grinning.

"Okay, fine. I'll pop one in there just as soon as I've finished eating your mum's yummy sorbet," Daisy concedes with a smile.

"Here we go, Toby," I say, passing him a bowl, and dishing up some to Drix too.

"Thanks," Drix replies, giving me a soft smile as they both tuck in.

A couple of spoonfuls later, a tiny furrow appears between Drix's eyebrows, and he inhales sharply, his tongue running over the split in his lip. "Damn," he mutters.

"Oh no, the lemon. I didn't think," I say, knowing that the acidity from the lemon juice would likely cause some discomfort. "I'm sorry, Drix.

"Don't be. It tastes delicious," he replies, resting the spoon back into the bowl and giving me a smile, "But I think I should avoid eating more of this until my lip heals."

Daisy reaches across the table, grabbing Drix's bowl. "Well, that just means more for us then," she says with a wink, sharing what's left of his dessert with Toby.

"Knock yourself out. I'm gonna head up to my room, see to this," Drix says, pointing to his lip as he gives me a brief glance. "Thank you for dinner, Lia. It was delicious."

As I listen to the creaking of the stairs under Drix's weight, I exchange glances with Daisy. "Maybe I should fetch him a painkiller?" I suggest, chewing on my lip as I try to shake off this feeling of unease. He's been acting weird since he got home, and I wonder if it's because he's in more pain than he's letting on or maybe he's just had a bad day. I haven't met Robert Blade yet, but if he's anything like Carl Gunn, he can't be an easy man to work for.

"Top shelf on the right," Daisy says, pointing to the cabinet in the far corner of the kitchen. "Though I'm sure he can look after himself, unless you *want* to of course," she adds, glancing up at me with a smirk.

"I'll only be a minute," I reply, ignoring her suggestive tone as I grab some painkillers and fill a glass of water from the tap.

"Take all the time you need," Daisy calls after me, laughter in her voice.

As I enter Drix's bedroom, the sound of water running in his ensuite bathroom fills the air. I pause at the threshold, hesitant to disturb him.

"Drix, can I come in?" I ask softly.

"Sure," he replies.

In the mirror above the sink, I see him dabbing a cotton pad against his lip, his gaze meeting mine in the reflection. My stomach churns at the look in his eyes, it's a mixture of pain and vulnerability that I haven't seen before.

"Darn thing won't stop bleeding," he mutters in frustration.

Concern washes over me immediately, and I remember the painkillers and glass of water I brought with me. "I thought you might need something for the pain," I explain, offering them to him.

"Thank you," he says, turning to face me so he can take them from my outstretched hand, quickly popping the pills into his mouth and washing them down with a gulp of water.

As he sets the glass down on the counter, his gaze lingers on me for a moment, and a palpable tension hangs between us. It's a mix of emotions—worry, gratitude, longing—that makes my heart beat faster.

"Lia, I–"

"Are you in a lot of pain?" I say, my cheeks heating as I realise I've just cut him off. "Sorry, you go first," I quickly add.

"I'm just fine, Lia," he reassures me. "I'm sorry if I seem a bit off. Just a little stressed, that's all."

"With the security plans? Is Robert giving you a hard time? Is there anything I can do?" I ask, chewing on my lip as I step closer to him, wanting to bridge the gap between us, having this sudden urge to comfort him like he's comforted me on so many occasions.

"Just being able to come home to you is more than enough," he murmurs, lifting his warm brown eyes to meet mine. "I love having you here."

"I like being here," I admit, my heart aching at his words, this feeling of longing settling deep within me. I take a step closer, our bodies almost touching, and I reach out to gently trace the bruises forming on his jaw and cheek. His short beard is rough beneath my fingers, and I feel a jolt of electricity run through me at the contact. Drix's breath hitches at my touch, and I can't help but notice the way his eyes seem to darken with desire.

"Let me take care of you," I say.

He exhales slowly, his eyes searching mine. "You already are."

"I meant your lip," I add, fumbling over my words as his hand comes up to cover mine, pressing my palm against his cheek. The warmth of his hand seeps into me and for a moment we just stand there lost in each other's gaze.

A huge part of me wants to kiss him, to press my body against his and see where this leads, to allow myself to indulge in these growing feelings. But the other part of me, the part that is insecure, uncertain, afraid, won't let me.

I quickly pull away, embarrassed at my sudden boldness. "I'm sorry," I mumble, taking a step back. "I didn't mean to overstep."

"You haven't," Drix says softly, his voice laced with tenderness as he takes a tentative step towards me, closing the distance I had just created.

"Drix," I caution.

"I'm fighting really hard against these feelings I have for you, Lia," he says, gently brushing a strand of hair behind my ear as we stand, caught in this magnetic pull drawing us closer together. "But being near you, it's becoming impossible to deny how much I want you."

I close my eyes for a moment, trying to calm the racing of my heart. Being this close to him is both torture and temptation. I can't deny I'm drawn to him, to his kindness, his strength, his unwavering support.

"I'm scared," I admit quietly, forcing myself to look up at him.

Drix's gaze softens. "Me too, he says softly, his head dipping closer.

My breath catches in my throat as I feel the heat of his body against mine, the soft whisper of his breath against my lips, but he makes no move to bridge the gap, allowing me to make that decision for the both of us.

My mind is screaming at me to step back, but every inch of me wants nothing more than to lean into him and lose myself in this moment. Do I follow my heart, and embrace this growing tenderness between us? Or do I listen to my head that's cautioning me to be careful, to wait.

Before I can make a decision either way, Toby's voice calls from the hallway and we jump apart, the moment gone as he comes running into the ensuite.

"Mama, we're going to play a game of charades! Daisy said Drix is terrible so he should be your partner!" he says, grinning up at us both.

Drix laughs, and I drag in a tremulous breath as he says, "I'll have you know that I am excellent at charades so you might want to reconsider partnering with Daisy."

"Nope," he replies, shaking his head. "Daisy said if we win, she'll let me choose one of her unicorns to keep forever!"

"Is that so?" I ask him with a playful smile, glad for the interruption that has saved me from making a rash decision.

Toby nods enthusiastically, his excitement radiating from him. "Yep! And she has like, a million unicorns, so I really want to win!"

Drix chuckles, ruffling Toby's hair affectionately before glancing over at me. "Well then, Lia, we'd better start strategizing. Can't have my little sister and this genius besting us, now can we?"

"I guess not," I agree.

Toby giggles, tugging on Drix's hand. "Come on, let's go!"

"Just give us a moment, okay?" he asks. "Got to finish up here."

"Okay," Toby replies, his hurried footsteps pounding on the floor as he rushes out, leaving behind a charged tension that still lingers in the air between us.

"Lia," Drix mutters, a hint of apology in his voice as his fingers brush against mine. "I didn't mean to make things so intense."

"It's honestly fine," I say. "It's not all on you."

Drix takes my hand in his, his touch comforting and warm. "I promise to take things slow," he says sincerely. "We don't have to rush into anything if you're not ready."

I let out a breath of relief, grateful for his understanding. "Thank you, Drix. That means a lot."

He smiles at me, his eyes shining with affection. "You don't have to thank me. I care about you, Lia. And I want us to explore whatever this is between us at a pace that feels comfortable for you. I just got caught up in the moment. Can you forgive me?"

"There's nothing to forgive," I reply, feeling a flutter in my stomach as our fingers intertwine. "Now, shall we show Toby and Daisy how it's done?"

"Let's do this," he agrees eagerly, grinning.

As we make our way downstairs, the charged tension between us slowly dissipates, replaced by a sense of ease. Drix's hand in mine feels familiar, a comforting presence that I can't help but relish.

Entering the living room, we find Toby and Daisy waiting, their excitement palpable. Daisy is wearing a mischievous grin, her eyes twinkling.

"Are you two ready to lose?" she taunts, wiggling her eyebrows playfully.

Drix chuckles and squeezes my hand before letting go. "We'll see about that," he replies, his voice filled with playful determination.

Toby jumps up and down in excitement. "Come on, Mama! Time to play!"

I smile at him and take a deep breath, trying to shake off the residual effects of our interrupted moment. This is just a game, I remind myself. Just an innocent way to spend time together. But deep down, I know that there is something more lingering beneath the surface, something that can't be easily dismissed. This is beginning to feel like a family, and I can't deny how happy that makes me.

As we split into teams and prepare for the game of charades, I find myself stealing glances at Drix when he isn't looking. The game begins, and Toby is surprisingly good at acting out his chosen phrases. Laughter fills the room as Daisy contorts her face comically while attempting to mimic words without speaking. But all the while, my attention keeps gravitating back to Drix – his infectious laughter, the way his eyes crinkle at the corners when he smiles.

With each passing turn, I feel my guard slowly melting away. The walls I had built so carefully around my heart are beginning to crumble in the face of his unwavering support and genuine affection. Perhaps it's time to take a leap of faith, to let go of my fears and embrace the unknown.

It's the final round, and Toby and Daisy have been relentless opponents, but Drix and I are determined to claim victory. We exchange knowing glances, a silent promise to give it our all.

Drix steps forward for his turn, and his eyes lock with mine for a brief moment before he begins to act out his phrase with enthusiasm, using exaggerated gestures and facial expressions. The room erupts in laughter as I struggle to decipher his message. But amidst the chaos, I find myself captivated by the way Drix effortlessly commands the attention of everyone in the room. How at ease he makes me feel.

And suddenly, it hits me – this is what it feels like to be truly alive, to embrace vulnerability and seize every opportunity for happiness. I may be scared, uncertain of what lies ahead, but I'm willing to see where this goes.

SEVENTEEN

FOR THE NEXT couple of weeks we all fall into a comfortable routine. Lia works her morning shift at the hotel whilst I look after Toby, and either myself or Daisy drive Lia to work depending on Daisy's shift patterns. In the afternoons I work on finalising the security for the upcoming wedding, and in the evening we all sit down to a home-cooked meal prepared by Lia.

Every day Lia opens up more and more, and I've begun to see glimpses of the woman she talked about once being. It's a good feeling, and nothing makes me happier than listening to her talk animatedly about her day. Cooking, and more specifically, baking, isn't just a job to her, it's what lights her fire, and in all honesty, her happiness and growing confidence lights mine too.

Today, three and a half weeks after Lia and Toby appeared in my life, the three of us are visiting the gym I own so that I can introduce Lia and Toby to my good friends and coworkers.

"How long have you owned the gym?" Lia asks me as we head inside the gym named after the man I owe everything to, Hubert.

"Bought the place a few months after Hubert was diagnosed with cancer. The previous owner wanted to sell up for his retirement. So I took it over, revamping the gym and adding more up to date equipment. I hired more instructors to provide a variety of classes to our growing members. I wanted Hubert to see what I was capable of, to make him proud of me, I guess," Drix explains, holding open the door as we step inside.

"I'm sure he must've been proud," Lia replies, Toby's hand held in hers as she follows me into the bright and welcoming reception area where Clementine sits. She grins up at us, her smile as dazzling as her dark copper hair and whiskey coloured eyes.

"Drix, hi!" she says, brushing a rogue curl away from her face and tucking it behind her ear.

"Hey, Clemmy, good to see you. These are my friends Lia and Toby. Lia, Toby, meet Clementine, the woman who keeps all the men here in check," I say with a wink. A black belt in karate makes her well equipped in that department.

"Hi Clementine," they both reply in unison.

"Busy today?" I ask.

"As always. Ten new members joined this week! I think that has a lot to do with the fact that Baxter has started taking pilates classes. He's very popular with the gym bunnies, if you know what I mean?"

"Yeah, that'll do it," I agree with a laugh.

"He's on shift right now, but the others are in the staff room on their break. Let me buzz you through," she replies, waving at Toby who gives her a shy smile.

When we pass through the door, Toby giggles. "She's *pretty*."

Lia and I exchange looks, grinning. "She sure is. She's also sworn off men for life, apparently. "

Toby puffs out his chest. "I could be her boyfriend."

"You've got a few years left until you can even think about having a girlfriend," Lia says with a chuckle.

"Wow!" Toby exclaims, his steps faltering as his attention is caught by Baxter, one of my good friends and employees, as he strides towards us from the other side of the gym. Pretty sure the whole room takes a collective breath as he moves, attracting glances from both male and female members alike.

"He's a powerhouse, that's for sure," I say, patting Toby on the head. "Not sure how he manages to take pilates classes though."

Now, I pride myself on my own muscular physique, but Baxter takes the cake. Standing at six foot six, he's built like a mountain, with muscles to match. He could be seen as intimidating with his shorn hair, long brown beard and brightly tattooed arms, but he's a good guy with a heart of gold that shines through when he smiles.

"Yo, Drix! Slacking looks good on you," he jokes, slapping me on the arm as he greets us all with a smile. Not one for keeping himself hidden away, he wears bright red shorts and a matching gym shirt that hugs his muscles, leaving very little to the imagination.

"A man could get a complex around you," I say, chuckling.

"If you've got it, flaunt it. Am I right?"

"You're even bigger than Drix!" Toby exclaims innocently as he looks up at the beefcake.

"In all the ways that count, little fella," Baxter replies with a chuckle, throwing a wink at Lia.

I side-eye her, noticing how her cheeks pink up and her lips jerk up in a smile. Well, fuck, now I feel a stab of jealousy at her obvious appreciation.

Baxter grins, glancing back at me. "We've missed you around here, mate."

"Been a little busy sorting out the security for Robert Blade's wedding. Are you still up for some overtime covering the biggest social event Princetown has seen since you beat AJ's arse at last year's heavyweight championship?" I add jokingly, shoving the jealousy aside.

"You know I'm good for it," he grins, turning his attention back to Lia and Toby.

"And you must be Lia and Toby, Drix has told us all about you. Pretty sure he could write a full on soliloquy about his feelings for you. The texts messages he's been sending are like poetry—"

"Thanks mate," I groan as Lia blushes an even deeper shade of pink.

"Nice to meet you," Lia says politely.

"We're heading to the staff room. I wanted to introduce Lia and Toby to you all, given they're going to be sticking around a while," I explain, hoping I'm not speaking out of turn.

Since our conversation at the shopping centre, she hasn't mentioned leaving again, and I'm hoping that means she's considering staying for longer than just a few short weeks, that she's beginning to trust her feelings like I asked her to do.

"Awesome, the guys will be glad to see you. But unlike those lazy buggers, I got work to do," Baxter replies, turning on his feet to move away. He hesitates, turning back. "Hey, why don't we meet for a drink at Bandits this weekend to have a proper catch up. The band is playing Friday night, and Ben's got some guy from a label coming in from the city to check them out."

"Yeah, he mentioned that," I reply noncommittally. It's not that I don't want to support Ben and the band, it's just that I enjoy spending all of my time with Lia and Toby, and I don't want to go swanning off on a night out when I'd rather be with them.

"He wants the place packed out. You should come too, Lia," he adds with a quirk of his brow and a twinkle in his eye, because he knows that'll needle me.

"Maybe," she replies, looking at me hesitantly.

I relax my face, plastering on a smile because the bastard is obviously intent on winding me up today. "Catch you later."

"Sure thing, boss," he says with a chuckle, stepping aside as we move past him.

"Do the men you're about to introduce me to all look like that?" Lia whispers under her breath as she glances over her shoulder at Baxter.

"What, you mean like a giant gnome?" I ask, bristling.

She snorts out a laugh. "That wasn't what I was thinking at all."

"Yeah, yeah they do," I mutter, reconsidering my choice to bring her here after all.

Pushing open the door to the staff room, we head inside to be welcomed by a wall of muscle in the form of Riley, Troy and AJ. The three men help me to run this gym alongside Baxter, as well as back me up when the family heads want us to deal with the local riff-raff. Riley is the first to get up from the large sectional in the corner of the staff room.

"Hey man, you good?" he asks, bumping my fist in greeting before turning his attention to Lia and Toby.

"Hello, lad," he says, crouching down in front of Toby and holding his fist up.

Toby immediately curls his fingers, gently bumping Riley's hand right back.

"You're not as big as Baxter," Toby observes.

Riley laughs. "No one is as big as Baxter," he agrees amiably, rising upwards to hold his hand out to Lia.

"Hi," she says, shaking it.

"This is Riley," I explain, his blonde hair almost as long as Lia's, reaching his shoulders. He normally wears it up in a man bun, but every now and again he keeps it down. The guy looks like he'd be better suited in an episode of Vikings than teaching boxercise in my gym.

"And this is Troy," I add, as our weights expert unfurls himself from the couch and gives Toby and Lia a terse nod. "Don't mind him. He doesn't say much."

"We've already met," Lia says softly as she gives him a tight smile.

"You have?" I ask, feeling both bemused and a little bit territorial as AJ throws me a look from the couch. Pretty sure he's trying to hide a smirk as he pushes to his feet, the bastard.

"At Bandits, the night Toby had a stomach upset," she explains, her smile faltering .

"You didn't say anything," I remark, looking at Troy who glides his dark eyes from Lia to meet mine.

"It didn't occur to me that I should," he shrugs.

"And I'm AJ, the one with the manners," AJ says, throwing a glare over his shoulder at Troy. "Nice to meet you both."

He grins at Lia and she smiles back. A little more uncertain now as he stares at her in that curious way he seems to do with anyone he meets for the first time. The shortest of the three, standing at six foot, his dark hair is a mess of curls on his head, offsetting his pale green-blue eyes.

"Do you all eat your vegetables? Is that why you're so tall?" Toby asks, peering up at the three men. To him they must seem like giants, so I lean down and draw him into my arms, picking him up.

"There, now you're just as tall," I say, and he grins.

Out of the corner of my eye, I see Troy throw me a look as he shifts in his seat. I don't know if it's because kids make him uncomfortable or if he's got something else on his mind, but I ignore it. For now.

"Anyway, I wanted to introduce you because Lia and Toby are staying with me and Daise for a while, so you'll probably see us out and about together."

"Awesome," AJ says, eying me, and I'm not sure I like the

conniving smile he gives me. "Have you shown Lia and Toby your collection of Funko Pops yet?"

Ah, fuck.

Riley covers a laugh with a cough, and even Troy lifts his lips in a smirk.

"You actually *collect* Funko Pops?" Lia asks me, her eyes widening with surprise. "So that's where the toy you gave Toby came from."

"I *used to* collect Funko Pops when I was a *kid*," I reply, glaring at Riley who's grin just widens.

"Funny, coz I'm pretty sure you received a delivery here a month ago of ten new ones."

"*Motherfucker!*" I whisper under my breath, my damn cheeks heating.

"That's another coin for the swear jar," Toby pipes up, wriggling on my hip with happiness that he just caught me out.

"I think we should head out," I say abruptly, ready to get the hell out of here.

"Wait. I want to hear more about the Funko Pops," Lia says, her eyes twinkling, and if it wasn't for the fact her smile beams like a ray of fucking sunshine, I'd be out of here like a shot.

Sighing, I plonk down on the corner of the sofa with Toby on my lap, making room for Lia beside me as I tell them both about my ridiculous obsession with Funko Pops. They sit listening, enraptured, whilst I glaze over the real reason I collect the stupid things. It's better that she thinks I'm some kind of closet nerd than a man who's childhood was so fucking destroyed by a violent man that I still seek comfort in the joy those damn things seem to bring me.

"So Funko Pops, huh?" Lia asks me in the car as we head back home.

Toby is fast asleep in his seat, worn out from our afternoon spent together. After visiting the gym we stopped off at the park, sitting in comfortable silence as Toby blew off some steam. At least this time he didn't hurt himself on the slide.

"It's kind of embarrassing," I admit.

"Why? They're collectors items. I can understand your interest."

I throw her a curious look. "You can?"

"I used to collect china dolls. So I get it. They made me happy. Silly, right?"

"Not at all," I say, wanting to open up to her, but somehow not able to find the words.

"Not that it matters now. Martin destroyed them all."

"Well, I know they're not made from china and wear pretty outfits, but you're more than welcome to play with my toys," I offer, realising too late how that sounded.

Lia laughs, and it's so carefree, so pure, that my heart fucking soars at the sound. "Now that's an offer I can't refuse."

"And if you're really good, I'll even let you touch my Fred Flinstone," I add, biting back a laugh.

Lia shakes her head with amusement. "Hendrix Hammer, I do believe you're flirting with me."

"Hey, you can't blame a man for trying."

EIGHTEEN

"ARE YOU SURE I LOOK ALRIGHT?" I ask Daisy as I check myself over for the hundredth time in the mirror. It's Friday night and Drix and I are about to go to Bandits Bar to watch the band play.

"You look incredible, Lia," Daisy replies, nudging Toby who is clutching hold of the Spiderman Funko Pop Drix gave him. Despite having bought him a full set of Marvel action figures, Toby prefers the Funko Pop. He hasn't let it go, taking it with him everywhere he goes, completely forgetting about his first love, Blue Bear.

Toby looks up at me, his eyes bright. "You look pretty, Mama," he adds, smiling sweetly.

I blow out a breath, looking back at my reflection in the full length mirror. I'm wearing a simple black dress I borrowed from Daisy that hangs loose from just beneath my breasts, skimming over my tummy and thighs. The top is a little tight over my breasts, with ruching that seems to accentuate them more, but I trust Daisy's word that it's not too revealing.

"Are you sure?" I ask, swiping my hand over the skirt, the hem of which sits a few inches above my knee, given Daisy is a few inches shorter than I am. It was the only dress in her wardrobe that actually fits me. The style on her would be looser, but because I'm much curvier, it hugs me around the top way more than it would her.

Daisy pushes up from the bed and steps up beside me as I stare at my reflection. "Lia, you're absolutely stunning." She lowers her voice, whispering in my ear. "Drix is going to have a coronary when he sees you."

"I should definitely change then," I reply with a soft laugh, my stomach twisting in knots from nerves.

Even though Drix insisted that this is just two friends going out to enjoy some music, it sure feels like a date to me. I can't remember the last time I went out without Toby, let alone with a man who's as handsome as Drix is, and who is slowly becoming more than just a friend.

"And your makeup is perfect too. That cherry red lipstick really suits you, and that emerald shade of eyeshadow really brings out your eyes. You sure are one hot mama!" she says, sliding her arms around me and giving me a quick squeeze.

"Thank you. I appreciate the loan of this dress," I reply, sliding my feet into my black pumps with a two inch heel.

I usually avoid wearing heels because at five foot nine I'm tall already, but on this occasion I felt the outfit needed a lift, and so did my confidence. I find that there's something about wearing heels that immediately makes a person walk taller, literally and figuratively, and tonight I want to at least feign some confidence, even if I don't really feel that way.

"To be fair, it looks a million times better on you than it did on me, you're welcome to keep it."

"There's no need–"

"Shush, it's yours," she grins. "Besides, I wore that dress when I was experimenting during my very short-lived emo stage, and I'm kind of into brighter things these days," she says with a laugh as she looks down at her rainbow striped corduroy dungarees and fluorescent green socks.

"You were emo?" I ask, grinning.

"For about a week. Then I realised the style didn't really suit me. Some people might think I'm quirky, but I like the me I am when I dress this way."

"I love your style too," I reply.

"You might be the only one," Daisy shrugs. "Dalton loves to rib me for my fashion choices."

"Dalton's an idiot."

Daisy smirks. "You're not wrong."

"Thank you, Daisy, for this. For everything. Are you sure you're okay staying in and watching Toby for me?"

"I told you, it's absolutely fine. You go on and have a lovely evening, Lia, and don't worry about Toby. We've got a date with the Smurfs Christmas movie and a huge bowl of toffee popcorn waiting for us."

At the mention of popcorn and Smurfs, Toby jumps to his feet, grabbing hold of Daisy's hand. "Come on, Mama, time to go, we've got a date!" he says proudly.

"We sure do, buddy," Daisy agrees as they both follow me from the bedroom.

With my heart beating like a bass drum, I grab hold of the railing and descend the stairs. Waiting by the front door is Drix, who has his back towards us, talking quietly on his phone. Dressed a little more smartly than I'm used to seeing him, I falter on the stairs, my eyes dropping to his tight arse and strong thighs hugged by black jeans. He's wearing that same deep brown leather jacket he always does, that moulds perfectly to his upper body.

"Oh God," I mutter, feeling extra insecure given how incredible he looks.

"She's ready," Daisy sings out, giving me a gentle push in the back, forcing me to keep moving.

With his phone still pressed against his ear, Drix turns around and my whole body flushes with heat as his gaze lifts slowly upwards from my feet, coasting over my legs, my waist, breasts, until he finally rests his gaze on my face. Tingles rush down my spine at the look in his eyes and for the first time in my life, I understand what it feels like to be truly desired. It's disconcerting, and also confidence inducing.

His mouth parts, and for a second there's silence as he drinks me in, his eyes flicking from my lips to my chest and back again.

"Fuck," he mutters, and behind me Toby giggles.

"Another pound for the swear jar," he says happily. "It's almost full!"

"Doesn't she look amazing?" Daisy asks, passing me with Toby who is looking between us both, no doubt wondering why we have seemed to have lost the power of speech.

"You look... Fuck..." he shakes his head, realising he's still got the phone pressed to his ear. "We'll be there in fifteen," he quickly adds, flicking off the phone and tucking it into his jacket pocket.

"Well?" Daisy presses, trying and failing to hide a smile.

"That was Ben asking where we were," Drix says.

"I wasn't talking about your phone call. What do you think of Lia? Doesn't she look good enough to eat?" she adds cheekily.

"You look incredible, Lia," Drix agrees as I step towards him.

"Thank you. You look incredible too," I say, my cheeks flushing at my response. "Handsome. You look handsome," I correct myself.

"Well, as much as I'm enjoying watching you two stumble for words," Daisy says with a laugh. "You should get going."

"Wait, before we go, I have something for you," Drix says, striding over to the side table on the other side of the room. He picks up a huge bunch of red tulips, edged with orange, handing them to me.

Drix drags his gaze away from me, clearing his throat. "Yes, right. Do you have a coat? It's cold out."

I move past him, picking up my black woollen coat hanging on a hook by the front door. I'm about to put it on when he takes it from me, holding it open.

"Here, allow me," he says roughly.

I slide my hands into the sleeves, and his hands linger on my shoulders, his body close to mine as he lowers his voice and says, "You really do look beautiful, Lia."

"Thank you," I reply softly, my heart squeezing as a different kind of warmth pools down low at the gruffness of his voice.

"Have a nice time, Mama," Toby says as I step away from Drix and crouch down to draw him in for a quick hug, glad for the distraction.

"Be good for Daisy. No staying up past eight o'clock, okay?" I say, rising upwards.

"Don't fear, he'll be tucked up in bed eight o'clock sharp," Daisy assures me.

"You have my number, so just call me if you need to."

"Don't worry, we'll be fine. Now you two go on and have a great time," Daisy says as Drix rests his hand on my lower back, pulling the front door open. "And don't do anything I wouldn't do," she adds, wriggling her brows as we both turn to look at her.

"See you later, Daise," Drix says, shooting her a glare as he steps aside so I can pass by him.

The whole drive Drix is thoughtful. My anxiety seems to increase with every mile. He's never been so quiet around me. Automatically my hands reach for the hem of my dress, tugging at it as I pull it down.

"Drix, is everything okay?" I ask. "We could go back if you've changed your mind."

"No, absolutely not," he replies, swiping a hand through his hair. He side-eyes me, his gaze dropping briefly to where my hands fiddle with my dress, before quickly snapping his head back around. The car lurches forward as he presses on the gas.

"You're acting strange. What's wrong?"

"I'm good. Nothing's wrong," he replies tightly.

I stiffen in my seat, uncertain what's happening. Despite my nerves, I was looking forward to tonight. Now I don't know how I feel. An uneasiness settles inside of me, and I feel that growing confidence diminishing with every mile.

Five minutes later we're pulling into the car park of Bandits Bar. Drix parks the car, switching the engine off. People are already gathered outside, and I see Baxter and Riley talking animatedly outside the entrance, their laughter quite a contrast to the sudden tension in the car.

"It's honestly okay if you don't want to be seen with me. I can get a cab back home," I say softly, trying to hide the tremble in my voice.

"Fuck. No. Lia..." he says, shifting in his seat to face me. I force myself to look at him, and my stomach lurches at the tortured expression on his face.

"Am I overdressed? I probably should've just worn my jeans. I haven't been out for a long time and I guess I wanted to put on something nice," I ramble, pulling at my skirt, but it just keeps riding up my legs, showing off my thick thighs.

"I meant what I said, you look absolutely stunning, Lia," he says, blowing out a breath.

"Then what is it? I don't understand what I did."

"You've done absolutely nothing. I'm just having trouble..." His voice trails off, a muscle in his jaw jumping as he grits his teeth, holding back whatever it is that's on his mind.

"Trouble?" I hedge, turning to face him. My skirt slips higher, and his eyes drop to my legs once again.

"Keeping my hands off you, Lia," he rumbles. "I'm really trying so fucking hard not to touch you."

"Touch me?" I croak.

"Jesus, fuck," he grinds out, swiping a hand over his face. "From the moment I met you I've wanted to kiss you, and every day that has passed that feeling has only gotten stronger. Tonight, when you walked down the stairs looking like a damn goddess... I just wanted to..." His voice trails off as Baxter notices us, waving as he approaches the car.

Heat flashes through me at his words, all that uncertainty falling away and being replaced with a warm feeling that just grows more intense as he continues to stare, his eyes rising from my legs all the way up to my face.

"The whole way here I've been thinking about how I'm going to get through the night with a raging hard on. It's more than a little uncomfortable."

"Oh..." I shift in my seat, feeling both incredibly flattered and a little unsure how to act.

He gives me a rueful grin. "Sometimes being a man is a fucking curse."

"I'm sorry," I say, a little helplessly. No one has ever said anything like this to me, and I honestly don't know how to act. I'm sure other, more confident women would come up with a suitable response, but I'm not one of those women. Besides, I'm saved from saying anything at all when Baxter raps his knuckles on the window.

"You guys coming in or what? The band is about to start playing."

"I guess we should go inside," I say.

Drix looks out the window at Baxter. "I'll be coming in two minutes," he says, holding up his fingers.

Baxter ducks down, grinning through the window at me. He lets out a low whistle, then looks back at Drix. "Yeah mate, I reckon you will."

A smile pulls up my lips as Baxter barks out a laugh and jogs back over to Riley. Pretty sure Drix mutters *fucking arsehole* under his breath.

"I'm going to apologise in advance on behalf of my friends. They can get a bit... raucous."

"I like your friends."

"That's what I'm worried about," he says, rubbing at his short beard.

"Worried?" I ask, wholly confused now.

"You know, that you might be interested in one of them..."

"Interested?" I say, frowning.

"Sorry, ignore me."

It finally dawns on me what he's getting at. "Drix," I say gently, reaching for his arm and squeezing gently. "I'm not interested in your friends like that."

"You aren't?"

"No. I'm not." My voice trails off as he covers my hand with his.

"Lia, there's something you should know about me." He pauses, gathering his thoughts as he takes my hand, brushing his thumb over the spot where my wedding ring once sat. "I can be a little possessive."

"Possessive?"

"I know you're not mine, and I have no right to behave like you are, but I can't help feeling that way about you. When Baxter flirted with you at the gym I got jealous."

"You did?"

"I did," he admits. "I know it's a red flag, but I *can* control myself. If one of my friends asks you to dance, you're free to do whatever makes you happy. I won't act like a dick, but I might need a stiff drink to get me through it. Please, just bear with me."

"I see."

"You probably wish you hadn't come," he says, sounding defeated.

I think about what he's just said, but it doesn't make me fear him. His honesty about his feelings is strangely comforting, and I do trust his word. I know he wouldn't do anything to hurt me. He's already proven that over and over again.

"Firstly, thank you for being honest with me. It means a great deal," I say, shifting closer. "Secondly, if I was interested in any man, it would be you."

Suddenly our faces are only inches apart, and my attraction to Drix that I've tried hard to ignore seems to ignite as he closes the gap between us, his mouth mere centimetres away from mine.

"You really shouldn't say something like that to me, Lia," he warns, reaching up and cupping my face. "It might give me the wrong impression."

"And what impression is that?" I ask, the sultry sound of my voice surprising me as his thumb hovers over my parted lips.

His eyes flash with more heat. "That you could like me back."

"Well that all depends on how good you can dance," I flirt, surprising myself.

"I happen to be a very good dancer," he smirks, eyes flashing with mischief, as his fingers slide into my hair, tugging gently, scattering goosebumps down my spine.

"We'll see," I whisper back, "Because I happen to really like men who can dance."

Time stills, neither of us breaching the gap, and that makes me bold knowing he is respectful enough not to push me despite how he feels. Leaning in, I ever so slightly brush my lips against his. A groan parts his lips, his fingers tightening in my hair.

"Fuck, Lia," he mumbles as I draw back, biting on my lip. "You sure could give a man a heart attack."

Christ knows what's gotten into me, but whatever it is, I like it. "Don't die on me just yet, we still need that dance," I joke. "Shall we go inside?"

"We better had," he says, shaking his head with a rueful smile.

NINETEEN

TRUE TO MY WORD, I don't act like a possessive prick when Lia dances with my friends. She even accepts Dalton's offer of a dance, and it takes every last bit of self-control not to rip her out of his arms and punch him for daring to touch what's mine.

Fuck, I've got it bad.

But her happiness, her laughter, her smiles and the way she sings along to all the covers the band plays stops me from acting like a prick. I've never seen her so alive, and I've spent most of the night watching her in awe. I won't lie, the four shots of straight vodka have helped. It's just as well I'm built, because despite the high alcohol content I'm tipsy, not drunk. Still, I make a mental note to get us a cab home. I'm not stupid enough to risk driving with such precious cargo.

And, fuck, she sure is precious to me.

That day when Carl had treated her like shit, I'd wanted to rip his damn head off. I almost did, but the way she stood up to him stopped me in my tracks. Fuck, I'd been so proud to stand by her side as she ripped him a new arsehole.

"Want to tell me why you're sitting here drowning your

sorrows and not on the dance floor with that beautiful woman?" Walter asks as he drops onto the seat beside mine.

"Wasn't expecting to see you here tonight," I reply, raising a brow at Benedict's dad and pointedly ignoring his question. "Did Carl send you to spy on me and Lia, or is this purely a social visit?"

"I heard he was a little unwelcoming."

"Unwelcoming? He basically accused her of being with me for my money, the fucking arsehole."

"That sounds about right coming from Carl. Sorry you had to deal with that."

"Don't be sorry for me. It's Lia who's owed an apology, and that needs to come from that prick not you," I grind out.

"I'll have a word with him."

"You do that," I say, not giving a fuck if he does or doesn't, because it won't make a difference to how I feel about Lia. I don't need his permission or approval.

Like most of the men in this bar, Walter's attention is drawn to Lia. Her hips swaying to the music as Dalton dances with her. My teeth grind just seeing her in his arms, and I crick my neck trying to relieve some of the tension. Dalton glances over at me, probably feeling the daggers I'm shooting from my eyeballs. He gives me a wary smile, and despite his usual manwhore ways, he's being respectful, his hands staying well away from all the places I'm desperate to touch her.

"She sure is beautiful, Drix. I can see why you're drawn to her."

"It ain't just her looks. She's an incredible woman, a damn fine mother, and most of all too fucking good for the likes of me." I sigh, reaching for my fifth shot, ready to down it when Walter places his hand on my arm.

"Don't you think you've had enough?"

"I'm not drunk... *Yet*," I counter, placing the shot back on the table. Despite hating to admit it, he's right, I should stop drinking.

"How serious are you about her?" Walter asks.

"As serious as a man can get. I think I might be..." My voice trails off as I groan.

"Might be what, Drix?"

"Falling in love with her," I admit, shocking myself with that revelation. I hadn't admitted it to myself until just now, let alone someone else.

"You are?" he asks me with a soft chuckle.

I swipe a hand over my face. "Yeah, I am," I reply, certain now that I've voiced my feelings out loud. "You know me, Walter, I don't say something I don't mean, and yeah, you're probably thinking it's too soon but I'm telling you, the second I laid eyes on her I knew she was special. What the fuck should I do?"

Walter grips my shoulder. "Son, I know I'm not Hubert, but I care about you so I'm going to give you a piece of advice."

"I sure could use some," I reply.

"When I met Dorothy, like you I knew immediately there would be no other woman for me."

"You did?"

"Yeah, but I spent a long fucking time arguing with myself about all the reasons why I was the wrong man for her, until one night she gave me an ultimatum."

"What was that?" I ask, eying him.

"Either I get over myself or she walks. I got over myself pretty damn quick."

"What did you do?"

"I took her home and made love to her, and the following week we eloped. That's what I did."

"She ain't ready for that. Her situation is complicated. I can't just throw myself at her, let alone put a ring on her finger."

"But you'll sit here and watch all your friends dance with her instead? You're wasting time, son, and God knows that's not a given. Take action. Do it now."

"I'm fucking nervous, okay? I ain't used to feeling like this."

"That's not the only reason. Why are you sitting here like a bear with a sore head, instead of claiming what's yours?"

"Because—"

"You're not good enough for her?" he says, giving me a thoughtful look.

"I said so, didn't I? Fuck, Walter, she's so incredible, and I'm a just man with blood on my hands..."

"Wrong, you're your father's son. Hubert did a good job bringing you up."

I laugh bitterly. "It doesn't change the fact I've hurt people."

"For good reason," he counters.

"No, for *your* reasons. Yours, Robert's and Carl's, not mine. I do as I'm fucking told because I have no choice not too."

Walter frowns. "What do you mean by that?"

"Ask Carl, I'm sure he'll enlighten you," I reply, making a decision as I push up from my seat. "Now if you'll excuse me, I'm about to make a complete fucking fool of myself and dance with the woman I intend on making mine."

Without waiting for a response, I stride over to Lia just as the band begins to play a cover of *Love On The Brain* originally sung by Rihanna. I'd laugh if I wasn't so damn nervous.

"Can I cut in?" I ask, tapping Dalton on the shoulder.

"I was wondering when you would," Dalton replies, slapping a hand on my back with a smirk before pecking Lia on the cheek. "Thank you for the dance, Lia, and the advice. I appreciate it."

"Advice?" I ask as he heads towards the bar.

"Apparently someone's caught Dalton's attention."

"Every woman catches his attention. The guy might be my best friend, but he's still a fucking cad."

Lia screws up her nose, and I have this sudden desire to press a kiss against the tip.

"This seems different," she says.

"So who's the lucky woman?"

"He didn't tell me, but he wanted to know how to approach her. For a man who seems very confident of his abilities, he's pretty nervous. Seems like she's caused quite a stir with him. "

"That'll be the blood rushing to his dick. Don't be fooled into thinking Dalton actually has the ability to commit to a relationship, Lia."

"Perhaps," she shrugs. Then tipping her head to the side says, "Are you okay? You seem a little tense."

"I'm four shots down," I explain, referring to our earlier conversation in the car.

She winces. "I'm sorry."

"Don't apologise to me. My issues are mine alone to deal with," I reply, drawing her into my arms as Owen's husky voice begins to sing. He's the lead singer of the band and a legend around here, despite only being twenty-two years old. The kid's got talent, that's for sure, just like the rest of the band members. "I'm *glad* you're having a good time."

"I am having a good time, but I'm having a better time now that you've finally decided to dance with me. I've been waiting all night, Drix," she replies, pressing her body against mine. My bastard cock stiffens at the way she feels so damn good in my arms.

"Had to pluck up the courage," I admit, my heart fucking skipping a beat as she wraps her arms around my back.

"Well, I'm glad you did," she replies softly as she stares up at me, her warmth seeping into my body as we sway together. "This feels good."

"It sure does, doll," I say.

"Doll?"

My cheeks flare with heat at the pet name. I shrug, smiling. "You look as pretty as one of those china dolls you love so much," I explain.

She chuckles. "If we're giving each other nicknames, what should I call you?"

"Yours?" I immediately reply.

Her eyes flicker with heat, a sensual smile pulling up her lips. "Yours," she murmurs, sounding it out on her lips.

"Yeah, mine," I mutter back, and as Owen sings about a man needing to be loved, everyone else in the bar seems to disappear and all I can concentrate on is this fucking beautiful woman before me. Her eyes are bright as she looks up at me, her porcelain skin flushed, jewels of perspiration dotting her forehead. I have the biggest desire to sweep my lips against her skin, tasting them.

"Thank you for this, I haven't had this much fun in a long time."

"I'm happy *you're* happy," I reply, meaning it with every fibre of my being.

She nods, biting on her plump, cherry-red lips. Fuck, I want to kiss her.

Her gaze flicks from my eyes to my lips, and her mouth parts on a soft breath as she softens in my arms. If she were anyone else I would've leaned down and kissed the breath from her body, but I can't seem to bridge the gap, my own feelings running rampant in my bloodstream.

I love this woman.

I fucking love her.

And for that reason I don't kiss her, because I might scare her off, and I can't fucking bear the thought. *Slowly*, I need to take this slowly, I remind myself.

So we dance, and as I hold her in my arms, I feel this strange concoction of peace, desire, and longing surging through me. My fucking cock grows with every damn step, and there's no hiding my burning attraction as her breasts press against my chest. I've gone to bed every damn night dreaming about how they might feel in my hands, both soft and heavy. I've wondered about what sounds she would make when I touched her, kissed her, licked her in all the places I know would make her wet, pliable in my hands. I've imagined how it would feel to sink my cock inside of her... I already know it would be fucking bliss, like coming home.

"Lia," I groan, needing to kiss her but knowing I can't. I pull back a little, distancing myself.

"Please," she whispers, her grip tightening as she stares up at me, her eyes heavy-lidded as though she feels as drunk on this feeling between us as I am. If I could bottle this feeling I would, I'd sip from it every day of my godforsaken life just to feel this way forever.

"Please?" I whisper, slowly coasting my hand up her back, my fingers curling around the back of her neck. It's a fucking possessive move, but damn, I want to own her. Every last inch.

"I need this," she whimpers, her hands sliding around my front, her palms burning like fire as she slides them over my chest. My heart pounds, throwing itself against my ribcage. It beats so fucking hard for this woman, desperate for her love in return.

"Fuck, I want to kiss you. I'm not sure I can hold back any longer," I admit, forcing space between us, the crowd around us coming back into focus.

I hear whistling and glance over my shoulder at my friends. Troy, AJ, Riley, Baxter, Dalton, and Ben are all watching us from the bar with interest, varying looks of amusement on their faces. I can't see Sterling anywhere, but six of my friends watching me fucking squirm is quite enough of an audience already.

"Oh God," Lia laughs shyly, burying her head in my shoulder.

"Do you want to get out of here?" I ask, hoping to fuck she says yes.

She nods, replying breathlessly. "I do."

Grabbing her hand, I guide her through the crowd, my friends hollering dirty remarks as we grab our coats from the hook by the door and head out into the cold winter night. I flip them off, their laughter following us out into the night.

Pulling out my phone, I order a cab, warm puffs of air leaving our mouths as we wait. Lia stands beside me, her arms wrapped tightly around herself. There's a nervousness to her body language, and I briefly rest my hand on her lower back hoping it reassures her.

"You okay?" I ask, brushing a few flakes of snow from her hair.

"I'm... Christ," she laughs, shaking her head as she turns her body towards mine. "I'm nervous, Drix. It's been a long time since I've been with a man."

I swallow hard, both at the way she leans into me, and the trust in her eyes.

"We take this as slow as you need," I murmur, cupping her cheek as I lean down, running the tip of my nose against the bridge of hers, my own nerves making mincemeat of my insides.

"Martin always made me feel so..." Her voice catches, and I get her meaning well enough.

My fingers slide into her hair, digging into her scalp, this feral need roaring inside of me. "A real man knows how to appreciate his woman, he knows how to adore every inch of her. I promise you right here and now, I will worship you, Lia. If you'll let me."

"I trust you, Drix," she replies, and in that moment it feels like she's just offered me the whole damn world.

Her breath hitches.

My pulse thunders in my ears as I inch closer, ready to kiss her into next week.

She moves towards me, hesitant, hopeful.

I drink her in, fucking love-drunk.

Her scent lifts up into the air, a mixture of apples and mother-fucking sunshine.

I drag in a deep breath, breathing her in.

Her mouth parts, the tip of her tongue wetting her bottom lip.

A horn sounds. "Fuck," I mutter, pulling back.

"You ordered a cab?" the driver asks through his rolled down window.

"Yes, mate," I reply, holding the door open for Lia. She slips inside, her skirt riding up as she moves, stirring every animal instinct inside of me.

I give the driver my address, then settle onto the backseat next to her, neither of us saying a word for the entirety of the journey home. The sexual tension is intense and it takes every single bit of self-restraint I have not to pull her into my arms right here and now, but I respect Lia way too much to instigate a makeout session in front of a stranger. The only contact I allow myself is my hand covering hers, my thumb rubbing gentle across her knuckles.

When we reach home, I pay the driver, and hold my hand out for Lia to take. She slides her warm palm into mine, glancing at me shyly as the cab pulls away. Silently we walk to the front door, and I pull out my keys, my damn hands shaking as I attempt to put the key in the lock.

"Smooth, Drix. Fucking smooth," I mutter with a laugh.

"Here let me," Lia says, sliding her hand gently over mine, taking the keys from me as I move aside for her. That simple touch ignites a fire within me that burns so bright instinct just takes over.

"Fuck it," I grind out, caging her body against the door with mine, unable to hold out a second longer. She gasps as I slide my arm around her stomach gripping her hip as my hand comes up to squeeze her throat gently. "I could fuck you right here and now against the door."

"Drix," she whimpers, turning her head to the side as I slide my lips against her jaw, licking at her skin, my cock rock hard as I press against her back, blind with passion, need.

"Tell me to stop, Lia. Fucking tell me stop," I grind out, capturing her lips with mine, but she doesn't tell me to stop, instead she whimpers into my mouth, opening up to me.

"Your mine," I say, repeating out loud those two words pinballing inside my head.

"Yours," she whispers back, her tongue sliding over mine as my thumb presses against the thrumming pulse in her neck. It beats wildly, matching the rhythm of my own heart.

"Mine, my beautiful doll," I growl as our lips meld, and all the feelings I've kept bottled up come flooding out full force as I steal the air from her lungs, kissing her with a hunger no other woman has ever stirred within me.

"Drix, God," she exclaims, panting as my fingers dig into her hip and I spin her around, parting for mere seconds before slamming her back against the door. I grab her hands, holding them up above her head, fisting her wrists with one hand as the other moves to grip her chin tenderly, angling her face up to meet mine. My whole body is vibrating with this intense, overwhelming need to claim her.

"I mean it, Lia. Tell me to fucking stop," I growl against her lips, my fingers dropping to tug at her coat buttons, desperately seeking the warmth of her body.

"I don't want you to. Don't stop, Drix. Please just kiss me. *Touch* me. Make me feel like a woman again," she pants, her chest heaving beneath my hands as I undo her coat, the cool tortoiseshell buttons giving way in my frantic need to give her exactly what she wants.

"I'll never stop. I'll give you everything I am, all that I have, Lia."

My mouth slams against hers once again as my hand slides up over her hips, across her soft stomach, I squeeze her flesh and she jolts against me, a sensual gasp parting her lips that I drink down greedily.

"Fuck, I love your body," I say, and she lets out a sob that almost fractures my heart.

Our teeth clash as I press my hips against her, wanting her to feel what she does to me, how hard she makes me, how fucking desperate I am, how turned on.

Fuck, this woman is killing me, the salt from her tears making me both furious at how she's been made to feel in the past, and desperate to show her that I love every single thing about her.

"Forget everything that arsehole ever said to you, and trust me when I say you're sexy as hell, Lia. I haven't even seen you naked yet, but I could come right here and now I'm so turned on by you."

She smiles through her tears, her head tipping back against the door as she presses her eyes shut. I lower my lips to her neck, lapping up the salt of her tears, replacing her sadness with liquid heat. She doesn't reply with words, but her body speaks volumes as she arches her back, her legs sliding apart as she gives me access.

Reaching up, I palm her breast, her nipple hard beneath the material as I curl my fingers over the neckline of her dress and bra tugging it down, freeing her breast. Within seconds, my mouth is on the mound of her pillowy flesh, sucking her into my mouth as I gently lick her flesh, my tongue moving in slow circles over her skin.

"Drix, please," she cries, her pinned hands fighting to touch me.

I growl against her skin, holding her wrists tighter, my other hand gripping her heavy breast. She has so much beautiful flesh even my large hands can't capture it all as my tongue flicks across her erect nipple right where she needs me to taste.

"Drix!" she cries out, her hips jerking against mine, seeking relief from the hard ridge of my oversensitive cock.

"I want to come," she whimpers, and I let her hands go, dropping to my goddamn knees right here on the doorstep of my home. Her hands fly to my hair, her fingernails scraping over my scalp as I run my palms up the back of her legs, beneath her skirt, gripping her arse as I look up at her.

"I'm going to make you come all over my face, Lia, then I'm

taking you up to my bedroom and I'm going to fuck you so good you're gonna have to smother your screams with a pillow so we don't wake the whole damn house up."

"Jesus," she whimpers, her head rolling against the door as I push up the skirt of her dress with my free hand, bunching it up over her waist. She's wearing black lace knickers, and I press my nose right against her mound, breathing in deep.

"Fuck, your scent is incredible, I want it all over my face so that even in my dreams I'll be reminded of this moment," I say, drawing my tongue against the seam of her pussy lips. She quakes, her moan music to my ears.

"Drix, no one has ever..." her voice trails off as I slide my finger along the elastic of her knickers, pulling it to one side.

"Fucked your pussy with their tongue?" I ask.

"Never," she whispers.

"Believe me when I say that no one else ever will. Now open up for me, doll. Put your leg over my shoulder," I demand, letting her breast go so I can guide her thigh over my shoulder, before burying my face in the soft curls of her pussy.

"Drix, oh God," she cries, her fingers curling into my hair as I part her pussy lips with my tongue and eat her out.

I don't hold back. I feast on her, her taste exploding over my tongue as I lap at the wetness, drinking every damn drop. Licking, sucking, fucking her pussy with my tongue, I unleash all my pent-up need as she bucks against my face. Reaching up I grab her breast again, my finger rolling over her nipple as snow begins to fall around us, the soft flakes melting against the heat of her skin.

Her legs begin to tremble, her hands clenching my head, pressing me further into her. I don't give a fuck about breathing right now, all I care about is making her come. Slipping my finger inside of her, I search for that spot I know no one else has ever bothered to find. She shudders as I press against the tender flesh, moving my finger in a come hither motion, before dragging my teeth lightly over her clit, flicking it with my tongue over and over again until her breath comes quickly, and she soaks my face and hand.

"Come for me. Come all over my face, doll."

And she does.

She comes.

Jerking, writhing, fucking calling my name, she comes.

It's a sound I'll never forget. Music to my damn ears.

A sound that is drowned out by Toby screaming for his mama.

TWENTY

"TOBY? TOBY!" I call, kicking off my shoes and running up the stairs towards our bedroom, adjusting my dress as I go. Drix follows close behind me, our moment of passion overshadowed with concern.

"Mama!" he cries.

I find him standing in the middle of the bedroom, the light from the hallway cutting across him as he blinks up at me. I notice the wet patch on his pyjama bottoms right away, and I rush towards him.

"Shhh, it's okay, I'm here now. I'm here, Toby," I murmur, dragging him into my arms as Drix hovers behind me.

"He was hurting you, Mama," Toby cries, sobbing against me, his small fists gripping my coat.

"Who was hurting me?" I choke out, fear rushing through my blood.

"Papa. Papa was hurting you," he croaks, trembling.

Tears spring to my eyes, and I look up at Drix helplessly. Our eyes meet and he understands what I don't say. Toby knows. He's more aware of the abuse I'd endured than I'd thought.

"Is everything okay?" Daisy asks, stepping into the room. Her hair is mussed up from sleep as she looks between us, her bright pink fluffy dressing gown pulled tight around her.

"Go back to bed, Daise. Toby's had a bad dream, that's all. We got this, okay?"

"Are you sure? I could get him some hot chocolate or something," she asks worriedly.

"We'll be okay," Drix reassures her, even though I feel far from okay.

"Let's get you cleaned up and changed, sweetheart," I murmur, shaking off my coat. I hand it to Drix who takes it wordlessly, placing it with his own coat on the ottoman at the end of the bed.

"I'm sorry, Mama," Toby whispers, tears sliding down his cheeks.

"It's okay buddy," Drix says. "Happens to the best of us."

"You wet the bed too?" Toby asks, eyes wide as he blinks back his tears.

"When I was kid, yeah, I did that a lot," he replies softly.

My heart aches at the pain on Drix's face, the honesty of his confession. As a child who grew up in a violent household, he understands only too well what it means to be truly afraid, and the terrible consequences of that fear.

"Can you grab me a fresh set of pyjamas and pants for Toby?" I ask, taking his hand as I lead him into the ensuite bathroom, flicking on the light.

I wordlessly help Toby to remove his clothes, and he just looks at me with such sorrow I can barely hold it together.

"Papa hurt you, Mama," Toby says as I grab some wet wipes and wipe him down.

"It was just a dream, Toby. I'm fine."

Toby shakes his head, his tiny hands cupping my face. "No, Mama. He hurt you. You were screaming."

"Toby—"I croak, my voice catching as tears pool in my eyes. I turn my head away, unable to answer him.

"Here, let me," Drix says, resting his hand on my shoulder and squeezing gently. "Why don't you go and grab Toby a drink of water? I'll dress him and get him back into bed."

"Thank you," I murmur, rising to my feet.

Drix reaches for my hand, brushing his fingers gently against mine. "I've got this," he says, meeting my eyes.

I nod, wordlessly slipping out of the bathroom. When I step inside the bedroom, I lean against the wall, pressing my eyes shut as tears slip from my eyes. How could I believe that I had protected Toby from the violence? He's such an intuitive little boy, and there were nights when Martin had forced me to have sex. I thought Toby had been sleeping.

A sob releases from my throat, and I stuff my hand over my mouth, curling over as I try to prevent him from hearing my distress. It takes me a good couple of minutes to pull myself together, and whilst I remain where I stand, drawing in deep, calming breaths, I hear Drix quietly speaking with Toby.

"You don't need to worry, kid, your Mama is strong, and she's safe now. You both are," he reassures him, the deep rumble of his voice soothing.

"Why did he hurt my mama?" Toby asks, his voice so filled with hurt I can barely keep my legs from buckling beneath me.

"I don't know, kid. But I do know that I will never let him hurt your Ma again. I promise."

"Pinky promise?" Toby asks, sniffling.

"I promise with my pinky, my big toe, my hand, my whole body, Toby," he replies earnestly.

There's a moment of silence before Toby responds, but what he says next has me wanting to scream at the top of my lungs for everything we've been through at the hands of his father.

"Will you hurt my Mama like Papa did?"

I have to pinch my lips together to stop myself from crying out, my heart shattering, bleeding with pain and overwhelming grief. It shudders through me, a tidal wave of debilitating emotion.

"Toby, I swear on everything I hold dear that I will never, *ever* hurt your mother like your father did. You have my word."

"Drix, do you love my Mama like I do?" Toby asks after a beat.

There's a long pause, my throat tightening as I listen.

"Yes, Toby. Yes, I do. Very much."

"Good," Toby replies

"And do you know what?"

"What?" he asks.

"I happen to love you too, kid," he replies.

Tears flood from my eyes and I push off from the wall, stumbling towards the door, an overwhelming mixture of sadness and hope buffeting against me. I can barely see from all the tears cascading down my cheeks as I make my way downstairs and into the kitchen. Thoughts ricochet inside my mind as I robotically grab a glass from the cabinet and fill it with water.

Toby knows that Martin hurt me.

I didn't protect him enough.

My God, he knows.

He knows.

How will I ever recover from that knowledge? How will he?

Placing the glass of water on the counter, I rest my hands on the surface and drop my head, shaking with grief, with guilt, with shame. It takes me a long time to pull myself together, the only spark of hope in this God awful situation is Drix's confession.

He loves me, he loves us both.

And it's with that knowledge that I'm able to gather the broken pieces of my heart back together, because buried beneath all the trauma, the pain and sadness, is a blossoming feeling that has grown stronger with every passing day in his company.

I think I might love Drix back.

"Is everything okay, Lia?" Daisy asks, stepping into the kitchen behind me.

I swipe at my eyes, forcing strength into my spine as I turn to face her. "Toby had a bad dream."

"I'm so sorry, perhaps it was the movie?" Daisy says, a look of guilt on her face. "Even for a Smurf movie it had some grown-up themes..."

"It wasn't the movie, Daisy," I say, shaking my head.

"Then what was it?"

"He was crying because he remembers Martin hurting me. I didn't protect him enough, Daisy. I didn't protect him," I cry, more tears falling unbidden down my cheeks.

"Oh no. I'm so sorry," she replies, striding over to me and pulling me into her arms.

"How will I ever forgive myself?" I whimper, clutching hold of her as she strokes my back.

"This isn't on you, Lia. Don't blame yourself."

"Who else should I blame? I'm his mother. I should've done more to protect him. I should've left earlier!"

Daisy pulls back, her fingers gripping my upper arms as she says fiercely, "This isn't your fault. None of it, you hear me?! That man deserves to rot in Hell for what he's done to you both."

"But–"

"No, no buts. This isn't your fault. You are a wonderful, kind woman. An incredible mother, Lia. God, how I wish I had a mum like you growing up. There isn't anything that you could've done differently. I know you tried your best to protect Toby, and you have protected him. You found the courage to leave that bastard."

"It hurts so much," I whisper.

"I know, but it will get better," she insists. "From this moment on you will let go of this terrible guilt I know you feel. You will dry your eyes, and you *will* get through this."

"How can you be so certain?"

"Because you have my brother, and that man will do everything in his power to put you back together again."

"This must be so traumatic for him," I counter.

"Maybe so, but I think he finally needs to face his past, and perhaps this is the best way to do that with you and Toby to help him. You can heal together."

"It isn't fair to expect that from him."

Daisy smiles gently. "Trust me when I say Drix will do whatever it takes to make you feel safe again. He spent his own childhood doing that for me." She shakes her head. "I would never have made it through without him. He's my rock, and he deserves someone to care for him, and some happiness of his own."

"I can see that," I agree, my heart aching for him, for all that he's had to endure.

"And he cares for you a great deal," Daisy replies, tucking a stray strand of hair behind my ear, before gently swiping at the tears on my cheeks. I can't tell her how I feel about Drix, not before I'm brave enough to tell him myself. So I remain quiet, contemplating everything she's said.

"Don't let your past cloud your future happiness, Lia. Don't let that bastard take any more of your power."

"That's easier said than done."

"I know, but you're strong. I see that strength in you. I believe in you. Just like Toby does, just like Drix. Whilst you will always carry the scars of your past, Lia, you *will* learn a new normal, and live a beautiful life despite the trauma of your past."

I nod. "Thank you for this."

"One day you're going to stop thanking me, and I know when that time comes it's because you'll finally understand that my friendship comes without expectations or requirements."

"Thank–" I cut myself off, giving her a wavering smile. "I appreciate you. If there's ever a time you need to talk about anything, I'll be here for you too."

"I know." She grins, releasing me from her hold. "Now, you go back upstairs. Get some rest. Tomorrow is a new day..." Her voice trails off as she tips her head to the side. "We could have a girls' day. Go for lunch at the hotel, maybe a spa treatment, on Dalton of course," she winks.

"Why on Dalton?"

She frowns. "He owes me for being a dick."

"How so?"

Daisy waves her hand. "It's too late to go into it today, but if you want to hear all the details, then spend time with me tomorrow and I'll tell you all about it."

"I'd like that very much."

"Good. Now, I'm going back to bed. See you in the morning, Lia."

"See you then, Daisy," I reply.

By the time I head back upstairs, the bedding has been changed, Toby is tucked into bed, and Drix is lying on his side, curled around him, stroking his hair.

"Is he okay?" I ask softly, and Drix lifts a finger to his lips.

"He's just fine, Lia," he whispers.

Placing the glass of water on the bedside cabinet, I watch Drix lean over and press a tender kiss against Toby's temple. That simple act of affection has my heart bursting with gratitude, and as he pushes off the bed, he opens his arms to me. I don't hesitate, walking straight into them.

"That was awful," I whisper, my arms circling his back as he hauls me close, pressing soft kisses against the top of my head.

"He's going to be okay," Drix quietly says. "You're going to be okay, Lia."

Pressing my eyes shut, I nod, feeling so much comfort from the strength of his arms, from his words, his actions. Everything about him makes me feel as safe as Daisy promised he'd make me feel.

"We'll talk in the morning. It's been a long night. Sleep, okay?" he requests, drawing back.

I reach for him, my hands cupping his face. There are no words I'm able to say to express everything this man makes me feel, so all I can do is rise up on to my toes and press a heartfelt kiss against his lips.

It's tender, lingering, and probably the most beautiful kiss I've ever experienced.

And it's over way too soon.

"Goodnight, Lia," Drix says, taking my wrists in his hands and stepping back.

"Goodnight, Drix," I reply, watching him leave.

Stripping out of my clothes and putting on my pyjamas, I lay down next to Toby, one hand on his hip as I stare up at the ceiling. I lay there like that for what seems like hours thinking over all that we've been through. I think about the woman I was before Martin, the hollowed out version I was whilst I was with him, and the woman I'm slowly becoming now. I think about how much upheaval Toby has had in his short life and how, from tomorrow things are going to be different.

Eventually, after I'm positive Toby won't wake up again, I slip out of the bedroom and take the first step to a future I'm desperate to have with a man I'm falling in love with.

TWENTY-ONE

I CAN'T SLEEP.

Lying on my bed I stare up at the ceiling, thinking about everything that's happened tonight. The way Lia had felt in my arms dancing with her, the taste of her lips, her skin, her goddamn beautiful pussy. The heady scent of her still lingers, a reminder to my cock just how much she turns me on.

But what keeps me awake is the way her face crumpled when Toby had shared what his bad dream was about. She had broken at that moment, and I had wanted so badly to tell her how I feel. To explain to her that I would never, ever hurt her like that bastard had. That I love her. That I love him. Instead I'd told Toby, and the way he'd looked at me in that moment will forever be burned into my memory.

A fierce kind of need to protect them both rushes through me, and I push up on my bed, knowing that sleep won't come for me tonight. Instead, I draw my legs up, resting my elbows on my knees as I cup my head, trying to figure out what to do. Daphne had been right, I need to tell Lia the truth about who I am. I can't betray her trust like her ex had. She deserves to know everything about me. I decide that first thing in the morning I'll do just that.

A knock at the door has me lifting my head. "Daisy?" I question.

When the door pushes open and Lia stands before me, my heart fucking sumersaults in my chest.

"Is it Toby?" I ask, shifting on the bed, ready to help.

She shakes her head, her long hair slipping over her shoulders. "He's fast asleep. Can I come in?"

"Please," I reply, watching her closely as she steps into the room. The light from my bedside lamp throws the room in a soft golden glow, and I swear to fuck her hair glimmers in a halo like some kind of fallen angel.

Gently closing the door behind her, she presses her back against the wood, uncertainty crossing her features. "I can't sleep," she explains, and I can't help notice the way her hands tremble.

"You and me both," I reply with a smile that falters as she steps toward me.

There's something about the way her eyes are smudged with mascara from her earlier tears, and the simplicity of her pale blue cotton pyjamas that has my heart constricting.

"Drix, I want to say something," she says as she walks towards me.

I shift to the end of the bed, my bare feet resting on the carpeted floor. Wearing only boxer shorts, I momentarily wonder if I should put more clothes on, but when she reaches me, her legs pressing against my knees, I'm too distracted by the way she stares at me to do anything about it.

"Toby never saw Martin hit me. I think maybe he heard some things he shouldn't have when I thought he was sleeping..." her voice trails off as her lips tremble.

"Please don't tell me that bastard..." I can't bear to even think of the words, let alone say them out loud.

"I've lost count of the times he took from me when I didn't want him too," she admits. "When I told you earlier it had been a long time since I've been with a man, I meant willingly."

My fingers grip onto the duvet cover. "That bastard," I hiss, my whole body vibrating with rage as I drop my head. I want to find that man and fucking kill him.

"But I don't want this moment clouded by those memories. Please, Drix," she begs, reaching for my chin, tipping my face upwards. "Right now, I need you to..."

Her voice trails off as she stares down at me, and I force my fingers to uncurl, dragging in a steadying breath. "I need to tell you something, Lia," I say, ready to confess all my sins, to bare my soul to her.

She shakes her head. "Not now. Please, I just need you to be with me here. Just us together in this moment. No more talk of the past. No more heartache. Not tonight. I can't take it."

"Anything you want, I'll give it to you, Lia. Fuck, I'd go and find that areshole and squeeze the life out of him if you asked me to."

She cups my face, her thumb brushing over my cheek tenderly. "What I need now is to feel adored, treasured, Drix. I *need* you so damn much."

"You have me, Lia. Now, tomorrow, forever, if you want. You have me," I whisper back.

Our gazes clash and she nods. "Then make love to me. Erase what he did to me. *Please.*"

"All fucking night long," I reply. "I'll make you forget that man ever existed. I will erase his memory from every inch of your skin and replace it with my touch, my kisses, my everything."

She nods, her fingers trailing from my skin as she reaches up, and with shaking fingers slowly begins to undo the buttons of her top. I watch her, caught in the moment of sheer vulnerability as she reveals herself to me, inch by precious goddamn inch. My gaze trails down her neck to the expanse of skin bared for me. Her breasts hang heavily, two stunning globes of flesh, resting just above the curve of her stomach.

Lifting my hands, I trail my fingers against her skin, gently pushing the cotton aside, revealing her beautiful breasts fully to me. Her nipples are puckered, surrounded by the softest pink areola, and I groan, unable to hold back what she does to me. My dick hardens painfully as my thumbs brush against the tips of her nipples, fucking jerking in my boxers as she moans softly.

"Fuck, you're stunning," I whisper, cupping her in my hands, gently massaging her heaviness.

Leaning forward I press a wet kiss between the centre of her breasts, right over her heart. Then I wrap my arms around her back and tug her between my legs, resting my cheek against the softness of her chest.

"Drix," she stutters out as my breathing hitches and my hands slide up her back, holding her against me.

"I've never felt like this," I admit, fucking choking on the words as I nuzzle against her.

"Me either," she replies softly, her fingers gliding through my hair.

A huge part of me wants to let go of the passion coursing through my blood, to fuck her hard, to bury myself so deep inside of her that we're one living, pulsing being. But tonight she asked me to make love to her, and that's exactly what I'm going to do.

Drawing in a ragged breath, I look up at her, my hands sliding around her front, up over her breasts as I push her top off her shoulders. It falls to the floor, revealing her to me. Gazing up at her, my eyes locked on hers, I hook my fingers beneath the waistband of her pyjama bottoms and knickers, pushing them over her hips, the softness of her curves making me want to fucking weep with gratitude. My cock strains against my boxers, the tip pushing against the confines of the material, wanting her. I need her so damn much it's painful.

She rests her hands on my shoulders, her fingers delicately pressing into my muscles as she steps out of the material until she's completely naked before me.

"Look at you, Lia," I murmur, my hands reaching for the softness of her stomach, my fingers trailing over the silvery stretch marks scattered across her skin.

"I try not to," she whispers quietly, her voice quaking as her hands fall to cover herself, but I shake my head, gently grabbing them.

"Don't hide yourself from me," I say, pressing soft kisses against each knuckle before gently placing her hands at her sides. "You. Are. Beautiful," I add vehemently.

The look in her eyes as I lift my gaze up to meet hers kills me. Her confidence from earlier is so thoroughly shattered by Toby's distress, caused by a man who deserves to be six foot under. I need to do something about that. Standing, I take her hand and silently lead her to the full length mirror in my bedroom. Resting my hands on her shoulders, I stand her before it.

"I want you to see what I see," I say when I see her questioning look reflecting back at me. She remains quiet, uncertain as my hands circle her waist and rest on the softness of her stomach. Pressing my whole body against her back, I want her to feel how she turns me on. "My cock is aching for you, doll. I'm so damn hard for you." She lets out a broken sob, her chest heaving with emotion as my fingers curl into her skin. "This body grew a life inside of it, Lia. I love how soft your tummy is, how it makes me ravenous for you."

Fuck, I love you, I repeat silently inside my head.

A tear slips down her cheek as I slowly lift my hands to gently cup her breasts, feeling the perfect weight of them. "Your breasts are so fucking full, so heavy in my hands, Lia. I want to slide my cock between them. I want to cover them in my cum," I confess, my dirty words making her gasp.

"You do?"

"Christ, yes. I've fisted myself thinking about this moment," I admit, trailing kisses over her bare shoulder whilst keeping my eyes fixed on her in our reflection. Heat flashes over her skin, her gaze alighting with desire as I roll each of her nipples between my fingers and thumbs.

"Drix," she murmurs, her eyes stuttering closed as I run my teeth over the curve of her neck, biting gently.

"And these nipples..." I let out a low groan, fucking overwhelmed with desire. "They make me so thirsty to taste you again. Fuck, I want to suck on them so damn bad."

"I need you to," she says softly.

"I will," I promise. "But not yet."

Releasing her, I drop to my knees behind her, my hands flying to her hips as she sways before me. "And your arse. Fuck me, Lia, it's so perfectly curvy," I say cupping her, biting each cheek gently before swirling my tongue over the little indents my teeth have made.

"Drix, this is... I'm... God," she whispers, her whole body trembling in earnest now.

My hands slide down the back of her thighs, my thumbs pressing into the back of her knees as I urge her to part her legs for me. She widens them, her breath as heavy as my dick feels.

"I ache for you, Lia," I continue, rising to my feet, my fingers trailing over the heat of her skin as I slide one hand around her front, cupping her pussy whilst the other glides over her breast and up to her throat, gently squeezing. Like a butterfly's wings, her pulse flutters beneath my fingers, delicate yet powerful.

"I ache for you too, Drix," she gasps as I slide my finger through her folds, finding her clit and circling it gently. She rocks against my hand as my fingers tighten around her throat. I don't hold her this way to scare her, but to possess her, to show her that she belongs to me, always will.

"I will never hurt you like he did," I promise, releasing my hold slightly as she draws in a ragged breath. "But I will worship every part of you... with your permission, of course," I add.

"You have it, Drix. You have me."

"Thank fuck," I nod, nuzzling against her neck, kissing, licking, gently biting as I finger her wetness. She floods for me, her body reacting so beautifully to my touch. The slick sounds of my fingers drawing out an orgasm is bliss to my ears, and as she throws her head back against my shoulder, her eyes fluttering shut, I vow to myself that I will love her with every inch of me.

"Drix I'm going to..." her voice trails off with a moan as she jerks against my hand, her own covering mine as I draw out every last drop of her orgasm.

"That's my beautiful woman," I praise her.

As her body turns liquid I release her, moving around her so that I can draw her into my arms and kiss the love I feel for her right into the very marrow of her bones.

She opens up to me, her hands flying to the back of my head as she softens against me. Willing, welcoming, pliable in my arms. Ducking down I grasp her under her arse, lifting her upwards as she wraps her legs around me.

Carrying her to the bed, I lay her down, dropping my body over hers and continuing to kiss her, taking my time, so fucking drunk on her as my tongue strokes languidly against hers. She writhes against me, the heat of her core rubbing against my aching dick. I feel her wetness through my boxers, and I let out a feral growl as she grasps my arse, pushing me harder against her heat.

"I need to be inside of you," I rasp, breathless, mindless, pulling back as I cup her face and shower her with soft kisses.

"I have an IUD," she replies, blinking up at me, her cheeks flush.

"I'm clean," I reply, hoping she trusts my word.

"I am too," she whispers back.

"Fuck, Lia." I stand, removing my boxers.

Her gaze lowers over my body, eyes widening at the sight of my dick, which is so fucking angry that it's not already balls deep inside of her. It leaks pre-cum as I climb back up her body, caging her head with my forearms as I let my dick rest against the seam of her pussy. It pulses there, desperate for entry, her wetness sliding against my too hot skin.

She reaches up to cup my face, her fingers curling into my hair. "The way you look at me, it feels like..." Her voice trails off as she laughs softly.

"Like I love you?" I ask, the words slipping from my mouth like the soft quietness of the snowflakes dropping from the sky outside. "I know it might be too soon for you to hear those words, and you don't need to ever feel like you have to say it back. But fuck, Lia. I goddamn love you."

"Drix," she murmurs, lifting her head to press a heartfelt kiss against my lips. She doesn't tell me she loves me back, but I feel her willingness to fall in that moment, and that's all I need to finally bridge the gap between us.

"I'm going to make love to you now," I say, adjusting my hips, the tip of my dick pressing against her. It's all I can do not to ram inside of her up to the hilt.

"Please, Drix."

Inch by inch I slowly sink myself inside of her, and she quakes against me, her legs sliding around my arse, holding me in place. My whole body shudders at how perfect she is for me. I'm not a small man, and she takes every single one of my eight inches. From the tip of my toes to the top of my head, an all-consuming fire burns in my muscles, my heart pounding a frantic rhythm against my ribs.

"You feel like home," I say, my voice thick with all the things I want to say to this beautiful woman who came into my life and made it a million times more meaningful.

"You've helped me to love who I am," she confesses against my lips.

Gently easing my head back, I stare down at her as she looks up at me. Time passes, maybe it's just seconds, but it feels like an eternity as I rest inside of her, filling her with my thickness. The warmth of her against my skin and her core tightening around me is the most intense, profound feeling. I've fucked other women before, I've enjoyed it, but this? This is so much more. As she blinks up at me, her cheeks flushed, her mouth parting on soft breathes, words fail me. All I can give her at this moment is my body.

Wholly, fully, completely.

I circle my hips, my pubic bone grinding against her clit, never once taking my eyes off hers. She moans, her internal walls gripping me tight, as though her body can't bear to let me go either. "Drix," she cries out, throwing her head back, exposing her neck to me. I kiss her from the hollow of her throat to her chin, my lips coasting up to meet her mouth as she licks her tongue against my parted lips.

Joined like that, kissing with the kind of passion powerful enough to change a man, I slowly move my body, pulling out inch by torturous inch before sliding back in.

She whispers my name.

I groan into her mouth.

She lifts her hips to meet mine, giving me deeper access.

Easing my cock out of her, I slide it over her swollen clit, once, twice, three times, before finding her entrance and sliding back into her once more.

"Please, don't stop!" she begs as my hips rock in a steady, even rhythm.

A part of me wants to let go and pound into her, but I hold

back, controlling my movements, needing to treasure her. I could fuck her just like this for hours and hours and hours.

I will do that. Forever, if she'll let me.

"This is what heaven feels like, Lia. You're so fucking perfect for me," I say, as breathless as she is. I rock my hips, electricity sparking deep inside of me, building, growing with every second.

Her fingers curl into my hair as she tugs on me, pulling me close, kissing me deep. Her body is so soft, so warm, so damn perfect.

"I need to come," she moans, a tear sliding from eyes. I kiss it away, brushing my lips against her temple.

"Then you take control. Take it back, doll. Take what you need from me," I demand, wrapping my arm beneath her and rolling to my back, moving her on top of me. Instinctively, I know that's what she needs, to take back control, and I want to be the one to help her get it back.

She gasps, still joined together as she lays on top of me, chest to chest, beating heart against beating heart. She stares down at me, caught in the moment, frozen.

Reaching up, I stroke my knuckles against her jaw. "I want to see you. Sit up, Lia, Take what you need. Fucking use me," I urge her.

She bites her lip, her eyes grazing mine as she slowly lifts upwards and my hands fall to her rounded hips. Slowly, tentatively, she begins to rock her hips, her internal walls gripping my cock as she moves, and I swear to all that's holy, I go blind for a second.

"Fuck, Lia. You feel so good. Your pussy hugs me so damn tight," I groan, my mouth falling open as I watch her from hooded eyes, drinking in every curve of her body.

"This feels... I feel... So *full*," she cries, her big, beautiful tits bouncing as she gathers confidence and begins to fuck me the way we both need.

"That's it, doll. Use me. Fuck me into next week, I can take it, baby."

Reaching up I grasp her breasts, squeezing them gently, my cock jerking as she rises up on her sexy-as-fuck thick thighs before sinking back down. I watch my cock drive into her, the apex of her thighs glistening with lubrication. I'm fucking mindless with desire as she cries out and I roll her nipples, pinching them between my fingers and thumbs.

Up and down she slides, the sounds of her arousal conjuring up an intense feeling in the bottom of my spine. My impending orgasm builds there, gaining in size as my fucking toes curl and I drag in a breath, holding it in my chest, not wanting to come yet. I have to wait. I have to wait until she comes first, but damn she's making it so fucking hard.

"Look at you. Look at how fucking stunning you are," I exclaim, overwhelmed by her beauty, her power over me as she rides my cock. "You're a goddess. I could die a happy man right here and now."

"Please don't," she murmurs, laughter in her eyes, quickly eclipsed by the desire that runs rampant across her features as she flops forward, arching her spine and pressing her pendulous breasts in my face.

Not one to ignore what's offered, I take her nipple in my mouth, sucking on her, my hands sliding around to her arse as she rocks back and forwards. Her thighs squeeze my hips and I urge her to move faster, my cock drenched with her wetness, engorged, fucking aching to come.

"Drix! God, I'm going to come," she moans, using me so fucking good.

Lost to the moment, Lia lets go, her movements jerky, shaky as she rides me. Her pussy greedy as it tightens around my cock. Reluctantly I release her breast, saliva pooling in my mouth as I reach up to grab her hair, my fingers curl into the strands.

"Then come, doll. Come all over my cock."

The guttural moan that releases from her lips, and the tightening walls of her pussy has my own orgasm barrelling out of me as we come together. She cries out my name, both of us lost in each other, in the excruciatingly beautiful orgasm that takes me to another place momentarily. Bright, white light blinds me as I press my eyes shut and succumb to her completely, my balls tightening as I release a stream of hot cum deep inside of her.

"Lia," I breathe, blinking back the aftershocks of my orgasm as she presses her forehead against my shoulder.

"That was... that was everything I needed," she whispers, her breath warm against my skin, her body quaking against mine as she rests her whole weight against me.

I hold her close, my arms wrapping around her. I already feel bereft at the thought of sliding out of her. I don't want this moment to end.

"I want to hold you like this forever. I never want to let you go, Lia."

"Thank you, Drix," she murmurs back, her soft hair falling around us both in a shroud as she pushes upwards, looking down at me. She brushes her lips against mine, softly, almost shyly.

"Lia, I meant what I said earlier."

"You love me?" she questions, frowning a little.

I reach up, easing my finger between her brows. "I do. There's nothing that I don't love about you."

She smiles then. It's tentative, a slow curve of her lips, a light in her eyes that warms me from the inside out.

"I feel it," she says, running her hand down my cheek, my neck, resting on my chest. "You make things better, Drix. You make me feel as though I can be me again. Thank you," she adds emphatically.

I grin, and the laugh that rumbles up my chest is so damn

cathartic. "Don't thank me just yet. I'm still not done with you," I playfully warn her.

"Really?" she challenges, biting on her lip as I push upwards, holding her in my arms.

Straddled over my lap, my hands fall to her hips, my fingers squeezing her flesh as I press kisses against her collarbone, lavishing my tongue in the hollow of her neck.

"Really," I confirm, wanting to keep us joined together for as long as possible.

"You're not tired?" she asks, gasping as I reach up and cup her breasts, rolling the pad of my thumb over her nipples.

"Not even close. In fact, I've never felt more energised, more alive," I reply, ducking my head to capture her in my mouth.

"That feels so good," she gasps, her hands flying to the back of my head, holding me in place.

"Do you want to know something really fucking dirty?" I ask her, my cock filling with more blood, more than ready to go again.

"What?" she asks, her mouth tilting up in a small smile.

"I've thought about your beautiful breasts, and what they would've looked like when you were pregnant with Toby. I've thought about what it would be like to suck on them and taste the sweetness of your milk. Tell me what they were like, describe them to me," I demand, holding her breasts in my hands and drawing her flesh together so I can lick her cleavage and nuzzle against them.

"They were at least two cup sizes bigger," she says eventually, her cheeks flushing.

"Fuck," I groan, taking her nipple into my mouth and sucking on it momentarily. "What else?"

"They were achy, heavy, and had blue veins running beneath the surface of my skin."

"Jesus." My cock jerks at her description, and she lets out a soft moan as her internal walls squeeze around my length.

"And when Toby came, they would leak so much milk I'd have to constantly change my clothes. If I ever got aroused, which wasn't often, and only by my own hand, they would leak then too."

"I would've liked to see that," I admit, fucking turned on by the thought.

"Drix, do you have a boob fettish?" she asks with a soft laugh.

I shrug. "Doesn't every man?"

"Perhaps," she agrees, her mouth parting as I slowly circle her nipple, the wetness from my saliva glistening on her skin.

"I know what I do have, Lia," I say, running my teeth over my bottom lip as I look up at her, my hands coasting over her belly.

"And what's that?"

"I have a *you* fettish," I reply, gripping her around the waist and flipping her back over, grinning down at her as my cocks slips out of her, our combined release glistening on her thighs and pooling on the covers between her parted legs. She laughs out loud, her eyes shining with happiness as I bury my face in her breasts, kissing them both.

"This tummy. God, how I love it," I say lowering my mouth to her belly and grasping a handful of flesh, fucking groaning at the way she feels in my hands. "I want to cover it with my cum. You make me feral, Lia."

"You make me feel beautiful, Drix."

"Because you are. You are so fucking stunning. Are you ready for more orgasms?" I ask, rearing upwards and gripping my slick cock. It's rock hard, needy for her.

Her gaze drops to my erection, eyes widening as she drags in a shaky breath then slowly coasts her gaze back up my body. "Everything about you is so attractive to me, Drix. I want you to know that."

"Ditto, doll. Ditto," I murmur as I grip myself, smoothing her wetness over my length. Once, twice, three times, I stroke my cock and the aching need grows more intense.

"So what now?" she asks teasingly, her body is blushing with colour, little drops of perspiration covering her skin.

"Now I make you come all over again," I promise, before dropping between her legs and swiping my tongue along her pussy in one firm stroke, tasting me on her.

She cries out, back arching, and I spend the next hour loving her all over again until eventually she falls asleep in my arms, satiated, happy, content.

TWENTY-TWO

"WOULD you mind just waiting for me here for a moment?" Daisy asks, dropping her bag at my feet as we stand in the reception of the hotel after checking into the spa.

It's the following morning after the best sex I've had of my life, and in all honesty I'm still a little dazed by what happened between Drix and me. I'd woken up in his arms, feeling safer than I have in a very long time. It was the most comforting feeling, and I've not been able to stop smiling. I'd left Toby happily playing with Drix, a warm feeling blooming in my chest as he'd picked him up in his arms and they waved us off at the door.

"Sure thing," I reply, shaking away the memories as I take the key for our locker from Georgia, another one of the hotel receptionists.

"Great, won't be a tick," Daisy says, striding towards Dalton's office, her knuckles rapping on the door. She doesn't appear to wait for a reply, shoving open the door and slamming it behind her.

"What's that all about?" Georgia asks, glancing at me wide-eyed.

"I have no idea," I reply, a little startled myself.

"Seriously, I'm surprised Daisy hasn't been fired already for the way she talks to Dalton. They really don't like each other very much." Georgia leans forward in her seat, looking right then left, making sure the coast is clear, presumably. "Though I do admire her gumption. He can be a total arse. Devilishly good-looking, but an arse."

"So I've been told," I laugh as she winks at me.

"So, spa day, huh?" Georgia asks, settling back in her seat, moving on to safer ground.

"Daisy persuaded me to come along. I've never actually been to a spa before. Is it nice?"

Georgia flips her long brown hair over her shoulder. "Oh it's amazing! I've used the spa a couple of times, the salt room is the best."

"Salt room? What's that?"

"It's salt therapy basically."

I frown, scrunching up my nose. "Salt therapy?"

"So the air inside the room exposes you to microscopic particles of salt. Apparently it helps to relieve tension and is great for your lungs and skin, and the room is so soothing. All soft lights and relaxing music."

"Wow, that sounds great," I agree, eager to try it out.

"It sure is. Oh, and then you've got to try the plunge pool after the sauna. Ice cold water, but so invigorating. Good for blood flow!"

"Not sure that the plunge pool is for me," I reply with a grin. "But Daisy has arranged for us both to have a full body massage, so I'm looking forward to that."

Georgia glances at the screen before her. "Oooh, Daisy has Tomasz doing her massage, the lucky duck."

"Tomasz? I don't think I've met him yet."

"Believe me, you'd remember him if you had. He's gorgeous!"

"Who do I have?" I ask, a little nervous to have a stranger's hands on me. Drix might have coaxed out some confidence in me last night, but I don't think I'm ready for another man's hands on me, even if it is in a purely professional manner.

Georgia checks her computer screen. "You have Melinda. She's excellent."

Relief floods through. "Great."

"That absolute prick!"

Georgia and I exchange looks as Daisy comes striding towards us both, her expression furious.

"Oh dear," Georgia laughs, hiding her smile as Daisy swoops down and picks up her bag.

"Come on, Lia, if we don't head into the spa now I might just commit murder."

Pulling a face, I wave goodbye to Georgia and follow Daisy into the spa.

Ten minutes later we're lying on two loungers next to the pool, wearing our swimsuits and wrapped up in soft towelling robes, a bottle of chilled champagne sitting on the small table between us. We're alone, ambient lighting and soothing music playing. It would honestly be bliss if Daisy wasn't as tense as I've ever seen her.

"Want to tell me what's bothering you, Daisy?" I ask tentatively. She's been out of sorts all morning, and she doesn't appear to be calming down despite the relaxing atmosphere.

"I'm not sure where to start," she replies, sitting up and grabbing a champagne flute, filling it to the top. "Do you want some?"

I shake my head. "I'm good with water for now."

"It's Dalton," she eventually says after downing the whole glass and filling it up again.

"I figured. What's he done?"

"What he always does," she spits out with a shake of her head.

"And what's that exactly?"

"Meddling."

"Meddling? How?"

She lets out a long breath, her eyes meeting mine. "Swear you won't repeat this to anyone? Especially not Drix. Only because he'll side with Dalton, and then I might have to murder him too, and I rather like my brother," she adds with an annoyed shake of her head.

"Okay, so what gives?"

"I was already furious with Dalton last night, hence the spa date on him, but now I'm livid," she explains. "This morning he fired Lewis."

"Lewis, as in the guy you..."

"Went on a date with, yes," she nods, anger blooming across her features in a flood of pink.

"Why did he fire him?"

"Apparently because he wasn't doing his job well enough! It's absolute rubbish. Everyone knows he's good at this job."

"Then why would Dalton fire him?"

"Because he's a prick, that's why."

"Wait, hold on. You didn't mention this last night."

"Because last night Lewis still had a job. Yesterday Dalton pulled him aside and gave him a dressing down. According to Lewis, Dalton said someone had complained about him."

"And this morning he fired him because of it?"

"Yep. Lewis texted me, said that he'd turned up for work and Dalton gave him the push. No warnings, other than the one he gave him last night. Which, again, is utter fucking rubbish!"

"Wow. That doesn't seem right."

"It isn't. Even if there was a complaint, which I know there wasn't, there are procedures that are supposed to be followed. Dalton is an arsehole. He doesn't like him because *I* like him," Daisy says, pouring herself another glass, the champagne spilling onto the table with her anger.

"Why would Dalton fire Lewis because you like him?" I ask, trying to follow but failing miserably.

"Because Dalton thinks he has a say in who I date, apparently."

"Okay, just back up a minute," I say, sitting up in my seat as I cock my head at Daisy. "Firstly, if he's firing Lewis because you like him, that's gross misconduct on his part. Secondly, I still don't understand why he would do that."

"Because, like Drix, they still feel like I need protection from all the men in the world. It's infuriating. I'm a grown-ass woman. I can go on a date with whoever the hell I want."

"Yes, you can," I agree.

"It's complete bullshit!" she exclaims.

"Has this got something to do with that guy you dated back in college?" I ask tentatively.

"Drix told you about that?"

"He mentioned it."

Daisy lets out a long breath, rubbing at her eyes before swallowing another mouthful of champagne. "It always does. Between the pair of them they've scared off four potential boyfriends. I can't even go on a bloody date without them conniving together to mess it up. Either Drix turns up on my date with his chest puffed out acting all protective and asking all these dumb questions, or Dalton does something sly, like firing a person!"

"That doesn't sound like Drix," I say, a little confused to be honest. I mean I know he's protective of Daisy, he's said as much, but I thought he had enough respect for her as a woman to be able to make her own decisions about who she chooses to be with.

"To be fair, Drix isn't as bad as Dalton. The last guy I dated he was okay with. Kind of. I think he's beginning to learn that I can look after myself now. Dalton, however, is still a dick. I don't even like him as a person, so why the hell he thinks he can act like he's my brother too, is beyond me. He has no right. What happened to me in college was shit, but that was years ago and I'm over it. I can look after myself."

"What exactly happened in college?" I ask. "If you're willing to share."

"I went out with this guy, Jonathon. He was the captain of the college rugby team. You know the type, gorgeous, fit, a little arrogant. I thought he liked me. He was my first..."

"You lost your virginity to him?"

"Yep. Though Drix and Dalton don't know that, not that they need to, but you know..."

"I get it," I reply, waiting for her to continue.

"I fell for him hard. I thought he loved me, but it was all a lie. Apparently his friends dared him to ask me out, to see how far he could take it with me." She lets out a shuddering breath at the memory. "He said all the right things, wined and dined me, made me feel special. Of course I fell for it. I gave him the most precious thing I could. Then he made a fool of me at the Summer Ball, dumped me in front of everyone. He was cruel with it. God, I can still remember their laughter."

"Their laughter?"

"The people he hung out with. His rugby friends and their girlfriends. You know, the popular ones. They all thought it was hysterical. I still see them out and about occasionally now, and I get thrown back to that moment of humiliation all over again. Pretty sure Dalton's fucked most of the girls too."

Her head drops in defeat, and I get up, sitting down next to her. "What a bunch of arseholes," I say, feeling anger rising inside of me as I put my arm around her shoulder.

"It took me a long time to recover from that," she admits. "It cut me deep, Lia."

"Of course it did. You trusted him. I'm so sorry."

"I really like Lewis, but now he won't answer my calls. I'm so over Dalton thinking he can interfere. Who does he think he is?"

"Honestly, I don't know," I say, at a loss for words or an explanation for his appalling behaviour.

"Anyway, enough about dickface," she says, wafting her hand in the air. "So, you and Drix..."

"What about us?" I ask, heat flooding my cheeks, hoping to God she hadn't heard us last night.

A grin spreads across her face, and I know instantly that she must've. "Oh," I mutter.

"Hey, don't be embarrassed. I'm happy for you both. I couldn't want a better person for my brother. You're perfect together."

"It's all so new," I say carefully.

"But you like him, right?"

I nod, unable to hold back my own grin. "Very much."

"Good. It's about time he settled down."

My smile fades. "I'm still married, Daisy."

"Only legally, right? Besides, what's a bit of paper to get in the way of true love, eh?"

"I wish it were that simple."

"It'll work out. You'll see," she replies, giving me a hug that I return in kind.

"Daisy, it's time for your massage," a tall man with unruly black hair and a smile to match says as he steps into the pool room. We break apart, both of us eying him.

"Wow," I whisper. Georgia was right, he is gorgeous.

"Wow indeed," Daisy whispers back, her eyes twinkling as she climbs to her feet. "See you in the sauna room in an hour?"

"I'll be there," I reply, resting back against the chair, waiting to be called for my own massage as Daisy strides towards Tomasz. He holds the door open for her, and Daisy throws me a wink before disappearing out of sight.

"I FEEL SO RELAXED. That was amazing, Daisy," I say, my stomach full from the delicious lunch we've just eaten and my heart happy from having spent the morning with someone I now call a friend.

"Tomasz has magic hands," she replies, sipping on her sparkling water. "I feel like a whole new woman."

"I bet," I laugh as she mimics an orgasmic face.

"Unfortunately for me he was very professional, and didn't do anything I was secretly hoping he might–" Her suggestive smile drops as she looks at someone behind me. "Oh, please. I really don't need this right now," she complains, her expression darkening.

Looking over my shoulder, I see Dalton approaching, his own expression thunderous.

"Daisy, a word," he snaps, focussing entirely on her.

"I have nothing to say to you," she snaps back, folding her arms across her chest.

"Too bad, because I have a shit ton to say to you," he hisses, completely oblivious to my presence, apparently, as he glares at her.

"Hello, Dalton," I say, trying to prevent an all out war from taking place right here in the middle of the restaurant.

Dalton swings his attention my way, clearing his throat. "Did you enjoy your spa experience?" he asks, his shoulders tense as he side-eyes Daisy.

"It was lovely. I had a great massage too. Thank you for your generosity."

"You're welcome," he replies tightly.

"You know, Tomasz was exceptional," Daisy adds, letting out an exaggerated sigh. "I don't think I've ever felt this *taken care of*. You should give him a pay rise. Better still, book yourself a massage. It might help with all that pent-up aggression you seem to carry around with you lately. Who knows, it may even help to rearrange some of your brain cells so you don't fire a person for absolutely no damn reason!"

Dalton snaps his head around, a muscle flickering in his jaw as he narrows his eyes at her. "I've already explained quite clearly why I let Lewis go, Daisy."

"Yeah, because we fucked," she hisses. "And you somehow think you have a right to say who I sleep with, that's why!"

Dalton flinches at the rise in her voice. "That's not why I fired him."

"Bullshit!" Daisy snaps.

"I'm not having this conversation here. Come with me to my office. Now," he adds with a jerk of his chin.

"Go to hell, arsehole," she snarls back.

Around us the conversation seems to fall away as the other people in the restaurant take notice. "Maybe this isn't the best place to discuss..." I begin.

"Why not? Everyone needs to know what an absolute turd he is," she counters with an angry shake of her head.

"You know what, Daisy? If you want to have this out with me in public, let's do this," Dalton snaps. "I'll tell you *exactly* why I fired him."

"Go on then, enlighten me," she taunts him.

"Lewis has been playing around with another woman at the same time he's been seeing you."

"What?" Daisy blanches, her face paling.

"Dalton, don't do this," I plead.

"If you don't believe me then ask Samantha because this morning I found out that after he spent the night with you, he fucked her in the staff room," Dalton continues.

"You're lying!" Daisy replies, her eyes cutting to me. I see the hurt in them and I reach for her across the table. She pulls her hand away, wrapping her arms around herself.

"I have the video footage to prove it," Dalton explains, a little softer now.

She stares up at him, her eyes filling with tears. "You just love this, don't you? Stupid, *trusting*, desperate little Daisy who can't seem to find a man who doesn't want to shit on her."

"I don't love anything about what he did to you," Dalton counters, shame creeping over his features.

"You know what, I've had enough. I don't need this. I'm going home," she says, standing abruptly.

"Daisy," Dalton says, reaching for her. She flinches away from him.

"Don't! Don't you dare look at me with pity, Dalton Gunn. You're just as bad as Lewis. You fuck and discard women like they're nothing, so don't pretend you're any different."

"This *is* different," he says, barely able to look at her.

"How? You hurt women all the time. How are you any different?"

"I don't hurt you," he whispers.

She barks out a laugh, the tears she's been holding back pouring down her cheeks. "You hurt me just by existing!"

"Daise, please," he begs, the confidence he always seems to have falls away at that moment.

"Don't *Daise* me, and don't expect me to be at work this week. I need a break from this... from *you*!" she adds vehemently.

He nods, squaring his shoulders and meeting her gaze. "Take all the time you need."

"Fuck you. I'm going," she adds, swiping at her face and looking pointedly at me.

"I'll come with you," I say, grabbing my bag and coat.

"See you in the car," Daisy replies, storming off without a backward glance.

Dalton wavers on his feet as though wanting to chase her.

"She's fucking infuriating," he admits, swiping a hand through his hair as he watches her leave.

"She's a grown woman, Dalton. No matter the intention, what you did was wrong."

"Clearly I did the *right* thing," he replies, throwing his hands up in the air. "The guy is a cheating dick."

"I'm talking about how you handled this situation."

"How the hell else should I have handled it?"

"Telling her the truth from the get go might've been the best idea, and not in front of a whole restaurant of people either."

"I'm just looking out for her," he replies.

"Why?" I ask as he sits down at the table opposite me, his shoulders dropping as he lets out a breath. The look on his face gives me pause, and I drop my bag and coat back onto the seat beside me.

"I thought that was obvious. I fired him because he's a dickhead."

"No, I get that now, but I mean why are you looking out for her, specifically?"

"Because..." his voice trails off as he focuses his attention on the table, a frown deepening on his forehead.

"Because?" I ask gently.

For a long time he doesn't answer, until eventually he looks up at me. "Because she's my best friend's little sister and has shit taste in men, that's why."

"I don't know much about the men she's dated, but I do know Daisy has a good head on her shoulders. I don't want to see her hurt anymore than you do, but being honest with her about what you found out would've been a better approach. She would've dealt with it in her own way."

He laughs. "You don't know her."

"I know she was hurt badly in the past. I also know she's capable of learning from that experience, *and* from this one."

"You're wrong. She's gone out with one loser after the other since that dick broke her heart. Lewis wasn't good enough for her. *None* of the arsehole's she's spent time with have been good enough for her," he adds.

"So you're going to just scare off every man she chooses to date even if one of them could turn out to be just what she needs?"

"If I have to," he snaps.

"Why?" I press.

"I told you why. I'm just looking out for her. She can complain about it all she likes, but I won't stop."

"Is that really the only reason?"

"What other reason would there be?" he counters, eying me.

Suddenly the conversation I had with Dalton last night replays in my head. Could it be that Daisy is the woman he's interested in? I decide that the only way to find out is to ask him directly. "Dalton, do you like Daisy?"

He barks out a laugh. "She's a pain in my arse."

"Is she the woman you wanted advice about?" I ask, being more specific.

He meets my gaze, something flickering in his eyes before he shuts it down with a biting laugh. "Fuck, no. She's absolutely not my type in any way, shape or form."

I nod, not believing him for a second. "Either way," I continue, "Scaring off men she likes is only going to make her hate you more. You must see that."

"She hates me?" he asks, his frown deepening.

"Can you blame her?"

Dalton rolls his eyes. "Daisy doesn't hate anyone. It's her one major flaw. She can't tell the difference between a good person and someone who's a wolf in sheep's clothing. That much is obvious."

"Perhaps you don't know her as well as you think," I reply, gathering up my coat and bags once more. "I'm pretty sure she's got you sussed."

He bristles. "I know all there is to know about Daisy Hammer. She's like my little sister."

I shake my head, giving him a pitying smile as I stand. "I think we both know you don't see her that way, Dalton."

He opens his mouth to reply, then slams it shut. "See you at work tomorrow," he says instead, pushing upwards from the table. "Now if you'll excuse me, I have work to do."

With that, he strides off and I'm left wondering whether Daisy has any idea that Dalton Gunn is secretly harbouring feelings for her, because from where I'm standing it's as plain as day.

TWENTY-THREE

"THE WEDDING IS in ten days time, I need to be certain the security is tight," Robert says, looking up at me from behind his huge walnut desk. Placed before him are ten pages of my meticulously written plans. I've left no stone unturned. I'm good with the security side of my job, at least this part of it doesn't make me feel like I'm just some mindless thug.

"You have nothing to worry about, I have everything covered," I reply, certain of my abilities. "I have ample security arranged. The press have been given accommodation at Walter's B&B in town, and will be watched closely by a member of my team. All of them have been thoroughly vetted."

"Good, I don't want any two-bit hacks sneaking into the ceremony thinking they can get a cheap shot of my bride before the news establishments who've paid for the privilege have released their pictures."

"We will also have blocks on all the roads leading in and out of town, and everyone will be thoroughly searched, guests included. It's highly unlikely that any uninvited guests or unauthorised press will slip through, but we have contingencies in place just in case. It's watertight."

"I can see that," he says, easing back into his seat as he eyes me. "I appreciate the work you've put into this. It's an important day for me and my new bride. I can't have any mistakes."

"I understand."

"Will you be bringing a guest to the wedding?" he asks me, changing the subject slightly.

"If you're fishing for information about Lia, then just ask me outright, Robert," I counter.

Robert nods, leaning forward in his seat as he presses his hands against the desk. "Carl, Walter and I had a discussion about you the other night."

"About me, or about Lia and Toby?"

"Both," he admits. "Despite Carl's approach to the situation–"

"Again, Lia and Toby are not *a situation*. They're important to me."

"Yes, Walter said as much."

"So what did you conclude from your conversation?" I ask, leaning back in my seat, waiting for whatever bullshit he's got to say.

"That Lia and her son should come to the wedding as your guests. If you're serious about her, then they should be a part of this celebration, don't you think?"

"If that's what you want."

"What I *want* to know is whether she's trustworthy. If you've chosen her to join your family, then she needs to be. Walter seems to think she is. Carl isn't so certain."

"Carl is an areshole," I snap back.

"And I'm yet to make my mind up given I've not met her yet," Robert continues. "Bring her to the wedding, her son too. Let me decide for myself whose opinion is right about your lady friend."

"With all due respect, Robert, I honestly don't give a fuck

what any of you think. The only opinion that counts is mine. Lia is a good woman. She's not a gold digger, and she's not some undercover cop here to investigate your nefarious shit."

"*Our* nefarious shit. You are the head of the Hammer family, Drix, and as such this is your legacy too," Robert reminds me.

"You don't need to worry. Your businesses and reputations are safe, because let's face it, that's all you really care about."

Robert shrugs his shoulders. "You don't get to be sitting where I am without being cautious. I have to protect my family, my businesses, and my fortune. It isn't personal, you understand?"

"Lia is important to me," I warn.

"Apparently so," he muses, pouring himself a shot of brandy from a crystal decanter sitting on his desk. "And I take it you've checked out her background too? Just to be on the safe side."

"Like I said, Lia isn't someone you need to worry about," I say, my hackles rising.

He cocks a brow, taking a sip of his brandy "But you *have* done a thorough search?"

"She's clear," I reply. The truth is I haven't done a full background check. Why would I? She has nothing to hide, and I trust her implicitly.

"Excellent."

"If that's all?" I ask, wanting more than anything to get back to Lia.

It's been a few days since that incredible night, our work commitments preventing us from spending as much time together as I'd like. I've arranged for Daisy to take Toby to the arcade tonight to spend the money in the swear jar so that we can spend some time together. Daisy is looking forward to taking Toby out, Toby can't wait to win some unicorns, and I need to lose myself in Lia for the night. It's a win-win for everyone.

"Sterling asked if you could stop by his studio before you leave," Robert says as I move to stand.

I nod. "I can do that."

"Check back in with me after Christmas break," he adds, his attention drawn to a message on his phone. A smile pulls up his lips as he reads the text. I don't bother to ask what it's about. Firstly it's none of my business and secondly, I honestly don't care what's got him so amused.

"No problem."

With that, I turn on my heel and head to Sterling's studio situated in the converted stables half a mile from the main building. Not only does he paint there, he sleeps there too, choosing to live in the small studio flat attached to the art studio over his palatial suite back at the mansion. I don't blame him. Like Carl, Robert is a cold-hearted man who's only interested in what people can do for him. He's never supported Sterling, using his talents only for his own gain.

Eight minutes of brisk walking along the snow-cleared path, I reach Sterling's art studio. Music blares from the open doorway, and as I push my way inside I'm confronted by a cacophony of colour splashed across a huge six foot by six foot canvas. My friend stands bare-chested in front of it, wearing a pair of threadbare blue jeans, covered head to toe in splashes of multicoloured paint.

With his back to me he has no idea I'm here, and for a few minutes I watch him work, his creativity and talent mind-blowing as he paints like a conductor might lead an orchestra.

Benedict let slip once that Sterling has a neurological condition called synesthesia where information meant to stimulate one of your senses, stimulates several. According to Ben, whenever Sterling hears music, he sees vivid colour and from an early age has used his gift to paint extraordinary artwork. He spent most of his childhood and teen years battling against his gift. It made him an outcast, laughed at, ridiculed as he desperately tried to fit in. I know for a fact his dad tried to beat the difference out of him with harsh words, never understanding that what he has is a gift not a curse. It's little wonder he hates the man.

"Mate, that's outstanding," I say, stepping into his studio as I turn down the volume on his speaker. A sultry woman's voice belts out a cover of *When the Party's Over* by Billie Eilish; whoever is singing, her voice is incredible.

"Drix, good to see you," he replies, dropping his paintbrush in a jar of water at his feet. "I take it you've seen Robert?"

"Yeah, we just went over the security for the wedding."

Sterling nods, swiping a hand through his hair as he pulls up a stool and sits. "Still can't fucking believe the arsehole is going through with this sham of a wedding."

"Have you met his fiance yet?" I ask, leaning against the huge table covered in tubes of paint, different sized paintbrushes scattered across the surface.

"Nope. Apparently she's not arriving until the night before the wedding. Won't lay eyes on her until the ceremony. Not that I particularly want to meet her. I'd rather be anywhere but here. But duty calls," he says with a roll of his eyes.

"You know who she is by now I take it?" I ask him.

He eyes me. "Yeah, I know. Melody Richards. Apparently back in the late eighties she was some famous Hollywood actress in a popular TV series that ran for a few years in the US."

"*Through the Eyes of a Child*, I think it was called," I say, having looked it up whilst doing my background checks. Robert might be marrying this woman he purportedly loves, but he wasn't foolish enough not to ask me to do some thorough checks on his bride-to-be. Apart from the fact she has a daughter not much younger than Sterling himself, and a list of three failed marriages, she's clear.

"Never heard of it. Don't care much either way. As soon as the wedding's over, I'm out of here."

"And Robert's okay with that?" I ask, eying the painting he's working on. Beneath the swirls of colour is a beautiful woman's face. She's got chin length blonde hair, her purple-lipsticked mouth wide as she sings into a microphone.

"Of course he isn't, but I don't need to be here to do my job," he retorts.

"Fair enough. Wish I could say the same."

Sterling meets my gaze, understanding brewing in his eyes. "I'm sorry. I know you wish things were different."

"It is what it is. I can't walk away from this life, not until Hubert's debt is paid off and I know Daisy is taken care of."

"You'd think, given their years of friendship and how much money Carl has, he'd let that debt go," Sterling says, shaking his head in disbelief.

"We both know Carl doesn't care about the money. This is about him controlling me."

"I know the feeling," Sterling agrees. "I think the only one okay with this life is Ben, and that's only because his father isn't a controlling, narcissistic bastard."

"Yeah," I agree wishing, not for the first time, Hubert was still around. If he'd known his actions would've left us in this predicament he would've done everything in his power to change it. If *I'd* have known, I would've made a different choice so he wouldn't have felt the need to protect me. Ultimately, this is all on me. "So, the woman..." I say shaking off the guilt I feel as I admire his painting.

"Someone I met in New York on my travels," he explains, looking at it a little wistfully. "She's the woman singing this track. Met her in a bar one night when she was performing."

"Good night was it?" I ask, tipping my lips up in a smile.

"Best fucking night of my life," he replies, shaking his head with a smile.

"You still in contact with her?"

"Not for lack of trying," he replies, cocking his head as he scrutinises his work.

"What do you mean? Didn't you get her number?"

"She gave me a dud number," he shrugs. "Don't even know her real name."

I frown. "How come?"

"She sings under a pseudonym. *Sunday Love* is her stage name. I know nothing else about her apart from the fact her voice inspires me to paint, and she's fucking incredible in bed."

"You want me to do some digging?" I offer.

He eyes me. "Believe me, I've considered it, but in the end I figured if she didn't want me to know the real her then there's a good reason for it. Besides, what do I have to offer her?"

"A great fucking deal, mate," I encourage.

"We both know I'm as trapped in this life as you are. Why would I make someone else suffer?"

"I get it," I reply, my gut churning.

Sterling must hear the change of tone in my voice, and he turns to me. "Ben told me Lia is something special. Sorry I wasn't there to meet her at Bandits, I wasn't really in the mood for socialising. You know how it is."

"S'alright, mate, you've got a lot going on, and yeah, she's incredible."

"Does she know...?" his voice trails off as I shake my head.

"Haven't told her about what I do."

"Are you going to?"

I wince. "I owe her the complete truth. I tried to tell her on a few occasions, but I just can't bring myself to share it just yet."

"Afraid she'll walk?" he asks.

"Scared shitless," I admit.

"Fuck, man. I wouldn't want to be in your shoes."

"Her ex was a violent bastard. Beat her, treated her like shit. If she knew what I did for the families she'll see me differently, and I'll lose her. I don't want to lose her, Sterling."

"I hear you," he nods, giving me a sympathetic look. "So what's your plan?"

I scrape a hand over my face. "Once we've got the wedding out of the way I intend on telling her everything. I won't stop her if she walks."

"You'll let her go?"

"It will kill me, but I'm not going to force her to stay," I say, hating the thought. Truth be known, the fact I've been a selfish bastard has been playing on my mind, but selfishly I want more time with Lia and Toby, even if it is only a matter of days. "Never felt like this before. Fuck knows, I want to keep her, and her son."

"He's a good kid?"

"The best. I care about him a lot."

Sterling blows out a breath. "I wish I had some words of wisdom, Drix, but I guess, in the end, it's better she hears the truth from you than someone else. What she chooses to do with that information is up to her."

"Yeah, I know," I reply, pushing off from the table. "I'm gonna head off. Have a good Christmas?" It comes out as a question rather than a statement.

He lifts a brow. "Unlikely."

"See you at the wedding then."

"See you there," he replies, turning the volume back up on the music as he picks up another paintbrush, dips it in some paint and loses himself to his creativity.

As I walk back to my car, I try to shake the feeling that in a few short days the woman I can't imagine being without is going to leave, knowing that the truth will send her far, far away from Princetown, from me.

TWENTY-FOUR

"BE sure to stick by Daisy's side. No running off, Toby," I say, as he beams up at me, his eyes bright with excitement.

"Don't worry, Mama, I'll be good," he replies, taking Daisy's proffered hand.

"You ready to go win some unicorns, little man?" Daisy asks him, her smile as bright as her pinafore dress that's covered in rainbows and multicoloured unicorns. "I've got my lucky dress on. Always win when I'm wearing it."

"She's not wrong," Drix comments, sliding his mobile phone into his pocket just as the doorbell rings.

"You look very pretty," Toby says, hopping from one foot to the other as Daisy's smile slips into a frown.

"Expecting a visitor?" she asks, as Drix strides past us, opening the door.

"You've got to be kidding me," Daisy groans, as surprised as I am to see Dalton standing on the threshold. He's dressed down in jeans and trainers, with a black turtleneck sweater and a long grey, woollen coat. His hair isn't as styled as it usually is, and an unruly few strands fall over his forehead.

"Afternoon," he says, his gaze flicking from Drix to Daisy and back again.

"Well, that'll be our cue to leave," she says tightly, helping Toby into his coat before grasping his hand.

"Excellent. The car's still running," Dalton adds, dropping his gaze to Toby who just looks up at him curiously. "Hello again, Toby."

"Hello," he replies.

"What do you mean, the car's still running?" Daisy asks, her eyes narrowing at Drix who just shrugs.

"Dalton offered to take you both to the arcade when I told him your plans. We're due more snow in a few hours, and his car is better equipped to deal with the roads should you get caught out."

"My car has snow tires, and I happen to be a very safe driver," Daisy retorts, bristling.

"Even so, I'd feel more comfortable if Dalton drove you," Drix says, looking between the pair.

"Need I remind you that Dalton has a history of being a boy racer. Pretty sure he's still racing about in cars when he's not messing with women he shouldn't be or poking his nose in other people's business. So I'm not sure he deserves the safe driver of the year accolade," she snarks, arching a brow.

"I am not a complete jerk, Daisy. I race *motorbikes* as a hobby on a *track*. I don't race cars on the roads, and especially not when I have a kid in the car," he adds, ruffling Toby's hair.

"Not to mention the fact I *don't want* to spend any time with you," Daisy continues pointedly.

"If you think there's going to be some heavy snow, perhaps you should postpone the outing?" I suggest, wincing when Toby pulls a face. "Sorry, sweetheart. Maybe another time?"

"Mama, you promised!"

"The snow's not forecast to fall until later," Drix reassures me. "And even if they get caught in the first flurry, despite what

Daisy has insinuated, Dalton is a very competent driver. He took the advanced driver's test, and aced it. I also happen to know he's also pretty damn good at the arcades. Aren't you, mate?"

"I've won a few things in my time," he says, winking at Toby who grins back at him.

"I don't know," I hesitate, not because I don't trust Drix's word or Dalton's capabilities, more because Daisy seems incredibly uncomfortable with the idea.

"Please don't worry, Lia, I'll take care of them. I promise."

Them, not him.

Daisy scoffs, mumbling something under her breath.

"It's only a ten minute drive into town. We can leave early, if need be," Dalton reassures me.

"Okay," I nod. "If you're sure?" I say this more to Daisy than Dalton.

"It doesn't look like I have a choice," she mutters.

"Excellent, see you in a couple of hours then? Lia and I are cooking a roast, so get them back for dinner at six sharp," Drix says.

"I'll make sure they're home safe and sound," Dalton adds as Daisy strides past him, scowling.

"Bye, Mama," Toby says, giving me a wave over his shoulder, far too excited about spending the afternoon at the arcade to notice the tension between the two.

"You're welcome to stay for dinner too," I say to Dalton, who watches Daisy pull open the door to his car, helping Toby inside. I notice he already has a car seat situated in the back seat. I give him a questioning look.

"Drix said Toby needed a car seat," he explains.

"You could've just borrowed mine," I reply.

He shrugs. "It's no big deal."

"Well, thank you. I appreciate you looking out for him."

"See you later then," he says, moving to step away.

"You should use the time to clear the air with Daisy," Drix urges Dalton, who falters, resting his eyes on him.

"Who told you?" Dalton questions, looking at me.

I hold my hands up. "It didn't come from me."

Drix swipes a hand through his hair. "AJ's friend was at the restaurant, he told him what happened. That information got back to me," he explains. "Just make amends, okay?"

He nods. "I'll try," he says, before twisting on his heel and striding towards the car.

Drix closes the door, leaning back against it as he eyes me.

"Daisy asked me not to say anything," I explain, feeling immeasurably guilty.

"Hey, I understand. They're always arguing. Been like that since we were kids," he says, shaking his head. "I love them both. I just wish they'd get on."

"Can't be easy being caught in the middle," I offer.

"Sometimes I think..." His voice trails off as he shakes his head.

"What?"

"Never mind."

"I'm really sorry, Drix. I didn't want to break Daisy's trust. I figured she'd tell you in her own time."

He shrugs. "She would've eventually, but I didn't feel like playing mediator for weeks on end like I usually do. Figured it couldn't hurt throwing them together so they could sort their shit out once and for all."

"I'm not sure a few hours at the arcade is going to cut it," I muse.

"It's worth a shot."

"I guess."

Drix pushes off from the door. "So..."

"So...?" I reply, heat flooding my cheeks at the mischievous look he gives me.

"Do you want to see my Fred Flinstone?" he asks, a flirtatious smile pulling up his lips.

"I've already seen it," I flirt back with a grin.

"Not this one you haven't," he says, striding towards me, and twining his fingers with mine.

"YOU REALLY DO like Funko Pops, don't you?" I ask, gazing at the shelves filled to the brim with them in his office. There are so many, and all of them are in pristine condition.

"Not nearly as much as I like you," he replies softly, reaching up for a box situated in the corner of the room. "*This* is Fred Flinstone."

I take the box from him, staring at the toy inside. "Is this special to you?"

"Hubert bought it for me when I was a kid. First toy I ever owned," he explains, leaning against the far wall, his eyes guarded as he watches me. "Started my obsession with the damn things."

"Your mum never bought you any toys?" I ask.

He shakes his head. "We were poor. Any money she did have went to the essentials after my father took most of her earnings to pay for his drug addiction. We were lucky if there was enough left over to buy food, let alone keep our home heated and the rent paid."

"I'm sorry, Drix. That must've been hard for you," I reply, placing it on the table as I approach him.

"I tend not to think about that time all that much. Better that way."

"Do you want to talk about it?" I ask, resting my hand against his arm, my thumb gently rubbing his skin right over the tattoo of a bird flying free from a cage. It seems significant given our conversation.

"Not particularly," he responds quietly, his hand reaching up to cover mine as he glances up at me, the faintest wisp of pain stuttering across his features before he shuts it down. "Hubert spent a lot of money on therapy for me. Can't say it helped all that much."

"I'm not a therapist, but I am a good listener. Sometimes talking about the hard things can make them easier to bear."

"So everyone tells me. Thing is, whenever I've tried to talk about that time, I just get..." His voice trails off as he heaves out a sigh.

"You just get what, Drix?" I press, cupping his face and urging him to look at me.

"Angry."

"That's understandable."

"I don't like feeling that way, Lia. I'd rather forget those years of my life. Especially the night that arsehole..." He shudders, his mouth slamming shut as he presses his head back against the wall and closes his eyes on the memory.

My thumb trails across his cheek as I gaze at him. "Daisy told me what your father did. I'm so sorry, Drix," I whisper, my voice cracking with emotion. His pain cuts me deep, reminding me that if I hadn't left Martin when I did, Toby could be without a mother, my life ended with a violent act just like Drix's mum's had been.

"It was a long time ago," he replies as I press my body against his, hugging him close.

He leans into me, his arms wrapping around my back, and we stand like that, just holding each other, seeking comfort in each other's arms. Eventually, we pull apart and I take his hand in mine.

"Come with me," I say, leading him to the kitchen. He follows me, quiet, thoughtful, then gives me a questioning look as he settles on one of the stools at the kitchen island.

"I find that baking is a good distraction. Want to help me make a chocolate cake?" I ask him, giving his hand a gentle squeeze before gathering a mixing bowl, a wooden spoon and two cake pans from the cupboard, as well all the ingredients needed to make the cake from the pantry and fridge.

"Not sure I'll be of much use," he replies, watching me as I stir together flour, cocoa powder, baking soda and powder, plus a pinch of salt into the glass bowl. "You've already experienced my poor culinary skills."

"Hey, it was a good effort. You just need a little practice."

"I'd rather watch an expert at work," he counters, leaning his hand on his chin. "So what made you want to do this for a living?"

"My mum. She taught me how to bake. It was something we enjoyed doing together, and I rather like making something from scratch and watching people enjoy the fruits of my labour," I explain with a soft laugh as I mix the ingredients together with a wooden spoon, cracking three eggs, some butter, milk and sugar into the mixture.

"What was she like?" he asks me.

"Kind, warm-hearted," I smile at the memory of her. "She had a wicked sense of humour too. Was in love with Tom Jones. I'm pretty sure she threw her knickers at him at a few of his concerts. I think you would've liked her."

"She sounds like a wonderful woman," he comments with a chuckle, watching me as I grease the cake pans and add half of the mixture into each one.

"She was. I miss her terribly. Every time I bake, I'm reminded of her. So it makes her loss a little easier to bear."

"I don't have a single memory of my mum happy," Drix blurts out.

"Not one?"

He shakes his head. "She was always so stressed. So on edge all the time. I tried so hard to make her smile, but in the end I think she lost her joy. My father stole it from her," he explains.

"I can sympathise," I say, then quickly add, "But I also know how hard that must've been for you. I'm so sorry, Drix."

His gaze meets mine. "I would bet on my life that even through the midst of all your trauma, you still managed to smile for Toby."

"I did, but it was hard, Drix. It took all my strength to be present, to find joy in the simple things. I'm sure you mum loved you as best she could given the circumstances."

"She did what she could," he whispers, blowing out a tremulous breath, before eying the empty bowl smeared with cake batter.

"Do you want a taste?" I ask, offering him the wooden spoon. "Don't worry you'll be fine. I grew up licking the bowl and spoon clean and I'm still here," I add when he hesitates.

"That's not what I was thinking," he replies, canting his head at me.

"What were you thinking?"

"You really want to know?" he asks, his warm fingers brushing against my hand as he takes the spoon from me, licking a little of the batter. He hums with appreciation at the taste.

"Yes," I reply, a little breathlessly if I'm honest.

Reaching for me, he takes my hand and tugs me towards him, a sexy smile pulling up his lips as he grasps the neckline of my t-shirt, his knuckles brushing against my nipple. That simple touch makes my core contract, heat pooling between my legs.

"I want to spread this all over your breasts and lick them clean," he admits. "Can I?"

I nod, my breath hitching as he swipes some of the cake batter between my cleavage, before leaning forward, his hot mouth and wet tongue sweeping across my skin.

"God, Drix," I shudder, my body reacting to his touch.

"You said baking makes you happy. Well, seeing you happy makes me so damn hard, Lia. Can I fuck you?"

The way the words trip off his tongue feel like hungry flames across my skin. I nod. "Please, Drix. Please, fuck me."

"Take your clothes off," he demands, his voice gruff as he rests the spoon back in the bowl.

"Shouldn't we go upstairs?" I counter, biting on my lip.

"I have a feeling this might get a little messy," he replies, reaching for the hem of my t-shirt and easing it upwards. "Now, be a good girl and strip for me."

Heat rushes from the tips of my toes to the top of my head. No one has ever called me a good girl. *This man.*

With trembling fingers, I help him to remove my t-shirt, placing it on the counter. He groans, his mouth immediately finding my nipple through my lace bra as he reaches behind me and unhooks it. Within moments, that too is discarded.

"The rest of your clothes too, Lia," he adds, watching me as I peel off my leggings, knickers and socks. I stumble a little, heat flooding my cheeks with embarrassment as he steadies me with a hand on my elbow.

"Sorry, I'm not being very seductive," I murmur, acutely aware that in the broad light of day, there's no hiding my flaws as I stand bare before him. A momentary feeling of embarrassment comes over me, but it doesn't last long, not when he's looking at me like I'm good enough to eat.

"Don't ever apologise to me for being so perfectly *real*. It's one of the things I love most about you."

"It is?" I whisper.

"Lia, I don't want a fake, vacuous woman. I've been there, done that, and it left me fucking empty. What I want is you. Real, honest, naturally beautiful. I want to feast on a body that has curves and dips, that's rounded and soft. I want to fuck a woman who isn't afraid to feed her body, who has scars and stretch marks, dimples and grooves that I can lick, kiss and worship. There's nothing about you I don't love."

"You really know how to flatter a woman, don't you?" I say

with a soft smile, his words healing those parts of me broken by a man who thrived on making me feel ugly.

"It's God's honest truth. Fuck, Lia, I want to do so many dirty things to you," he grinds out as he grabs the wooden spoon once more and presses it against my breasts, trailing cake mix over my nipples and lower down towards my aching pussy.

"I want you too. I want you to do dirty things to me, Drix," I reply, my clit pulsing as he flips the wooden spoon around and angles the handle downwards, gently pressing it against my clit.

"Jesus," I whimper, finding myself rocking against the smooth wood.

"I'm going to make you come with the handle of this spoon, Lia. Then I'm going to spread you across this counter and lick every single drop of batter off you," he continues, rubbing me delicately.

"We might need to buy a new spoon," I whisper, my cheeks flushing as a moan parts my lips and wetness floods my pussy.

"I'll buy you anything you want," he replies, adding a little more pressure. "I'd do anything for you, doll." Our gazes meet, and his free hand finds my hip as he urges me to rock against the spoon. "But first I want to see you flush that pretty pink knowing it's me who's turning you on, knowing you're mine."

"God, Drix," I moan, gripping his shoulders and throwing my head back as I let the sensation take over.

What we're doing is filthy, it's erotic, and it isn't long before my chest is heaving and my clit is pulsing, an oncoming orgasm building deep inside of me. Just when I'm on the precipice, Drix drops the spoon and pushes back the stool, kneeling before me.

"Come on my face, Lia. Flood my tongue with your cum," he demands, lifting my thigh over his shoulder so he can press his mouth against me.

I grip the counter, and the second his lips close around my clit, sucking on it, my orgasm barrels out of me and I'm clutching his head to me, riding his face, jerking against him.

"Drix. Oh my God!" I scream.

He groans, his tongue flicking against my clit, drawing out the pleasure until stars glimmer behind my closed eyelids and I shudder against his face. He doesn't give me a chance to recover, because the next moment he's standing, lifting me off my feet and dropping me on the edge of the counter.

The cool surface makes me suck in a breath as he says, "Don't move."

Half a minute later, the counter is cleared, and he's standing between my parted thighs, his hands on my hips as he stares at me with an intensity that makes my breath catch and my heart stutter.

"Lia, I want you to know that the man I am with you is who I *truly* am. I'm more myself with you than I am with anyone else."

"I believe you," I say, folding my arms around him and pressing a kiss against the base of his neck, feeling his pulse thunder against my lips.

"You make me want to be a better man," he continues, his hand sliding up my back as his fingers curl into my hair. Tugging gently, he urges me to look at him. "When I'm with you the past doesn't hurt as much. I can see a future for us, Lia. I want it so fucking bad."

"Drix..." I begin, but he quiets me with a gentle press of a kiss against my lips. A kiss that soon turns from searching and languid into heated and desperate.

TWENTY-FIVE

"FUCK, I need to be inside of you," I mutter against Lia's mouth, my fingers tangling into her hair, pulling on the strands as my free hand strokes down her chest, cupping her breast, the cake batter sticky beneath my fingers.

Lowering my head, I duck down, licking at the sweetness, the taste exploding in my mouth as I slide my tongue over her skin. She moans, her hands flying to my head, pressing me against her as I cup her breasts and suck her flesh into my mouth, my fucking cock aching with need.

"Don't stop," she cries, and I smile against her skin, so fucking happy I could burst.

A sharp stab of guilt penetrates my heart, but I ignore it. I don't want to think about what will happen when I tell her the truth, I can only live in this moment now, and by fuck, I'm going to enjoy it. Does that make me selfish? Yes, but a part of me is hoping that by the time I do tell her the truth about me, she'll know me well enough that she doesn't need to fear me, that she'll realise what I do is out of obligation, not because I'm a sick bastard like her ex.

Following the trail of cake batter, I lick her clean as she moans, her legs widening, her core pressing against the hard ridge of my jeans as I reach up and press my palm against the top of her chest.

"Lie back for me, Lia," I command, my voice guttural even to my own ears.

Slowly Lia eases herself back, her cheeks tinted with spots of pink as she rests back against the counter. My gaze trails over her beautiful body, my hands following the movement as I grasp her breasts, then slide my palms lower, coasting over her stomach, before resting on the inside of her trembling thighs.

"Spread your legs. Let me look at you." I coax, my voice laced with desire.

With eager compliance, Lia spreads her legs, revealing her perfect pink pussy to me. It glistens from her earlier arousal, the centre a deeper pink that drives me wild with want. My cock throbs painfully in my pants, begging for oblivion in her tight cunt.

"You're fucking beautiful," I mutter, tracing my fingers against her delicate skin. She gasps when I dip a finger inside of her, pumping languidly in and out whilst I watch her face contort with pleasure. Every moan and whimper fuels the fire burning within me.

"Please, Drix," she begs, arching her back, causing her breasts to bounce enticingly. My mouth waters to taste them again, my dick leaking pre-cum in anticipation. Reluctantly I remove my finger from her pussy, and she lets out a needy whimper.

"Look at me," I grind out, lifting my finger to my mouth as she blinks up at me, her pupils dilating as I suck my finger into my mouth, tasting her arousal. "Fucking delicious."

Releasing my fingers with a pop, I deftly undo my zipper, freeing my cock from its confines as I push my jeans and boxers down over my thighs, kicking them free.

"Look at what you do to me," I say, fisting my cock, pumping up and down whilst her eyes remain fixed on me, heavy lidded and hungry as I stroke myself slowly, relishing in the way she drinks me in. "I'm so hard for you."

"Drix, stop teasing me," she whispers, her lips glistening as she licks them in anticipation.

Fuck, what I wouldn't do to have her lips around my dick, but first I need to sink inside of her. I need to lose myself in the warm embrace of her cunt, to feel the bliss of her tight walls clenching around me as we fuck each other into oblivion.

"The other night we made love," I remind her, the memory of our passionate encounter still fresh in my mind. "It was the single most perfect experience of my damn life. But..." I pause, letting the tension build before continuing.

"But?" she whispers, her chest heaving.

"Now I'm going to fuck you. *Hard.*"

She sucks in a breath at my promise. Desire and a glimmer of fear scattering across her features.

"I won't hurt you, Lia," I add. "Everything I'm about to do is with your pleasure in mind. I want you to feel every inch of my cock whilst I'm fucking you, and I want you to fall into mind-numbing bliss when you come with my release filling your pussy. I want you to feel the weight of my love knowing that there isn't another man on Earth who can make you feel the way I do. I want you to go to sleep tonight with a desperate ache between your legs, and when you wake up tomorrow I want you to know that there will never be a man who will love you like I do, that no matter what, you're safe with me."

"I'm not afraid, Drix. Just fuck me," she demands.

"Oh doll, those dirty words are music to my ears," I growl, grabbing her hips and pulling her to the edge of the counter. She's at the perfect height for me to slide into her, and I swipe the head of my cock over her clit, the sensitive slit of my dick hugging her nub.

Then, with my fingers curled into her hips, I slam into her

right up to the hilt, the force driving her back across the counter. She gasps as I let out a primal roar, and with my body curled over hers, I fuck her just like I promised I would. Pounding into her, my hips piston, ramming, rutting as I let go. She screams, clawing at my back, her nails drawing tracks across my skin as she anchors herself to me, her legs wrapping around my arse, holding me tight.

"Yes, Drix. Yes, fuck me like that," she cries, her breasts pressing against my chest as she bites down on my shoulder.

But it's not enough. I need to be deeper. Pulling back, I draw myself out of her, my cock glistening with her juices, the head a dark, angry red.

"Feet on the floor," I command, dragging her off the counter and gripping her by the hips before pressing a rough kiss against her lips. She lets out a startled gasp as I twist her around, so she's facing away from me, then I press my lips against her ear and roughly say, "Bend over, chest on the counter, Lia. I want to go deep. I want you screaming my name so damn loud everyone will know you're mine."

She nods as I release her, her cheek and chest pressing against the cool surface, her peachy arse, wide hips and thick thighs fucking bliss to look at.

"Like this?" she asks, looking back at me.

"Just like that, doll," I reply, smoothing my palms down her back and across her beautiful arse.

"Widen your legs."

She shifts her feet, giving me a perfect view of her slit, the tight hole of her arse and dripping pussy making this feral kind of need rise up in my chest. Grabbing my dick I press against her hole, intending to ease inside of her, but she drives back against me, taking me to the hilt.

The air in my lungs escapes with a rough breath, and I know at that moment she can take what I'm about to give her.

Without a second thought I pull back and slam into her, over and over and over again. Fucking blind with need to claim her, to keep her, to make her come. Her back arches on a scream as she takes me, her soft arse cushioning my roughness.

"Fuck, Lia! Fuuuuccccckkkk!" I roar, my balls tightening, a rush of adrenaline and endorphins flooding my system as we fuck.

She matches my energy, slamming back against me as I ram into her. Reaching for her hair, I grip a handful, anchoring her body, driving into her with ravenous, unquenchable need until my balls draw tight against my body and this wild tsunami of pleasure builds in the base of my spine.

"Come for me, Lia. Come for me before I blow my load in your spectacular cunt," I grind out, drawing in sharp breaths as I try to stave off my impending orgasm.

"Fuck me harder then!" she commands, and damn, if I didn't already love this woman, I would've well and truly fallen in that moment.

Giving her what she wants, I drive into her, oblivious to everything but the way her internal muscles squeeze my cock, and how she feels so damn perfect beneath me bent over and spread wide.

"I'm coming," she cries out, her pussy clenching tight, milking my cock, and that's all it takes for me to lose control over my body. Hot cum spurts from my dick as I pulse inside of her, my body jerking as I fold over her, fucking mindless as my orgasm takes hold.

"Fuck, fuck, fuck," I mutter, breathless, boneless, fucking overcome with this intense feeling of love as I cover her body with mine, my cock still jerking deep inside of her as I kiss her cheek, her shoulder, the nape of her neck. "God, I fucking love you."

"Drix, I can't breathe," she laughs, placing her palms flat on the counter and pushing upwards.

"Shit, fuck. Sorry!" I exclaim, sliding my arm beneath her stomach and drawing us both upright.

My legs buckle a little, and I laugh. "God dammit woman, you've made my knees weak."

"You and me both," she replies as I ease out of her, our combined arousal sliding down her thighs as I turn her in my arms and cup her face, pressing kisses over her face.

"Are you okay?" I ask, my chest heaving as I try to steady my own racing heart. It beats as fast as a wild stallion running free.

"I feel thoroughly and blissfully fucked," she replies, a sweet laugh parting her kiss-bruised lips.

I swallow her joy with my mouth, kissing her until we're both ready to lose ourselves in each other again.

"THAT SMELLS AMAZING!" Daisy says as she enters the kitchen a couple of hours later.

Her eyes are bright, her cheeks tinged pink from the cold. Outside the snow begins to fall heavily, and I'm grateful to Dalton for getting them home safe.

"We've set the table in the dining room, I thought we could all eat there today," I reply as I begin to carve the roast beef that has been resting for the last half an hour. Lia places the roasted, honey-drenched carrots and parsnips into a dish next to the fluffiest, crispiest roast potatoes I've ever laid eyes on. My stomach rumbles, and I grin. Lia and I have most definitely worked up an appetite, that's for certain, and part of the reason we're eating in the dining room is that despite thoroughly cleaning the kitchen island after fucking on top of it, I could do with eating dinner without a raging hard on at the memory.

"Sure," Daisy replies as Toby comes running into the kitchen holding the biggest, cuddly toy unicorn I've ever seen. It's bright blue with a silver horn and tiny white stars embroidered into its soft body.

"Look what Dalton won for me!" he exclaims, practically tripping over the thing as he stumbles into the room.

"Wow! That's a gorgeous unicorn," Lia exclaims, reaching for him and taking the toy from his arms before giving him a hug.

"Won it on the first attempt," Dalton explains, leaning against the door frame as he watches Lia interact with Toby. "Looks like I am good for something," he adds, sliding his gaze to Daisy who pointedly ignores him.

"So you had a nice time then?" Lia asks Toby, but I'm pretty sure the question is aimed at Daisy who is removing her coat and avoiding answering.

"We had the *best* time ever!" Toby says, hopping on his feet as he reaches for the unicorn once again. "I'm going to put it in my room!"

With that he rushes out of the kitchen, leaving the adults to deal with the tension that's left behind. Jesus, I could cut it with a knife. So much for the intervention.

"You're staying for dinner, right?" I ask Dalton, who looks more than a little uncomfortable.

He shakes his head, pushing off from the door frame. "I should head off before the snow gets too heavy and I can't get home."

"You can stay here for the night. Wait for the roads to get cleared in the morning?" I suggest. "There's so much food, we'll need some help getting through it." Lia adds.

"He said he wanted to go, let him go," Daisy says, giving him a look that confirms my plan for them to at least call a truce had failed miserably. Dalton slides his gaze to her and she stares at him unflinchingly, a challenge in her gaze.

"You know what, I think I'll stay. I'm off work tomorrow anyway before things get too busy with Robert's wedding."

Daisy huffs out a breath, shaking her head as she storms towards him. "Coat," she demands, holding her hand out.

He gives her a dazzling smile. "Thank you, Daisy," he says, pulling off his woollen coat and handing it to her.

"Oh shut up," she grouses, snatching it from him and storming off down the hallway.

"I think I'll go check on... Toby," Lia says, eying me. I'm pretty sure that's code for *'talk to Dalton, find out what went on'*. "Would you mind taking everything through to the dining room once you've finished carving the meat? I'll only be gone for a moment."

"Of course," I agree, waiting for her to leave before I question my best friend.

Dalton walks towards me, swiping a hand through his hair. "Lia's good for you," he observes.

"Don't try to change the subject. I take it you and Daisy are still at war?"

"I tried," he replies with a shrug, grabbing a slither of meat and stuffing it into his mouth. "Damn that's good."

"Well?" I insist, refusing to let this go.

"What can I say, she still hates me."

"Daisy doesn't hate anyone," I say, knowing that in his case, that isn't exactly true.

Dalton barks out a laugh. "Except for me..." he replies, his voice trailing off as he frowns.

"Look, I get why you did what you did. Firing the arsehole was a kindness because if I'd have gotten hold of him, I'd have kicked his arse."

"There's a but in there somewhere," Dalton assesses.

"*But,*" I continue, "Dropping that bombshell in front of a restaurant full of people wasn't the smartest move, mate."

"She antagonised me," he replies, but he has the good grace to look guilty.

"Even so. That was a shitty thing to do," I point out.

"I tried to apologise, but she just accused me of being a fraud.

Said I needed to take a long hard look at myself before interfering with her love life."

"She's got a point," I say.

"Don't start acting holier than thou with me, Drix. You're just as bad when it comes to the men she dates."

"Yeah, but I'm her big brother, it comes with the territory. What's your excuse?"

Dalton grits his teeth, a muscle feathering in his jaw. It takes him a moment to respond, and I'm left wondering what, exactly, is the deal here.

"I've known Daisy as long as I've known you. I care about her, okay?"

"Care about her?" I question.

"Yeah, like a *sister*," he adds pointedly. "Don't go giving me that look. You've got no worries there."

"Hey, I have an invested interest in Daisy's happiness, and you, my friend, are not for her."

"Did I say I was?" he snaps.

"So what's the deal then?"

"It pisses me off that she chooses the wrong guy every single time. I don't get it. She's not fucking stupid, but she sure acts that way."

"Thanks for that," Daisy snarks, stepping back into the kitchen as she glares at Dalton.

"I didn't mean—" Dalton begins, but Daisy cuts him off.

"I'm really not interested, Dalton. Just keep your opinions about me to yourself, stop interfering in things that don't concern you, and," she adds, glaring at me, "Stop trying to fix something that will never be repaired. Dalton is your friend, not mine. Stop trying to force us to like each other, because we're never going to get along, okay?"

"Daisy, he's my best friend and you're my sister," I protest. "I don't need you to be best mates, but a little civility would go a long way."

"I can be civil," Dalton offers.

"Really? So you'll stop being an infuriating oaf who sticks his nose in my business then?"

"If that's what you really want," he retorts.

"Are you joking? I don't need you to *look out for me,*" she replies with finger quotes. "What I need you to do is leave me the hell alone. Am I understood?"

"I hear you, loud and fucking clear," he snaps back. "But the next time someone breaks your heart don't come running to me for sympathy because you won't get any."

"I wouldn't fucking dream of it!" she shouts, storming over to the counter and picking up the dish filled with carrots and parsnips. "Now shut up, and gather the rest of the dishes. Lia and Drix have cooked us a beautiful meal and I won't let you ruin it for them."

With that she heads towards the dining room, taking her wrath with her.

I blow out a long breath. "Well, that went well."

TWENTY-SIX

IT'S CHRISTMAS EVE, and Toby, Drix, Daisy and I have all headed over to the shopping mall for some last minute gift buying. After a hectic few days of work, and juggling Toby between us, it's the first opportunity we've had to spend some quality time together.

Thanks to my part-time job, and not having to pay towards our keep, despite my insistence, I've managed to put aside enough money to gather a small nest egg and buy Toby some presents. For the first time in a long while I'm really looking forward to Christmas. One way or another, Martin had always managed to spoil Christmas, so this time I want to make sure it's special. It isn't about the presents themselves, more the act of giving and being surrounded by people who I adore, and who care about me and Toby deeply.

"Mama, is that *Santa's* grotto?" Toby asks me, stalling as he points to the cute set up in the centre of the mall. The wooden shed has been decorated with fairy lights and Christmas decorations, whilst two women dressed as elves are entertaining the children lined up waiting to see Santa.

"It sure looks like it," I agree, eying the long cue and wondering whether we have time for a visit.

"Can I see him? Can I?" Toby asks, tugging on my hand.

"Santa looks very busy," Drix observes, a soft smile spreading across his face as he absorbs Toby's excitement. "But I reckon he's got time for another special little kid before he needs to gather his reindeer and start delivering presents."

I wince, looking at the hoards of people and the queues in every store.

"I can take him," Daisy offers, noticing my hesitation. "I mean, if you don't mind?"

"Are you sure?" It's not that I don't want to, it's just I haven't got anything for Toby yet and I really don't want him to wake up on Christmas morning without at least a few gifts.

"Yep, I've got everything I need anyway. I was just coming along for the fun of it. Get in the Christmas spirit and all. This will be the perfect opportunity to do that."

"Thank you. I'd appreciate it."

"Sure thing! Come on then, Tobes, let's meet Santa!"

Before I'm able to reply, they've disappeared into the crowd and have joined the back of the queue.

"Pretty sure Toby would happily follow Daisy anywhere she'd go," I say, smiling.

"He adores her," Drix replies, sliding his hand into mine, tugging me towards the toy store.

"Toby adores you too," I say as we step into the store and are confronted with rows upon rows of toys. There are shelves stacked with handmade wooden toys, puzzles and boardgames, soft toys and electronics, dolls and action men. Not to mention a whole section dedicated to Funko Pops.

Drix's eyes light up when he sees them, and I can't help but grin. "This must be heaven for you."

"Heaven is wherever you are, doll," he replies with a wide grin.

By the time we've finished, my hands are full of bags filled with toys for Toby. Drix reaches for them, taking them off me.

"I'll take them to the car. Go find Daise and Toby, and I'll meet you at the coffee bar in ten minutes?" he suggests, leaning in to brush a soft kiss against my lips.

"Thank you," I murmur, and before he's able to slip away, I grip his arm and whisper. "Drix, Toby isn't the only one who adores you. I adore you too."

Our eyes lock and my heart stutters at the look of absolute devotion in his eyes. "The feeling's mutual, doll," he says, before turning on his heel and slipping out of sight.

Even though we hadn't talked about getting a gift for one another, I want to do that for Drix, so I head back into the store, and towards the counter that says 'design your own Funko Pop', grinning widely when the shopkeeper explains what I need to do.

"MAYBE WE SHOULD GO FIND HIM?" Daisy says, looking out of the cafe window at the crowd of people passing by. "It's been almost forty-five minutes. It shouldn't take that long to drop stuff off at the car."

We've already drunk our own coffee and Toby is getting restless. The one I bought for Drix is now stone cold. "Is he still not answering his phone?" I ask, an edge of concern coursing through my veins.

"No. It keeps going to voicemail. Probably ran out of battery or something."

"Okay, let's see if we can find him. Perhaps he got caught up with someone, and lost track of time?" I suggest, ignoring the churning feeling in my stomach.

"Yeah, must be that," Daisy replies, giving me a worried look.

After checking all the other eating establishments and the

stores Daisy suggested looking in, Drix is nowhere to be found and my anxiety is steadily growing. It's not like Drix to just up and disappear without at least calling first.

"Let's head out to the car. Perhaps we went to the wrong cafe and he couldn't find us so is waiting for us there?" Daisy says as we step outside into the wintry air. Snow is falling once again, adding to the chill scattering down my spine.

"Is that an ambulance?" Daisy whispers, her attention caught by the flashing lights and the bright yellow truck on the other side of the car park. "You don't think...?"

My gaze follows her, my heart lurching.

"Wait here with Toby," I say, shoving my shopping bag at her and running towards the ambulance before she's even able to respond.

By the time I reach the ambulance, my mind has already gone to a dark place. Thoughts of Drix hurt and in pain have my eyes welling with tears.

"Drix!" I shout, recognising his leather boots and jean-clad legs as he lies on the gurney in the back of the ambulance. He's partly obscured by the paramedic, but that doesn't stop me from pushing my way into the back of the ambulance. "What happened?" I ask, my hands trembling as I reach for him, noticing immediately the bandage wrapped around his head, blood seeping through the material at his temple. He appears to be unconscious.

"You need to step out of the vehicle whilst I attend to him," the paramedic says.

"I'm not going anywhere," I snap back, gently touching Drix's cheek with my fingers. He doesn't even react to my touch. "Tell me what happened."

"We're not sure. Got a call saying that a man with a head injury was needing assistance. Nasty gash on his head. It will need a few stitches, I'm sure. Can you give me his name?"

"Drix Hammer. Hendrix Hammer is his full name," I correct.

"And you are?" the paramedic asks, jotting the details down on his pad before checking Drix's vitals on the machine. It makes a regular beeping noise, and whilst I'm not a medical professional, his pulse rate appears to be steady.

"Miss?" the paramedic prompts, eying me.

"I'm the woman who loves him," I reply instantly, feeling that love squeeze my heart in a frantic embrace.

"Lia?" Drix mutters, his eyes blinking as I snap my head back around, leaning over him.

"Drix. Oh my God, you scared me to death!"

"You love me?" he retorts, a smirk pulling up his lips.

The paramedic laughs. "Looks like your secret's out."

"I thought you said he had a concussion!" I accuse the paramedic, shaking my head as the tears pooling in my eyes slide down my cheeks.

"Pretty sure I said nothing of the sort, though given the details from the passerby who found him, it seems as though he did lose consciousness for a while," the paramedic replies, winking at Drix who smiles up at him.

"You were pretending just now?" I accuse, swiping at my tears, laughing despite everything.

He shrugs. "I was just resting my eyes."

"Don't do that to me ever again!" I half-shout, half-sob.

"Come here," he says, holding his arms out and I fall against his chest, pressing my lips against his neck, internally cursing him for scaring the crap out of me.

"I thought something terrible had happened to you," I whisper, the anger quickly subsiding and replaced with a swell of love that almost takes my breath away.

"Slipped and fell on some damn ice after I dropped off Toby's presents in the car. By the time I came too, the ambulance was here and my phone had run out of battery. I'm sorry I scared you."

"You should be more careful!" I scold him, without any heat

behind it as I nestle in his arms, completely oblivious to everything else apart from how warm he feels, how alive, how very, very mine.

"A man could get used to this," he says, pressing his mouth against the top of my head, his strong arms holding me tight.

"What, cracking your head open, ending up in an ambulance, and scaring the shit out of me?" I counter, pushing upwards so I can look down at him.

"No," he replies, brushing his lips against mine. "Hearing the love of my life admit that she loves me back."

"Oh that," I say, letting out a quiet laugh.

"So you love me then?"

I nod. "Have since you showed me your Fred Flinstone."

"So that's what did it?" he grins. "I knew it would come in handy one day. Funko Pops for the win."

"I wasn't talking about *that* Fred Flinstone," I reply, pressing my lips against his and kissing him deeply.

The paramedic clears his throat and we pull apart, breathless, happy, in love. "We should get you to the hospital. You need stitches and a CT scan just in case," he says.

"Let me just call Daisy and tell her what's happened," I say, reaching for my bag.

"No need. I think we got the gist of it," Daisy says as the paramedic steps aside.

She's standing at the foot of the ambulance, Toby in her arms, a wide grin on her face. "Talk about attention seeking," she says, chuckling. "You should win an Oscar for that performance."

"Funny," he replies.

"Are you okay, Drix?" Toby asks, his little face crumpling with worry.

"It'll take more than some ice to finish me off, buddy. I'll be just fine," Drix replies, giving him a wave.

"Would you take Toby home? I'll go to the hospital with Drix," I say, thinking ahead.

"No problem," Daisy agrees, turning her attention to the paramedic. "Just make sure they sew him up well. I can't have my brother's beautiful face ruined with shoddy work."

"I'll be sure to pass that on."

By the time we get home, it's gone eight, Toby's tucked up in bed and Daisy is waiting for us in the living room with four cups of cocoa on the coffee table.

"Thanks, Dalton. I appreciate you dropping us home," Drix says as he plonks down on the stool, Dalton taking the armchair opposite Daisy. When I called him to explain what happened he insisted on picking us up and dropping us home.

"Of course, I couldn't resist the opportunity to call you Bambi," he replies with a mocking grin.

"Bambi?" Daisy asks, then realisation dawns and she giggles. "Oh, you mean the scene where he slips and slides on the ice."

"Yep," Dalton replies, popping the p and chuckling to himself. "Wish I'd been a fly on the wall when you dropped, Drix. I'm still laughing at the thought."

"Well, I'm glad I could be of amusement, you arsehole," Drix grumbles back, and we all laugh, even Drix.

"Thank you, Lia, for going with Drix to the hospital," Daisy says as the laughter dies down. "He means a lot to me."

"He means a lot to me too," I say, reaching for Drix's hand and squeezing it gently.

"And thank you, Dalton, for getting him home safe. I appreciate it," Daisy adds, flicking her gaze to Dalton who nods.

"Of course." He gives her a gentle smile, and this time she smiles back.

"Well, shit, if I'd known all it would take is a crack to my head to get you two to be friends, I would've done it sooner," Drix says, chuckling.

"Hey, I wouldn't go as far as friends," Daisy pipes up, her cheeks flooding with heat. "At best we're *frenemies,* and only for the Christmas period. I've no doubt he'll do something to piss me off,and we'll be back to hating each other after the festivities are over."

"I can do frenemies," Dalton says, reaching for his mug of cocoa and taking a sip.

Drix yawns, swiping at his face. "As much as I'd like to sit here and dissect your annoying as fuck relationship, I really just want to sleep. Are you good to drive home?" he asks Dalton.

"Of course. I'll just finish my drink first if that's alright?"

"Sure, mate," he replies, glancing at me. "Bed?"

My cheeks heat at the offer. "I think we've all had enough fun for one day," I reply, but take his hand nonetheless, standing with him.

"Watch out, Lia," Dalton says with a smirk. "Drix will be using this accident to garner sympathy at every opportunity. Don't fall for it."

"It's too late for that, I've already fallen," I reply, throwing Drix a warm smile.

"Good luck with that," Dalton replies, winking at Drix so he knows he means no harm, though I suspect that there's a whole host of complicated reasons why the idea of love is so offensive to him.

"You know, you should try it sometime. You might even like it," I add, pointedly looking at Daisy who has suddenly found the flickering flames in the hearth more than a little interesting.

"Nah, love isn't for me," he says with a shrug.

"No, you just love the temporary rush of fucking without any emotion attached, isn't that right, Dalton?" Daisy interjects, but there's a lot less anger behind her words.

Drix rolls his eyes. "That'll be our cue to leave."

Half an hour later, Drix has fallen fast asleep, the events of the day wearing him out. Instead of joining him in bed, I go to check on Toby who is cuddled up to his toy unicorn, still wearing a santa's hat. Undressing out of my clothes, I pull on my pyjamas and slip into bed behind him, hugging him back against my chest.

"I think we've found a home here, Toby," I whisper against his cheek, knowing that I'm utterly in love with Drix Hammer, and he's in love with us too, but completely unaware that in just a few days time that love will be tested to its limits.

TWENTY-SEVEN

SURROUNDED by a heap of wrapping paper, and watching Toby bubbling over with happiness as he stares at his gifts, I grin, feeling that same joy buzzing inside of me. Christmas morning has never felt so special, and despite Toby getting us all up at six am, I don't need a coffee to wake me up like I usually do. Right here and now, this feeling is all I need to keep me energised.

"Look at all my things!" Toby says, grabbing Lego set Lia bought him at the toy store yesterday, his eyes are like saucers as he stares at the dinosaur on the front. "It's a diplodocus!"

"It sure is. I can help you build it later if you want?" I offer, glancing over at Lia who smiles gently.

"Yes please!" he replies, jumping up and dropping himself in my lap. He curls into me, his cheek pressing against my chest as he lets out a happy little sigh as I hug him close.

God, I love this kid.

"What about your presents?" Toby asks me.

"You being this happy is my gift, kid," I reply, bopping his nose with my finger as I glance over at Lia. "And having the love of your Ma."

"Ahhh! Drix Hammer, you big softy," Daisy says, her eyes sparkling as she wraps an arm around Lia's shoulder and hugs her. "You two are goals."

"It's the honest truth. I'm so damn happy," I reply.

"Me too, Drix," Lia says, her smile the best fucking present I could receive.

"Well, I probably can't match the gift of love in quite the same way," Daisy says after a beat, "But I can give you this."

Reaching behind her she pulls out a present, and passes it to me, a mischievous look on her face. At Christmas we tend to buy each other novelty presents, nothing too expensive, but meaningful nonetheless. The box she hands me is similar in size and shape to Funko Pop packaging. I grin, and say, "I wonder what this is?"

"You'll just have to open it and see!"

Toby hops off my lap, and sits down beside Lia, and the three of them watch me unwrap Daisy's present. As per usual it's wrapped in brown paper covered in hand drawn artwork. This time it's Christmas trees. She does it every year, personalising the wrapping paper with her terrible art. She doesn't know it, but I've kept every single sheet of wrapping paper ever since our first Christmas after we were adopted together, the wrapping almost more special to me than the gift itself. Last year it was snowmen, the year before holly, the year before fat little Santa's with stick arms and legs.

"Just rip it!" Toby yells, bouncing on Lia's lap as he watches me.

"I don't want to tear the paper and ruin Daisy's lovely artwork," I reply with a wink, pulling at the sellotape carefully, then resting the paper on the side table next to me so I can put it away later when she isn't looking.

When my eyes land on the object inside I chuckle. "This is the most ridiculous present ever," I say, holding up the box to show Lia and Toby the contents. "But I love it. Thank you, Daise. Every year I'll be reminded of what a handsome man I am."

Daisy bursts out laughing as Lia and Toby stare at the Christmas tree bauble inside. My face has been printed onto the surface but disguised as the Grinch, and because it's spherical, my features are even more distorted. It's hysterical.

Lia's hand comes up to cover her smile as she giggles, and Toby's mouth drops open as he takes the box from me.

"You make a terrible elf," he says, frowning.

"That, my friend is *The Drinch*," I say, smirking.

Lia can no longer hold onto her laughter any longer, and Daisy loses it, cackling as she falls back on the sofa, tears streaming from her eyes. Pretty soon I'm joining in too.

Toby wrinkles his nose. "What's a Drinch?"

"He means a Drix the *Grinch*, so a Drinch" Daisy explains, pushing upright.

"I don't know what that is," Toby says, pulling a face.

"You've never seen The Grinch movie?" I ask.

Toby shakes his head. "No."

"Well then, after we've stuffed ourselves full of turkey and Christmas pudding, we're going to watch it together!"

"Yay!" Toby claps his hands, the box of Legos on his lap sliding to the floor. He jumps off Lia's lap and grabs it. "Can we build this now?"

"Give me a minute, kid. I've got some presents to hand out first," I say, getting up as I head to the cabinet on the other side of the room to grab the hessian sack I'd stored inside of it. Pulling it free, I grab the Santa's hat I left next to it, and put it on. "Ho, ho, ho."

"You're such a dork," Daisy remarks with a snort.

"I thought it matched my outfit," I shrug, looking down at my red flannelette pyjamas as I settle back on the sofa. Dipping my hand into the sack, I reach for Toby's present first. "Here you go, buddy," I say, handing it to him.

"Drix, that's so kind," Lia says softly.

"There was no way I wasn't getting my little pal a present."

"We got you one too!" Toby exclaims taking his gift from me and plonking on the floor.

"You did?" I ask Lia.

"Of course," she replies, biting on her lips as her cheeks flush pink.

Our eyes meet and I hold her gaze, desperately wanting to drag her in my arms and give her more than a chaste Christmas kiss. Heat flickers in her eyes, and I clear my throat, internally begging my twitching cock not to embarrass me.

"So, what do you think?" I ask Toby as he pulls the last of the wrapping paper off to reveal a pair of rollerskates.

He gasps. "I've always wanted these, but Mama always said it was too dangerous!"

I pull a face. "I'm sorry, I should've checked with you first."

Lia shakes her head. "No, don't apologise. They're perfect. I'm sure with practice, he'll be just fine."

"I was planning on helping you to learn how to skate," I say to Toby. "I thought you could use the hallway to practise before we head outside. When the snow finally clears, of course."

"Thank you, thank you, thank you!" Toby exclaims, jumping up, and throwing himself into my arms. A breath whooshes out of my chest, partly from his exuberance, and partly from being so overwhelmed by his affection. I wrap my arms around him, hugging him close.

"You're so welcome," I mutter.

Eventually he untangles himself, peering at the sack as I reach for Daisy's present next. Grabbing the tiny box, I pass it to her. "Merry Christmas, Daise," I say.

"Ooooohhh, what's this?" she asks, her fingers running over the box as she tears off the paper. Within seconds she's popped the lid and is reaching for the necklace inside. It's a rose gold chain with a unicorn pendant that has tiny diamonds embedded in its body. There are matching earrings too. She lifts her gaze to meet mine. "You said token gifts, Drix! This isn't a token gift."

"I saw it months back in the jewellery store and knew you'd love it," I say with a shrug. "Besides, there isn't anything I need, and I happen to love your present. So we're good."

Jumping up, Daisy steps over the pile of wrapping paper and bends down to give my cheek a kiss. "You are a sneaky bugger. I love it. *Thank you.*"

As she settles back down, I suddenly feel extremely nervous. Lia's gift is last, and I'm having second thoughts about my decision to give her it. But not giving it to her now would look even more suspicious. Dragging in a breath, I reach inside the sack and pull out the box, passing it to her. It's pretty heavy, given the contents.

"I happened across these at a consignment store. I think they're, well..." my voice trails off, I really hadn't thought this through all that well. I just sure hope she believes my story.

Lia frowns, her smile wavering a little as she tries to get a read on me. "Are you alright, Drix?"

"Maybe you should just open it," I mumble.

Her eyes drop to the present on her lap, and she starts to pull at the paper, Toby watches her, enraptured. When she lifts the lid on the box, her eyes widen and she gasps as she reaches inside the box and pulls out the first recipe book. She places it next to her on the sofa, grabbing each of the recipe books in turn. There are five in total. The last one is the one that has her mum's handwritten note, a note I've memorised having read it several times over.

To my dear Lia, when you bake with love, that love will feed the hungry with more than just sweetness, Love Mum.

"How?" she whispers, blinking back the tears welling in her eyes.

"That night at Bandits, when I got Toby's pyjamas from your car, I noticed that recipe book in a box nestled behind the driver's seat. It was sitting on top," I say, pointing to the one she's holding now, the one with her mother's handwritten note. At least that part of my story is true, I *did* see it then. What she doesn't know is that I kept them all in my flat since the night Fraser stole her car. Guilt surges inside of me, but I ignore it, pushing on. "I happened to be passing the consignment store in town a week or so ago, and saw it displayed in the window. So, I went inside, and asked to look at it. When I opened it up and read the note, I knew it belonged to you."

"And the others?" she asks, "They're *all* mine."

"I asked the shop assistant about it, she said that the recipe book was brought in with some others at the same time, so I put two and two together, and bought them all."

"Drix this is..." her voice cracks, and she shakes her head. *"Thank you."*

"It's nothing," I reply, clearing my throat, hating the fact I'm lying to her, *again*.

"It's *everything*." Placing the recipe book on top of the others she leans over and presses a kiss against my lips. *"You're everything."*

"Lia, I—"

But my response is smothered with her lips on mine, and I'm lost to the sweetness of her kiss, a kiss that turns more intense as the seconds pass. We only pull apart when Daisy clears her throat.

"Not to spoil your fun, but there's a kid in the room," she reminds us with a wink.

"Gosh, sorry," Lia says, her cheeks flooding with heat.

"That's okay, Mama. I don't mind having a younger brother or sister," Toby says with a grin.

"A younger brother or sister?" I ask, chuckling.

"Yes, silly. Kissing makes babies," he replies.

Daisy snorts with laughter, but quickly recovers when Toby frowns. "I guess kissing *is* part of it."

Toby frowns, turning his attention to Lia. "But you said–"

Lia pulls a face. "There's a little bit more to it than that."

"Oh boy," I say, looking between the two and wondering how on Earth Lia is going to explain her way out of this.

"Why don't you grab Drix's present, sweetheart? It's still under the tree," Lia says, and the whole baby making conversation is forgotten as he claps his hands and turns on his feet, grabbing it from beneath the tree.

"This is for you!" he says proudly, handing me the gift.

"I wanted to get you something special," Lia says softly as she draws Toby onto her lap. "I hope you like it."

"It's from the two of you, of course I'll *love* it," I say, ripping open the wrapping with enthusiasm. When my eyes land on the four figures sitting inside the Funko Pop box, I'm rendered speechless momentarily. There's no mistaking who they are.

"That's you," Toby says, pointing to the largest one with blonde hair, brown eyes, wearing jeans and a brown jacket. There are even tiny drawn replicas of the love and hate tattoos I have inked across my knuckles. "This is me and Mama, and that is Daisy," he adds, pointing to each one in turn.

"*I'm a Funko Pop?*" Daisy asks, squealing as she leans over Lia's shoulder and grabs the box from my hand. "Look, I've even got a dress with unicorns on it. How did I not know about this?"

"The toy store had a section for personalised Funko Pops," Lia explains. "All I had to do was choose the right bodies and heads, and ask them to add the little details. Apparently it was a new idea they started this Christmas."

"Well, crap. You've totally earned the title of *best gift giver* this year! This is awesome, Lia. Isn't it, Drix?" she replies, handing the box back to me.

"It's the perfect gift, Lia," I say, meeting her gaze with mine, feeling this rush of love flooding my veins, and making my heart fucking soar.

"You know what is perfect?" she replies. "This. Us. I'm so happy, Drix."

"Me too, doll. Me too."

TWENTY-EIGHT

"SWEET DREAMS, MY DARLING," I murmur against Toby's temple as he sleeps peacefully.

Worn out from a magical day surrounded by people who adore him, he cuddles up to his toy unicorn. The Lego diplodocus that Drix helped him to build after dinner, sits on the side table next to the bed.

Happiness is a warm feeling in my chest, and for a moment I just enjoy how *good* that feels. I know that, eventually, I would've clawed back that happiness just being away from Martin and the toxic, abusive relationship I had with him, but I'm so glad that I chose to stop in this town, and not drive through it like I had so many others before. Call it serendipity, call it fate, either way, I'm so grateful to have met Drix, and Daisy. They've made both of our lives so much richer.

"Hey, doll, you okay?" Drix asks from the doorway, a pinafore wrapped around his waist after I left him and Daisy cleaning up in the kitchen so I could put Toby to bed.

The light from the hallway highlights his handsome features, and my heart stutters in my chest as he leans against the doorframe with a goofy smile on his face. Today, just like every day I've spent with him, he'd been so attentive, so present in the moment with us both, and that has been such a soothing balm to my healing heart.

"I'm really, really good, Drix," I reply, pushing to my feet as I stroll towards him, my bare feet sinking into the plush carpet. "Thank you for this beautiful day. You've made Toby so happy."

"And you?" he asks as he reaches for my hand, grasping it in his.

"I'm happy too."

He nods, brushing a stray strand of hair off my face, tucking it behind my ear, his thumb caressing my cheek. "I have something for you," he says softly.

"You do?"

"It's in my room…" he replies, his eyes sparkling with promise.

"What about Daisy?" I ask, laughing softly.

"This is a gift, Lia," he adds with a wry grin. "Besides, Daisy is in the den eating chocolate liqueurs and watching her favourite movie, Stardust. She won't notice our absence for a bit."

"But you've already given me a gift, Drix, and I'm not just talking about the recipe books. I don't need anything else but you."

"Even so, I wanted to get this for you. Will you come with me?" he asks, dropping his mouth to mine and brushing a sweet kiss against my lips.

"Yes," I reply, my insides turning liquid.

Taking my hand in his, we walk side by side to his bedroom. Inside he guides me to the bed, and I sit as he reaches for the bedside table, pulling open the top drawer. Grabbing a small silver gift bag from it, he sits down next to me.

Dragging in a breath, he hands me the gift bag and says, "I know that what we have is still so new, but I'm certain about how I feel for you, Lia. Believe it or not, I don't love people easily, but falling for you has been the easiest thing in the world. You and

Toby mean a great deal to me, and I wanted to get you something so you know how special you are."

"Drix, you've given me enough," I repeat.

"Please, just open it," he urges quietly.

Dropping my gaze to the gift bag, I untie the bow holding it together and pull out a small black velvet box. Placing the bag on the bed beside me, I open the lid with trembling fingers, the heat of Drix's gaze penetrating my skin.

"Drix this is a..." my voice trails off as I stare at the beautiful ring inside.

"It's a claddagh ring," he explains.

"What does this mean, exactly?" I ask him, my heart tripping in my chest.

"It doesn't have to mean anything other than what it is," he says gently.

"And what is that?" I whisper.

"The heart represents my love for you, the crown, my loyalty, and the hands, my friendship. You don't have to wear it, I just wanted you to have it. Call it a promise of sorts."

"A promise?"

"Yes. A promise that even if I fuck up," he explains, swallowing hard when I look at him, "That you will always know how loved you are."

"Drix this is—"

"Please, let me finish," he requests, resting his hand on my leg, my knee length skirt riding up a little from his touch. I shiver involuntarily, overwhelmed by the look of pure love in his eyes, but it isn't that which scares me the most, it's the whisper of fear that shadows it.

"Drix, what is it?"

Squeezing my leg gently, he continues. "I want you to know that I'd lay my life down for you and Toby. I'm so in love with you."

"Drix, why am I afraid?" I whisper, feeling like there's so much he isn't saying.

"I need you to know that you will *always* have my friendship, my love, and my protection."

"Is there something you're not telling me?" I ask.

For a moment, he presses his eyes shut and swipes a hand across his face. "This is so... *Fuck*, I can't..."

"Can't what?" I question, angling my body towards his, our knees touching as I reach for him, my fingers trailing up his arm.

"Can I ask you to bear with me?" he replies, meeting my gaze once more. "I want to explain, but I need more time."

His expression is so full of pain that I quieten all the questions burning inside of me, and nod instead. "I can give you that," I reply, trusting him not to hurt me, trusting my heart, believing in what we have.

"Thank you."

"Whatever's troubling you, I promise you we'll face it together."

He nods, dropping his eyes and reaching for the box, as though to set it aside. I shake my head, resting my hand over his. "I want to wear it," I say.

"You do?"

"I do."

Taking it from him, I reach inside for the ring and pull it free, sliding it onto the fourth finger of my left hand. It's a little too big, so I move it to my middle finger and it fits perfectly.

"I had to guess your ring size. I was a little concerned I might've got it wrong," he explains, tipping his lips up in a faint smile.

"It's perfect. Thank you," I whisper.

Grasping my hand, he brings it to his lips, pressing a kiss against the ring, his eyes never once leaving mine. "Will you let me love you?" he asks, and my breath catches as he presses another kiss against the back of my hand, then higher as he turns my hand in his and kisses the sensitive skin of my wrist.

"As long as you let me love you back," I reply, heat warming my cheeks.

"*Fuck yes*, Lia," he mutters against my skin.

Tingles rush down my spine, as he drags his mouth up the inside of my arm, whispering his lips against my elbow crease. My fingers curl into his hair as he moves his attention to my breasts, his hot mouth seeking out my nipple beneath the cotton of my shirt and lace of my bra.

He groans, his teeth grazing over the nub before sucking me into his mouth.

"God, Drix," I moan, heat pooling between my legs.

"I've been waiting all day to peel your clothes from your body," he admits, drawing back as he presses one last kiss against the back of my hand, resting it on my lap. "Fuck, you make me ache for you, Lia." His gaze drops to his lap, and his erection pushing against the confines of his jeans. "Look at how hard I am for you."

I reach for him, my fingers coasting over his erection. "Knowing how much you want me gives me so much confidence, Drix. You're not the only one aching to be touched," I say, reaching for the buckle of his belt and undoing it. He leans back on his hands, making it easier for me to free him.

"Touch me, Lia."

"Stay there," I command softly, pushing off the bed and dropping to my knees in front of him, resting my hands on his knees and urging him to make room for me.

"Fuck, Lia," he replies, his voice rumbling out of his chest as he stares down at me. "Look at you on your knees for me. So fucking beautiful."

"I want to make you feel as worshipped and adored as you've made me feel. I want to taste you."

Cupping my face, he slides the pad of his thumb across my

bottom lip. "I can't lie, I've thought about these plump lips wrapped around my cock. I've wondered how well you'd take me. If you'd lick me slowly, or suck me down deep."

"I've imagined it too," I admit, his mouth parting on a groan as I undo his zipper, grazing my fingers gently over his dick.

"Jesus," he mutters, his cock jerking against my hand.

"These need to come off," I say, reaching up and gripping the waistband of his jeans and boxers.

Lifting his arse off the bed, he steadies himself as I pull down his jeans, his cock springing free. The head is a shiny, deep red, a pearl of pre-cum beading on the slit. Adjusting my position, I remove his clothes, freeing them from his body, and discarding them on the floor. Automatically, his legs widen, allowing me to settle between them as my palms slide up his shins, over his knees and along the tops of his thighs. His powerful muscles contract beneath my touch, the soft, dark-blonde hair on his legs tickling my palms and sending shivers of pleasure up and down my spine.

"Take off your t-shirt," I urge him. "I want you bare when I take you in my mouth."

He grins, reaching for the hem of his t-shirt and pulling it off. "I like you giving me orders, doll."

For a moment, I just drink him in. His beautiful body is exquisite, cut to perfection. His intricate tattoos, stunning, only adding to my attraction to him.

"You turn me on so much, I'm so wet for you, Drix," I whisper, my fingers wrapping around his erection, my clit pulsing as I gently hold him. Despite being on my knees, I feel powerful, his desire for me destroying all the bad memories I had with Martin, replacing them with new ones. Better ones.

"Keep saying things like that to me and I may just come before you even wrap your pretty lips around my cock," he admits roughly.

I let out a soft laugh, then rise on my knees, licking the tip of his cock, tasting him for the very first time. He groans, muttering curse words under his breath as I press the flat of my tongue against him and fold my lips over the head of his cock, sucking him into my mouth.

"Jesus fucking Christ," he mutters, jerking, more salty pre-cum exploding on my tongue.

I hold him in my mouth, laving my tongue against his sensitive flesh, enjoying the feel of his thickness before sliding him deeper into my throat. He's so long, I can't take him all the way, my lips meeting my fist as he hits the back of my throat.

"That feels so good, doll. So fucking good," he praises as I suction my lips around him, hollowing out my cheeks and slowly bobbing my head up and down his length.

Every time I reach the tip, I run my tongue around his glans, paying particular attention to the thick, throbbing vein that runs along the underside of his cock.

He groans and I moan around his dick, my knickers flooding with arousal, my nipples scraping against the lace of my bra, edging me further. God, I need him inside of me. I've never been more turned on.

But first, I want him to unravel just like he's made me unravel from his talented mouth and tongue. So I pick up my pace, sucking him as deep as I can go, my saliva dripping down his length covering my fingers as I move my hand up and down his cock.

"Lia, fuck!" he grinds out, his hand wrapping around the back of my head, urging me to move faster, to take him deeper.

Humming around his length, I rub my thighs together, trying and failing to ease the need between my legs. I feel him thicken, and my jaw aches from stretching so wide to accommodate him. Then I remember what he told me about his fantasy, and I pull back, releasing his dick.

"Lia," he pants, a questioning look in his eyes. "Was I too rough?"

I shake my head. "No, just give me a second," I say, kissing the tip of his cock as I release him and reach for my top, pulling it off.

"Lia, what are you...?" his voice trails off as I unhook my bra, my breasts falling heavily, feeling achy as I hold them in my hands.

"Look at you," he groans, reaching for his dick and holding the base as I rub one nipple, then the other, up and down the length of his dick.

"You've taken my pussy, and my mouth, now I want you to fuck my breasts. Sit on the edge of the bed," I say, guiding his dick between my cleavage. "I want you to come all over me, Drix. I want you to mark me as thoroughly on the outside as you've touched me so deeply on the inside."

"Fuck. Yes," he pants, mouth parting on a breath as he slides his thick length between the globes of my breasts. The slickness from my saliva helping his cock to slip easily against my skin. The sound he makes as he starts to rock his hips has my clit pulsating, and my core gasping for him.

"That's it," I whisper, dropping my chin against my chest, gathering more saliva in my mouth and letting it drip from my lips onto the head of his cock. I don't know what possesses me, but damn, do I feel sexy doing it. I like this side of me, so I embrace it with a man I feel safe with.

"That is so fucking hot," he cries, eyes widening as I glance up at him.

"I feel so damn powerful. Now fuck my breasts, come all over me, Drix."

"Fuck, Lia!" he exclaims, as I hold his length between my breasts and he pumps his dick, mindless now. "I'm going to come. I'm going to come all over your beautiful tits!"

Easing back slightly, I release him, so he can grab his dick, and aim it at my chest. He lets go with a roar, jerking his cock as streams of hot cum spurt from the tip, hitting the top of my breasts and chest. It slides over my skin as his mouth drops open, his chest heaving as he stares at the beautiful mess he's made.

"Better?" I ask with a soft laugh, feeling this sense of pride at making him come undone, or should I say, all over me.

"You surprise me every single day," he replies, shaking his head as he presses his finger against my skin, swirling his cum around my nipple before gently pinching it. "I'm going to live off this moment for a very, *very* long time."

"You don't have to live off the memory, when you have me already," I remind him. "I'm here for the taking, Drix."

"Now that is an offer I can't refuse," he replies huskily.

"I should probably clean myself up first," I suggest, dropping my gaze to my chest. The me 'before Drix' would never have done something like this. The person I am now wants to do it all over again, and again, and again.

"If you think I'm going to let you walk out of this room without giving you an orgasm or five, you're sorely mistaken, doll."

"Five?" I grin.

"You think I won't?" he counters with a suggestive smirk.

"I'm not sure I'm capable," I laugh.

"Doll, when I say I'm going to make you come five times, I will make you come five times," he assures me with confidence, "Now stand up and take off your knickers, I want to feel how wet you are."

"Jesus, Drix," I murmur. "You could make a woman turn to jelly."

"That's the plan," he replies with a wink. "Up you get."

Pushing to my feet, I ignore the way his cum drips over my skin, and slide my hands to the waistband of my skirt, about to push it over my hips.

"No. Keep your skirt on, just take your knickers off," he instructs, watching me with hooded eyes as I follow his commands.

With my knickers bunched in my hand, I stand before him and he holds his hand open. "Give them to me."

I hesitate. "You want my underwear?"

"Lia, now."

I pass my knickers to him, my cheeks flushing at how damp they are as he lifts them to his nose, breathing in deep.

"Fuck, doll, I could get high just off your scent alone. Now turn around, put your arms behind your back, and cross your wrists."

Trembling with need, I turn away from him, offering him my wrists. He uses my damp knickers to bind them together, before grabbing my hips and turning me back around to face him. Slowly, he runs his fingers up my thighs, pushing up the material of my skirt as he does so. His touch sends shivers down my spine, soft yet certain.

"You feel like silk, Lia," he murmurs, looking up at me as his fingers coast along the top of my thighs, drawing electrical currents across my skin as one hand dips between my legs, parting my folds gently. I gasp as he finds my damp entrance and slides two fingers inside of me, right up to his knuckles.

"Drix, that feels so good," I murmur as he grasps my arse with his free hand, squeezing, pumping me languidly with the other.

"You are the sexiest woman alive, Lia. I could fuck you until there's nothing left in me to give, and then I'd fuck you all over again. Now stand there and take my fingers, let me hear you call my name," he orders, pulling me closer, still pumping his fingers inside of me.

I can't even utter a word, too overcome with sensation, my greedy pussy weeping for him, my clit desperate to be touched. He must sense my need, because he releases my arse, grips the material of my skirt with his free hand and tucks it into the waistband, pressing his thumb against my clit and rubbing against it. I'm already so turned on by giving him a blowjob and watching him release all over my chest, that the orgasm I've been teetering on the edge of detonates, and I cry out his name, jerking against his hand as I come.

Bliss spreads out from my core, leaving me weak-kneed, and I stumble into his arms as he pulls his fingers out of me and grasps my hips, holding me steady. My sticky chest is still covered in his cum, but he doesn't seem to care. In fact, he swipes his lips over my skin, no doubt tasting the saltiness of his cum as he sucks one of my nipples into his mouth, dragging on it, his tongue licking, his teeth grazing over my nub. My core tightens, drawing out the last dregs of my orgasm.

"Drix," I moan.

"I'm not finished with you yet. Sit on my cock, Lia," he demands, shifting back slightly so that I can kneel on the bed on either side of his hips.

With my hands tied behind my back, I'm a little unsteady, but I needn't worry as he supports me with one hand, whilst gripping his dick with the other. Slowly I position myself above him, feeling the head of his cock tease my entrance. Softness against slickness. Hardness against openness. Unable to hold on to him, he wraps his arm around my lower back as I slowly sink down onto his glorious cock, seating myself fully.

"You were made for me, Lia. You fit me so perfectly," he says, taking my tied wrists in his hand, holding me steady as I adjust to him.

"You feel so right. Everything about you is so right," I reply, my heart hammering against my ribcage as he pulls me tighter against him, taking all my weight. With him I feel both powerful and delicate, like a solitary flower in a field full of thorns, blossoming under his affection, his attention, his undeniable love.

Leaning down, I kiss his mouth, sliding my tongue between his parted lips as I begin to rock against him. Heat blooms deep inside my womb, my internal walls squeezing him tight. This time I don't bounce up and down on his cock. No, I keep him clenched tight within me, savouring how deep he feels, how *full* I am.

My pussy hugs him tighter, my heart swells bigger, my happiness grows infinitely as we make love. Kissing, rocking, fucking, loving, we move as one, until I don't know where he begins and I end. In this moment, here and now, there is only him and I. Two people brought together by circumstance, bound together by friendship, tied together by love.

Time stands still, this moment stretching on and on and on, until eventually his grip tightens on my wrists and his dick swells. I groan, my desire making us slick, my tongue plundering his mouth as I swallow the sounds of his release, mine following moments later.

TWENTY-NINE

IT'S New Year's Eve, the morning of Robert's and Melody's wedding, and I'm waiting by the Rolls Royce for Robert and Sterling. The sun is shining in a cloudless blue sky, heralding new beginnings as the snow glistens beneath its rays. Or at least that's how it feels as I stand in my smart black suit, waiting for the world to fucking end.

Tonight, after the wedding, I plan on telling Lia everything.

I can't live with the secrets a moment longer.

She'll know the truth about me, and I'm scared shitless.

I've spent every spare minute since Christmas with Lia and Toby, falling more deeply in love, and agonising over my decision to keep the truth from them both. Lia will hate me when I tell her, she will run, and I have no one to blame but myself. A better man than me would've been honest from the get go, and I hate myself from hiding the truth from her. There's little I can do about it now other than be honest, and hope that by some miracle she chooses to stay.

"We're a go," comes the deep rumble of Baxter's voice in my earpiece. "The roads are clear. We're ready when you are."

Just like I've planned, Baxter is waiting in another car at the gates of Robert's home at the end of the half-mile long drive. He's ready to guide us through town to Carl's hotel where the wedding is being held. The guests are all waiting at the venue, the press have been thoroughly vetted and are in position. Every road leading into Princetown has been blocked with security checkpoints, questioning anyone trying to get in or out. Together, we've got shit locked down.

"Five minutes," I reply, speaking into the mic attached to my earpiece as I glance at my watch.

"Roger that. Over and out," he replies, laughing.

"You're enjoying this, aren't you?" I ask him.

"Listen, it's not everyday you get to fulfil your fantasies. I feel like James motherfucking Bond."

"Baxter Bond doesn't have quite the same ring to it. Sounds more like a pornstar name to me," AJ interjects with a laugh. He too is connected to us through the earpiece; he waits at the hotel with Riley and Troy for our arrival.

"Tell you what, why don't you both keep the lines clear and do your jobs," I reply tetchily, feeling the strain.

"Yes, Boss," they reply, clearing the line.

I shake my head, blowing out a tense breath just as Robert steps out of the front door, Sterling following behind him. In matching grey Savile Row suits, they very much ooze money and glamour. But, going by the look on their faces, things are still tense between them. Just goes to show that money doesn't necessarily buy you happiness. Pulling open the passenger door, I wait for them to join me.

"You have the rings?" Robert asks Sterling as they approach.

"No, I sold them," Sterling replies sarcastically.

"Funny," comes Robert's tight response as he slides into the backseat without so much as a nod of acknowledgement, the rude bastard.

"Good luck, mate," I mutter to Sterling as he shakes his head at his dad's shitty behaviour.

"Fuck knows I'm gonna need some luck to get me through today," he replies under his breath. "That and a flask full of brandy," he adds, opening up his jacket and showing me the silver flask tucked into his inside pocket.

"I'm with you there, mate," I say, nausea churning in my stomach at the thought of what I've got to do later.

He gives me a knowing look, and squeezes my arm before taking a seat in the backseat next to his dad. Slamming the door shut, I pull open the driver's door and slide behind the wheel. A couple of minutes later we're following Baxter to the hotel.

Along the way, the residents of Princetown line the streets, waving as the car passes them by. You'd think Robert was royalty given the way everyone applauds and cheers. It's fucking ridiculous. If only they knew how he came by his riches, maybe they wouldn't be so enamoured by the bastard.

When we pull up at the hotel, the flashlights from all the cameras start going off. Contained behind rows of metal fencing leading up to the entrance, the press jostle for the best picture of the groom and his son. Over the years Robert has used the press to his advantage, and hasn't given too shits that Sterling has been hounded by the press for the best part of his adult life.

Touted as one of the richest, most eligible bachelors in all of England, Sterling has an intense dislike for the press. It's part of the reason he's so reclusive, choosing to keep himself out of the limelight as best he can. Doesn't seem to matter to the press, however, they're like circling vultures, just waiting for a juicy story they can feed the public.

I don't envy him, not one fucking bit.

"Shall we get this shit over and done with then?" Sterling says, as he opens the door to the car and steps into the frey.

Almost immediately the press clamour for a photo, pushing

and shoving at each to get the best shot. Thank fuck for Riley, AJ and Troy who have the unenviable job of keeping the fuckers in check. Not that they're bothered, they know how to handle themselves. The press have been forewarned with what is expected of them. Anyone who breaks the very long list of rules laid out will be escorted from town, so it's in their best interests to behave. Only one magazine has been given the opportunity to photograph the entire wedding, these fuckers are from the tabloids, and will be drip-fed photos as and when Robert deems appropriate.

Switching off the engine, I step out of the car, waiting for Robert to emerge. His shiny, buffed to perfection shoes emerge first, followed by a lean body clad in his bespoke grey suit.

The smile he failed to give me is plastered on his face as he rises upwards and strides towards the waiting press. I slam the door of the Rolls Royce, following them both, hanging back as he poses for pictures with Sterling.

"Mr Blade, are you looking forward to getting hitched?" one of the press asks, the flash from his camera blinding.

"Yes, very much so," Robert replies, throwing his arm around Sterling's shoulder, who just grits his teeth.

"And Melody? Is she excited too?" another asks.

"Why wouldn't she be, she's marrying one of the richest men in the UK," he replies obnoxiously.

"And your ex-wife? How does she feel about today? Have you invited her to the wedding?" another cheeky bastard asks.

The crowd laughs, and I see Sterling tensing up further. If Robert doesn't get him inside soon he might just lay one of them out. Sensing blood, a short, fat, balding man eyes Sterling.

"What about you, Sterling? How do *you* feel about your new stepmother and stepsister?"

"Can't say I'm all that–" Sterling begins, but Robert cuts him off.

"He's delighted, aren't you, Sterling?" Robert prompts, his grip on Sterling tightening.

"Yeah, over the fucking moon," comes Sterling's terse response.

"Well, I think we'd better get inside. It doesn't pay to be late to my own wedding. Time is money, chaps," Robert adds with a sleazy smile, and the crowd laughs, bolstering his ego further.

What a crock of shit. This is a fucking circus, not a wedding.

Following the pair inside, I hang back as Robert and Sterling exchange a few heated words. I use the moment to quickly tap out a text to Lia.

Just arrived. Are you and Toby okay?

We're just fine. She replies immediately, the three little bubbles telling me she's still typing out a message. **Toby is a little overwhelmed. I'm glad we all decided to stay at the hotel last night with Daisy. We missed you.**

I smile, forgetting for a moment that this ease we have with one another will all soon come to an abrupt end. Blowing out a breath, I type a response.

I missed you both too. Five minutes and I'll be by your side, I reply, tucking my phone back into my pocket when Robert motions me over.

"Get a call up to Melody's suite, let her know we've arrived," he instructs, before striding off to the function room where the wedding will take place.

Sterling swipes a hand over his face. "Fuck this bullshit," he grumbles, reaching for the flask in his jacket. He unscrews the lid, knocking back a mouthful.

"You might want to go easy, mate," I say. "Last thing you need is those vultures getting photos of you half-cut."

"Don't really give a shit," Sterling replies, swallowing another mouthful.

"Just get through today, and then you can get out of here," I remind him.

He nods. "Just one more fucking day."

Gripping his shoulder briefly, I head to the reception desk where Dalton is waiting.

"Everything good?" he asks me.

I raise a brow. "If you're talking about security, then everything's wrapped up. If, however, you're talking about Sterling," I say, glancing over at my friend who is heading towards the function room, "Then no. We're going to have to keep an eye on him today. He's spiralling."

"Yeah, I figured," Dalton acknowledges. "Lia and Toby are waiting with the other guests."

"I know, I just texted her."

Dalton grins. "Not going to lie, she looks fucking incredible."

"Don't piss me off, Dalton," I warn him.

"You haven't seen her in her dress yet?" he asks, cocking his head with a sly smile.

"She wanted it to be a surprise after Daisy took her shopping to the boutique in town a couple days ago. I gave Daisy my credit card and instructed her to buy them both a dress on me, and Toby a suit."

"Well, you're going to shit yourself when you see her. She's stunning."

"Dalton!"

"Just stating a fact. You're a lucky son-of-a-bitch."

"I hope you've been treating Daisy with respect," I say, changing the subject before I get the urge to punch him for even daring to look at my woman.

Dalton laughs. "She's gone back to ignoring me, if that helps? I haven't seen her yet this morning. Figured she's already in the function room with Lia and Toby."

"You two are a pain in my arse," I grumble. "Now do me a

favour and make a call to Melody's suite, tell her Robert and Sterling have arrived."

"You got it," he replies, picking up the phone and dialling the number.

I crick my neck, waiting for Dalton to finish his conversation before heading into the function room with him. His voice trails off mid-sentence as he looks over my shoulder at someone.

"Fucking hell," he mutters, then quickly apologises before placing the handset back onto the cradle.

"What?" I ask, slowly twisting around to see Daisy rushing towards us both from the elevators, the skirt of her pretty pale pink dress fluttering around her legs as she moves. She's holding the material of her skirt in her hands, showing off her slim ankles wrapped in the delicate straps of her silver heels.

"Daise, you look beautiful," I say, my smile spreading wide as pride fills my chest. I particularly like the fact she's wearing the necklace and earrings I bought for her for Christmas. The necklace rests against her chest, the sweetheart neckline showing off the smattering of freckles covering her skin.

She grins, her cheeks flushed pink, her hair piled up on her head, tendrils framing her face. Daisy usually wears thick black liner on her eyes, but today she has gone for brown eyeshadow and soft pink lipstick that compliment her skin tone, and highlight her natural beauty.

"I'm running a little late. Had a fight with the straighteners trying to deal with my unruly curls so I had to put my hair up," she explains, a little breathlessly as she glances at Dalton, eyes narrowing. "What's up with you?"

He clears his throat. "This isn't the Daisy show," he retorts sharply.

"What's that supposed to mean?" she snaps back.

"It means you're *late*. Get your arse in the function room with the other guests," he replies.

"Dalton, are you looking for a punch to the face? Have a little respect," I grind out.

Daisy rolls her eyes, waving her hand in the air, completely unperturbed by his rudeness. "Ignore him, it's probably the *Just For Men* he used last night to cover the greys, must've poisoned his mind a little, right arsehole?"

With that she throws Dalton a sweet smile, the sound of her heels clicking against the marble floor echoing around the reception hall as she strides off.

"She's—"

"Be very careful of what comes out of your mouth next," I say, raising a brow.

"Never mind," Dalton mumbles. "Shall we go?"

"Yeah."

The second we step into the function room, I search the crowd, taking in the decadent display of cream roses dripping from the ceiling in long garlands twined with fairy lights, crystals and white feathers. Every seat has a cream silk bow tied at the back, a small bouquet of lilies, tucked between the knots. There has been no expense spared, and the decorations in this room alone must've cost thousands of pounds. I can only imagine what the ballroom is going to look like. It's a huge space that will hold the reception party. I'm pretty sure Robert spent a cool million on this wedding. Which, for a man like him, is nothing.

A harpist plays, the soft notes lifting up into air, entertaining the two hundred guests that are seated either side of the aisle whilst they all wait for the bride to arrive. At the front of the hall, Sterling and Robert stand slightly off to the side of a huge arch of cream roses that the wedding officiant is standing beneath. According to my background checks he's a retired captain of a naval ship, and an old friend of Robert's.

"Drix!" a sweet voice shouts, and my attention is drawn to Toby who is standing in the aisle, about three rows back from

Robert and Sterling. He grins at me when I wave, my eyes searching for Lia, who is partially obscured from my line of vision by the guests standing behind her.

"Get ready to be blown away, Drix," Dalton mutters as we approach, a smile in his voice.

To my left, I spot Ben and his father Walter, acknowledging them both with a nod as we pass. Walter smiles but Ben barely notices, his attention fixed on the woman who broke his heart. She sits on the other side of the aisle next to her husband several rows back, her own gaze fixed ahead of her.

Man, that's gotta hurt.

Unlike most traditional weddings where it's a free for all in terms of where people sit during the ceremony, so long as the bride guests are on the left of the aisle and the groom on the right, Robert made sure that each seat was labelled very clearly with his guests' names. The nearer to front you are, the more valued in his eyes you are as a guest, no matter which side of the aisle you're placed. As members of the founding families we have prime position at the front of the hall. It pleases me that Lia and Toby have been invited to sit beside Daisy and I. If Robert had put them at the back, away from us, then there would've been hell to pay.

"Just try not to trip over your dick when you see her," Dalton continues when I don't respond to his earlier statement.

"Funny," I mutter as he chuckles, taking his seat next to his father on the opposite side of the aisle.

"Hey, Drix," Toby says, grinning up at me.

"Hey, buddy," I reply, ruffling his hair before finally laying eyes on Lia.

My steps falter, struck dumb momentarily at just how fucking incredible she looks. Even as Daisy takes Toby's hand and moves aside so I can sit down next to Lia, I can't seem to move my feet. My gaze roves over her beautiful face, her pretty eyes accented with soft green eyeshadow and black mascara, her plump lips shiny with clear lip gloss.

"Hello," she says as she smiles up at me, her fingers rising to her cheek as she brushes a tendril of hair off her face, tucking it behind her ear. She's wearing it down, curled in soft waves. It falls just below her shoulders, and I have this sudden urge to run my fingers through the strands.

"Lia, you're stunning," I say, my gaze following the slope of her bare shoulders, resting on her beautiful cleavage that's encased in a blood-red bustier covered in tiny black crystals that scatter across the red layered chiffon of her floor length dress. The dress code for the wedding was decadent elegance, and she sure meets that requirement and then some. There's a certain kind of synchronicity in the fact that her dress happens to match my red tie, the Hammer family crest embroidered onto it.

"You should probably sit," Daisy giggles, dragging my attention back to her as a string quartet begins to play, heralding the entrance of the bride.

Edging past Daisy and Toby, I sit beside Lia, pressing a kiss to her cheek, my lips coasting toward her ear. "I wish I was alone with you," I say, my cock thickening at the thought.

"The feeling's mutual," she whispers back.

"This is going to be a long fucking day," I grumble, momentarily forgetting that there's an important conversation that needs to take place between us. That thought is like a bucket of ice-water over my head, and all thoughts of making love to Lia leave my mind, replaced instead with a churning sickness in my stomach.

Concentrating on the here and now, I wrap Lia's hand in mine, my thumb running over the ring I gave her. Focussing on Sterling and Robert, a woman begins to sing. Her voice is familiar to me for some reason.

"Wow," Lia breathes, her arms covering in a scatter of goosebumps as she reacts to the sound.

She's not the only one entranced by the ethereal voice, the whole room falls into stunned silence, but that is nothing in comparison to Sterling's reaction.

He stumbles into his dad, his head snapping around as he looks for the woman singing. The hope in his eyes is plain to see, but that soon turns to shock as he looks past the guests, realisation dawning.

"What the hell?" I mutter, as shocked as Sterling clearly is as I twist in my seat following his gaze. The woman singing does so as she walks down the aisle in front of Melody, Robert's bride. Dressed in a silver, floor length gown, and holding a bouquet of flowers, there's no mistaking who she is. She's the woman in Sterling's painting.

She's Friday Love.

"What's the matter?" Lia whispers.

"Please don't tell me that woman singing is Melody's daughter," I plead, twisting my head back around as I stare at Sterling who, given the range of emotions passing across his face, has come to the very same conclusion.

"Yes, we met her last night. Her name is Harlow, she's lovely."

"Oh fuck," I exclaim.

"WHAT'S WRONG WITH STERLING? He's been acting strange all day," Lia observes a few hours later, her hand resting on my thigh as we watch the bride and groom step onto the dance floor.

The room is drenched in soft candlelight, the dance floor of the ballroom surrounded with round tables where the wedding guests sit watching the newlyweds take their first dance after finishing an extravagant five course meal.

Sterling is still seated at the head table, a troubled expression on his face. Harlow sits three seats over, her attention focussed on her mother and Robert as they begin to dance. She looks as tense as Sterling, her hand grasping the delicate stem of her champagne glass as the magazine photographer starts snapping pics of Robert and Melody, as well as members of the wedding party. I can only imagine the thoughts running rampant through Sterling's head. The woman he slept with is now his stepsister. You couldn't make this shit up.

"It's complicated," I begin, chewing on my lip.

"That doesn't sound good," Lia observes, tapping Toby's arm as he reaches for another cake from the tiered cake stand. "That's enough, Toby."

"But Mama, they're so good," he replies, smacking his lips in a way that makes me laugh. He has thoroughly enjoyed all the food we've eaten tonight, including the two small cakes he's already demolished.

"No more, okay? I don't want you getting sick," she warns him.

"Okay, Mama," he agrees, withdrawing his hand as she presses a kiss to the top of his head.

A rush of pride floods my veins as I watch them. Toby has behaved impeccably today, and I couldn't love him any more even if he were my own flesh and blood. When Robert introduced himself to Lia after the ceremony and started firing questions at her, she had held her own with grace and humility. I know he was impressed by her, and his offer of joining them both for dinner at his mansion once they'd returned from their honeymoon is the equivalent to winning the lottery to some of the fuckers in attendance here tonight. I've never felt more proud to stand by her side, not because of the invite, but because she had shone with confidence and self-worth.

It only makes what I'm about to do even harder.

I glance at my wristwatch, it's almost eight pm, and in a few minutes Lia and I will take Toby up to the suite we're staying in tonight to put him to bed. My plan is to tell her everything once Toby's fallen asleep, and every second that counts down to that moment feels like a dagger piercing my heart. I rub at the ache in my chest, trying to ease the swelling pain.

Daisy's laughter drags me out of my depressing thoughts as she talks with one of the wedding guests seated at our table. He's a business associate of Robert's. Some twenty-something entrepreneur who's as obnoxious as most of the other guests here tonight, and just as fucking vacuous. I don't dislike him because he's taken an interest in Daisy, I dislike him because he's bragged nonstop about his achievements. I can respect confidence, but arrogance? Not so much.

Across the table, Dalton watches their interaction with a scowl on his face, clearly feeling the same about this man as me. He has completely ignored the woman sitting next to him, despite her flirting with him all night. Frankly, I'm surprised he hasn't slipped off with her already. She seems like his type. Tall, slim, model-esq, and from a well-to-do family, I've no doubt Carl had some influence over the fact she has been placed next to him at the table.

"So... Sterling," Lia says, resting her arm on mine.

"I'll tell you about it later. Too many people," I reply, covering her fingers with my own.

She nods in understanding. "Okay."

"Ladies and gentlemen," Walter suddenly announces into the microphone, drawing our attention his way. "The bride and groom ask that you now join them on the dance floor. So gather your loved one and let's get this party underway!"

My gaze flicks to Sterling, who pushes up from his seat, trying to make a swift exit, but Walter notices, and says, "Sterling, your father and stepmother would like you and Harlow to join them too."

"Jesus Christ," I mutter, feeling for my friend.

Sterling grips the back of his chair and for a second I think he's going to bolt, but instead he strides towards Harlow, holding out his hand. Their eyes meet, and if you didn't know their history like I do, you'd assume that they were acting this awkwardly because of their new relationship, not because they'd fucked. She takes his hand, and I force myself to look away. He doesn't need me ogling them just like the rest of the arseholes here are doing.

"Would you like to dance, Daisy?" the prick, who's been chatting up my sister, asks as some of the other wedding guests walk onto the dance floor.

Daisy grins. "Sure, I'd love to"

I glance at Dalton who understands what I don't say. He gets to his feet, rounding the table, before clearing his throat. "Actually, I think the honour is mine. Daisy?"

Daisy looks between the two men, and for a moment I think she's going to take up Dalton's offer, but instead she slides her hand into that creep's, and silently follows him onto the dance floor.

"Motherfucker," I grind out under my breath.

"Drix, she's a grown woman," Lia reminds me. "Come on, dance with me?"

"He's a creep," I grumble. I'm already on edge, I don't need to lose my shit tonight.

"She can make her own choices," Lia whispers back, as I take her hand and step onto the dance floor.

"I just worry about her, that's all," I explain, dropping my gaze to Lia and forcing myself to be with her in this moment, right now. She deserves my undivided attention, and that's what I'm going to give her.

"I know, but you also need to respect her choices. Dalton too," she adds, pressing her body against mine as her arms circle my back.

I blow out a breath, drawing her tighter against me, matching her step for step. "You're right."

"You know, I've really enjoyed today," she says after a beat, her warm breath fluttering over my skin as we sway together.

I nod, suddenly lost for words as I gaze at her. She's so damn beautiful, and I'm so fucking afraid. With my heart ramming against my ribcage, all I can do is lower my lips to hers and kiss her. I don't care who sees, I don't care what anyone else in this goddamn room thinks. I don't even give a shit that the photographer is snapping pictures of us as we kiss. I love this woman, and I want to savour the moment.

Eventually, reluctantly, I pull back and she sighs contentedly, leaning her cheek against my chest as I wish for a fucking miracle, knowing that I don't deserve one.

Over her shoulder I spot Sterling dancing with Harlow. He's tense, holding her stiffly and I frown, catching his eye. "You alright?" I mouth.

He shakes his head. Of course he isn't. Stupid fucking question.

Behind them, on the far side of the room, I notice Benedict talking with his ex Elodie and her husband, Councillor John Hoxton. The tense way he holds himself and the look of disbelief on Elodie's face as Ben and John shake hands has me questioning exactly what's happening there. But honestly, I'm not sure I want to know.

Next Dalton appears in my line of vision, and I watch as he strides across the room towards Daisy and the creep who has his hands far too close to her arse for my liking. Dalton taps him on the shoulder, saying something to him. The creep steps back, holding his hands up before twisting on his heel towards the bar. Dalton attempts to dance with Daisy, but she just shoves him in the chest, scowling up at him. Her lips are moving rapidly, and whilst I've no idea what she's saying, it's obvious from their interaction it isn't good.

"Ah, fuck," I groan.

"What's the matter?" Lia asks, following my gaze. "Oh."

"I should probably intervene."

"Don't you dare. Daisy can handle herself. Just let them be," she advises, reaching up to cup my cheek, her eyebrows drawing together in a frown as she looks at me. "Sterling isn't the only one who's been acting strange today. Are *you* alright?"

My hand slides up Lia's back, coasting over the tiny crystal buttons that hold her corset together, knowing that I won't get the chance to drag my lips down her spine as I remove this beautiful dress from her body.

"Lia, once we put Toby to bed, I want to talk with you about something."

"Is this about what you were afraid to share with me on Christmas day?" she asks, cocking her head.

"It is," I confirm, my gut twisting painfully.

"Do you want to go now? It looks like you need to get whatever this is off your chest, and I need to stop Toby from filling his tummy with more pudding. I really don't want him throwing up."

"Yeah, let's do this," I nod, taking her hand in mine, feeling like a criminal on death row waiting for his execution

"Come on, kid. Time for bed," I say, dropping Lia's hand as we reach Toby, so I can haul him into my arms and hug him tight. The thought of losing him is just as painful.

"But I was having so much fun!" he protests.

"I know, buddy. But there's a big comfortable bed waiting for you, and me and your Ma are pretty tired too. Been a long day all round," I say, trying to placate him.

"Alright, you should probably get some beauty sleep anyway," he shrugs. "Right, Mama?"

"Exactly," she replies with a grin, grabbing her purse from the back of the chair and following us out.

To anyone watching we look like a perfectly happy family, a family I'm about to destroy with my truth.

THIRTY

"NIGHT, KIDDO," Drix says, dropping a kiss against Toby's temple, his large hand resting on Toby's arm as he sleeps deeply, completely worn out from a long day.

I watch from the doorway as Drix eases upright. Yet, he doesn't move to leave, instead he remains seated on the edge of the bed, staring at Toby, his thumb rubbing gentle circles on his arm. I'm reminded in that moment just how much affection and love Toby was denied by his own father, how easily Drix has stepped into that role, and how Toby has blossomed from it. Heaving out a sigh, Drix moves to stand, and I can't help but notice a heaviness to his shoulders as he twists on his feet. It worries me.

"Sorry, I didn't realise you were standing there," he says, moving towards me.

My heart clenches, the small smile he gives me not quite reaching his eyes. Having already discarded his suit jacket, Drix's white shirt is pulled taut across his chest, the top two buttons undone, revealing a glimpse of his tattoos that I've already committed to memory.

"I didn't want to wake Toby up," I reply, holding my hand out to him. "Come on, let's have a drink. You look like you could use one."

"Sure," he replies, sliding his palm against mine as I guide him down the hallway to the living area in this huge suite he booked us in. With three bedrooms, it's big enough to accommodate Daisy as well as give Toby his own room to sleep in.

"What would you like? There's whisky, brandy, wine, vodka?" I ask as he settles on the leather couch, watching me as I look through the contents of the bar. Heat flashes across my skin at the intense look he gives me.

"Brandy, neat... *Please*," he adds.

"Coming up," I reply, grabbing the small bottle of brandy and two crystal glasses from the cabinet.

Pouring us both a shot each, I carry them over to the leather couch, passing him his glass whilst I sit down next to him. Muttering his thanks, he takes it from me, knocking it back with one swift flick of his wrist before resting the empty glass on the coffee table.

"That bad, huh?" I joke, only the smile slips from my lips when his expression remains troubled.

Taking a fortifying sip of brandy, I relish the burn as the liquid slides down my throat.

"So, there's something you want to get off your chest?" I begin.

"There is," he agrees with a nod, and despite the fact that he has his body angled towards me, he has his arms crossed over his chest, closing himself off.

"Do you want to tell me what that is?" I ask tentatively.

"I don't know where to start," he admits, flicking his gaze away as though he can't bear to look at me.

"How about from the beginning?" I suggest.

He nods, swiping a hand through his hair, his thick fingers running through the strands. "When I was twenty, Hubert brought me into the Hammer family business," he begins. "Up until that point I didn't really know where his riches came from. I guess I assumed he inherited that wealth given he never really spoke about what he did for the founding families of Princetown."

"And what did he do exactly?" I ask, taking another sip of my brandy, cupping the cool glass in my hands whilst I wait.

"Security mainly, much like what I've done today. If there were any big events involving the families, he would arrange the security detail, completing background checks on any guests invited, staff employed, and press covering the event. He trained me well, and I found that I was good at it. I enjoy taking care of people and running a team. Hubert always said I was a natural leader, that people respected me, and that I knew instinctively what was needed to ensure everyone was kept safe."

"I can see that," I admit. "You make me and Toby feel safe, Drix."

His eyes meet mine, and I can't quite interpret the emotions held within them. All I know is that a seed of worry begins to grow inside my chest with every passing moment.

Clearing his throat, he continues. "It wasn't long before I was taking over Hubert's role more and more, especially when he began getting sick. By the time he'd died, I was head of security for the families, as he was before me, and his father was before that."

"Okay, so what's troubling you about all of this? Are you concerned you've made a mistake tonight? Has something gone wrong? Is Robert displeased in some way?"

"No, nothing's gone wrong. Everything has gone to plan. This part of my role is a breeze..." His voice trails off and he winces.

I frown. "This part of your role? What do you mean by that?"

Drix leans forward, taking the glass from my hands and placing it onto the table, then folds my hands in his. "I want you to remember the man that I am when I'm with you and Toby, Lia. I need you to know that I *am* that person. That is the true me. The real Drix Hammer. Not..."

"Not?" I question quietly, hating how the worry starts to sprout roots and tangle inside my stomach, churning it up.

"Not this other person."

"Other person? What are you saying?"

"Remember when I told you about that guy who hurt Daisy back in college?"

"Yes, he moved away, right?" I ask, hating the look he gives me when he slowly shakes his head. There's shame swimming within his beautiful brown eyes. There's also worry, pain, fear, and anger too. It all swirls together.

"No, he didn't move away. Carl paid him and his family off. They left Princetown with a cool ten million in the bank, and signed a contract to state they'd never step foot in this town again or mention what happened."

"Why did Carl pay him off?"

"Hubert lost his fortune on an investment deal gone wrong about a year before the incident when that bastard broke Daisy's heart. I only found out when it all blew up. Daisy still doesn't know that the family was paid off. All Huburt had left was our family home, and a few hundred thousand in the bank."

"So Carl stepped in and paid the family to move away to protect Daisy? That seems rather extreme? I mean, I know he hurt her, but it wasn't as if she was going to go back out with him again. I don't understand."

Drix fingers squeeze mine tightly, his eyes meeting mine. "No, Carl didn't pay off the family to protect Daisy, but to protect *me*—"

"Wait, why would you need protection?"

"You have to understand, Lia, I acted on instinct. I couldn't bear to see Daisy destroyed by that prick. She was devastated by what happened, and withdrew into herself. It triggered things from her past, her sense of low self-worth, all of her abandonment issues. I didn't think she'd pull through it. A couple of weeks after he dumped her, I went looking for him. I wanted him to understand how badly he fucked her up. I wanted him to apologise..."

"Drix, what did you do?" I whisper out, my throat tightening as the worry inside of me twists and turns, transforming into something ugly, turning into *fear*.

"I beat him. I beat him so badly he almost died," he admits quietly. "He ended up in hospital on life support. By some miracle he pulled through. Carl paid off his family because Hubert asked him to, so that I wouldn't go to prison for what I did."

"You almost *killed* a man," I whisper, tears springing to my eyes as bile rises up my throat. How can this kind, attentive, thoughtful man I've fallen in love with be capable of almost killing someone? How could he be that violent? I jerk backwards, and he drops my hands as I try and fail to rationalise what he'd done.

"I know it's a lot to take in," he rushes on, "And I wish so fucking badly that's the end to my story, but it's not Lia."

"There's more?" I choke out.

"After Hubert died, and Carl realised he wasn't ever going to get that money back, he said that I had to work for him to pay off the debt."

"You already work for the families though."

"I do, but he wanted someone who could deal with the less glamorous side of their businesses. Once Hubert had passed away he made me their enforcer."

"Their *enforcer*, as in...?"

"Wealthy men like Carl, Robert and Walter have enemies, Lia. Sure, on the surface they appear to be successful businessmen, and they are. They have legit businesses now, but they gained most of their fortune in the early days doing illegal shit."

"What kind of illegal things?" I ask, not really wanting to know the answer, but asking anyway.

"Drugs mainly, but also theft of high value items. Jewels, paintings, that kind of thing."

"Oh my God," I mutter, shaking my head, trying to clear the wayward thoughts catapulting inside my head like one of those silver balls in a pinball machine.

"I hurt people for them, Lia. If I don't, Carl will take our home as payment towards the debt. No, *Daisy's* home, because it's hers not mine, I don't want it. She'll have nowhere to go, and nothing left. Don't you see, I couldn't allow that to happen to her. She's been through enough in her life. You don't know half of what she had to live through as a kid. I did it for her, I *do* this for her."

I shake my head, pushing up to my feet as I stumble over the skirt of my dress, trying to put as much distance between us as possible. "You've hurt people, Drix."

He rises to his feet, holding his hands out, stepping towards me. "Please, Lia. You have to know that I wish it were different. I wish I'd made a different choice back then. It's not an excuse, but I am fiercely protective of the people I love, and I won't lie to you and say that if I ever came across your ex, I wouldn't want to do the same to him as he's done to you. That part of me—"

"The *violent* part you mean?" I snap back, wishing I could turn back time, wishing he could still be that beautiful, kind, caring man I'd fallen in love with and not someone I no longer recognise. When he'd said before that he'd kill Martin for what he's done to me, I just thought it was words. Now I know he truly would.

"That part of me is still here," he continues, pressing the flat of his hand against his chest. "But there's a difference between me hurting someone to protect the people I love, and being forced to hurt someone to pay off a debt. I don't want to be their enforcer, but I have no choice."

I shake my head furiously. "Violence is violence, Drix. There are no grey areas, it's black and white. You lost control and almost killed a man. You hurt people at the behest of others."

"So you're telling me that if your ex, Martin, had hurt Toby the way he hurt you, that you wouldn't have tried to protect him?"

"I *did* protect him. I left before he could," I counter angrily.

"You did," he agrees, "But that's not what I meant. If Martin had hurt Toby, can you honestly say that you wouldn't have acted with violence to protect him?"

"Of course I would've, hurting someone in self-defence, and seeking out someone to hurt because they've wronged you or someone else are two different things. It's *not* right, Drix," I reply, doubling over as the truth of who Drix is hits me like a sucker punch to my stomach.

"Lia, please..." he begs, stepping towards me.

I hold my hand up, shaking my head as I rise. "No, don't come near me. You're not who I thought you were."

"I'm still that man you love, Lia," he pleads.

"God, I've done it again haven't I? I fell for your lies, just like I fell for Martin's." I let out a broken laugh, tears streaming down my face now.

"I'm nothing like him. I would never, *ever* hurt you or Toby. I love you both, so fucking much. I've never lied about that. I'm sorry I didn't tell you sooner. I wanted to. It's been cutting me up inside."

"You made me love you, Drix. You made Toby love you. I *trusted* you."

"I'm sorry I've hurt you. Fuck, I'd do anything to make this right..." He swallows hard, stepping closer.

"I ran from violence, Drix. You knew that, and yet you let me believe that you were different."

"I *am* different. Fuck, Lia. Who I am with you and Toby, that's the man I *want* to be, who I am. I can be that man with you by my side."

"I can't... You lied to me. What else have you lied to me about?" I ask, seeing him flinch, knowing there's more.

He drags in a deep breath. "Your mum's recipe books—"

"What about them?" I cut in.

"I know who stole your car. He's a thief, a troublemaker, a problem for the founding families," he explains. "Carl sent me to... speak with him."

"*Speak* with him?" I spit out.

"Carl and Robert were concerned he'd try to steal from the wedding guests. They sent me to warn him not to make trouble. When I got to his place, he had your car in pieces. He'd stolen it, pulled it apart for parts to sell on. Your things were there. I knew if I told you the truth about how I'd come across them, I'd have to tell you the truth about me. So I kept the recipe books at my flat above the gym whilst I figured out what to do. When you told me what they meant to you, I made up the story about finding them at the consignment shop."

"Another lie. How many more are there?"

"That day I came home from checking the security cameras at the hotel..."

"You didn't fall off a ladder did you?"

He shakes his head. "No, I—"

"I don't think I want to know. Christ, who are you?" I ask, cutting him off.

"Ben called me from the bar, needing my help," he continues, ignoring my question. "He was in trouble, and Dalton and I went to help."

"What kind of trouble?"

"That night you took Toby to Bandits and I stepped outside to get his clothes, there was a guy who Ben was chucking out of the bar because he was trying to force himself on a woman. He was threatening Ben, so I stepped in. He pulled a knife. I dealt with him, sent him on his way. Only he came back with some men..." His voice trails off as I stare at him.

"So you dealt with them too?"

"We did."

"God, how stupid of me. I believed your lies, trusted you were telling me the truth that night, even though deep down inside I sensed there was something more."

"I'm so sorry, Lia. I was quiet that night because I hated that I'd lied to you. I've struggled so much with wanting to tell you, and knowing that if I did I'd lose you. I was selfish, ashamed, fucking scared to death, Lia."

"Is there anything else?" I bite out.

"That's it. That's everything."

"And the man who stole my car, did you hurt him too?"

"I thought about it. I wanted to," he admits. "But I didn't. Thoughts of you and Toby stopped me."

"Christ!" I exclaim, striding away from him, needing to put space between us.

"I fell for you, Lia. You *and* Toby. I wanted... Shit!" he exclaims, swiping a hand over his face. "I wanted a family of my own. I *want* you both."

"No!" I snap.

"No?"

His question remains unanswered because Daisy enters the room, Dalton following her close behind.

"I swear to everything that's holy, Dalton Gunn, if you don't leave this instance I'm going to mur–"

Her sentence cuts short as she takes one look at me. I burst into another flood of tears, and they fall unbidden, running in rivulets down my face.

"What's going on?" she asks, looking between us both. "Drix?"

"Daisy, this isn't a good time," he replies.

"What the hell?" Dalton asks, stalling as he enters the room.

A sob escapes my throat, and the little strength I had left in me drains out of my body as I drop to the floor, crying in earnest now. I shove my hands over my mouth, trying to stifle my sobs. I can't let Toby hear me. He'll be devastated if he sees me like this.

"Oh, Lia, what's wrong?" she asks, running to my side, dropping to the floor next to me as she hauls me into her arms.

"I can't do this," I cry between sobs.

"Do what? What happened?"

"What the hell is going on?" Dalton asks.

"Do you know what he did? What your father has done?" I accuse, glaring at Dalton.

He blanches, his face paling.

"You do, don't you? My God, you're all the same!"

"If someone doesn't tell me what the fuck is happening right now, I'm going to lose it!" Daisy warns, hauling me closer as I press my face into her neck and cling to her. I realise in that moment how much she means to me, how desperately I'm going to miss her friendship. This is all so messed-up.

"Fuck," Dalton mutters, dropping onto the couch.

Drix heaves out a sigh. "I'll tell you everything, Daisy. But not here, I think Lia needs some time alone."

THIRTY-ONE

"THIS IS A BAD IDEA," Dalton says, trying to prevent Daisy from knocking on the door of the suite his father is staying in tonight. "Just calm down."

"Don't you dare tell me to calm down. Your father is a bastard, and I'm going to tell him as much."

"Daisy, this isn't going to help," I say, grabbing her arm and forcing her to look at me.

After leaving Lia to give her some space, we headed to Dalton's suite to talk further. The pair of us have spent the last hour trying, and failing, to get Daisy to calm down. She's determined to give Carl a piece of her mind.

"You can be quiet too, Drix. How could you keep this from me?" she accuses, her cheeks flushed with anger, her eyes rimmed with angry tears.

"To protect you. I've done everything to protect you."

"When will you learn that I don't need protection? We could've figured something else out, Drix. You didn't have to do this for me."

"What choice did he have, Daisy? My dad's an arsehole. Everyone knows that," Dalton points out.

Daisy wrenches her arm from my hold and rounds on Dalton, pressing her finger into his chest. "And you're an even bigger one for keeping this secret. Christ, *you* could've helped Drix. He's your best friend, for crying out loud. All that money you've spent on being a playboy, you could've used it to do some good. Instead, whilst you were living it up in the Maldives for months on end, Drix was forced to hurt people to pay off this debt!"

"He wouldn't have needed to pay off a debt if you had some common sense and saw that prick for what he was!" Dalton snaps back.

Daisy reels back, flinching. "So this is my fault because I fell in love? Because I trusted someone, just like Lia trusted you," she snarls, turning her attention back to me. "How could you be so stupid, Drix? You lied to her. You lied to me!"

"I know, Daisy. I know, alright! I messed up, and now I'm going to lose the woman I love," I croak, my throat thick with regret, my heart fucking breaking.

"Not if I've got anything to do with it!" she retorts, twisting on her feet and slamming her fist against the door. "Carl Gunn, open this door right now!"

"What the fuck is this?" Carl shouts as he pulls open the door and Daisy shoves past him into his room.

If this wasn't such a fucking mess, I would've laughed at the expression on Carl's face, instead I follow Daisy inside, Dalton behind me.

"There better be a good fucking explanation for this," Carl says, slamming the door and heading into the living area of his suite where Daisy waits, her hands on her hips, her anger blazing brightly.

"You, Carl Gunn, are going to release Drix from his debt, right this fucking second," she shouts.

"Ah, so you know. I did wonder whether he'd ever tell you," Carl says evenly, dropping onto the sofa as he looks up at her. Still dressed in his suit, he crosses one leg over the other and smiles.

"Did you hear what I just said? Drix will no longer be your enforcer. It ends. *Now.*"

"It ends when he's paid off his debt which, as you clearly now know, is a rather substantial amount of money."

"I heard. Ten million, yes?"

"Well, eight point five. He's paid off some of it already."

"Then take Brownstone Estate to pay off the rest. Sell it. You'll have your money," Daisy says, her whole body trembling with anger and barely suppressed hatred.

"Daisy, no. That's your inheritance. It's your home," I say, shaking my head.

"No, you're wrong, Drix. *You're* my home," she says, meeting my gaze before focussing back on Carl. "Take it. Sell it."

Carl has the audacity to laugh, and my fingers curl into fists. "Wipe that goddamn smile off your face, you bastard," I shout, lunging for him and grabbing him by the lapel of his jacket. I raise my fist, fucking furious, ready to knock him the fuck out.

He just smiles at me in that snakelike way off his, and threatens, "Do it, and see what happens."

"Drix, don't," Dalton says, grabbing my arm.

I let the arsehole go with a shove, backing off.

"Sell our home. You'll have your money," Daisy insists, a hell of a lot calmer than I am.

"Brownstone Estate isn't worth eight point five million," he tells her, straightening the lapel of his jacket. "At the most, you'd get four, maybe four and a half."

Daisy blanches, looking across at me. "He's right, Daise. I'm sorry."

"Okay, so we get four and half million for it, then we only owe you four million. We'll find a way to get that money," Daisy says, looking pointedly at Dalton.

Carl follows her gaze, cocking a brow. "Oh, you think my son has that kind of money, do you?"

"Don't try and tell me he doesn't. He's constantly flashing his wealth around for everyone to see," she snaps back.

"*My* wealth," Carl corrects her, his eyes narrowing on a sly smile.

Daisy frowns. "What?"

Carl tips his head back and laughs. Beside me Dalton scowls.

"Should I tell her, or will you?" Carl asks, flicking Dalton a smug smirk.

"I don't have an allowance anymore, Daisy. I earn my living as the manager of this hotel," he explains.

"And a *good* living, I might add. There aren't many hotel managers who earn two hundred and fifty thousand pounds a year. You should count yourself lucky, son."

Dalton swipes a hand over his face. "Yeah, Dad. *Thanks.*"

The fight Daisy entered the room with seems to drain out of her all in one go, and she sits down heavily on the couch opposite. When she looks up again, her eyes are flooded with tears.

"Please, Carl. Hubert was your best friend, don't do this."

"You're right, he was. Which is precisely why I helped him when he asked me to."

"Drix made a mistake. He was looking out for me, this shouldn't be his debt. It should be *mine.*"

"Absolutely fucking not!" I argue. "I chose to beat that prick up. Not you. This has nothing to do with you, Daisy. I will deal with it."

"And lose Lia and Toby?"

"I've already lost them. She wants nothing more to do with me," I reply, hating that it's true.

"You're wrong. She's just angry, *scared* right now. She knows who you truly are, Drix. She'll forgive you."

"I wish I could believe that, but she won't, Daisy. It's over. A man like me was never meant to have a woman as incredible as her. I don't deserve their love. I'm no good for them."

"No!" Daisy shouts. "Don't you dare do that. Don't you dare let her go. You have to fight for Lia, Drix! You have to show her how much you care, just like you did for me every day since we met. I didn't trust anyone. I didn't believe that there was anyone in this world who could love me until you came along. You can make this right. I *know* you can." Her voice wavers and she blinks back the tears threatening to fall.

"Daisy, just let this go," Dalton says, his tone softening as he stares at her.

"Don't talk to me," she snaps, holding her hand up to him. "Don't say another word!"

"You can't wave a magic wand and make this all go away," he persists. "This is the real world we live in, not some fairytale. People hurt each other, they fall out of love just as quickly as they fall into it. They fucking walk away."

Daisy glares at him, baring her teeth. "I'm well aware of what happens in the real world, Dalton. I grew up knowing all too well what it feels like to be shit upon. Don't you dare tell me to let this go, or play down what Lia and Drix feel for each other. *I* happen to care about Drix's happiness more than anything, more than my own. You should too."

"I do care," he counters. "But I'm realistic. I know when it's time to let shit go."

She scoffs then, her gaze trailing over him scornfully. "Oh wait, I forgot, you don't give a shit about anything other than *yourself*, and *your* selfish needs, right? It's easy for you. You pick women up and discard them the second you tire of them. You wouldn't know love if it whacked you across the fucking face!"

Dalton opens his mouth to respond, but Carl holds his hand up, silencing him. I don't like the way he's looking between the pair, and my hackles rise, sensing he's about to say something none of us are going to like.

"I have a proposition, one which might solve all of our problems," he begins.

Daisy frowns. "What proposition?"

Carl turns to Dalton, raising a brow. "You know what I need from you, son," he says, and Dalton's face pales. "And if Daisy truly wants to help you, then this would most certainly pay off your debt," he continues looking at me.

"Absolutely fucking not!" I grind out, knowing exactly where he's going with this.

Dalton shakes his head. "No, Dad."

"Come on, Daisy. We're leaving," I add, holding my hand out to her, but she bats it away, looking at Carl.

"What proposition?" she repeats.

"It's no secret that I want Dalton to settle down and marry, that I want a grandchild to carry on the family name."

"Stop fucking talking, Dad! That's enough!" Dalton snaps, turning his attention to Daisy. "Get up. Just fucking go with Drix."

She ignores him, instead straightening her spine and nodding. "Go on, Carl. Finish what you've got to say."

He smiles then like he's already won. "You agree to marry my son, give me a grandchild, and I will wipe Drix's debt the second that child is born."

"No!" Dalton shouts.

"Don't even think about it, Daisy!" I warn.

She turns to look at me, then at Dalton, before levelling her gaze with Carl's. "If you write off Drix's debt *immediately*, and release Drix from his obligations, I promise that I will marry Dalton and give you a grandchild," she says.

"The hell you will!" I shout.

"How do I know you'll go through with it?" Carl asks, ignoring me and narrowing his eyes at her.

"Draw up a contract. So long as Drix's debt is written off now, I will sign it. At that point he'll no longer be your enforcer. We will keep Brownstone Estate, and the only tie we'll have to your family will be our child. Dalton's and mine."

Dalton strides towards Daisy, stepping in front of her. "This is not happening! You've no idea what you're agreeing to here."

She draws herself upright, and despite being almost a foot shorter than Dalton, she stares him down, fierce in her intention. "I will do the right thing, for *all* of us. You will marry me, we will have a child, and Drix will be free to love Lia and Toby. I refuse to believe this is over for them."

"This is fucking ridiculous," he argues. "I am *not* marrying you."

"Over my dead body," I add, fucking vibrating with anger. "You're not doing this."

Stepping around Dalton, she faces me. "I am, and I will."

"Daisy, I don't need you to do this. Not to mention the fact I will kill Dalton if he lays one fucking finger on you."

"Precisely my point," Dalton adds, agreeing with me. "This isn't just a fake marriage, this is a *child* we're talking about. Need I remind you how they're made."

"All I need is your sperm. I don't need to fuck you to have your baby, Dalton," Daisy snaps.

Carl tips back his head and laughs. "You know what, Daisy Hammer, you've got a lot more spunk than I've given you credit for. I think I'm going to enjoy having you as my daughter-in-law."

"No," I persist.

"If you're free from your obligations, you'll have a chance to win Lia back, Drix. I know you can do it. I believe in you. I believe in your love," Daisy continues passionately.

"I can't let you ruin your life on a chance we *might* be able to save our relationship, Daisy. I won't let you do this," I say, shaking my head.

"Drix, when I was a kid, *you* saved *me*. Now I'm saving you. You need Lia. You need Toby. I love you, and I'm doing this for you with or without your approval," she croaks, reaching for me, her hand pressing against my chest. "I want you to be happy. Let me do this for you. *Please.*"

"And what about your happiness? What about that, huh?" I ask her.

"You know I've always wanted a family of my own. This baby will be my family. At least I know what I'm getting into with Dalton, and I'll be getting something precious out of it too."

"Even if by some miracle I manage to persuade Lia to work things out with me, I can't lie to her again, Daisy."

"I'm not asking you to lie to Lia. *I* will tell her why I'm doing it, and even if she still chooses to leave, I will go through with this because you're my brother and I don't want you to have to hurt people to pay off a debt for something you did out of love for me."

"You're going to do this no matter what I say, aren't you?" I concede, knowing that she will, that once she's made her mind up there is nothing I can do or say to stop her.

"Yes," she replies, giving me a small smile. "I'm okay with it. Truly."

"I'm fucking not," Dalton says, looking between us both, panic-striken, furious.

"This is happening," Carl intercedes. "As long as I can get a grandchild out of it, I really don't give a shit whether you're okay with it or not. But you're going to have to make this convincing for everyone else. We have a reputation to uphold. I can't have anyone suspecting your relationship is a farce. That won't do at all. "

"What reputation?" Dalton argues. "The one where you've had three wives, all of whom married you for money, and not love? Even Mum couldn't wait to leave. She practically skipped out of our home with her divorce settlement, and hasn't looked back since."

"Which is precisely why you're going to give the performance of a lifetime. At least until I have what I want," Carl says, offering a smile to Daisy. "Once the child is a year old, you'll be free to divorce Dalton, although there will be a stipulation in the contract that there will be no personal settlement for you, given the fact this is already costing me eight and a half million pounds."

"I don't want your money, I just want full responsibility for the care of our child. You and Dalton will be able to see him or her as often as you like."

Dalton shakes his head in disbelief. "So what you're basically saying is that you'll happily pretend to be in love with me, enter into a fake marriage, use me for my sperm, then divorce me a year after the baby is born?"

"I think that's about the gist of it," Daisy says, tipping her chin up, challenging him with her gaze.

"What am I, just some vessel for you to use then dump as soon as you've got what you want from me?" Dalton grinds out.

"I guess you'll know what it feels like to be on the receiving end for once, won't you?" Daisy shrugs, and Dalton flinches as though she's slapped him.

"I don't care much for babies, anyway," Carl adds with a wave of his hand. "So long as we have an heir, that's all that matters to me. I'm more than happy to provide for the child so it grows up accustomed to the lifestyle afforded to an heir of the Gunn family fortune."

"If I knew you just wanted an heir, I wouldn't have used a condom with the women I've been fucking. By now you'd have dozens of grandchildren running around," Dalton sneers.

"You misunderstand, son. I don't want *bastard* heirs. This marriage *has* to happen to make it official. Besides, I like the fact that Daisy is a Hammer. It works out rather nicely, don't you think?"

"Daisy," I grind out. "Please reconsider."

"Well that's settled then," she replies with a firm nod of her head. "Get the contract to me. I will review and sign it."

"And what if I don't agree. What if *I* refuse?" Dalton asks, folding his arms across his chest.

"Then you'll have to live with yourself knowing that you had a real chance to help your best friend out, and refused because you're too damn selfish to think about anyone other than yourself!" Daisy shouts, glaring at him.

For a moment Dalton doesn't respond, a muscle in his jaw flexing as he grits his teeth. They glare at each other, and I fucking pray Dalton denies her.

"Fine, we'll get married," he eventually says. "But if you think, for one second, that I won't be a part of *our* child's life every minute of every day after we've divorced, you've got another thing coming. You may think I'm a selfish bastard, Daisy, but I will *not* be a selfish father."

"I'm glad to hear it," Daisy replies.

"Excellent," Carl grins, getting to his feet and slapping his hand on Dalton's back. "I shall get the contract drawn up as soon as possible."

THIRTY-TWO

"LIA, CAN I SPEAK WITH YOU?" Daisy asks, rapping her knuckles on the bedroom door as I pack up mine and Toby's clothes. It's been almost a week since my heart shattered into a million pieces. For all that time, I've tried, and failed, to come to terms with what Drix had told me.

I've been a mess, missing him, hating him, wanting him, still loving him, needing to run.

He hasn't come back to Brownstone Estate, deciding instead to stay at his flat above the gym. The morning after the wedding he'd told me that he was moving out, that there was no need for us to rush off, that he was willing to offer us his home to stay in whilst I figured out what to do.

Another kindness, and yet the secrets he kept from me taint it now.

I can't trust him. But worse than that, I can't trust *myself*.

"Where's Toby?" I reply, placing Blue Bear on top of the suitcase.

"He's in the den, playing," she replies, stepping into the room. "Lia, we should talk."

"I really don't think there's much to say," I respond, hating how I sound because none of this is Daisy's fault. But I feel raw, exposed, and the only way to protect myself, to protect Toby, is to move on, to leave, even if that means leaving Daisy too.

"There's plenty to say, Lia," Daisy argues. "You need to hear me out okay? You're my friend, I care about you. I know that you're hurting, but there are things I need to tell you..."

"Hurting?" I release a broken laugh, forcing myself not to cry. I've done too much of that already. "I'm angry, Daisy. I'm scared. I'm *heartbroken.*"

"Drix is heartbroken too. I've never seen him this cut up. He's not himself without you."

"He's never been himself around me, Daisy. It was all a lie."

She sits down on the edge of the bed, reaching for my hand, taking it in hers. "No, it wasn't."

"How can you say that?"

"Because it's true. Drix is still the man you fell in love with," she insists. "His kindness, his big heart, his warmth, his love for you, none of that was a lie. I *know* him."

"I thought I did too," I whisper out, casting my gaze away, dragging in a deep breath.

"I know it's hard to come to terms with what he did. It was difficult for me to hear too, but I've had years of loving Drix, and I can categorically say that he is a good man. He did what he did out of love for me, just like he took on this debt and became their enforcer to keep looking after me."

"It's hard for me to get my head around all of this," I admit.

"All of the good he's done far outweighs the bad. He is *not* like your husband," she insists. "He would never hurt you or Toby, me, his friends, *any* decent person. The men he's hurt, they aren't good people."

"So you're saying that I should just turn a blind eye, forget that he almost killed a man? That I should stay with him and ignore the fact that when he's not home with me and Toby he's out there, somewhere, hurting someone? I *can't* do it. That kind of violence has a habit of rubbing off on others. I didn't just leave Martin because he hurt me, because he would've eventually hurt Toby, I also left because I didn't want Toby to have that kind of toxic influence in his life. I don't want Toby growing up thinking that violence is okay, because it isn't. Look at how much damage it's already done, to me, to Toby, to you, to Drix."

"Which is why I've made a deal with Carl Gunn to write off Drix's debt," she says.

"What are you talking about? What deal?"

"Lia, Drix needed a way out, and I've found the solution. I'm willing to do whatever it takes so that he can be done with that life. I did it so that you three can be a family, if you choose to stay that is. I really, truly, hope that you do."

"Daisy, what have you done?" I ask, a chill running down my spine.

"What I'm about to tell you goes no further. Even if you decide to still leave after everything I tell you, you must promise never to speak a word of this. I'm about to tell you some things about my past, and it's important to me that you don't speak about it to anyone. Please, Lia."

"Daisy—"

"You have to *promise* me," she urges. "It's important."

"Okay," I agree, terrified of what she's about to tell me.

"Okay." Letting out a breath, she levels her gaze with mine. "Before I explain what I've agreed to do, I want to tell you about how I ended up in care, and how Drix saved my life."

"He saved your life?"

"Yes," she replies softly.

"How, Daisy?" I ask.

"I was five when I went into care," she begins, her fingers tightening around mine. "I arrived at the foster home a month after

Drix. I was malnourished, suffering from the effects of emotional, physical and mental abuse. I wasn't a child, I was barely even a functioning human. I was utterly broken, as broken as any person could be."

"Daisy, I'm sorry," I whisper out, feeling for her, hating what she's been through.

"The day I arrived, Drix was kicking a ball in the backyard of our foster parents' home. The social workers introduced me to him briefly, leaving me to sit and watch him whilst they gave our foster parents my personal file. At this point, I was beyond terrified," she explains, her eyes glossing over from the memory. "I was an empty shell. Hollow. I had no idea of the concept of suicide at that age, but I knew that I didn't want to live, that I didn't know what living even was. All I knew was pain, sadness, and despair. All I felt was this gaping hole, this emptiness inside of me."

Releasing one of my hands, she rubs her palm over the centre of her chest, her fingers trembling.

"I didn't move from the spot on the step they'd left me on. I just sat and watched Drix kick that football around. He asked me to play with him, but I couldn't. When he realised I wasn't going to join in, he came and sat down next to me. He didn't say a word. He simply put his arm around my shoulder and held me. I cried in his arms for an hour, Lia, and he just held me until I was spent, knowing instinctively that's what I needed the most. To be held with kindness."

In that moment, I'm reminded of all the times Drix has held me in his arms, how safe he'd made me feel, and a lump forms in my throat. Neither one of us speaks as she lets that information slowly sink in.

"At the time I had no idea about the level of trauma *he'd* been through, because on the surface he seemed like any other kid his age. It wasn't until I was sixteen that he finally told me what happened the night his dad murdered his mum."

"Oh God, I'm not sure I'm ready to hear this," I admit.

"Drix saw everything, Lia. He witnessed his father stab his mum multiple times with a knife. The post-mortem revealed that she had twenty-seven wounds. The only reason Drix survived is because he hid in his mum's wardrobe. When his father left, he tried to bring her back to life..." Daisy's voice trails off as she chokes on the words, and I have to stifle my own sob. "He blames himself for her death, you know."

"He was just a child, what could he have done?" I ask.

"We both know he couldn't have done anything, but he's been left with the scars of that night, and has carried them with him all these years. He holds on to so much guilt, Lia. Yet, despite that, he still has this big, beautiful heart. This huge capacity to *love*. Please don't undervalue that."

"I understand he's been through something horrific. I do, Daisy, and I hate that for him. I hate that he had to experience so much trauma, but..."

"But?"

"But the way he lost it with that guy who hurt you, I'm afraid of that kind of violence. I've lived in fear for so long. I spent years walking on eggshells around Martin. He would turn at the flip of a switch. What if...?" I can't even bear to say the words, to express them out loud.

"Drix wouldn't hurt you. He couldn't. He loves you, so, so much, Lia. You and Toby."

"You can't know that for sure."

Daisy heaves out a breath, blinking back her tears. "I do know that, and let me tell you why. For the next five years when we lived in foster care together, Drix took it upon himself to look after me. He kept me company, he coaxed me out of my shell, and slowly but surely I became a little girl again. In the day at least."

"In the day?" I frown, not understanding.

"The only other people who know what I truly suffered as a

child are Drix and Hubert. Even the social workers and the family who fostered me didn't know half of it. I was picked up by a stranger on the side of a motorway and eventually handed over to social services. Most people believe I was abandoned by my parents, and whilst that is true, it's not in the way they assume."

"You don't have to tell me if it's too painful," I say.

"I'm telling you because you need to understand why Drix is so protective of me, and why he did what he did."

"Go on," I say, softly.

"With Drix's love and affection, I began to blossom. In the daytime, when the light was shining, I was able to claw back some happiness. Everything seemed so much better in the daylight, but at night, when darkness fell, I was thrown back into my past."

"Nightmares?"

Daisy lets out a tremulous breath before pushing on. "More of a living nightmare. My parents used to keep me in a dark room, all day and all night, Lia."

"My God, how evil," I exclaim.

"They kept me chained to a bed, made me shit and piss in a bucket, and on the odd occasion when they remembered they had a daughter, they fed me scraps. I was no better than an animal to them. So at night, when darkness fell I became that tortured, caged little girl all over again. All the progress I made in the day evaporated until Drix figured out how to help me."

"What did he do to help you?"

"He used to wrap his body around mine and hold me all night long. He gave me the warmth and the kindness I needed to get through those dark nights. He protected me, cared for me, became my rock all whilst he carried his own trauma within him. He never expected anything in return."

Daisy gives me a tremulous smile, and I don't have the words to express how bad I feel for her, how gutted I am that she had to endure so much, that they both did. Instead, I wait for her to continue.

"The night Jonathon dumped me so cruelly, something inside of me broke. It triggered all my past trauma and pain, and I spiralled into a very dark place. Drix witnessed me disappearing before his eyes, and two weeks after that night I overdosed on painkillers. I tried to kill myself, Lia. Drix found me, and because of his quick thinking I'm still alive today. He forced me to be sick, held me whilst I threw up. He wouldn't leave my side. For a week he stayed with me in hospital. He loved me back to life, Lia. First as a child, and then again as an adult. That is why I know he'd never hurt you. The very core of him is *good*, Lia."

He loved me back to life...

Her words penetrate somewhere deep inside, and I choke back another sob, because that's exactly what he's done for me. Drix has loved *me* back to life.

"My decision to try and end my life had terrible consequences," she continues. "I know now that Drix sought out Jonathon, told him what I'd done, tried to get him to come and see me, to apologise in the hope I'd find some peace in that. Apparently Jonathon just laughed in his face. Drix lost it... And, well, you know the rest of the story."

"Daisy, I'm so so sorry. I don't know what else to say."

"There's nothing you can say, but you can try to understand why he acted the way he did. He lost control in a moment of vulnerability and despair. Don't you see, he wasn't able to protect his mum from a despicable human being, but at that moment when Jonathon laughed in his face, he was trying to protect me from future pain and heartache."

"This is a lot to take in," I admit, my head whirling with so many emotions as I try to unravel my own feelings.

"So later, after Hubert had died," Daisy pushes on. "Drix agreed to pay off the debt. He could've sold Brownstone Estate to help clear the debt—God, I wished he had—but instead he stepped into a role he despises, hating himself for the things he's had to do. Which is why I've made a deal with Carl so Drix is free from that debt."

"What's the deal you've made, Daisy?"

"I'm going to marry Dalton and have his child."

"You're going to *what?*" I exclaim.

"Carl Gunn wants a legitimate heir to carry on the family name. I'm going to give him one so long as he releases Drix from his obligations."

"You can't do that. This is unbelievable."

"I'm going to do it because I want Drix to find happiness of his own with you and Toby, and he can't do that so long as he works for the families. This is my way of saving him, Lia, just like he saved me."

"And Drix is okay with this?" I ask.

"No, not at all. But he knows that I will do it regardless if you stay or go. I'm going to marry Dalton. I signed the contract, it's already done. Drix is free."

"You're willing to sacrifice your own happiness to do that for him, *for us?*"

She gives me a gentle smile. "I'm willing to do whatever it takes. Drix's kindness saved my life, and now I'm paying that kindness forward. The question is, are you willing to see past what scares you the most? Are you willing to do the same?"

THIRTY-THREE

THE GYM IS EERILY QUIET, the only sounds coming from the clanking of weights, and my heavy pants as I work out. Sweat drips over my skin, my muscles screaming at me to stop, to rest, but I can't. I need to rid myself of the stress, the pain, the anger, the frustration that's been building over the last week. Hell, for years now.

It's agony being away from Lia and Toby. It hurts so damn much.

For seven days straight, this has become my routine, keeping myself busy at the gym throughout the day and night, working out my stress until exhaustion takes over. Anything to keep from turning to the bottle like my father did. I won't go there.

But my workout is interrupted by the door to the gym slamming open. I grind my teeth not wanting to have a conversation with anyone, let alone Dalton, who steps into the room.

"What the fuck do you want?" I growl, side-eying him as he strides towards me. It's well past closing time, and I'm not in the mood for him. Not in the slightest. Fuck, it's all I can do not to punch his lights out.

"Riley let me in," Dalton replies calmly, unperturbed by my anger.

"I told him to go home," I huff, dropping the weights onto the mat and snatching up a towel from the floor. Every night my friends here at the gym have been taking turns watching over me. I've told them time and again I don't need babysitting, but they insisted. Frankly, I can't stand the look of pity in their eyes. It makes me feel worse than I already do.

"He has. Look, he's worried about you. We all are," Dalton says, sitting down on the bench press, watching me.

"I'm fine!" I snap, running the towel across my damp forehead.

Closing my eyes, I push away thoughts of Lia and Toby, trying to ignore how much I long for them. Every time I've let myself think about them, I've had an overwhelming urge to go to them, but I know that would only make things worse. Lia needed space to figure things out and I promised to give her that. It's the least I can do after everything I've put her through.

The tension cracks in the air between us as Dalton unbuttons his coat, revealing a crisp white shirt and perfectly tailored pants. I drop the towel to the floor feeling exposed and vulnerable under his gaze.

"You're a mess," he states bluntly, his eyes roaming over me.

"What the hell do you expect?" I shoot back, my anger rising. "Not only have I fucked up my relationship with Lia, my stupidity has meant Daisy is marrying you!"

"I never wanted that," he admits, his voice tinged with regret.

"Yet you're still going through with it!" I counter, my fists tightening at my sides. "Daisy told me she signed the fucking contract yesterday, Dalton. That you did too!"

He blows out a breath, his expression pained. "Your debt is clear, Drix. I did it for you."

My anger boils over at his words. "Don't you dare say that you're doing this for me. Let's be real here, we both know that you're only doing it for the damn money!" I spit out each word like venom.

For a moment guilt flashes in his eyes, before being replaced by another emotion I can't quite decipher. There's something deeper there, hidden beneath the surface of his perfect facade. But it doesn't last long, nothing ever does with Dalton. He's always quick to push aside any emotions, just like he does with all the women he's fucked. I'm the only relationship he's stayed faithful to, and our once solid friendship is on very shaky ground. I can barely look at him.

"Partly, yes. But, I'm *also* doing it for you."

I bite out a harsh laugh, my voice dripping with bitterness and hurt. "And what about Daisy? What about her happiness, huh? Jesus fuck, Dalton, what about her?"

His eyes flicker away from mine. "She's made her choice," he replies stoically. "Besides, you heard what she said. She's getting something out of this too. Pretty sure she's going to be using me as much as my dad is using her to get what he wants.

My heart aches at the thought of Daisy being manipulated in such a way. Dalton can play martyr all he wants, we both know this is a win-win for him.

"Yeah, a child!" I shout in frustration. "Don't you fucking get it? The only thing Daisy has ever wanted was to love and be loved in return. You can't give her that. We both know that you're fucking incapable."

He flinches at my words, but he doesn't try to deny it.

"I'll do my best by her," he replies with a hint of defeat, dropping his gaze to the floor.

"How? How will you do your best for her?" I demand, my anger fueling my words. "You're a fucking sex addict. You'll be shagging the next woman who offers herself to you without a second thought. You've probably just come from fucking someone right now. You're incapable of keeping your dick in your pants, let alone staying faithful. Daisy deserves better than that. She's worth so much more than having to suffer in a loveless marriage."

My voice breaks with emotion as I think of Daisy trapped in a relationship with a man who cannot give her the love and loyalty she deserves, all because of *me* and *my* choices.

With my feet firmly planted and my legs spread to a comfortable hip width, I bend at the waist and wrap my calloused hands around the cold metal barbell. My fingers grip tightly as I prepare to unleash my pent-up frustration and anger on this weight. I avoid looking at Dalton, too afraid of what I might do if I catch his gaze. Instead, I focus on the task at hand—lifting the barbell. The weight feels heavier than usual, but I push through it, determined to punish my body instead of taking out my emotions on my best friend.

As I finish my second set, every muscle in my body is screaming for me to stop, but I can't. The adrenaline and fury coursing through me demands that I continue. Without hesitation, I replace the barbell on the rack and reach for the dumbbells once more.

"I give you my word, Drix," Dalton finally speaks up, his hand raking through his hair as he watches me with concern. "I won't sleep with anyone while I'm with Daisy."

I scoff bitterly. "You're telling me you can last that long? You're looking at almost *two years* before she can divorce you after you get married." I pause, feeling the weight of my sadness and frustration crushing down on me. "And let's not forget that the only way you'll be able to have a child together is through jerking off into a cup because you aren't touching my sister. Understand?"

Dalton meets my angry gaze head on, his jaw set in determination. "I *can* do it. And yes, Daisy has already made it very clear how we plan on having a baby."

"Well, at least we're all in agreement on that fucking point," I growl, dropping the dumbbells with a loud clatter as I throw my hands up in exasperation. "This is complete and utter horseshit."

A heavy sigh escapes Dalton's lips. "I suppose we've both made our beds, and now we have to lie in them."

I can't help but scoff at his words. "In your case, it's your own motherfucking bed."

"I've got the message, Drix," he throws back.

"So when's this farce of a wedding taking place?" I ask, wiping the sweat from my forehead with the back of my hand, my heart pounding with dread.

Dalton pauses for a moment, as if weighing his words carefully before answering. "Soon."

"How soon?" I press, my voice tight with barely suppressed panic.

"Six weeks time," he says, and the weight of those two simple words nearly knocks me off my feet.

"Fuck," I exclaim, running a hand through my hair in frustration.

"Yeah," Dalton replies, his own expression grim. "Daisy is going to be moving in with us next week."

I feel like he's just punched me in the gut. "She's *moving in?*"

"We have to make this look real, Drix," Dalton continues, his voice low and serious. "But don't worry she'll have her own suite."

"That does *not* make me feel any better," I mutter, my mind reeling with the implications of all this.

Moving to stand, Dalton reaches into the inside pocket of his coat, pulling out a magazine and dropping it onto the bench. "This was published two days ago," he says, gesturing to the glossy cover featuring Robert and Melody smiling on the front steps of the hotel. "According to Robert, the magazine sold just as many copies covering their wedding as it did when the latest Royals tied the knot."

I let out a humourless laugh. "That man is delusional. What a dick."

Dalton shrugs nonchalantly, but then locks eyes with me as his expression turns serious once again. "I have one more thing I want to say before I leave."

"Yeah, and what's that?" I ask, bracing myself for whatever truth bomb he's about to drop.

"Don't you think you owe it to Daisy to at least try to salvage your relationship with Lia?"

Dalton's words hit me like a sledgehammer. It's a reminder of all the things I've been avoiding. "Don't tell me what to fucking do, Dalton," I snap, my anger flaring up again.

"Then don't be a selfish prick," he retorts, his voice sharp and unyielding. "Stop hiding out here when you have a real chance at happiness. Some of us don't have that luxury—believe me, I should know," he adds bitterly before turning on his heel and striding out of the gym leaving me speechless.

EXHAUSTED AND JITTERY, I plop down on the sofa in my flat above the gym and cradle a steaming cup of black coffee in my hands. Letting out a heavy sigh, I try to process Dalton's advice, but my thoughts are a chaotic mess. The impending wedding between my best friend and my little sister swirls through my mind, a tempest of conflicting emotions that leaves me feeling overwhelmed and disoriented. On one hand, Daisy's sacrifice has already benefited me greatly—it has lifted me from the crippling debt and has given me the opportunity to find happiness. But at what cost? How can I justify allowing Daisy to tie herself to someone else for my sake? Selfishness gnaws at me, threatening to consume any sense of rationale or morality. And yet, here I sit, miserable and lost in this whirlwind of complicated feelings because ultimately I want a chance to make things work with Lia and Toby. I want them in my life for good.

Placing my cup on the coffee table, I pick up the magazine Dalton left behind in the gym and flip through the pages. Each picture tells a story of a perfect wedding between two people in love. Their happy expressions caught on camera, the written article accompanying it spinning a story of romance and devoted love. In contrast my life feels like a messy, unedited draft of a story.

As I flip through the pages, my eyes lock on to a picture of Lia and me, caught in an intimate dance with our lips locked in a kiss. At the sight of it my love is like a spark inside of me that grows into a blazing fire.

God, how I love her.

As much as I hate to admit it, Dalton is right. I would never forgive myself if I didn't at least try to set things straight with Lia. No more putting off the inevitable, I need her to hear what I have to say. Getting into bed, I vow that first thing in the morning I'm going to fight for the woman I love.

Early the next morning, the sharp trill of my phone drags me out of my sleep, and I push upright, blinking as my eyes adjust to the light. On my bedside table, the LED light from my alarm clock tells me it's just after seven am. Reaching for my phone, I glance at the screen. A sharp pang of dread shoots through my stomach when I see that it's an incoming call from Daisy. Is she calling me to say that Lia has left already?

"Daisy?" I grunt into the phone, my voice strained.

"Drix, you need to come home now," she whispers urgently. "Martin's here."

Martin? Fuck, no!

And then it hits me, the photo in the magazine.

"Shit!" I blurt out, fear creeping into my veins, a sudden wave of panic washing over me. "Where are you now?"

"With Toby. I heard the commotion and locked us both in his

bedroom, but Lia is downstairs with him. He barged his way in, Drix. He's going to hurt her!."

I hear the sound of Toby's sobs in the background, and it's all I can do not to lose my damn mind. "Stay right where you are, and as soon as you hang up, call the police. I'm coming."

THIRTY-FOUR

"YOU FUCKING WHORE, shacked up with another man!" Martin shouts, his voice filled with rage as I back up against the sofa, my whole body trembling with fear as my gaze locks onto his. I can only thank God that I'd been up to get a glass of water, and it wasn't Daisy who'd answered the door. She would've heard the commotion and taken Toby somewhere safe.

"Calm down. Let's talk like rational adults," I reply, trying and failing to hide the tremor in my voice as I stare at the man I once foolishly loved dressed like he's someone from the post office, he's even wearing a baseball cap with the logo printed on it. That's what I saw in the security camera attached to the doorbell. I just assumed it was a delivery. I'm an idiot.

"Did you honestly think that I wouldn't find you?" he asks, ripping off the baseball cap and chucking it to the ground. "Where's your new man now, huh?"

I blanch as he eyes me knowingly.

"Yeah, that's right, he isn't here, is he? You think I haven't done some investigation of my own? So don't even think about pretending he's here, because I know full well he isn't."

"Please, don't do this, Martin. Think of Toby," I beg, the weight of his anger compressing the space around us, narrowing down the world to this single, desperate moment.

"I *am* thinking of my son," he snarls back, stepping towards me as my heart pounds wildly against my rib cage, each beat a desperate plea for escape from this nightmare. "You took him from me, and you will fucking die knowing that you brought this on yourself."

"You don't have to do this. I made a mistake. I will come home with you. We can be happy again," I lie, hoping to subdue him, at least until help arrives. Daisy isn't stupid, she would've called for help.

"You think I'm a fucking fool, don't you?" he sneers, his words a deadly hiss. "You think you can just run off with my son, and whore yourself out to another man and there wouldn't be any consequences? I'm going to fucking kill you!"

"Please, Martin," I beg, my heart pounding in my chest, the echo of each beat deafening in my ears as I back up. I try to swallow, but my throat is as dry as sandpaper. "You have to think of Toby."

He laughs then, a cold humourless sound that sends chills down my spine. "You thought that you could just leave me and live happily ever after?" he growls as he closes the gap between us.

"I... I never meant for this to happen," I stammer, trying to buy as much time as possible. "We can work this out. We can be a family again, just like before."

"Where's my son?" he snaps back, eying the stairs.

"In bed, asleep. Please, Martin, let's just talk," I say, forcing the tremble from my voice, knowing that my fear will only fuel his hatred. "We can figure this out."

"Talk about what, how you upped and left in the middle of the night? How I find out that you've been fucking another man after seeing you draped all over him in a magazine? Do you know how fucking humiliating that is?"

"I'm sorry," I say, holding my hands up as I edge towards the china lamp sitting on the side table next to the sofa. If I can get to it, maybe I can use it as a weapon.

"You're sorry? You're fucking sorry?" Another maniacal laugh escapes his lips, and it takes everything in me to remain strong, to not cry.

"Let me make it up to you," I whisper.

"And how do you plan on doing that?" he asks.

I take a deep breath, trying to steady my nerves. "I'll come back home, and we can go to counselling. We can work through our issues together," I say, hoping that my words will calm his anger. It's all a lie, of course, I'd rather rip my own eyes out than go home with him, but it's all I can think of to say.

"Counselling?" he scoffs, fury burning in his eyes. "After everything you've done? You think that's going to fix things?"

"Please, Martin," I plead. "Just give me a chance to make things right."

He shakes his head, his dark hair falling into his eyes. "Fuck you, Lia. You're nothing but a filthy whore, I don't want you back. I want revenge, and I'm going to get it."

Tears spring to my eyes, but I quickly blink them away. "I didn't mean for it to happen like this," I whisper, hating how my voice betrays me.

"But it did happen," he snaps back. "And now you have to face the consequences." My stomach drops as realisation dawns on me - there is no talking or reasoning with him, this is it, this is the night he'll finally kill me. All I can think about is Drix and what he had to witness as a child. I can't let that happen. I can't allow Toby to go through the same trauma.

"Please," I beg one last time, my gaze flicking towards the lamp.

Sensing what I'm about to do, he lunges for me right at the

same moment my fingers wrap around the base of the lamp. I pick it up, ripping it from the socket, and throwing it at him with a cry of fear and blazing anger.

The lamp smashes against his chest, scattering to pieces as he reels backwards from the force. Seizing the opportunity, I run towards the kitchen, my heart pounding as I hear Martin's angry shouts behind me.

Running towards the utensil draw, I rip it open, my hands shaking as I search for something, anything to protect myself. My eyes land on a large chef's knife, its serrated edge gleaming ominously. Gripping it tightly, I feel a wave of determination wash over me as he bursts into the kitchen.

His eyes drop to the knife, then lift back up at me. "You don't have it in you," he smirks, edging closer, his eyes filled with malice and a sick satisfaction at the fear in mine. "You're weak. You're nothing but a pathetic sack of flesh."

At that moment something inside me snaps. I will no longer be a victim of this man's abuse. I refuse to let him hurt me or take my son. No more.

"Fuck you, Martin. I'm done being your punching bag, someone for you to abuse. If you dare lay another finger on me I will kill you!"

"Is that so?" he taunts, the scent of fear, rage and sweat filling the air.

"I mean every damn word," I grind out.

"You really think you can fight me?"

"I do," I reply, my voice strong and steady. "You took everything from me, Martin. My confidence, my self-respect, but you will not take my son, and neither will you take my life."

He looks at me, his face twisted in fury. "You've finally lost it, haven't you? You fucking crazy bitch."

I don't let him goad me into lowering the knife. I'm not backing down, not this time. Feeling a surge of courage rushing through my veins, I hold onto the knife with a tight grip, ready to defend myself.

"No, you're wrong. I've finally found my courage, and a decent, kind, incredible man who *loves* me and Toby. You have no power of me anymore, you fucking arsehole. Come at me, I dare you!" I shout, ready to end this now. I'm not just willing to fight, I'm ready for a full-on brawl.

Maybe it's the adrenaline rushing through my veins, or maybe it's the thought of losing everything I hold dear, but I can't let this monster take any more from me. My heart is pounding in my chest, and my hands are trembling, but I'm not going to let fear get the best of me. As he approaches me, I lunge, swinging the knife with all my might. The blade makes contact with his arm, drawing a deep gash that turns his skin crimson. His scream of pain fills the glaring silence, and I can't help but feel a sense of satisfaction.

"Don't you ever touch me again, Martin!" I scream. "Don't you fucking dare!"

Martin stares at the cut on his arm, his face twisting into a mask of pure evil, and the laugh that follows? God, it sends shivers down my spine.

"I'm going to fucking enjoy this," he rasps, lunging for me.

I swing the knife wildly at him, and in that moment I lose all sense of myself. All I care about is protecting Toby, and ending this once and for all.

A ferocious anger I have never experienced before consumes me, and the sound of my own pulse pounding in my ears drowns out all other noise. Every muscle in my body is tense, preparing to defend myself as he lunges at me once more. I manage to evade his attack, slicing the knife across his cheek. Blood spurts from the wound and he screams again, this time with a mixture of fury and pain.

"You bitch!" he snarls, but I can't react quickly enough as he grabs onto my arm and twists it painfully, attempting to wrench the knife from my grasp.

In a desperate move, I kick out at him, but his rage only seems to fuel his strength. The knife falls to the ground as he pushes me down and kicks me in the stomach.

The blows keep coming, and I fight with everything I have but Martin's rage seems endless. The tears stream down my face as I try to protect myself, but it's like trying to hold back a tsunami with my bare hands.

"You think you're so fucking tough now?" he growls as he straddles my chest, pinning me down. "You think you can just walk away from me?"

All I can do is whimper in response as he continues his assault. My vision is blurred from the tears and the pain as I hold my arms up to protect my face. I don't know how much longer I can last, and as I begin to slip into darkness, a familiar figure looms over both of us.

"Get off of her!" Drix roars as Martin is pulled off of me and forcefully thrown across the room.

Martin staggers to his feet, but Drix throws a lethal punch, knocking him to the ground.

"You dare to hurt the woman I love?" he shouts, bending over Martin and unleashing a barrage of punches as police sirens wail in the distance. I've never witnessed such brutal force, and the sounds of fists meeting flesh ricochets around the room creating a symphony of pain and anger.

"Stop. Please, stop!" I beg, as Martin soon turns limp in Drix's grasp.

I push up onto my hands and knees, crawling towards them both as Drix's fist is held mid-air, a wild look in his eyes as he registers my words. For a moment we just stare at one another, caught in this defining moment. Martin is still breathing, and as much as I wish he were dead, I don't want Drix to go to prison for murder. I couldn't bear it.

"Please, no more," I whimper.

"Oh, Lia!" he cries, dropping his fist and falling to his knees, dragging me into his arms. My body screams in pain but I ignore it, clinging to him tightly.

"You saved me," I whisper through my sobs.

"No Lia, you brave, beautiful woman, you saved yourself," he replies, his voice cracking with emotion as he presses kisses all over my face. "If I'd lost you..."

"Never. You have me Drix. It's over," I reply, pressing my lips against his.

"Mama?" I hear Toby calling my name, and I shake my head.

"He can't see this. Please, Drix."

"Go to him. I'll watch over this arsehole until the police arrive."

"Thank you." With tremendous effort I climb to my feet with Drix's help. He pulls me into his embrace once again, cradling my head with one hand as he stares at me with such reverence, my heart skips a beat.

"Mama? Mama?" Toby cries, and I pull back, ignoring the pain that seems to have enveloped my body.

"Go," Drix says, brushing the tip of his nose against the bridge of mine.

With one final lingering kiss, I untangle myself from Drix's arms, and force steel into my spine as I walk towards Toby and Daisy who are waiting at the top of the stairs.

"Is he?" Daisy asks, her eyes flying over me.

I shake my head. "No, but he's out cold. Drix came. He's here. We're safe now."

Toby pulls his hand free from Daisy's and rushes down the stairs. Hauling him into my arms, I hold him close as he sobs against my chest.

"I heard you screaming, Mama," he cries, his whole body trembling as Daisy drops onto the step beside us.

"Shhh, it's over, Toby. We're safe," I say determinedly.

"I should've come to help," Daisy whispers, her eyes welling with tears as she looks at me.

"No, don't do that. Don't you dare feel guilty. You did the right thing. If Martin had hurt him, hurt you..." My lips tremble as I realise how close I was to losing everyone I love.

"I'm so sorry, Lia," Daisy manages to choke out between sobs, tears cascading down her cheeks as she wraps her arms around me, seeking solace in each other's presence.

"We're going to be okay now," I reassure them both, and as Drix strides to the front door, letting the police in, I really, *truly,* believe it.

THIRTY-FIVE

STARING out of my bedroom window, the sky is a canvas of muted oranges and pinks, the sun just beginning to make its ascent above the horizon.

Behind me Lia sleeps peacefully, her arms wrapped around Toby on my bed. They're both exhausted, emotionally, physically and mentally worn out after a day and part of the night at the hospital where Lia was checked over by the medical staff, and the police had questioned us all about the events that unfolded. She has some deep bruising on her torso, back and cheek from Martin's punches, and a broken rib but no other injuries apart from the ones that only time and love can heal.

Apart from a few unsettled hours, I've barely had any rest, watching over them both as they slept. I'd come so close to losing them, and the thought makes my chest ache. Absentmindedly, I reach up and rest my palm over my heart, rubbing the pain that lingers there still.

"Drix?"

Lia's soft voice drags me out of my thoughts as her arms wrap around my waist and she presses her chest against my back.

"I didn't mean to wake you," I reply, twisting in her arms to face her.

"You didn't," she responds, looking up at me.

"How do you feel?" I ask, brushing my knuckles gently against her cheek, my stomach coiling at the deep purple bruise blooming there.

"Better now you're here," she replies, her eyelids fluttering shut as I uncurl my fingers and she leans into my open palm.

"I'm sorry, for everything," I say, dropping my forehead to hers, my heart aching for all that she's been through, that they've both been through.

"I'm not," she replies, tipping her head back so she can brush her lips to mine. "As horrific as this experience has been, it's brought me to you, Drix."

"Lia, I don't deserve you."

"You're wrong," she insists, her voice catching with emotion.

"I would've killed him, you know," I confess. Part of me wishing I had, needing to be completely honest with her.

"I know, but I would never forgive myself if you had. Martin is going to get what he deserves, and that's a very, very long time in prison. He no longer holds any power over me, Drix, and I have you to thank for that."

"How so?"

Lia's eyes meet mine. "Because you gave me the strength to find my own power, to fight back. Being with you, being *loved* by you has helped me reclaim my sense of self-worth."

"That means a lot to me, Lia."

"Will you take a bath with me?" she asks after a beat, taking my hand in hers.

I nod, my throat thick with love. "What about Toby?"

"He'll sleep for a while yet. Please, Drix, I just want to wash away the memories of last night. I want to start over."

"Okay."

Stepping into the ensuite, I gently close the door and reach for the taps, turning on the water. As it fills I help Lia to undress, her winces of pain cutting me deep. When she's naked before me and I see the extent of the damage Martin has done, it takes everything in me not to drop to my knees and weep. With trembling hands, my fingers trail over the deep purple bruises blooming across her chest.

"Look at what he did to you," I whisper, my head dropping as I try and fail to steady my voice.

"Don't do that, don't let him get inside your head. These will heal. I *will* heal," she replies, as I remove my own clothes until we're both naked.

"You're so strong, Lia. God, so fucking brave."

"I am now," she replies as I drop to my knees and wrap my arms around her, my legs no longer able to hold me upright. Her fingers stroke through my hair as I press gentle kisses against her bruises, wanting so desperately to take the pain away.

"Can I say something?" she asks after a moment, looking down at me as I look up at her.

"Of course," I reply, climbing to my feet and resting on the edge of the tub.

"Yesterday, I was ready to leave. I'd packed my bags, Drix. I was so afraid of the violence you'd committed that I couldn't see past what scared me the most, to the man you truly are."

"I don't blame you for wanting to leave. I understand. If you still want to go..." My voice trails off as I contemplate the thought of her walking away.

"I'm not leaving, Drix. I'm not going anywhere. Please, just let me finish."

I heave out a breath, forcing myself to look at her, to be brave in the face of her honesty. "Go on."

"Then Daisy came to me. She told me about what happened to her as a child, how her parents mistreated her, how much she'd been through at the hands of their cruelty, how broken she was."

"She told you?"

"Yes. She told me that with your love, care and patience she became happy again. You looked after her even when you were suffering from your own trauma." She pauses then, dragging in a deep breath. "I know what happened the night your father killed your mother, Drix."

"Fuck," I whisper, the pain of that memory like a battering ram against my chest. "I tried to bring her back. I tried to help her, Lia."

"I know," she replies, brushing her fingers over my cheek, tears welling in her eyes. "But you were just a child. You couldn't have done anything. I want you to know that none of it was your fault. That experience shaped you, and your need to protect the people you love, Drix. I see that now. I was wrong to even consider for a moment that you could hurt me like Martin had. That came from a place of fear, and from my own experiences, and I'm sorry for letting that cloud my judgement."

"You never have to apologise to me, Lia."

"Daisy explained what happened after Jonathon humiliated her," she continues, pressing on as I reach for her, my hands resting against her hips. "That she tried to commit suicide, that you saved her life, and stayed with her at the hospital until she recovered."

I shudder at the memory. "I almost lost her, Lia."

"But your quick thinking saved her, Drix, and your love helped to heal her once again."

"Anyone would've done the same," I reply.

"Not everyone, Drix. We both know there are many cruel people in the world."

"I guess," I concede.

"She told me that you tried to get Jonathon to apologise, that he mocked Daisy, laughed at her pain, and that is why you lost it. I can understand why, Drix. Again, you were protecting her from the pain, from someone deeply cruel, and you continued to protect her taking on the debt and becoming an enforcer for the families. Doing something like that comes from a place of love, and a deep sense of empathy. I see that now. I see you," she whispers.

"Lia..." I can't finish my sentence, overwhelmed with gratitude, with love.

"She told me how your kindness brought her back to life, Drix, and it reminded me of all the times you've been kind to me and Toby, how you brought *me* back to life, and I knew at that moment that you were still the man I fell in love with. The violence you committed isn't who you are, but a product of circumstance, of a deep-seated need to protect the people you love."

"Thank you," I say. "For seeing me."

"Thank you, for loving me back to life, Drix," she replies, silently taking my hand as she steps into the bath, easing herself down into the water. I climb in too, switching off the taps as I face her.

"I vow to you, Lia, that I will continue to love you the way you deserve. That I will be the best dad to Toby," I say, cupping her face and pressing a sweet kiss against her lips.

"And I vow to always trust in us, in our friendship, and in our love," she replies, grabbing hold of the body wash and taking my hand in hers, squeezing some into my palm, before adding some to her own.

Adjusting her body she slides her legs over my hips, the most tender parts of us touching as she begins to wash my body. I follow her lead, washing her skin, the touch of her hands stirring desire deep within me. As we continue to bathe each other, the weight of our pasts begins to lift into the air like the steam surrounding us, replaced instead with the warmth of our love and the promise of a future together.

"I love you, Lia," I say, brushing my fingers through her damp hair, marvelling at the way she looks at me now.

"And I love you, Drix. So, so much," she replies as she presses her lips against mine in a gentle, heartfelt kiss.

The water laps against us, its gentle caress providing a soothing backdrop to our intimate exchange. Lia's broken rib and bruises are a reminder of the pain she has endured, but it hasn't dampened her spirit or her desire. Her trust in me is unwavering as she places her vulnerable body in my hands.

With utmost care, I begin to explore her form, my fingers gliding across her damp skin. I move slowly, mindful of her injuries, tracing a path of tantalising caresses along her curves. Every touch is imbued with tenderness and yearning, an unspoken promise to bring her release despite the limitations imposed by her healing body.

"Drix," Lia breathes, her eyelids fluttering shut as my fingers slide over her stomach and between her legs, finding her core and transforming pain into waves of ecstasy.

"Look at me, Lia," I command softly.

Gazing into her eyes, I can see the flicker of both vulnerability and trust reflected back at me. She holds onto me tightly as sensations ripple through her body, giving herself over to the euphoria building within. In this moment, the throbbing pulse of pleasure merges with the profound love we share.

Lia's body responds eagerly to my touch, the beautiful sounds of her soft gasps and moans making my cock thicken. But this isn't about my pleasure, this is about hers, and as each delicate stroke brings Lia closer to the pinnacle of bliss, it binds us together in a union forged through shared experiences, unwavering support, and the sacred act of finding solace within each other's embrace. In this moment of intimacy, we are both healers and healed. The fragility of Lia's broken rib, and the deep bruises scattered over her body are no match for the resilience of her spirit.

"Drix, I'm going to come," she whispers, teetering on the precipice of release.

Her body arches against mine, an exquisite surrender mirroring the connection between us as I wrap my lips around her nipple and suck on her tender flesh. And finally, as her body convulses with her orgasm, I hold her close knowing that no man will ever love her as fiercely as I do.

ONE WEEK LATER.

"Mama, the snow is finally melting!" Toby exclaims as Daisy, Lia and I relax on the sofa in the living room. His face is pressed against the windowpane, soft puffs of air steaming up the glass as he stares out at the front drive.

"Is that so, buddy?" I ask, climbing to my feet as I head towards him.

"Yeah! Can we go outside and play before it goes for good?" he asks excitedly, turning to look up at me with big hopeful eyes.

I glance over to Lia and she grins. "I'll join you."

"Sure thing, buddy. Let's get our coats and boots on," I say with a smile.

Toby claps his hands together before running off to grab his coat from Lia, who is already standing by the front door waiting for him. We all pull on our coats and boots, and as Lia opens the front door, Toby grabs her hand pulling her outside.

As Lia and Toby's laughter fills the air around us, I turn to Daisy with a smile. "Daisy, you coming?" I ask, gesturing towards the door.

"Yeah, why not?" she replies, joining me at the door, slipping on her coat and shoes before resting her hand gently on my arm. My gaze falls to the engagement ring on her finger, a huge sparkling diamond set in a platinum ring. It's ostentatious, and not at all Daisy.

"Drix," she says softly. "I'm so glad you found happiness. Lia and Toby are truly the best thing that has ever happened to you."

"Hey, don't forget to include yourself in that statement," I reply with a gentle nudge of my arm.

"You know what I mean," she replies, a smile tugging at my lips as I watch Toby throw a snowball at his mum, hitting her chest with a soft thud.

"Yeah, Daise, I do. I'm a lucky man..." My voice trails off as I take in the scene before me—the laughter, the love, the sense of family. Yet, deep down we both know that this has little to do with luck. It's because of her sacrifice that I am able to experience moments like these.

"And they're lucky to have you," she replies, nudging me back, her smile sincere. "It feels good to see them so happy."

"Yeah," I agree, feeling my heart swell with love for the little family we've created.

"I'm so glad Lia decided to stay," she adds, but there's a wistful tone to her voice that doesn't go unnoticed.

"Are you certain about everything?" I ask, eying her suitcases that sit beside the stairs. Aside from a brief phone call to Dalton the morning after Martin was charged for attempted murder, when I filled him in on what happened, we haven't really spoken. Our relationship is strained to say the least, and I'm not sure it will ever get back to what it was.

"We've been over this, Drix. I'm okay with it. Dalton is..."

"Is what?" I ask guardedly.

"Is making an effort."

"How?"

"Just small gestures," she replies.

"What, you mean that huge fucking engagement ring? Is that

the small gesture you're talking about?" I ask, unable to hide the sarcasm in my voice.

She flinches, tucking her hand in her pocket. "Drix, this is happening. No use getting angry about it," she replies softly.

I open my mouth to speak but she shakes her head, cutting me off.

"He's doing his best, and even though things are... strained, I appreciate that he's trying."

"Taking you out on a couple of dates this past week, and flaunting you about to his rich friends is not what I consider trying. That's just surface level bullshit."

She glances at her wristwatch, ignoring my remark. "He'll be here in a couple of hours to pick me up. Perhaps you could use the opportunity to make peace with him, for my sake, if not for your own."

"I'm not sure I can do that," I admit.

She sighs. "Drix, you've been friends for years, I don't want this to come between you."

"It already has, Daisy, and I'm not saying that to make you feel bad, but because I need to be honest with you. I love you. I appreciate what you've done for me, for us, but I can't help but worry. This is your happiness we're talking about."

"*You're* worth it," she replies. "And please know that I went into this arrangement for my own reasons too. I *want* this baby."

"You'll be an incredible mother, Daisy, I have no doubt about that," I sigh, "But it feels like I've escaped a life sentence only for you to take it on."

"Don't think of it like that. Marrying Dalton and freeing you from your debt is my gift to you. Having a child is a gift to myself. I won't ever regret it."

"Even if being married to Dalton makes you unhappy?" I ask. "You don't even like each other."

"Maybe we can learn to?" she offers. "This isn't the first

arranged marriage, and it won't be the last. Besides, you always wanted us to be friends, this could be our chance."

"That's an extreme way to make friends, Daise," I laugh lightly, trying not to let my discomfort show too much.

"Well, you know me, I always try to find the good in people."

With that she gives me a quick squeeze then heads towards Toby and Lia, laughter bursting from her lips as Toby bounds towards her, throwing himself in her arms.

A couple of hours later, Dalton has packed up the last of Daisy's suitcases in the boot of his car and we're standing awkwardly together as Lia and Toby hug Daisy goodbye.

"They're going to miss her being around," I say, watching the three of them. "*I'll* miss her."

"She's only a ten minute drive away. Nothing's changed," Dalton says, swiping a hand through his hair, a muscle flickering in his jaw as he stares at his bride-to-be.

"*Everything's* changed. You are now responsible for my sister's happiness, are you certain you're up for the challenge?" I press.

"Honestly, I'm not sure."

I let out a bitter laugh. "That's probably the most honest thing you've ever said to me."

"Look, Drix," he starts, eying me cautiously, "I know this isn't what you want for Daisy. It isn't what I want either, but there's nothing I can do to prevent the inevitable. We're getting married in a few weeks with or without your blessing."

"I will be there for Daisy, but I can't give you my blessing."

"I understand," he replies with a nod of his head. "Will you be coming to the engagement party next week?"

"I will."

"I appreciate that," Dalton replies.

"I'm not doing it for you," I grind out.

He heaves out a sigh. "I want you to know, despite what you

think of me, that I *will* do everything in my power to take care of her."

His words catch me off guard, and I can feel the sincerity behind them. For a moment, I let myself believe that he might actually mean it.

"Are you ready to go?" Dalton asks as Daisy steps up to us both, ending our tense conversation.

"I guess," she replies with a small smile, her gaze drifting to me.

"Come here," I say roughly, pulling her into my arms.

"As much as I love you, Drix, I can't actually breathe," she laughs after a moment, and I pull back apologising.

Gripping her shoulders, I look into her eyes and say, "If at any point it gets to be too much, you come home, okay? No matter the consequences. You come home."

Out of the corner of my eye I see Dalton flinch, but he remains quiet.

"I love you," she retorts.

"Love you too."

With that, she unravels herself from my arms and pulls open the passenger door, shutting it quietly behind her.

"Don't let me down, Dalton," I say, and he nods, climbing into the car too. A moment later the engine starts and he's pulling off out of the drive.

"Bye, Daisy!" Toby calls, running after the car, his laughter lifting up into the air as he waves frantically, unaware of the sacrifice she's made for our happiness.

Lia's hand slides into mine as she leans her head against my arm. "Maybe things will work out," she suggests.

"You think?"

Lia nods, an air of certainty in her voice as she says, "Just over two months ago I met a man who extended me an act of kindness. That kindness blossomed into love. I never dared hope to find such happiness, but I did. Perhaps there's a chance for them both."

As Lia's words wash over me like a warm, comforting balm, I feel the sharp ache in my chest begin to subside. It is then that I understand that love is not merely an emotion, but a powerful force capable of mending even the most broken of hearts, and maybe, just maybe it can work its magic on Daisy and Dalton too.

EPILOGUE

FIVE WEEKS later

WITH NIMBLE FINGERS, I carefully spread a layer of smooth buttercream frosting onto the tiers of Daisy and Dalton's wedding cake, savouring the silky texture as it glides beneath my spatula, infusing each stroke with love and hope as I sing at the top of my lungs to some folk music playing on the radio. Suddenly the sound of hurried steps interrupts my concentration as Toby bursts into the kitchen, his cheeks flushed with excitement.

"Mama! Mama!" he exclaims breathlessly, bouncing on his toes. "Drix has a surprise for you!"

Intrigued by his enthusiasm, I wipe my hands on my apron and follow Toby into the living room, my heart skipping a beat when I see what Drix has prepared.

The coffee table has been moved aside, and in its place is a red tartan picnic blanket laid out on the floor covered in all of my favourite things to eat and drink, but that isn't the most wonderful thing because around the room there are dozens of vases filled to the brim with multicoloured tulips, my favourite flower.

"You remembered," I exclaim, stepping closer, my senses overwhelmed by the earthy aroma of aged red wine and richly flavoured cheese that seem to tantalise my taste buds even before I've indulged. There's also a huge strawberry cheesecake just waiting to be eaten, alongside soda bread and olives, sliced meat, and bowls of crisps.

"I've committed to memory every single thing you've told me, Lia," he replies roughly.

"How did you even manage to do this without me noticing?" I reply, shaking my head in bewilderment.

"You, Lia Pearson, get very, very engrossed in your baking. Daisy helped me to arrange all of this, she had everything delivered this morning. I snuck it inside with Toby's help. Besides, you were singing so loud, I could've brought in a herd of elephants and I don't think you would've noticed," Drix replies with a chuckle as he stands by the blanket, a mischievous grin playing on his lips.

"You, Drix Hammer, are a wonderful man," I exclaim, taking his proffered hand as his eyes sparkle with affection.

"I wanted to surprise you," he whispers, his voice carrying the warmth of his intentions. "Just call this a moment of respite amidst the whirlwind of wedding preparations. You've been working so hard on designing and making the perfect wedding cake, and I wanted to show you my appreciation."

Unable to contain my joy, I throw my arms around him, embracing him tightly. "You always know how to make me feel cherished," I murmur, my words a testament to the depth of my love for him.

"I might not be able to bring you warm weather, but I sure as hell can bring you all the things you love," he says as we sit down together, and Toby immediately reaches for a handful of crisps, stuffing them into his mouth.

Time ticks by, and as we talk and laugh, the fragrance of tulips mingle with the taste of rich cheese and smooth wine, creating a heady mixture that will forever be etched in my memory.

As we finish our impromptu picnic, I lean back against Drix's chest, my head nestled comfortably against his shoulder. Toby is sprawled out on the blanket beside us, content and sleepy as we sit in comfortable silence, savouring the love that envelops us.

"Lia," Drix whispers my name lovingly, his fingers tracing gentle circles on my arm. "I'm so damn happy."

"Me too," I reply, echoing his sentiment, feeling a surge of thankfulness for the family we've created and the love we share.

My body relaxes in Drix's embrace, and as I'm wrapped up in the warmth and security of his arms, I silently thank the universe for bringing us together. In this perfect corner of our world, where tulips bloom and love flourishes, there is a certainty that no matter what challenges lie ahead, we will face them with unwavering devotion, *together*.

THE END

THE ROGUE AND HIS FLOWER #2
PRINCETOWN HEIRS

Read on for an excerpt from **The Rogue and His Flower**

PROLOGUE

DALTON

THE AFTERMATH of last night's events weighs heavily on the four of us as we sit in the lavish bar of my father's five-star hotel. My friends, Sterling, Drix, and Benedict all wear troubled expressions, mirroring my own inner turmoil.

Dropping my gaze to the empty glass in my hand, the weight of my situation presses down on me more heavily than the whiskey I just swallowed. Empty glasses stand as evidence of our desperate need to numb ourselves, to escape from the tangled mess our lives have become.

We attempted to drown out our problems with alcohol, but it only brought them to the surface, each of us spilling our secrets, and none of us lighter for it.

Drix, my best friend, glances at me with a mix of pity, frustration and barely veiled anger, our friendship at risk from a decision neither of us are happy about.

"What a fucking night." Sterling's voice cuts through the quiet as he catches my gaze and swipes a hand through his glossy brown hair.

Drix shifts his attention to Benedict, who is lost to his own unsettling thoughts. "I'm assuming you've had just as little sleep as the rest of us," he remarks knowingly.

Benedict's silence speaks volumes as he looks up at Drix, his startling green eyes filled with turmoil.

"Yeah, that would be none then," Sterling says with a sharp exhale, his voice filled with bitterness and regret.

This morning feels like a cruel joke. We were supposed to be celebrating new beginnings after his father's extravagant wedding, but instead we've each been left with the repercussions of four women who have tangled our lives up in ways we never saw coming.

To make matters infinitely worse, lurking beyond the luxurious confines of this hotel, lies a world of outrageous headlines. The tabloids would have an absolute field day if they ever found out how the heirs of the four founding families of this town were embroiled in a web of forbidden love and deception.

On the outside, it may seem like we have everything we could ever want, but behind our polished exteriors lies a tangled web of scandal and vulnerability that threatens to undo us all.

Four sons. Four friends. Four men weighed down by our father's expectations, carrying secrets that could shatter the carefully crafted images we've maintained for years as the Princetown Heirs.

There's Sterling, an extraordinary but troubled artist who is expected to carry on the Blade family legacy, disregarding his own dreams.

Benedict, a man with genius level IQ who is set to inherit the Pike family's wealth that can buy a lot of things, but not a future with the woman he loves.

Drix Hammer, who carries the burden of a past mistake, and

has been forced into a role he never wanted, sacrificing his own happiness in the process.

And then there's me, Dalton Gunn, born into a life of privilege and trained to excel in high society, who's about to enter a fake marriage with my best friend's younger sister, to clear his debt so he can be with the woman he loves.

But where does that leave me?

Am I really willing to go through with this sham of a wedding to appease my father and secure my inheritance? Can I bring myself to marry the sweetest, most frustrating person I know, knowing I will hurt her deeply and ruin my friendship with my best friend of almost twenty years?

The truth is yes, yes I will. I am my father's son unfortunately, and love is a luxury I simply cannot afford...

Read Dalton and Daisy's romance in *The Rogue and His Flower*

ACKNOWLEDGMENTS

Thank you so much for stepping into the brand new world of Princetown with me. After spending so much time in the Academy of Stardom Universe, I knew I was ready to start something new.

The characters in this world are so incredible and deep-diving into all those juicy tropes we all know and love has been, and will be, so much fun! Just wait until you see what I have planned for the next three books, though by now I guess you might've figured out the tropes for book two already!

There are four books currently planned out in this series, and truth be known I wasn't going to start with Lia and Drix, but for some reason their voices were loud, and I followed my muse and ended up writing their story in just two months, which for me is pretty good going!

Have you guessed who the other stories will be about? If you've read the prologue to The Rogue and His Flower, I'm sure by now you'll know that the love story will revolve around Dalton and Daisy, and boy is it going to be fire!

But what about books three and four? I'm guessing you know who the men are, and I left some pretty big clues in The Thug and His Doll as to who their love interests will be!

For now, I hope you enjoyed reading Drix and Lia's love story. He is, and forever will be one of my most swoon worthy heroes! That moment when he stood Lia in front of the mirror and told her all the things he loves about her body was one of my most favourite scenes I have ever written.

I would like to thank my PA Courtney Dunham for holding my hand on this new venture into a brand new world. Believe me it is scary AF moving away from a universe that you have spent the best part of seven years writing in! But as always she helped my hand and talked me down from a cliff several times over. You're the best!

A special thanks must also go to my BETA readers, Gina, Claire, Jennifer and Lisa. All your comments and excitement bolster me, and help me to be the best writer I can be.

Also thanks have to go to the incredible artist, Samaiya Art, who has drawn all my characters and the crests for each family. You captured them so perfectly and I am addicted to your incredible artwork.

To all the book bloggers, bookstagrammers, book-tokers and ARC team who loved this books and shared your thoughts, graphics and incredible videos, thank you.

Finally, to you, dear reader, I'm forever grateful for your love and support and for continuing on this journey with me. I continually have to pinch myself knowing that I get to do the thing I love most in the world and bring you new characters to fall in love with.

Bea xoxo

ABOUT THE AUTHOR

Bea Paige lives a very secretive life in London... She likes red wine and Haribo sweets (preferably together) and loves to write about love and all the different facets of such a powerful emotion. When she's not writing about love and passion, you'll find her reading about it and ugly crying.

Bea is always writing, and new ideas seem to appear at the most unlikely time, like in the shower or when driving her car.

She has lots more books planned, so be sure to subscribe to her newsletter: www.beapaige.co.uk

Beyond the Horizon

Finding Their Muse

#1 Steps

#2 Strokes

#3 Strings

#4 Symphony

#5 Finding Their Muse boxset

Academy of Stardom

#1 Freestyle

#2 Lyrical

#3 Breakers

#4 Finale

#5 Encore

Their Obsession Duet

#1 The Dancer and The Masks

#2 The Masks and The Dancer

Grim & Beast's Duet

#1 Tales You Win

#2 Heads You Lose

The Deana-Dhe Duet

#1 Debts and Diamonds

#2 Curses and Cures

Short Story

Force of Gravity

(available FREE via my website if you signed up to my newsletter)

For all up to date book releases please visit

www.beapaige.co.uk